OUTER DARKNESS

A novel

by

Bart Brevik

This story is a work of fiction. All characters and religious

organizations described herein are the product of the author's

imagination, and do not represent any real persons, living or deceased,

nor actual religious organizations.

ISBN # 978-0-6151-6537-0

T o the Lord Jesus Christ, who has graciously blessed me in so many ways, and enables me to do the things I do. No matter what happens in this life, He is still on the throne.

Acknowledgements

I offer my special thanks to George Durgin and Merlin Puck for their significant contributions to this story, from start to finish. I also thank my beloved wife Carol Ann Brevik, Ernie Linz, Craig Nelson, Sherri Moreno, and Frank Sheets for their review and input of this work.

Author's Note:

During my growing up years in the Conejo Valley area of Southern California, there were a number of documented incidents of cat mutilation occurring in the small town of Westlake Village. According to news reports at that time, it was always the same result: cats surgically and deliberately disemboweled or dismembered, and dumped in the same residential neighborhood every time. No arrests were made, nor were any motives found. These unsolved crimes carried on sporadically for years, and generated much speculation about who might be responsible for theses heinous acts. Although practitioners of Satanism were suspected of being the perpetrators, it was never proven – nor disproved.

Similar bizarre incidents of cat mutilation have been reported in various locales throughout the country, as well as the UK and Canada. The gruesome details of each of these incidents are remarkably similar, regardless of where they occur. Satanic Ritual Abuse is implicated in many investigations, but no arrests or convictions have ever been made, to my knowledge.

PROLOGUE

In the war of good against evil, there are casualties. Some never recognize the enemy until it is too late.

***

She feels the darkness penetrating her bones as deeply as the cold, and she shivers.

The room is frigid, and dark as the grave. Not even a dim night light to shed a faint glow on the slender teenage girl, who stands bound and naked in the center of the room. Her arms are securely restrained above her head by handcuffs that are fastened around a rusty pipe, hanging low from the ceiling of the bare concrete basement. Her delicate wrists bear red witness marks from the cuffs, which dig into her supple flesh each time she struggles against her bonds. A piece of gray duct tape is sealed rudely across her mouth, making it more of an effort for her to breathe. Her fair skin tightens up into gooseflesh, shivering against the cold.

How did I get here? she wonders. *That lady, Bobbi, that I met outside the homeless shelter seemed cool; she let me stay at her place with her a few days. Her house was stocked with lots of food.*

I can't ...remember anything; one minute I'm at a bangin' party at her house with a bunch of her friends, then ...what happened? Did somebody spike my drink with something? This place is so dark. How did I end up here, and what happened to my clothes? These handcuffs are killing my wrists. Why would they handcuff me to this pipe up above my head?

Whoa – I'm so dizzy ...I can barely stand up straight. My head - it's killin' me! Oh man, I never should've run away from home ...I wanna go back.

Tears begin to flow down her pale cheeks and hit the hard concrete floor, her pretty face contorted with fear and anxiety. Her head slung downward, she sobs plaintively.

Footfalls approach - several people coming, by the sound of it. She lifts her chin up apprehensively. The door opens abruptly, and a column of bright light pierces the darkness of the room.

Through her squinting eyes, the girl sees a group of several people coming down the steps into the basement slowly and quietly, each one silhouetted by the light as they glide in. Their faces are obscured by the deep hoods of their dark purple robes.

Although bound with her hands above her head, the girl pulls her bare thighs together tight and twists her hips to the side, in a vain attempt at modesty.

Who are these people coming in now? The people from the party, maybe? And now they're all seeing me naked. But why are they wearing those robes? Must be some kind of kinky perverts. Oh, God, they're probably going to rape me. Maybe they already did while I was out of it. I told that lady Bobbi that I'm a virgin, but they probably don't even care. I haven't done anything to them, why are they doing this to me?

Her shivering abruptly gives way to a cold sweat as she realizes all at once the gravity of the situation. The hooded figures walk in single file around the outer perimeter of the empty basement room, until the last member of the group passes through the door. In his left hand, the enrobed man carries a dark, medium-sized suitcase. He closes the door behind him, and flicks a light switch on the wall. The room becomes illuminated in a gloomy amber glow.

Each member of the hooded group assumes a position along the wall, facing her. Not a word is spoken among them; everyone methodically follows this ritual in silence. The girl's increasing sense of dread is evident, her eyes darting frantically from one hooded figure to the next. She can't see their faces, which are obscured by the deep hoods. Muffled, unintelligible sounds of protest and pleading leak out from her taped mouth. She feels the tingle of sweat oozing from her scalp, further soiling her matted blonde hair.

A sense of deadly anticipation permeates the air, as the man carrying the suitcase sets it down on a small table near the door. He bends over to open the case.

Snap! Snap! The latches on the case spring open noisily, startling the girl, and cause her to jerk back like a spring suddenly released. Losing her balance, the unforgiving handcuffs lacerate her skin, but won't let her fall to the cold, hard cement floor. As the lid of the suitcase opens, the glint of stainless steel is unmistakable, even in the dim light.

Hey, w- what's that thing he's pulling out? Looks like some kind of machine. Oh, my God, look at the size of that needle. No, no, I don't want to be here. What are you going to do? Don't come near me with that thing! I ... can't move ...I can't even scream. Please don't hurt me. Somebody help me! ...Mommy!

CHAPTER 1

Chatsworth, California

He thought he'd already seen everything that the perverse underbelly of Los Angeles had to offer. But on this morning, his queasy stomach told him that he hadn't.

As a top reporter for KNLA TV in Los Angeles, George Tanaka had seen more than his share of crime scenes over the years. He had covered the gamut; drive-by gang shootings, domestic violence incidents that culminated in murder, a teenage girl found bleeding to death in a cheap motel after a botched abortion - you name it. But none of the previous atrocities could have prepared him for what he saw today.

The police usually tried to keep him at arm's length, with varying degrees of success. Today he had managed to find a way to snake through the police lines surrounding the warehouse, by using one of his scams.

The crime scene was in one of the newer industrial parks in the San Fernando Valley; one of a dozen or so cloned tilt-up buildings painted in neutral earth tones. The kind of generic-looking light industrial floorspace that looked like it could be planted anywhere in America - and probably had, for that matter. A very nondescript place, and empty as well. The sparse stick-like trees and small shrubs that dotted the industrial park landscape seemed to be the only living things in the area, besides the police.

George had donned his gray blazer and a necktie after parking his car down the street, out of sight. Brazenly walking into the taped-off crime scene like the cock-of-the-walk, his well rehearsed swagger and look of arrogance marked him as a police detective in the eyes of the cops on the scene, who were busily going about their business.

After all, he thought to himself, *you don't get the big story by hanging back with the crowd.*

In this case, though, he found himself wondering if he would have been better off if the officers standing around the perimeter had been a bit more diligent about keeping him at bay. With his tie loosely knotted and his travel coffee mug in hand, George was trying hard to look like the kind of hardened detective who saw murder scenes like this every day, and twice on Sunday. Once inside the warehouse, he noticed a couple of men in suits looking intently at the area where the roll-up shipping and receiving door was located.

Gotta be Feds, he thought. *The local cops don't dress like that.*

Casually walking up to the forensic tech who was examining the corpse with latex-gloved hands, he grunted "Watcha got?"

She looked young - probably not more than fifteen, although it was hard to tell with her color gone and the ghostly pallor of her face looking like a grotesquely distorted mask. George took a quick glance, not allowing his eyes to dwell too long on the macabre scene before him. According to the forensics tech, she had been dead for at least six hours or more. George had seen dead bodies before; the worst ones were the car crashes. But this one was different – and worse than any he had seen.

She was nude, yet according to Forensics, there were no indications of rape. It was worse yet, if that were even possible. The dead girl lying on the cold floor of this empty warehouse had two large incisions on her torso: One vertical down the center of her chest, another about three inches above the navel and to one side. There was also what appeared to be a large puncture mark at the base of one carotid artery in the neck.

The forensics tech who was thoroughly examining the body said that her heart and liver had been surgically removed, and there was very little blood left in her body. Strangely, there was little blood on the floor either. There were no signs of struggle, other than the scraped black and blue marks around both of her wrists.

Another oddity that the crime scene investigators on the scene were busy photographing and examining was a marking on the lower torso, separate from the two incisions. It appeared to be some kind of emblem that was burned into the skin of the victim, about two inches in diameter. The CSI's were buzzing about what it meant, and speculating as to whether a branding iron or similar tool had been used to make the marking.

As he tried to take in the scene with a dispassionate scan, George made the mistake of staring directly at the victim's face. Her eyes were stuck open by rigor mortis, but even in their lifeless state they had a look of horror in them. Her blue lips looked to him as though they had been plaintively screaming for help, but in utter futility. Disgusted, George tried to look away, but couldn't. He suddenly felt something well up deep within his stomach, and he quickly averted his eyes from hers. Too late.

He lunged for the warehouse roll-up door, and burst into the harsh morning sunlight. He hit his knees, just in time to hurl his breakfast into the sparse shrubs.

CHAPTER 2

Westlake Village, California

Jim read the headline of the story, and shook his head in disgust. A violent murder of a teenage girl had been reported only about thirty miles from his home.

I can't believe it, he thought, *she was only Chelsea's age.*

Jim DiMario grabbed a quick breakfast of bagel and coffee in his kitchen while he looked over his morning newspaper.

His coffee had long since gone cold as he perused the morning paper, looking for a grain of good news - some ray of light in this otherwise darkened world.

As the Senior Pastor of the largest church in town - Solid Rock Community Church, Jim knew that the only true good news was found in the bible, the gospels of Christ.

Is it too much to expect some kind of positive news, he asked himself, *something good actually taking place in the world every now and then? It seems like things are getting worse all the time. Is it just my imagination, or is the whole country going down the tubes at a dead run?*

It outraged him to think that there were sick people running around loose who were capable of these kinds of things. With a scowl on his face, he bit into his cinnamon raisin bagel like a shark, reviewing the rest of the headlines of the day, letting the crumbs fall where they may.

Jim took his plate into the kitchen, and washed it off before placing it into the dishwasher. Giving the countertop a cursory sweep with the dishtowel, he made his way to the front door, and headed out to the church office.

Jasmine DiMario woke up early on this dreary October morning to the sound of a door slamming downstairs. The DiMario children had just left the house for school - probably without breakfast, again. Garrett, age sixteen, and Chelsea, age seventeen, were students at Westlake High School.

Westlake Village was, by all accounts, a nice place to live; an upscale community with it's own private lake, and within commuting distance of Los Angeles. The DiMario home was a comfortable two-story Mediterranean style house with four bedrooms. The spare bedroom was for guests who would stop in; missionaries, vacation bible school teams, guest speakers, and others. Jasmine always tried to make it as comfortable as possible for visitors - always the perfect hostess.

After all, she figured, *isn't that expected of a pastor's wife?*

Their home was situated in a neighborhood known as The Greens, just off Triunfo Canyon Road. Although one of the older neighborhoods in town, it was still a desirable place to live. It's greenbelts of grassy space wove like a spider web throughout the neighborhood, between and behind the houses, with cement pathways adjoining the grassy areas and buffer zones.

On this morning, Jasmine lay in bed late, dreading the thought of getting up. Today was bible study day. It wasn't that she didn't enjoy the fellowship; Jasmine was well known and admired, and the church women were always eager to talk with her. It certainly wasn't a lack of interest in the bible - she loved the Word of God.

Her life seemed, to her, sometimes a dream and sometimes a nightmare. She had a great husband and two terrific kids. She was loved and respected by all the church members. But with the love and respect came a set of high expectations, she felt. She was the Senior Pastor's wife. She was expected to be a role model and a leader for the women - a touchstone to be emulated. A few of the women had even duplicated her hairstyle. In the three-thousand member Solid Rock Community Church, Jasmine was sought after for guidance and leadership - and public speaking.

She lay in bed fully awake, staring at the motionless ceiling fan above her bed. Knowing that she would probably be expected to "say a few words" to the hundred or so women attending the midweek bible study, she was hesitant. She didn't feel much like a leader – or a speaker, for that matter. It wasn't due to a lack of bible knowledge on her part - she had grown up in church. Her father had been a Lutheran pastor, and Jasmine had learned the bible more thoroughly by age ten than most adults ever do.

Jasmine's mother and the other pastor's wives had numerous talents and abilities. Musically, all of the wives of pastors and missionaries that she knew could sing beautifully, or play piano, or both. Jasmine couldn't carry a tune, nor did she ever learn the discipline of playing a musical instrument. The other pastor's wives were energetic and outgoing, but Jasmine was basically a shy homebody, scared to death of public speaking. Her main areas of giftedness were in the culinary skills, and organization. She was well-known for preparing outstanding dishes for potluck dinners, and for making exceptional meals when friends or guests came over. She also had a knack for putting together fellowship events, meetings, retreats, block parties – and for generally getting things done.

Jasmine was a pretty woman, but her size ten figure combined with her short stature of four foot - eleven and a half inches, often made her feel fat and body-conscious. Her long blonde hair was trimmed with long bangs in front, and sprinkled with a few silver hairs that were noticeable only to her.

The ladies at church didn't know how inadequate she felt. So many times, Jasmine was sure that God had picked the wrong woman for the job.

Nevertheless, it was bible study day. Emanating a soft moan, she slung her legs over the side of the bed, and staggered to the shower.

CHAPTER 3

Solid Rock Community Church: Westlake Village, CA

The electronic ring of the phone on his desk jolted Jim DiMario out of his daze.

Sitting in his office at church thinking about current events and daydreaming about the bass fishing boat he wanted, he'd almost lost track of where he was.

He used to be so busy and focused on the ministry, but now with the growth of the church, he had associate pastors and staff members to handle much of the day to day business. Although still responsible for the Sunday sermon and the overall leadership of the church, he had, as the church grew steadily over the years, delegated responsibility for much of the rest. He languidly picked up the receiver.

"Pastor Jim?" said the voice of Beverly Hanson, the church secretary. "Bjorn Nilsson is on line one for you."

Bjorn Nilsson - Jim's old seminary buddy was a missionary in Brazil, but he hadn't actually spoken to him in a long time - maybe even years. Jim eagerly punched the button for line one.

"Bjorn - Great to hear from you!" Jim enthused. "What are you up to?"

"I'm stateside on furlough right now," Bjorn replied, sounding uncharacteristically serious. "Jim, I need to see you."

"And I'd love to see you," responded Jim. "Are you planning on coming out this way while you're on furlough? I could sure use you as a guest speaker on missions night next week. We're having a potluck dinner and a video presentation, but I could still work it around your ministry".

"I'm planning to fly out there tomorrow night," declared Bjorn.

"Tomorrow…night?" Jim stammered. "You have meetings planned in California?"

"Just you, Jim – its important. I'll see you tomorrow night. If Jasmine can accommodate me on such short notice, great. Otherwise, I'll just check into the Howard Johnson's".

"I won't hear of it," Jim insisted. "Do you think I'd put my favorite missionary in a hotel?"

"I'll get a car at the airport. Tomorrow night then," Bjorn concluded tersely.

"Can't wait," said Jim. "Bye."

A puzzled look crossed his face as he carefully set down the receiver.

Jim had always looked forward to spending time with Bjorn, though it was rare these days. In spite of their radically different backgrounds, the two of them had forged a strong bond of friendship during their seminary years. Bjorn had been raised on a farm near Grand Forks, North Dakota. The worst trouble he had gotten into as a teenager was one occasion when he and two friends from school went cow tipping at several neighboring farms in the middle of the night.

Jim, on the other hand, had been raised in Burbank, California. He had found plenty of opportunities for trouble as a teenager, and trouble seemed to seek him out. As a youth, he had tried most every illegal drug available to him during those difficult years, along with any kind of alcohol he could get his hands on. But in spite of his flagrant indiscretions, he had somehow stayed alive and out of jail. It wasn't until a little later in life that he realized how gracious God had been to him.

During their two years rooming together at Maranatha Theological Seminary, there were a few times that Jim started feeling like he had taken a wrong turn on his career path.

Doubts had plagued him frequently - *Can I possibly live up to God's expectations for a pastor? Or the congregation's expectations, for that matter? Will I be able to make a respectable living? Will I be able to become someone who could actually be a spiritual guidepost for others?*

Whenever Jim was thinking about giving up and quitting, Bjorn reeled him back in.

Immediately after seminary, Bjorn had accepted a call to service at a small church in the town of Japeri, on the outskirts of Rio de Janeiro. In addition to the challenge of learning to speak and write fluently in Portuguese, the native language of Brazil, Bjorn had to assimilate into Brazilian culture - no small task for a six-foot four-inch tall Swede with blonde hair.

In the years that followed, he expanded his ministry by founding a training school for native missionaries. It had now blossomed into a complex of significant size, placing up to twenty trained native missionaries onto the streets each year. In a heavily superstitious country flooded with cults and the occult, Bjorn's ministry was making a significant impact.

So ..., Jim wondered to himself, *Why does Bjorn need to see me so bad? He sounded almost desperate on the phone. Our church supports him financially every year, so I doubt that it's money related.*

Perplexed and feeling strangely uneasy, Jim unconsciously furrowed his brow as he thought about their oddly brief conversation. With his elbows on the desk in front of him, he planted his brooding chin in his hands.

CHAPTER 4

Westlake High School: Westlake Village, California

In his tenth-grade social studies class this morning, Garrett DiMario was barely paying attention - at least not to the teacher.

One chair up and to the left, Darlene Jeffries was a much more compelling focal point for his attention than Mrs. McAllister. Darlene - she seemed to Garrett more like a work of art than merely a girl. Her long hair was shiny, straight, and intensely golden. Her altogether smooth skin looked like it had never seen a pimple or blemish. Her beautiful face could have been meticulously carved from solid marble. Everything about her was so perfect, so flawless, so...

"Garrett!" Roberta McAllister's voice hit him like an electric shock down the spine, jolting him back to the here and now. "Perhaps you could share with us some of the hunting techniques that may have been used by Nebraska Man."

"Um...maybe I could, but it would just be a guess on my part."

A few giggles made their way around the room.

"And why is that, Garrett?" Mrs. McAllister retorted sarcastically. "Have you not been paying attention to the lesson?"

"Well, actually," Garrett ventured, his voice slightly wavering, "I don't believe that Nebraska Man ever existed at all, so how could he hunt?"

More giggles.

"It wouldn't be in this textbook if it wasn't true," said McAllister, her voice rising. "I suppose you know more than the archaeologists who made all of these important discoveries?"

"Well, I know that Nebraska Man and a bunch of other so-called 'missing links' have been proven to be fakes. The Institute for Creation Science has investigated all of these so-called archeological finds, and found that ..."

"Enough!" McAllister shouted. "Garrett DiMario, I know very well who your father is. Don't you dare try to spread your religion in my classroom!"

"But, I'm not - I just..."

"Stop! Not another word from you. Class, open your textbooks to Chapter Four and start reading. We'll be having a test on the evolution of man next Thursday," said McAllister, while shooting Garrett a sideways glance. "And nobody is going to get out of it by claiming religious views."

Chelsea DiMario walked slowly and steadily down the empty corridor toward the Principal's office. It was the middle of fifth period, so it was quiet enough in the halls of Westlake High School to hear the gentle squeak of her skater shoes on the smooth linoleum as she cautiously approached the outer door of the administration office.

What could the principal possibly want with me? she wondered to herself.

Chelsea had never been in trouble at school, and was a hard working student. Anything that she may have lacked in natural scholastic ability she had learned to overcome through diligent effort. It was the start of her senior year, and the hardest academic work was now behind her. She had lots of friends, and no enemies - at least, none that she knew of.

It came as a surprise to her, then, to be handed a note from the office by her fifth period teacher - a summons to see the Principal. With trepidation in her heart, she reached for the door handle, and quietly slipped inside the cool and quiet environs of the administration office. The receptionist looked up as Chelsea approached.

"Chelsea DiMario here to see Mr. Brooks," she said quietly.

"He's expecting you. Down the hall to the right," the receptionist said in monotone.

Casually dismissing Chelsea with a wave of her hand in the direction of the Principal's office, the receptionist looked back down toward her desk at some papers that were apparently of more interest.

I wonder if she knows something about this, Chelsea wondered as she slowly moved down the hall.

She looked up while passing under a large black and gold banner with the school mascot, and the slogan "*Home of the Panthers*" emblazoned across it. Approaching Principal Brooks' office, she heard voices inside and saw activity through the watered glass window. Chelsea tentatively tapped on the door, and the talking inside stopped immediately. After an awkward silence, Principal Brooks opened the door.

"Chelsea! Thanks for coming," Brooks said with a smile. "Please, come in and have a seat. I believe you know Mrs. McAllister."

"Yes, of course," Chelsea said curtly, looking at the teacher. "I had her in tenth grade." *Yeah, how could I ever forget*, she thought to herself.

Chelsea slunk into the office, suddenly feeling like a lamb being led to slaughter. Roberta McAllister sat rigidly in a side chair with her legs crossed. Her auburn hair was pulled back tightly in a bun. She wore a gray business suit and a frown. She did not stand or smile when Chelsea acknowledged her.

"Chelsea," Principal Brooks started, "I understand that you submitted a request to the club committee to start a lunchtime bible study group."

"Yes, that's right, sir."

"Well, I'm sorry to have to tell you that we can't approve that request," Mr. Brooks said gently, looking a little embarrassed.

"Is…that what this is all about?" Chelsea asked in amazement. "I thought approval by the school administration was just a formality. We were planning to meet at lunch time. We wouldn't even…"

McAllister stood abruptly and cut Chelsea off in midstream.

"You must realize that we cannot allow the practice of religion at a public school," she said with the subtlety of a freight train. "It would violate the constitutional separation of church and state."

Chelsea turned to face Mrs. McAllister. Her body tensed, and she felt the anger rise in her stomach.

"Actually," Chelsea stated boldly, "my dad says that the idea of a so-called 'separation of church and state' is not in the constitution at all, but was taken from a misinterpretation of a letter that Thomas Jefferson wrote to a group of men known as the Danbury Baptists, who were afraid the government might establish a state church. A Supreme Court decision back in 1947 in *Everson vs. Board of Education* is what started the false idea that there can't be any involvement between the government and church. But even that court decision is usually misinterpreted by atheists".

As Chelsea was speaking, she imagined that she could see smoke starting to come out of McAllister's ears as the teacher grew redder and more agitated by the moment. Finally, she burst.

"Well! It seems your father has opinions about most everything, doesn't he? Is this the kind of nonsense he preaches every Sunday!? You've read the textbook in your eleventh grade U.S. history class – assuming you passed that class. You won't find any of the junk you just said in there!"

"I know," Chelsea replied matter-of-factly. "That kind of information is suppressed in public school textbooks."

McAllister stood fuming, her face red as a beet.

"How can you possibly ...," she huffed.

"Mrs. McAllister," Principal Brooks cut in.

"Who do you think ..."

"Mrs. McAllister!" Brooks shouted loud enough to make Chelsea jump. "Sit down!"

McAllister slowly retreated to her side chair, as Principal Brooks straightened his suit lapels and tried to regain his own composure. He took a deep breath before speaking again.

"Chelsea," he started, as gently as he could muster, "I'm afraid that we just can't move forward on this bible study. There would be too much controversy."

"Yes," Chelsea replied tersely, while looking directly at Roberta McAllister. "I can see that."

CHAPTER 5

Insomniac Café: Woodland Hills, California

George Tanaka settled into his favorite seat at the Insomniac Café on Ventura Boulevard in the Big Valley. The sun had just peaked above the Topanga Mountains a few minutes before, and held the promise of another beautiful clear autumn day in Southern California - at least, as far as the weather was concerned.

With a large cappuccino in one hand and a cinnamon roll in the other, he scanned the L.A. Times to see if any of the paper's reporters had picked up the story about the cut-up dead teenage girl in the warehouse. They had. On the third page there was a short piece about the murder. No pictures. No details, either.

They must have got to him, he figured. *Any good reporter would have worked that story to the max, just like I wanted to.*

After George had lost his breakfast at the crime scene yesterday, an FBI agent took him aside.

"It wouldn't be in the family's best interest - nor the community's, to give out the details of this murder," the agent had warned him, in a coercive tone. "In fact, it could jeopardize our chances of catching the perpetrator."

He had put the screws to George, and even suggested that George might be subject to criminal charges for impersonating a police officer unless he agreed not to report the gruesome details of the crime scene, and the condition of the body. George had been threatened before, both by police and criminals. He knew that the charge wouldn't stick, since he never actually claimed to be a detective, or showed a fake badge. But the FBI man had called George's editor, who reluctantly cut out significant parts of George's video segment that he had shot at the warehouse after the fact. George's training as a hard-nosed TV news reporter coupled with his human nature demanded that he report everything - all the facts. But sometimes the powers above him had to play politics.

Even so, he reasoned, *maybe there are some things that folks would just rather not know about. Blissful ignorance.*

After getting out of the army years ago, George had started at the TV station at the bottom, as a "gopher", doing all sorts of odd jobs and research for the reporters. With no college education, he gradually worked his way up the ladder, until he finally made it to reporter. As a rookie reporter, he was shocked again and again by the crime scenes that he covered, and the wicked people he came in contact with. But over time, he became more and more callused. He learned to bury his feelings deep inside, where they wouldn't get hurt. The few graying strands of hair on his head were a testament to the trouble he'd seen, and the lines in his face showed mileage that belied his thirty-nine years.

George's hardened heart had taken it's toll on his marriage as well. He and his wife of twelve years were separated. They had two girls together, along with a large, custom four-bedroom house with a swimming pool, and a dog. George tried to keep up on being an attentive father, but work often kept him out at night.

A glimmer of sunlight flashed momentarily across George's face, and he automatically looked up from his newspaper as the door opened. A uniformed figure strode confidently into the shop. The man was of average height, but his build was far from average. His large arm muscles strained at the short sleeves of his Sheriff's uniform, and his upper body bulk was reminiscent of Lou Ferrigno, who years ago played the role of *Incredible Hulk*. He had thin medium brown hair, and a matching Fu-Manchu style moustache. Cops came in here all the time, George knew, but this one looked familiar. As George stared blankly, the man turned his head toward him and nodded.

That's the guy, George realized. *One of the deputies from the crime scene yesterday.*

George watched as the deputy got his coffee and started to slowly head toward the door. The deputy looked back, and George kicked a chair out from the table and beckoned him over. The cop paused for a few seconds, then tentatively came over and sat down.

"I hope your stomach feels a bit better today," the cop said sarcastically as George folded his paper.

"George Tanaka," he said, reaching out his hand, while remaining seated. "Please, take a load off."

"Rich Harrison," the cop said, taking George's extended hand and squeezing it like a vise. He sat down in the chair opposite George at the small table.

The deputy was physically intimidating, and looked big enough and tough enough to run down most any crook who was dumb enough to try something on his beat. They shared small talk for a few minutes before George hit him with the big question.

"The FBI was pretty tight-lipped about what went down in that warehouse. What's your take on it?"

Deputy Harrison was silent for several seconds before offering a terse reply.

"Sexual assault and murder. It happens."

"Not like this."

The deputy shrugged. "Yeah," he admitted, "This one's a bit different."

"And …," George prompted, slowly waving his hand in a circular motion.

"I'm not a detective," Deputy Harrison said. "What do you want me to say?"

George looked down at the table for a moment, then lifted his gaze directly to Rich's eyes. "Look, I've never seen anything like this before, and I've seen plenty of crime scenes – bloody, gruesome crime scenes. This one didn't have any blood; maybe that's why it's so freaky. This wasn't a typical homicide – you must know that if you've been on the street more than a couple months. So, what do you think?"

"You don't really want to know what I think," Rich said solemnly.

"Try me."

Deputy Harrison pursed his lips and looked around the room. He paused for a moment, then spoke quietly.

"SRA," he said simply.

"What?"

Another pause. "Satanic ritual abuse," he said slowly and quietly, leaning toward George. "I've heard stories about it, even attended a lecture about it. But I'd never actually seen a case that fit the profile until yesterday."

"I'm listening," said George, fully engrossed. His hand automatically moved to the notepad in his jacket pocket, and he pulled it out.

"Hey," Deputy Harrison objected, waving him off, "Don't even think about quoting me on this - I'll deny everything."

"Okay, okay." George backed off immediately, eager to hear more. "But why the hush-hush?"

"Because the official story is that SRA doesn't exist," breathed Harrison, nearly whispering. "The FBI has gone on record as stating that there is no conclusive evidence of Satanic groups committing these kinds of crimes. The police and sheriff's departments follow that party line."

"But you think otherwise?" George's leading question sounded more like a statement.

Rich Harrison took a sip from his coffee. "Yeah, and I'm not the only one. The stories of these crimes are too persistent and well-documented. But neither myself or anybody else I know is going to come out and say so publicly."

"Why not? What are you afraid of?" queried George.

"Let's just say that it would be a career-limiting move."

George stroked the stubble on his chin thoughtfully. He deliberately fought down the impulse to smirk and make light of what Rich had just said. Instead, he kept a poker face as he continued.

"You know," George started, "That's a pretty wild explanation for this crime. Sounds like something from out of the *X-Files*. What makes you think that Satanists are responsible?"

"Look at the facts at the crime scene; the victim was naked, but hadn't been raped. In fact, the autopsy performed last night indicated that the victim was a virgin."

"So?" George asked, with a reporter's cynicism in his voice, "Maybe the killer couldn't follow through."

"There's more," continued Harrison. "Almost all the blood was gone from the body, but there was no blood at the scene. Her heart and liver were also cut out - surgically removed. Quite skillfully, too, according to the coroner."

"Maybe," countered George, "The perpetrator killed her to harvest her organs and sell them on the black market. It's happened before, according to reports I've heard coming out of some third-world countries."

"Urban legends," Harrison stated somberly, shaking his head. "So, then, how do you explain the *Sigil of Beelzebub?*"

"The … what?"

"The symbol that was burned into her torso. An inverted pentagram, with the goat's head inside. It's a symbol that Satanists use. You saw the body yourself - everything was done with great care; she wasn't hacked up."

George sat expressionless for a moment, suddenly at a loss for words. A sudden chill swept over his body, and he thought about what had happened to this girl. She was somebody's daughter, their precious little girl.

Why would anyone do something like that – marking the body? he wondered. *What kind of sick animal could even think of it? My God, what if she was alive and conscious while they were doing these things to her?*

The familiar cloying of nausea flirted with his stomach, and George pushed his coffee cup away from him. He took in a deep breath, and turned his attention to patrons ordering coffee at the front counter, in an effort to fight down the sensation.

The whole thing was sick and disgusting – but now he was hooked.

CHAPTER 6

DiMario Residence: Westlake Village, California

Jim could scarcely contain his enthusiasm at the sight of his old friend as he opened the door.

"Bjorn, old man - Look at you!"

Bjorn Nilsson's naturally pale skin had gradually tanned like leather during his years of evangelizing and helping the poor on the streets of Rio de Janeiro. Other than the weathered look, he appeared pretty much the same to Jim, only more mature and seasoned. His shock of white hair contrasted even more distinctively against his darkened skin. Jim eagerly strode onto the doorstep and embraced him warmly.

"Come in, don't stand on ceremony. Mi casa es su casa."

"No hablo Español, Jim," Bjorn replied. "It's Portuguese in my country, remember?"

Dinner time found them all sitting around the DiMario table.

"Jasmine, you've outdone yourself," Bjorn enthused, wiping a smear of marinara sauce off his chin with a paper napkin, "I haven't enjoyed a meal like this since the last time you had me over."

"That was a long time ago, Bjorn! Too long, in fact. I don't think we've had the honor of your company for a few years, now."

Bjorn was evidently enjoying the meal of lasagna and fettuccine alfredo, with garlic bread and asparagus tips, wolfing it down with gusto. Garrett and Chelsea didn't say much during dinner; they hadn't seen Bjorn in such a long time that he seemed like a stranger to them.

Laying his fork down on his empty plate, Jim pushed it away from himself. As he gently patted his full belly, he let out a satisfied sigh.

After helping clear off the table, Jim and Bjorn retired to the home office that Jasmine and Jim shared.

Jim shut the door behind them and beckoned Bjorn to sit down on the couch with him.

"Bjorn, do you really have to go back to Minnesota tomorrow?" he asked. "I could get used to having you around for awhile. I've got about a million things you could help with at church."

"Afraid so, Jim. You know how it is with us missionaries; I have to do the circuit of churches stateside in order to raise our support for next year before I go back to Brazil. But...," Bjorn confided somberly, with his jovial smile fading, "That's not why I came to see you."

Jim said nothing, sitting forward expectantly, waiting for Bjorn to continue.

"Jim," Bjorn began slowly, "ministering in Brazil has always been a challenge for me. There are constant financial pressures, of course. And then there are the cults; the *Church of Michael the Archangel* has been very active in their evangelism efforts. So have the *Messengers of Elohiem*."

"They're busy here too, Bjorn," Jim interrupted. "We have to address false teachings all the time."

"I know," Bjorn continued. "But that's not the half of it. We also have the native religions to deal with - *Santeria* and the other Caribbean religions."

"What's *Santeria*?" Jim inquired, furrowing his brow.

"Well basically, it's a pagan religion that originated in Africa, and worked it's way to the Caribbean many years ago, due to the slave trade. Actually, the proper name is *Regla de Ocha*, meaning Way of the Saints. In Brazil they call it *Candomble Jege-Nago*, but it's the same thing. It incorporates elements of Catholicism, since the African slaves were forced into the Catholic faith. They worship several gods, the chief god being *Olorun*. There are a bunch of lesser gods or guardians, which are called *Orisha*. Anyway, in order for these *Orishas* to be effective, they need food in the form of blood sacrifices. Typically, worship involves sacrificial killing of animals. The blood is collected and offered to the *Orisha* in some kind of ceremony."

Jim sat silently with a surprised look on his face.

"Anyway," Bjorn continued, "at first I thought it was the Santeria Practitioners that were doing it."

"Doing what?"

A long pause.

"The human sacrifices."

The silence in the room was complete, and Jim's jaw dropped in astonishment.

"W-what?" he sputtered finally.

"It started during *Carnival* this year, just a few months ago," Bjorn elaborated, "when the parades and parties are in full swing in Rio. I left Japeri where our ministry headquarters is, to go into Rio for four days of street evangelism. I had six native missionaries with me - we do it every year. As we were riding our bikes along the road, we noticed a bunch of ravens in a field next to the road. It looked like they were feeding on some dead animal. But suddenly, one of my men stopped his bike directly in front of me, and I couldn't stop in time. I ran into him, and we both fell down. That's when he shouted, "My God, it's a hand!"

Jim sat transfixed as Bjorn went on.

"We all went over to investigate and found - to our horror, that there was a child buried in a shallow grave. His hand was sticking out of the ground – it looked like an animal had partially dug it up. We dug with our hands just enough to expose the child's face – it was so awful, Jim."

He paused to take a deep breath, and let out a long sigh.

"Anyway, to make a long story short, we sent for the police as soon as we got to town. We found out later from my sources that it was an eleven- year old boy that had been murdered."

"That's terrible," Jim interjected. "I can never get used to …"

"It gets worse," Bjorn interrupted. "This information that I'm going to tell you now wasn't released to the public, and even the newspapers were in the dark about it."

Lowering his voice, he leaned toward Jim and began recounting the grisly details.

***

The young boy lay lifeless in the dirt, his skin showing the typical bluish pallor of the dead. His shirtless torso had two large cuts on it; one vertical down the center of his chest, another a few inches above the navel and to one side. Strangely, there was no blood coloring the dirt around the body, nor in the shallow grave that the Rio de Janiero Police pulled him up from. They would find out later that his heart and liver had been surgically removed through the gaping wounds that were now attracting a large number of flies. There was a large puncture mark evident in the carotid artery on the left side of the boy's neck, and a mark that appeared to have been branded into his skin. A symbol of some kind, impossible to make out, considering the partially decayed state of the body.

***

Jim sat spellbound, listening to Bjorn's graphic description of the odious find.

"H-how could you know all this, Bjorn?" Jim stammered. "Surely you didn't dig up the body yourself!"

"Of course not - but I do have my sources. One of our converts is in the police department. He tells me everything, including the fact that the Police Commissioner is clueless about who is committing these heinous killings."

"Killings?" blurted Jim, in amazement. "You mean, there are others?"

Bjorn paused momentarily, as if to keep from bowling his friend over with the gravity of his answer.

"Four others," he conceded. "All teenagers or children - and all found in the same condition. And all since *Carnival*."

Jim sat motionless, semi-catatonic as Bjorn went on.

"So that's why we suspected that it was one or more renegade *Santeria* practitioners who had graduated beyond animal sacrifices. But we were wrong. We did our own investigation. You know, Jim, we probably have better informants than the police do. So many converts for Christ in my area have come from the ranks of former prostitutes, drug dealers and users, thieves, smugglers, and so on. And many of them still know people that they associated with when they were living in the flesh. They were willing to find things out for us; as it is written: *'From whom much is forgiven, much is required'*. We learned that these killings were done by a very secretive Satanic cult known as the *Temple of Anubis*. They're hard-core. Those few informants that actually knew of their existence are all scared of them."

"Can't the police do anything to stop them?"

"The police are pretty much powerless in dealing with this," Bjorn admitted. "All they have been able to do is pick up the bodies and try to keep a lid on the publicity. These killings are not the acts of one or even two people - they must have a well-developed network of people involved. Nobody seems to know exactly who or how many there are. But I'll tell you this much - if things continue as they are, we'll have suspicions rising and finger pointing the likes of which haven't been seen since the Salem witch trials."

"If the police can't do anything about it, what can be done?" Jim wondered.

"I'm surprised you have to ask that!" replied Bjorn. "With man, it is not possible, but with God, all things are possible."

"Of course, we must pray for God to intervene in this situation," Jim acknowledged.

"Indeed we do. One of the reasons I came way out here to see you is because I remember how much of a prayer warrior you were back in seminary. I hope you still are."

"And ... another reason?" Jim tentatively inquired, convicted of his diminished prayer life.

"The other reason is ... my sources also tell me that the *Temple of Anubis* is not restricted to Brazil only."

An awkward pause.

"They're here, Jim. In Southern California."

Without another word, both men shifted from their chairs, and knelt to pray.

As he knelt, Jim thought to himself, *Thank God they're not in Westlake Village.*

He had no idea that his world was about to change forever.

CHAPTER 7

Solid Rock Community Church: Westlake Village, CA

In the church office the next morning, Jim held court as was usual for a Friday morning. The weekly staff meeting was a time to review the past week's activities, and plan for the coming week. Time to catch up on who in the congregation was sick, who had prayer requests, who had a new baby, and anything else noteworthy.

Jim and the rest of the pastoral staff gathered around a small rectangular folding table in the conference room. In attendance were the church secretary, Beverly Hanson, the new Associate Pastor, Pete LeTourneu, Music Pastor Rick Samuels, and Youth Pastor Dave Linnemeir.

Rick had been with Jim since the start of Solid Rock Church. He talked about the coming Sunday's song list, what the worship team was working on for new music, and the status of the new CD they were recording.

Next up was Dave, who presented his plans for the youth group winter camp in the San Bernardino Mountains.

Beverly mentioned some of the more important telephone calls that had come in to the office that week, as well as presenting a list of office supplies that was needed. An amiable lady in her late fifties, Bev had been in church all her life. She had been widowed a few years ago, when her husband unexpectedly suffered a brain aneurysm.

At last Jim took the floor. He covered a yawn with the back of his hand, and talked about his sermon theme for the coming Sunday, and the order of the worship service. Then he mentioned his visit with Bjorn Nilsson, including everything that they had talked about.

Jim suppressed another yawn, and said, "I couldn't sleep last night, thinking about what Bjorn told me."

"Those are some pretty wild accusations that Pastor Nilsson is making," Pete LeTourneu said. "But what evidence do we have that it's true?"

"I've known Bjorn a long time," Jim declared, "and I know his character to be beyond reproach. He wouldn't come all the way out here just to tell me this if he didn't know in his heart it was true."

"I don't doubt that he believes it," Pete countered, "but maybe his sources are wrong. There's a lot of superstition in his part of the world – maybe his informants have fed on that superstition. It's just so implausible. Allegations about Satanic-related crimes have rarely, if ever, been proven."

"It's shocking, I'll agree, but not that implausible," Jim replied. "The bible says that our enemy, the Devil, prowls around like a roaring lion, seeking who he may devour. We need to be wise as serpents, and harmless as doves."

"I just wish Pastor Nilsson could be here now to give us more details," Pete persisted. "Did he go back to Brazil already?"

"Actually, he's probably on his way to the airport right now. He's going to Minneapolis to visit some other churches before going back to Brazil."

"It would have been nice to meet him," Pete said casually, staring out the window.

"Let's lift him up in prayer," Rick interjected. The others nodded in agreement, and proceeded to bow their heads.

After their closing prayer, the staff went their separate ways, back to their offices.

Pete took Dave by the arm and whispered in his ear, "I can't believe Pastor Jim would fall for that devil cult junk. What a crock!"

Dave said nothing, and went into his own office.

Pete watched him go. Then he rushed out to his car and drove off, as if he were late for an appointment.

CHAPTER 8

Los Angeles International Airport

Fridays at LAX were usually a madhouse, and today was no exception. Business travelers waited in long lines at ticket counters and pushed their way in and out of the baggage carousel area, eager to get home to their families for the weekend.

Bjorn was just coming away from the check-in counter with his boarding pass when he looked up and was surprised to see a young man who appeared to be in his late twenties carrying a sign that bore the name "Rev. Nilsson". He cautiously walked up to the man and identified himself.

"I'm Pastor Nilsson," he said tentatively, "but I didn't call for a ride."

"Pastor Nilsson!" The young man smiled widely, and extended his hand to Bjorn. "I'm Pete LeTourneu, Associate Pastor at Solid Rock. It's my pleasure to meet you."

"Ah, yes, Pastor LeTourneu! What a pleasant surprise. Pastor DiMario told me about you, and it was my regret not to have been able to meet you in person."

"Please, just call me Pete. Jim - that is, Pastor DiMario, asked me to stop by and see you off. He was so glad for your visit, and wishes you the best of God's blessings on the remainder of your trip."

"How thoughtful. But he didn't need to send you way out here just for that."

"It's no problem. I also brought along a bag of cookies for you, in case you get a bit hungry while waiting for your plane. One of the ladies at church bakes them for the staff members from time to time."

"Hey, that's great!" Bjorn's eyes lit up as Pete produced a ziplock bag full of chocolate chip cookies from his backpack, and handed them over. "I'll put these to good use," he said, patting his belly.

"I'm sure you will," Pete said with a smile. "Well, I wish there was time to hear all about your ministry, and what's going on in Brazil, but it looks like your plane will be boarding soon. I'd better let you go through security and get over to your boarding gate."

Bjorn glanced at his watch. "Right - thanks for the cookies, and the send-off," Bjorn said. "It was a pleasure meeting you, Pete."

"The pleasure was all mine."

They shook hands, and Pete watched as Bjorn turned and headed toward the metal detector checkpoint that leads to the departure lounge. LeTourneu then walked into the men's restroom, and washed his hands thoroughly.

***

Halfway through the flight to Minneapolis, meals were being served by the blue-uniformed flight attendants, who made their way slowly down the center aisle of the Boeing 737 with their carts laden with substandard food. But Bjorn didn't feel much like eating. In fact, he was tingling with sweat and feeling strangely nauseated. The smell of the pre-made dinners that came wafting down to Bjorn's nose on the recirculating air current was decidedly unappealing, and only made him feel worse.

I knew I should have taken an air-sickness pill back at the airport, he thought to himself.

The flight was a little bumpy, but nothing beyond normal.

Maybe some peanuts and 7-up will help settle my stomach, he reasoned. He waved his hand, trying to get the attention of a uniformed crew member.

Twenty minutes later, the peanuts a 7-up hadn't helped. By the time the 737 was making it's final approach toward Minneapolis/St. Paul International Airport, Bjorn was feeling really ill. He looked it, too, judging by the fact that all the passengers sitting around him had already requested new seat assignments some time ago. His head was pounding, his stomach was grinding, and the sweat had soaked his cotton golf shirt to the point that he wished he had a spare to change into. He could even feel his scalp tingle the way that it did when he was out jogging, and every pore on his body exuded sweat.

If I sit real still and breath steadily, maybe I won't throw up, he thought to himself hopefully.

But as the plane was descending in preparation to land, that certain tumultuous sensation gripped Bjorn suddenly, like Mount St. Helens about to erupt.

It was as if a voice inside his head shouted, *"Get to the Lav - now!"*. He complied. Bjorn launched out of his aisle seat and set out for the aft lavatory like a bull in a china shop.

A blonde flight attendant in his path started to say, "I'm sorry sir, but you'll have to return ...," before being nearly trampled underfoot. A couple of businessmen who were chatting across the aisle from each other saw the look on Bjorn's face and dodged out of the way fast, as he charged past them and into the lavatory.

CHAPTER 9

Minneapolis, MN

O n the ground in Minneapolis, Pastor Dennis Heipler was waiting patiently for Bjorn's plane to arrive. Pastor Dennis remembered Bjorn as a big, robust Christian leader who brought his contagious enthusiasm for the Lord with him wherever he went.

That mental picture of the man didn't match what came through the terminal gate. Bjorn was riding in a wheelchair, being pushed by two flight attendants. They were the first off the plane.

"Bjorn!" Pastor Dennis exclaimed as he rushed forward to meet them. "Oh, my Lord!"

Bjorn's skin was pale and green, and he was still wet with sweat. His trembling hands held a large plastic bowl. He needed it; it was partially full of a thick, white liquid with some small chunks floating in it.

"I think this man needs medical attention," said one of the flight attendants nervously. Her disgusted facial expressions and mannerisms conveyed a deep-seated fear of typhoid, AIDS, cholera, TB, hepatitis, and a host of other undesirable communicable diseases.

"We had to nearly drag him out of the lav," added the other. "Is he with you?"

"Yes. Please, help me get him to the car," Pastor Dennis said. "I'll pull up to the curb."

Ten minutes later, they were in Pastor Heipler's car, on the way to Minneapolis Lutheran Medical Center. On the way, Dennis tried to keep Bjorn awake and responsive.

"Bjorn, what happened to you? I've never seen you like this."

"I don't know - I was fine when I left California," Bjorn moaned. He curled his body into a tight ball facing the door. "Ohh! Are we almost there? I think I'm going to need a restroom soon."

"We're there," Dennis replied, as they pulled up to the ER entrance. "Let me hop out and get some help."

***

Dr. Miles Anderson pulled his head back from the CRT monitor of the Scanning Electron Microscope in the pathology lab. He rubbed his eyes and squinted, and looked again. Standing up, he shook his head quizzically, and reached for the phone.

"Get me Dr. Berger in the ER, please".

After a moment, Dr. Berger came on the line.

"Berger here," he barked hurriedly.

"Miles Anderson in pathology calling."

"What's up, Dr. Anderson?"

"I'm looking at the blood specimen from patient Nilsson that was sent up."

"Right, the gastro patient in bed E-six," Dr. Berger muttered while sifting through his notepad. He cradled the phone precariously between his shoulder and ear.

"I think you need to see this. I need a reality check."

"Can't you just tell me? I've got patients."

"I know, but this is important. Come on up."

"Okay, I'll be there as soon as I can."

Dr. Anderson put the phone down and walked over to the bookcase, where he proceeded to dig through his reference books like a man searching for buried treasure. At last, he found what he was looking for just as Dr. Berger walked briskly into the lab.

"Okay, what's so mysterious about a guy with a stomach bug?" Berger asked impatiently.

"The bug itself. Come have a look at this."

He guided Dr. Berger to the Scanning Electron Microscope that held a slide containing Bjorn Nilsson's blood specimen.

"What do you see?" inquired Dr. Anderson expectantly.

"Bacteria."

"No kidding. What kind?"

A long pause.

"Not sure. I'm not familiar with this one. What do you think it is?"

"I've only seen it in books - never in person," Dr. Anderson said excitedly. "Take a look at this."

He passed the open textbook to Dr. Berger. As he looked at the picture, his eyes grew wide. He looked back at the monitor, then back at the book.

"You're right!" he exclaimed finally, "*Bacillus Anthracis* - Anthrax!"

"Who is this patient of yours?"

"Don't know - but I'm sure going to find out," he said, hopping out of his seat and striding to the door.

He turned to face Dr. Anderson, just before passing the doorway.

"Thanks! You probably saved his life."

"Don't mention it," replied Anderson, but Dr. Berger had already disappeared into the hallway.

***

"You're a very sick man, Mr. Nilsson," Dr. Berger stated matter-of-factly, while peering into Bjorn's ears and eyes with his otoscope. "But I think you'll be okay eventually."

"Thanks for the words of encouragement, Doc," Bjorn replied mournfully, as his body cramped into a tight fetal position on the gurney. Sharp pains stabbed his entire abdomen like a blunt knife point.

"What do you think is wrong with me? I've … never been this sick in my life," he said breathlessly, struggling to get the words out.

"Mr. Nilsson, I need to know everywhere you've been, and everything you've done for the past few days. Have you been out of the country recently; on a farm, perhaps?"

"I live in Brazil; but I've been in the U.S. for a little while."

"How long, exactly?"

"About three days."

"Hmmm. You must have picked it up in Brazil. It's virtually unheard of here. That's a pretty long interval of time for it to present, though."

"What's unheard of?"

"Woolsorter's disease," Dr. Berger declared with a serious tone. "It's caused by the Anthrax bacteria."

"Anthrax - but how could I have contracted that?"

"You must have eaten some contaminated meat. If you had inhaled the spores, it would have presented in your respiratory system. And ...," he added for emphasis, "you'd probably be on your way to the grave in that case."

"But I don't see how ...," Bjorn's protest trailed off, too weak to even finish the sentence.

"Have you been feeling sick for awhile now?"

"No," Bjorn croaked. "I was fine until I got on the plane."

"Strange," the doctor said, scratching his chin, and looking off into space. "You should have been feeling sick before now, if you picked it up in Brazil."

"Sorry to disappoint you," Bjorn moaned.

"Nurse!" barked Dr. Berger, turning toward the desk, "Give this patient two cc's of Zithromax, intramuscular, with Phenergan. Get him on a drip of Ringer's lactate. Then have him admitted, stat. He'll be with us for awhile."

CHAPTER 10

Westlake Village, California

Jim was out for an early morning jog when he saw it – and wished that he hadn't.

As usual, he was jogging through the green-belted area in his Westlake Village neighborhood. It was a large neighborhood of nice homes, with areas of grass interspersed with paved pathways. The homes adjacent to the grassy common areas had high walls surrounding them, to ensure privacy from people walking along the paths behind the homes.

He had just crossed Greenmeadow Drive, and jogged at a steady pace down the narrow pathway between the high walls of two luxurious homes. Rounding a gradual bend in the path, something unusual crept into his peripheral vision up ahead on the right. It was a cat, lying on the grass - but it wasn't moving. Nor did it look up at him as he approached. Jim jogged in place for a moment as he watched the cat. As he studied the cat's motionless body, Jim noticed that the calico mix was missing something - it's head.

"Oh, Lord - not again," Jim muttered out loud.

It had happened before, though Jim had never seen it himself. There were reports going back several years about mutilated cats being found in this neighborhood. Nobody ever saw who was doing it, although it appeared that this neighborhood of green belts was just a dumping ground for the eviscerated animals. The police took reports from the concerned homeowners, but there was nothing that they could really do. The occurrences were fairly irregular; there was no predictability to it.

Jim moved tentatively over to the headless feline. The hair on the back of his neck stood up when he saw that it had been mutilated beyond mere decapitation. There was a slice along the distended underside of the animal, traveling almost the full length of the body. From this clean and deliberate-looking incision, various internal organs had been pulled out and laid upon the grass. Viewing this grisly scene, Jim couldn't help but notice that it looked like a deliberate display.

"What kind of sick creep would do something like this?" Jim mumbled to himself.

Disgusted, he turned away and walked down the path for a short distance before falling back into a jogging pace.

Jim walked briskly down Westlake Boulevard to cool down from his run. A steady stream of late-model cars glided by him on their morning pilgrimage to the freeway, with billowing streams of condensation flowing out of their tailpipes like ethereal ghosts, dancing in the cool morning air.

Jim always looked forward to the reward of a good cup of coffee at the end of his run - the proverbial pot of gold at the end of the rainbow. As he pushed open the door at the local Starbucks Coffee House, the piquant smell of fresh-ground espresso beans filled his nostrils. He inhaled deeply as he strode to the counter. The scent was as effective at clearing his mind as eucalyptus vapors were at clearing the sinuses.

"Good morning, Pastor Jim, what can I get you today?" said the fresh-faced, brown-haired young lady behind the cash register, with a smile.

"Good morning, Shelly. I'll have my usual, thanks."

"One quad venti percent latté," she called to the matronly barista working the stainless steel espresso machine.

Jim looked over his shoulder and saw that there was nobody in line behind him. "What's new with you, Shelly?" he asked. "I didn't see you at church last week. You know, I could really use someone with your bible knowledge and people skills to lead the new young adult bible study that I'm planning."

"Thanks, Pastor Jim," Shelly replied, blushing slightly. "I appreciate you thinking of me. There's just so much to do between working here and going to college, too. I'm just not sure how I can fit it in right now."

"Well, think it over. I really think that you would make a great leader."

"I will think about it. So, what's new with you?"

"Well, I got more than I asked for on my run this morning. I came across a mutilated cat."

"Oh, no! I was hoping we'd seen the last of that," Shelly said, with a grimace. "You know," she added, lowering her voice, "Some of my friends think that Satanists are behind it."

Jim felt gooseflesh on his arms and neck, as if an Arctic gust had just blown in on him.

"Satanists! Really. What makes them think that?" Jim asked, as casually as he could manage.

"Well," said Shelly, lowering her voice further as she leaned toward Jim, "My friend Trey thinks that they use the blood for various ceremonies. The heart and head supposedly give some kind of power to the Satanist."

Sitting unnoticed in a corner with his back to a wall, a stranger had tuned in to their conversation, and was listening intently.

"Are we talking about Trey Simmons?" Jim inquired. "How does Trey know about this kind of stuff?"

"Yeah, Trey Simmons. He's actually done a lot of research on Satanism, cults and the occult. All the weird stuff. It's kind of a hobby for him, I guess."

"Is he a Christian? I don't really know him very well."

"Yes, Pastor - a strong Christian, too. Knows the bible real well. In fact, you might actually want to consider him for a bible study leader."

"Thanks for the tip. Do you have his phone number?"

"No, but you do."

Jim's face displayed a baffled look.

"The church directory. It has everyone's address and phone number, doesn't it?"

"Right," said Jim through an embarrassed smile. "I'll look him up. Thanks, and I'll see you Sunday, okay?"

Jim started to turn away and head toward the door. As he did, the stranger in the corner stood up abruptly and plotted an intercept course.

"Excuse me, Pastor?"

"Yes, can I help you?"

The stranger extended his hand.

"George Tanaka, KNLA TV."

Jim looked him in the face. Suddenly, a look of surprise crossed his own face as the realization hit home.

"Hey, you're that guy on TV!" Jim gushed. He immediately felt silly as soon as the trite observation had passed his lips. "Uh, what brings you to Westlake Village today? Must be a slow news day."

"Yeah it is, actually. I'm out here to do an interview with Aldon Brehm. You know, the candidate for County Supervisor." Then he added with a tone of sarcasm, "Election day is less than a month away, after all. I'm sure he'll make LA County a better place – if he's elected."

"Oh, yeah, Brehm," Jim acknowledged. He's a college professor or something, isn't he?"

"Right. Say, Pastor ..."

"Jim DiMario. Just call me Jim."

"Okay, Jim. You know, I happened to overhear you mention that you found a mutilated cat along your jogging path."

Jim noticed out of his peripheral vision a few pairs of eyes turning their way.

"Umm ... let's talk outside."

Leaving the aroma of coffee behind, they stepped out into the cool, crisp morning air. After casually looking both directions, Jim motioned to a green metal table with two chairs, and they sat.

"Yeah, it's true," Jim continued cautiously. "Not a pretty sight, that's for sure."

"And this has happened before?"

"I'm afraid so. Every now and then, there's a brief mention of a new occurrence in the local paper. It goes back a long time in our town - several years."

"What about the police? Have they ever arrested anyone in connection with these crimes?"

"Nah," Jim said, shaking his head somberly. "There have never been any witnesses. None that have come forward, anyway."

George had been warming up to drop the bombshell question.

"So, what's with the Satanism connection? Do you think that some Satanic cult is responsible for these mutilations?"

"Oh, I don't know about that," Jim said, averting his eyes away from George's piercing gaze. "That's what this one young man thinks."

"I'd like to meet him."

"What - who?"

"The young man that your friend Shelly was talking about. Trey something, wasn't it?"

"You don't miss much, do you?" Jim said suspiciously.

"Would you introduce me to him?"

Jim sat silently for a long moment, thinking. At last he spoke.

"Do you believe in the Devil and his demons, Mr. Tanaka?"

"Not really. I've seen a lot of evil deeds perpetrated over the years, that's for sure. I don't know if we can blame that on Satan, or if it's just the evil within men's hearts."

"Actually, we have three enemies, Mr. Tanaka; The World, The Flesh, and The Devil. Each of these enemies fights against what The Lord wants for our lives, so a combination of these ..."

"Can we save the sermon for another time, Pastor?" George cut in, "I'd really like to visit with this kid, and ...," he added with a wink, "I'll bet you would, too."

"I thought you had an interview with the candidate."

"I'll call to reschedule, no problem. Right now, he needs me more than I need him. So, then...," George said, nodding his head toward the parking lot "My car or yours?"

CHAPTER 11

Lake Sherwood, California

In the middle of a small clearing set within a dark forested area, six figures stand around a crackling fire. Their naked bodies are eerily illuminated by the flickering glow of the firelight. Four men and two women stand in the grassy glade, within the confines of a circle made of small stones.

One of the men strikes a gong once. The clear, mournful sound pierces the dark loneliness of this remote place.

"Hail, Anubis! Hail, Satan!" the leader exclaims loudly. "We call upon you now. Heed our call."

"Hail, Satan," the others intone in unison.

The leader strikes the gong again, allowing the sound to resonate around the glade.

"We demand that you fulfill our requests," he says. "Shemhamforash!"

"Shemhamforash," comes the reply.

The leader now picks up a sword from the ground, and points it at each of the four directions of the compass as he speaks.

"We call upon the four Princes of Hell – Satan, Lucifer, Belial, Leviathan – come forth!"

At this, the leader places the sword back on the ground, and picks up a paintbrush, and a small plastic container. He opens the lid of a plastic container. He holds the container above his head.

"May this sacrifice be found worthy!" he shouts.

The man turns and steps between the fire and the woman on his left, facing her. Dipping the small paintbrush into the dark fluid in the container, he quickly raises the brush and draws it across her forehead. She smiles through the blood dripping down her face, and he replenishes the brush in the container. He returns the sodden brush to her again. This time starting at her left shoulder, he draws it slowly and deliberately across her torso to the other shoulder. The crimson fluid glistens in the firelight as it flows down her breasts and drips to the ground.

Turning himself to the left, he steps slowly to the next participant, and repeats the process. Working his way around the circle, he finally returns to his place, where he is anointed in like fashion by the woman on his left.

Bending down again to set the container of blood on the ground, he now picks up a second container and lifts the lid. Reaching inside, he seizes the contents, and pulls it out.

"Behold!" he shouts, lifting a severed cat's head above his own. "We offer this animal as a worthy sacrifice, Lords of Darkness. We offer it's suffering for your pleasure, we offer the suffering of it's owner to you."

At this, the other five figures become more animated. Raising their hands above their heads and throwing their heads back, they call out to their favorite demonic entities. As their entreaties become louder and more feverish, they start to move to the left around the circle in a trance-like state.

"You who dwell in the outer darkness, come forth to do our bidding," implores their leader. "Shemhamforash!"

"Shemhamforash," the others echo.

A low-pitched whistling sound can be heard through the trees, as the wind suddenly picks up.

"Grant us victory over all who would oppose our great Satan," the leader declares.

"Hail, Satan!"

Putting the cat's head back into it's container, the leader again takes the container of blood and dips his hands into it. Approaching the entranced woman next to him, he begins rubbing the blood every which way about her body, until her pale white skin is covered with red smears.

The wind rises in intensity, and dark shadows begin to faintly take shape outside the circle. Amorphous shapes and outlines of various sizes stand or hover above the ground, seemingly weightless. A foul sulfurous stench suddenly envelops the participants, but they hardly seem to notice.

"Go forth, and torment our enemies!" the leader cries.

"Hail, Satan!"

CHAPTER 12

Simmons Residence: Westlake Village, California

Jim DiMario rapped the knocker loudly on the door of the Simmons house three times.

What am I doing? he asked himself. *This is probably a big mistake.*

He turned to face his new acquaintance as they waited on the porch. "Remember, we agree that I will do the talking, and you will not use the boy's name in any article without permission, right?" Jim admonished.

"Of course, of course," George replied, "I already gave you my word on that."

"I know, and I'll hold you to it. After all, this young man is a member of my congregation. He needs to know that his pastor would not violate his trust, and ..."

"Okay, okay, I get the picture. Besides, he might not have anything Earth-shattering to tell us, anyway."

Presently the door opened, and they were greeted with a figure standing in the doorway somewhat reminiscent of a scarecrow. He was tall and lanky, with brown hair that stood up straight in a spiked fashion. He had earring studs in both ears, and wore baggy jeans that threatened to slip off his hips at any moment. His orange T-shirt was emblazoned with the name *Ezekiel*, one of the popular skateboard and clothing companies.

"Whoa! Pastor DiMario," he exclaimed, with a startled look on his face. "What's up? Are you here to see my mom? She already left for work."

"Hello, Trey," Jim answered, smiling. "Actually, we're here to see you. Do you mind if we come in for a few minutes?"

"No problemo, Pastor. Come on in."

The young man stepped aside to allow them entrance, while eyeing the stranger warily. They passed by him and into the dimly lit front room of the modest house. The old furniture was accented by a few inexpensive-looking pictures on the walls, which Jim figured to be swap-meet art. Jim noticed that in spite of the austere appearance of the room, the home was scrupulously clean and tidy.

Trey beckoned them with a flick of the wrist to sit on the worn brown sofa in the living room, and they obliged. Trey sat on a chair opposite them, fidgeting at the end of his seat until Jim spoke up.

"Trey, this is George Tanaka. He works for ..."

"KNLA News," Trey interrupted, snapping his fingers. "Yeah, that's it, I recognize you. Hey, is this about the big paintball tournament next weekend? Me and my crew are ready to bust out a win this time."

"Actually," Jim continued, "I could use your help in trying to understand something. I hear that you have some knowledge about Satanism. We were hoping that you could give us your take on what's happening to the dead cats that have been found here in town."

Trey's countenance brightened at this, and Jim thought that he suddenly seemed more relaxed.

"Yeah, it's true. I am kind of into Satanism and the occult - learning about it, that is," he clarified. "I mean, don't get me wrong; I'm a Christian - I'm totally sold out for Christ – I'm fireproof. But I think that any self-respecting Jesus Freak should know something about the enemy. After all, doesn't the bible say that our enemy, The Devil, prowls around like a roaring lion, seeking whom he may devour, or something like that?"

"Right," Jim acknowledged. "First Peter five-eight."

"Yeah, that's it. Anyway, I guess that it's kind of a hobby or pastime of mine the last couple years. I've learned a lot about different Satanic groups and their practices. I've even studied about witchcraft and other pagan religions. The 'Left-Handed Path', and all that."

"The Left-Handed Path?" George probed.

Jim shot him a stern look.

"Yeah," Trey replied. "It's kind of a generic term for those who practice ritualistic majick."

"But witchcraft?" Jim asked surprisedly. "Surely you're not suggesting that there are real witches running around killing cats?"

Trey chuckled condescendingly. "I *am* saying that there are modern-day witches. Shoot, they're not even very low-key. You could probably meet one face to face at that metaphysical bookstore down on Grand Avenue. And, of course, there's that best-selling author of kid's books from England, who's a self-proclaimed witch. But no, I don't think that witches are responsible for killing these cats. It doesn't line up with their creeds. Wiccans – or witches in general, claim to do no harm to anyone. They're just not into that kind of stuff – killing and dismembering animals."

"Who, then?" Jim pressed, "what kind of people would do something like this to helpless animals?"

Trey sat forward on the edge of his chair. He leaned forward and stared into Jim's eyes, and slowly answered, "The kind of people who believe that they gain power from the death of innocents. In a word, Satanists. They believe that all creatures have a life force, which is released at the moment they die. I hate to say it, but they probably torture the animal before they kill it to make sure it releases adrenaline into it's bloodstream. That supposedly makes the blood more powerful. They would probably kill the animal inside a *'majick circle'* so that they can absorb it's energy."

"What is this 'majick circle' you're talking about? There wasn't anything like that near the cat I found this morning."

Trey jerked his head back and raised his eyebrows, clearly startled. "Whoa, Pastor! You didn't tell me you found a cat yourself."

"Sorry," Jim replied, "I was going to get to that. I found it while I was jogging this morning through The Greens."

"Well," Trey started taking in a deep breath, "they wouldn't have killed it there. The Greens is probably just a dumping ground. All of those green belts are too close to people's houses to do anything there. The ritual sacrifices must take place somewhere else. They need plenty of room, away from prying eyes. Anyway, to answer your question, the majick circle is where the ceremony itself takes place. It would be clearly marked out on the floor - or the ground, if they're doing it outside. It would be exactly nine feet in diameter, and probably marked with paint, chalk, or stones. Satanists believe that it focuses their energy, and protects them."

"Protects them?" George asked. "From what?"

Trey shifted in his seat toward them again. "From the demonic forces they conjure," he said eerily.

Jim wondered if Trey was being sarcastic in his response, but the stony look on his young face told him that he was dead serious.

George broke the silence that was hanging in the air. "Why would they dump the bodies of the cats in The Greens?" he asked.

"Probably for intimidation, to gain some psychological advantage. They would never identify themselves, or plainly advertise what they're doing. But the fact that they are purposely leaving the remains where they will be found; they must be 'flexing their muscles' so to speak. They're letting us know that they're here."

"How ...how many people do you think would be involved in something like this?" Jim asked haltingly, while thinking to himself, *I'm not sure I want to know.*

"It's hard to say, without seeing more evidence. It could be the work of one self-styled Satanist working alone, or it could be a big, organized pylon or grotto of up to say, fifty people or so."

Jim paused to catch his breath. *Maybe it's just one person*, he thought hopefully.

"What do you think, Trey?" George pressed. "What's your expert opinion?"

Trey laughed out loud, seemingly enjoying his new role of consultant to the Senior Pastor and a top news reporter.

"Dude, I'm not an expert - just a college student," he replied, straining to put a note of humility in his voice. "But I've gotta say that, because of how clean the remains are – according to what I've heard, and how stealthy the acts are, and how often it's happened …it's got to be a group of people, not just one person doing it alone."

Just what I didn't want to know, Jim thought. "So, I'm still not understanding what would motivate them to these kinds of things," he said. "What do they want, anyway?"

"That's simple - power. Power over their career and standing in the community. Power to get money, sex, you name it. And especially, power over their enemies."

"Their enemies?" Jim repeated, entranced. "Who exactly are their enemies?"

Trey sat back abruptly and cocked his head in disbelief. "Pastor - I can't believe that you would have to ask a question like that. You are their enemy. I'm their enemy. Anyone who declares that Jesus Christ is Lord is their enemy."

Jim swallowed hard. He could feel the sweat start to ooze out of his pores, all over his body.

If I'm their enemy, he thought, *could I or my family be in some kind of danger? I wonder who these people are, and what else they're capable of.*

CHAPTER 13

Lake Sherwood, California

The midday sun shone down upon Lake Sherwood, making the surface sparkle like a tray full of diamonds. The lake and the rustic, spread-out community that bears it's name sits immediately to the west of Westlake Village, but it seems a world away. Where Westlake Boulevard ends, the smooth curves of Decker Canyon Road begin, as it winds it's way like a serpent past Lake Sherwood on it's circuitous path down to Pacific Coast Highway.

As the men pushed their way slowly through the dense brush that clawed at their legs, Jim started to have doubts about the wisdom of what he, Trey, and George Tanaka had come to do.

What in the world have I got myself into? he said to himself, *I'm wasting my day on a wild goose chase, that's what. Why did I let this reporter guy talk me into it?*

Trey was in the lead. For the last twenty minutes, he'd followed an almost invisible deer trail through the hills surrounding Lake Sherwood. The sun was up, but it wasn't too hot. The burning heat of the Southern California summer was past, and the smell of autumn air held the promise of more temperate weather.

Approaching the top of a hill, Trey stopped for a moment. "Where did your friend say this place was?" Jim asked breathlessly. He bent over and rested his hands on his knees.

"His house is right down there," Trey replied, pointing a bony index finger at a hillside home about a quarter of a mile to the south. "Jason said the fires he saw were about a half a mile away, looking straight out from his bedroom window. That would be right over in that direction," he said, motioning to a hilly area covered with dense chaparral.

"Like I said at the house, it couldn't have been campers – there's no camping allowed up here. And the fire went out after only about half an hour, according to what Jason said. There's no trailhead, really. This isn't even a hiking area, you know? Whoever was up here probably parked their cars on a side street and went up this little deer path. They must be real familiar with the area to be able to follow this path in the dark."

Jim felt the blood pumping through his legs and sweat forming on his body as he resigned himself to keep going.

Trey continued to lead the way, flanked by Jim and George.

Jim noticed that George didn't seem to be enjoying this nature outing any more than he was, judging by the flushed and frustrated look on his face and the sweat pouring from his brow.

They were working their way through the chaparral and bushes, when a limb that Trey was pushing past suddenly whipped back into Jim's face.

"Arghh!" he cried out, as the sharp limb stung him. "Trey! Watch what you're doing, will you?"

"Sorry, Pastor," Trey replied, without looking back.

"Hey, Rev," George piped up, "I thought I might hear a preacher swear just then."

"Not today," Jim said, continuing to plod along.

"How do you guys do it, anyway?"

"Do what?"

"You know - biting your tongue all the time. Keeping yourself from swearing, or giving people the finger when they cut you off on the road, or making off-color remarks and such."

"Well, I can't say that I've always been too good about that in the past. But I don't have to bite my tongue really. Jesus said, *'Out of the abundance of the heart, the mouth speaks'*. I'm not claiming to be especially holy just because I'm a pastor, but God has granted me a lot of victory in the area of my speech. Several years ago I started praying particularly for that. Still do, in fact."

Their conversation was interrupted when they suddenly broke out of the heavy foliage into a clearing. Trey stopped abruptly, causing Jim to bump into him. He stared at something in the clearing. George caught up, and he saw it, too.

"What is it?" he asked, panting.

"I knew it," Trey replied gloatingly. "Just like I told you. It's a ceremonial site."

Stepping slowly and deliberately into the clearing, Jim noticed the large ring of small rocks that made a circle on the ground. Inside the ring were the remnants of a small campfire. Approaching the ring, Jim noticed that the ground inside the ring looked darker than that of the surrounding area. George pulled out a small digital camera that he had stashed in his pocket, and took a few pictures of the site.

Trey squatted down outside the edge of the ring, and carefully examined it. Reaching inside the circle, he laid the palm of his hand on the ground, and wiped it across the earth slowly. Then he turned his hand over, palm up.

"Yo! - Pastor, check it out," he shouted.

Jim and George came over immediately, and found Trey's outstretched hand stained with dark red stripes.

"Is ... that what I think it is?" Jim asked. He immediately realized that his question was too obvious to require an answer.

"Something bad went down here, all right," Trey declared. "There's blood all over the place, mostly inside the circle."

Jim stood rigidly, looking down at Trey's bloody hand and the circle of stones. His face took on a blank stare, feeling the comfortable predictability of his day to day life starting to spin out of control. He didn't know how to put the brakes on. The reality of spiritual warfare was now staring him brazenly in the face. The smell of the blood-soaked earth and the buzz of the flies that were swarming around the area became too much for him.

"I've got to sit down," he said at last, finding a large lichen-covered rock nearby to park himself on.

George, meanwhile, was scribbling furiously in his notebook and taking pictures of the site from various angles.

"Hey," Jim called out, "make sure you don't get either of us in those pictures."

Jim's body felt like a wet noodle as he sat on the rock, surveying the scene. Just this morning before leaving the house, everything had seemed to be fine in his world. In spite of his great respect and admiration for Bjorn Nilsson, Jim had been allowing himself to think that maybe Bjorn was wrong, or just overreacting. But now, faced with both the disemboweled cat on the jogging path, and this bloody site, he had to come to terms with the unpleasant fact that all was not well. He had an unnerving sensation like he was waiting for the other shoe to drop. He didn't have to wait long.

"You know ...," George said casually, sauntering over to where Jim was seated, "I didn't really think that what the cop told me about that murder the other day was true. But now - I'm not sure what to think."

"What are you talking about?" Jim responded, still in a daze.

"Don't you watch the news? I'm talking about the teenage girl who was murdered. I reported it from the crime scene two days ago."

"Yeah, I saw that!" Trey chimed in as he walked over to join them. "That sounded like a sexual assault. But I gotta say, George, you were a little sketchy on the details."

"I didn't have a choice," George replied defensively. "The FBI was all over me about that. They didn't want the details to be made public, for fear of losing the advantage over the killer."

"So, what were the details?" Trey pressed.

For a split second, the bright red dot of a laser touched the rock that Jim was sitting on, but none of them noticed.

Unknown to the three of them, someone else was listening attentively, too. Hidden in the chaparral about a hundred yards up the hill from them, a pair of eyes watched through binoculars, and the observer's pair of ears listened to their every word through a high-tech directional sound amplification system.

***

"We've got a problem," the young man said, bursting into the dimly lit, smoke-filled office.

"What kind of problem?" asked the portly, gray-haired man seated behind a large mahogany desk. His large mouth wrapped around an equivalently large cigar, as he casually took a puff. Three others sat in chairs around the desk.

"The ceremonial site has been compromised," the young man answered breathlessly.

"By who?"

"That pastor, James DiMario. He had a news reporter with him, and some kid - I don't know who he is."

"Then find out who he is," demanded the gray-haired man, his voice rising in intensity. "I want to know exactly who is playing with us. But first, take some men up there and cleanse the site. Clean it up good - don't leave anything. And make sure you're not seen. I want it to look completely natural next time someone stops by. And I'm sure they'll be back. Get going."

The man turned and rushed out through the door as quickly as he came. After a moment of silence, a woman sitting opposite the gray-haired man at the desk spoke up.

"So, DiMario wants to start probing around now? Perhaps he has too much spare time on his hands."

"Perhaps we can change that," said a man next to her, with a sly grin. They all broke out in raucous laughter.

"I'm sure we can!" she replied. "But what about the reporter and the kid?"

The man behind the desk blew a smoke ring toward the ceiling. "Find out everything you can about them. I'm sure we can find things to keep them busy, too." He sat forward in his chair as he snuffed out the cigar in a heavy cut-glass ashtray on the desk. "But for now, let's focus on DiMario. As his bible says: *'I shall strike the shepherd, and the sheep will scatter'.*"

With a self-satisfied smile, he added, "This is going to be fun. Let the games begin!"

Almost in unison, the men and women seated around the desk began to laugh uproariously.

CHAPTER 14

Solid Rock Community Church: Westlake Village, California

Jim was in the office early to get a jump start on the day. Even though a couple days had passed since the outing in the woods with the reporter and Trey Simmons, he couldn't get his mind to quit thinking about what had transpired over the last several days.

"What's on the agenda today?" Jim asked Beverly Hanson.

"Let's see … you've got a ten o'clock meeting with …," Beverly paged through her day planner until she found today's page, "Angela Shepherd."

"Who's she?"

"I don't know. I don't think I've met her myself. Anyway, she's a member of the congregation who wants to see you about marriage difficulties."

"Is her husband coming?"

"She didn't say."

"Okay. Let me know when they get here. I'll be in my office."

Jim closed the door behind him and sat down at his desk. He knew he needed guidance on what action to take next – or if any action on his part was needed, for that matter. There was only one source he knew of to get it. Folding his hands on his desk, he slouched his head over and began to pray. Jim prayed for wisdom, for his family, his church, and for certain church members in particular.

He lost track of time when he was at last brought back to the here-and-now by the phone on the desk ringing. It was the inside line.

"Yes, Bev?"

"Pastor, Mrs. Shepherd is here to see you."

"Okay, thanks."

Jim hung up and said a quick *amen* before getting up to meet his visitor in the church office's small lobby, where Beverly sat. As he came out of his office at the far end of the complex and started down the hall, a woman who appeared to be in her late twenties stood up from her chair to greet him.

"Pastor," she said, taking his outstretched hand, "Thank you for seeing me on such short notice."

Jim didn't recognize her, but that wasn't so unusual for a church the size of Solid Rock. He couldn't help but notice, though, that she was strikingly beautiful, with wavy blond hair that came down to the middle of her back. Her shapely figure was tucked into a tightly-fitted business outfit that consisted of a light blue buttoned jacket with a matching skirt that was short enough to show off her athletic legs.

"Will your husband be joining us today?" Jim asked.

"No. He … well, he isn't willing to acknowledge that we have some real problems that need to be worked out."

"Okay, well, why don't you come on back to my office."

Jim motioned for her to go down the hallway. As she did, Jim turned to look at Beverly, who nodded knowingly.

Jim made it a policy to never be alone in the office complex with a woman; it was a matter of appearances. He did meet with women in his office occasionally if there was some personal issue to discuss, but never without other staff members in the vicinity.

Jim followed her back to his office, and shut the door. He motioned for her to sit in the chair in front of his desk. He pulled his own chair out from behind his desk, and sat down to face her.

"Well, let's start with a word of prayer, shall we?" Jim said as he bowed his head. "Lord, we ask your blessing upon Angela and her husband. You already know all about the difficulties that they are having. You have said in your Word that the very hairs on our heads are numbered; You know more about us than we know ourselves. I pray this morning that you would help bring reconciliation and restoration to the Shepherd family. In Jesus' name we pray, amen."

As Jim raised his head, he noticed that Angela was already sitting upright, looking at him. Taking a deep breath, he started with a gentle opening question.

"So, tell me what's going on in your life, Angela."

"Well, Pastor, I hardly know where to begin," she said tentatively, shifting uncomfortably in her seat. "I've been married to my husband, Dave, for about three years now. I'm at a point now where I just don't know if I can keep going."

"What seems to be the problem? You said that Dave doesn't really think that there is a problem."

"That's just his way of dealing with it. He thinks that if he ignores it, maybe it will go away. But it doesn't …" The pitch of her voice went up to a squeak as she started to sob. "It just gets worse all the time."

"And what exactly is that?" Jim inquired gently.

"He ignores me all the time," she continued, sobbing intermittently. "He barely talks to me at all when we get home from work, except to ask what's for dinner. He doesn't talk during dinner, and then he watches TV for the rest of the evening. Whenever I try to start a conversation, he just gives a one-word answer, or sometimes says nothing at all. I feel like I'm not even there."

Angela broke into a full cry, with tears flowing freely. The waterworks lasted for a minute or so before she composed herself enough to continue.

"Excuse me, Pastor," she said, casually undoing the three large buttons of her jacket. "I'm really hot."

She began to fan herself with her unbuttoned jacket. Jim noticed that she was wearing a thin white tight-fitted blouse underneath her jacket. Thanks to the polyester material, and her buxom form that pulled at the buttons of the blouse, he also couldn't help but notice that there was nothing under it.

"I've tried everything I can think of to get him to notice me," she continued, dabbing her eyes with a tissue.

How could he not notice? Jim thought to himself.

"I've bought nice lingerie to wear in the evening, I've tried to do all kinds of things to please him, but nothing works. He just doesn't seem to want to share himself with me."

She broke into sobbing again. While sitting in the chair facing Jim with her legs crossed, she had been fidgeting and squirming around so much that her short skirt was now riding dangerously high on her thighs.

"Pastor, we haven't even had sex in six months," she blurted out, with a tear running down one cheek. Now she indiscreetly uncrossed her legs in front of Jim, giving him a clear view of her inner thighs and points beyond. She leaned back in her chair, looking directly into his eyes. "Tell me, am I really so undesirable?"

Jim started to sweat, and alarm bells began ringing in his head. He stood up abruptly, signaling the end of the session. Angela slowly stood as well.

"I'm going to recommend a good Christian marriage counselor for you and Dave," he said. Picking up the phone, he quickly punched Beverly's number. "Could you come in here, please?" he said into the phone, with a note of urgency that he hoped Bev would pick up on.

"Oh, thank you so much for listening to me, Pastor," she said. Then she lurched toward Jim, and locked him in a tight hug.

Just at that moment, Beverly came into the room. Jim tried to gently push Angela off of him, and she finally disengaged.

"Bev, would you give Angela the phone number of Scott Corwin, please?" Jim asked. "Maybe you can set up an initial meeting with him for Angela and her husband."

"Of course," Beverly said, eyeing Angela up and down. "If you come out to my desk, I'll get you set up."

"Oh, look at the state of me!" Angela said, seemingly embarrassed.

She finished wiping her tears, then straightened her skirt and buttoned her jacket back up. Finally, she followed Beverly back out to the lobby. Jim came to the doorway a moment later after collecting himself and looked down the hall. He observed Beverly on the phone, and Angela was still straightening herself, while brushing her hair and touching up her makeup in the large mirror. About this time, Pete LeTourneu appeared at the door of his office, which was directly across from Jim's. He looked at Jim, then down the hall at Angela.

"Whoa!" he said, "what went on in here?"

He and Jim locked eyes, then Pete turned and went back into his office. Jim went back into his office, too, and sat at his desk. He took several minutes to gather his thoughts about what had just taken place, then picked up the phone and pressed Bev's extension.

"Is she gone yet?" he asked.

"Yes, Pastor, she is."

"Make out a work order for the church handyman. I want a window put in the wall here, between my office and where your desk sits."

"Will do. I understand, Pastor."

***

The ladies bible study morning at Solid Rock was a beehive of activity, judging by the busy parking lot. Jasmine pulled into a parking stall and started to get out of her car, but then paused for a moment to muster her courage before facing the roomful of women that she knew were waiting. She took a peek in the rear-view mirror to check her hair and makeup. Looking back at her was the image of a pretty, but solemn-looking woman approaching forty, without a smile on her face. There was barely a hint of crow's feet forming around her green eyes, and her blonde hair was perfectly styled in a way that flattered the shape of her slightly round face.

Get it together, girl, she said to her reflection.

She slowly got out of the car and made a deliberate effort to paste a smile on her face.

Jasmine walked through the main door and into the outer narthex, which was a sizable buffer zone between the huge main sanctuary and the outside. As soon as she walked in, Jasmine was sure that she could feel the gaze of several sets of eyes fall upon her.

Her friend Barbara Armstrong was sitting inside the main sanctuary, and she looked up from her bible study notes when Jasmine came in. She immediately got up and hurried over to greet Jasmine with a hug.

"I love that outfit!" Barbara gushed, scanning up and down Jasmine's black pantsuit with the animal print trim. "I wish I could wear something like that."

"So what's stopping you?" Jasmine asked. "You always have such good taste in clothes."

"About twenty extra pounds, that's what," she said, patting her own ample buttocks for emphasis. "I don't know how you can stay as thin as you do, considering the kind of delicious dinners you make."

Jasmine wrapped her arm around her friend's shoulder and drew her close.

Just then, Barbara looked up and noticed the bible study director walking over to the raised podium area in the main sanctuary. The room started to get quiet. "Oh, look, it's time. Come on, let's go in and get started."

Jasmine was glad to have Barbara as the leader of her bible study group. A mature Christian believer for many years, Barbara knew how to handle a bible study, and she was Jasmine's closest friend. She was also the only friend Jasmine felt that she could trust completely. Their group was also the largest, with eight regular members.

With so many women present that morning, few people noticed the new girl sitting in the group next to Barbara's. That group's leader, Tracy Singleton, a twenty-something redhead, introduced the newcomer to the other five members sitting in their own circle.

"Ladies, I want to welcome Angela Shepherd to our group. She's new to Westlake Village, and to the church, so I want to make her feel welcome."

All of the women took turns greeting her enthusiastically, introducing themselves and shaking her hand. After the introductions were over, they all turned in their books to the study for that week - *'Becoming a woman of Grace'*.

"I'm so excited about starting this study," Angela said, "I've been looking forward to it so much. And I've heard so many good things about your group. I'm glad you could fit me in."

"We're glad to have you," the leader said. "Who recommended this group to you?"

"Oh, it was Pastor Pete. He told me what a great supportive bunch you are. And I could really use the support of a group of solid Christian ladies like yourselves right now."

Jasmine was tuned in to the conversation in the neighboring group, without really knowing why. Out of the corner of her eye, she noticed Angela's nervous-looking behavior - looking down at her lap frequently, wringing her hands, the stressed look on her pretty face.

"Well," Tracy said, raising her eyebrows slightly, "we usually start the group study with prayer requests. Would you like to start today, Angela?"

Angela was silent for a moment before responding.

"Sure," she said haltingly. "I have a prayer request. It's kind of hard to talk about but - I'm ...having some serious marriage problems right now. Things just aren't going well between me and my husband. And then to make matters worse, a man that I went to for advice, someone I trusted ...," she paused to choke back a tear. " ... Tried to take advantage of me."

As she said this, she looked directly over at Jasmine, and the two locked eyes for a moment. Angela quickly looked away. Jasmine looked away too, feeling embarrassed to be caught eavesdropping.

As Angela broke into a quiet sob, the other ladies in the group silently began to exchange looks of concern and interest. After an awkward pause, Tracy finally spoke up.

"Let's just put it in God's hands, okay?"

The others in the group nodded in agreement, and bowed their heads.

"Hello, Earth to Jasmine," Barbara's voice jolted Jasmine back to her own group.

"What?"

"I said, would you read the passage of scripture that we're going to be talking about today - Proverbs thirty-one. Are you okay, honey? You seem a bit distracted this morning."

"Sorry, Barb. I guess I was thinking about something else." Jasmine took a breath and exhaled, while paging through her bible quickly. "Here we go; the passage is titled, *'The Wife of Noble Character'*."

As Jasmine began reading, Barbara gave her a concerned smile and a wink. She made a mental note to talk to Jasmine after the study was over.

CHAPTER 15

Saint Mary Adoption Agency: Canoga Park, California

Wednesday afternoon was busy at the Saint Mary Adoption Agency. In the waiting room were two visibly pregnant teenage girls - both of them unaccompanied.

The door of the small second-floor office opened, and another teenage girl entered the waiting room, accompanied by a middle-aged woman in business attire and a tightly pulled back hairstyle. The woman stepped up to the receptionist desk.

"This is Cherie Valdez, and we have an appointment," she said brusquely to the receptionist.

The receptionist looked up at the woman and replied, "Go on back to the conference room. The case worker will be right with you."

As the two walked slowly down the hallway leading to the conference room, the girl spoke up.

"I can't thank you enough, Mrs. McAllister, for arranging all of this for me. My parents would kill me if they found out I was pregnant. I know that California law will let me get an abortion without them knowing, but I don't want to do that."

"I understand your situation," Roberta McAllister replied, "and I think you're making the right decision. You realize that I'm really sticking my neck out for you here, don't you?"

"Yes, I know. I don't know what I'd do without your help."

Entering the small conference room, they were greeted by the caseworker, who beckoned them to sit down at the square table in the center of the room. After exchanging pleasantries, the caseworker began thumbing through the blue file folder on the table in front of her.

"So, Cherie, you are … four months along now?" she asked.

"Yeah, that's about right."

"You hardly show at all."

"My parents don't even know," Cherie said nervously, averting her eyes away from the gaze of the caseworker. "Nobody else does, either. I'm afraid to even tell my friends. I've been hiding it by wearing loose sweatshirts and stuff."

"You won't need to tell your parents, or anybody else. We can handle everything without parental interference. I understand that your teacher, Mrs.

McAllister, has made arrangements for you to be an exchange student for the duration of your pregnancy?"

"Yes. I've always been a good student, so nobody will think it's weird for me to get hooked up with an exchange program."

"And you'll be going to … Brazil?" she said casually, while continuing to sift through the file. "Do you think you're up for that, considering your condition?"

"I'll handle it. I've taken three years of Spanish, so I think I can pick up Portuguese pretty quick. I know it won't be easy, but I just want my baby to have a good home. I'll do whatever it takes - I just can't let my parents find out. Mrs. McAllister says I'll come back at the end of the semester after I give birth, and nobody has to know what happened. My parents can't afford to visit me in Brazil, so they won't find out."

"That's right, Cherie. It will be a fresh start for you – like nothing ever happened. Okay, then," the case worker continued, looking down at her papers, "I already have a few families who would like to adopt your baby, and I assume Mrs. McAllister has arranged for the overseas family and school, is that right?"

McAllister smiled and nodded.

"Then it looks like we're all set. I just need you to sign these papers to grant your permission for the adoption, then you can be on your way. And may I say, you're very fortunate to have the support of someone like Mrs. McAllister here."

"I know," Cherie said, wiping a tear from her eye with a tissue. She looked at McAllister, and impulsively reached out to hug her.

Roberta McAllister smiled as she hugged and lightly patted Cherie on the back.

CHAPTER 16

Tanaka Residence: Burbank, California

It was late in the evening, and George Tanaka was having a hard time just sitting around home by himself, without his wife and girls.

Sitting silently on the brown leather nailhead couch in the family room, he idly flipped the TV remote controller over and over in his right hand. The TV remained off.

Nothing worth watching, anyway. Just a bunch of junk to anesthetize the masses, he thought to himself.

George deliberately turned his thoughts to work - always an effective escape mechanism. Thinking about the cat mutilation case in Westlake Village, and the time spent with the pastor and the kid, he tried to put the pieces together in his mind.

A sudden ringing of the phone on his belt caused him to jerk involuntarily. Relaxing for a moment after the spasm, he let out a slow breath, and reached for his cell phone.

"George Tanaka," he barked into the phone.

"Mr. Tanaka? This is Rich Harrison."

"Who?"

"I'm the Sheriff's Deputy. We talked the other day at Starbucks, remember?"

"Oh, yeah - Sorry about that. Your name didn't ring a bell. But how did you get my cell number?"

"I'm a cop. We have ways to find information that most people don't. Just like you do, I suppose."

"Right. So, what's on your mind, Deputy?"

"Well, I was thinking about our conversation. You seemed interested in the Satanic aspect of the crime scene down at the warehouse."

"I am," George replied, sitting up abruptly. "Is there something new that you know?"

"First of all, Mr. Tanaka, let me be clear that I'm calling tonight not on official business, but on a more ... personal level."

"I understand – so why don't you just call me George. You made it pretty clear that the department takes a dim view of the whole Satanic-related crime implication."

"True. Any follow-up in that regard, I'm doing on my own. Nobody else in the department knows about it, or needs to know. So I was thinking … you've probably got connections that I don't have, and I've got some connections that you don't have. Maybe we could share information and … meet both our goals in the process."

"So," George said suspiciously, "you think you know what my goals are, then?"

"I suppose you're looking for an exclusive story. Something nobody else has done; something an audience would latch onto."

"Well, Deputy, you must be a prophet," George replied sarcastically. "So what's your goal in this? What are you hoping to find?"

"Simple. I want to put this Satanic cult out of business. If I can identify the perpetrators and get enough evidence to prosecute, I bet we can stop a lot of crime from happening."

"How do you figure?" George asked innocently. "You think that there are other people involved, and that they've done more than just this one killing?"

"Exactly. The killer couldn't have acted alone. Just look at the crime scene. There had to be a group of suspects, and I'll bet they're doing a lot more than just this one murder."

"Like what?"

"I don't really want to talk about it on the phone," Rich said. "If you've uncovered anything, we should talk face to face."

"I have, and we will. I also have someone I'd like you to meet. We've actually made a discovery together. He has a take on this you might find interesting."

"Good. Bring him and let's meet tomorrow evening. Say, Starbucks on Lankershim at eight?"

"That should work. I'll give him a call. See you then."

The phone made the usual click as Harrison hung up. George didn't even notice the second click, before he pushed the red END button on his cell phone.

George and Deputy Rich Harrison were already waiting for Jim when he pushed through the door at Starbucks Coffee House.

Jim looked around and spotted George and another guy he didn't know at a typical wood veneer table, up against the far wall.

Rich Harrison stood up as Jim approached, apparently waiting for George to introduce him.

Man, I wouldn't want to be on his bad side, Jim said to himself as he watched the large, muscular man rise from the chair and straighten up to his full stature. Jim slowly walked up and extended his hand.

George nodded a greeting at Jim and made the introduction, but remained seated.

"Jim DiMario, this is Sheriff's Deputy Rich Harrison."

"Good to meet you, sir," Rich said, clasping Jim's hand in an iron grip and gave it a jarring shake.

"Likewise."

"I just got here myself," George said. "Sit down, gentlemen, and let's compare notes."

"Hang on a minute," Jim said. "Let me get a café mocha first."

After Jim had procured his coffee, he returned to the table and sat down. George wasted no time in getting started. He began to recount in detail for Rich the story of their hike into the woods with Trey, and their discovery of the bloody ceremonial site. He looked over at Jim frequently as he went on, who nodded in agreement.

"Do you have anything to add, Jim?" George asked at last.

What a question to ask a preacher, Jim thought to himself. Then he replied, "I think you pretty much got all the details. Of course, I'm really outraged and upset about having practicing Satanists in our area," he said, shaking his head slowly in disgust.

"I'm afraid we can't bust them just because of their beliefs," Rich countered, raising his opened hand. "Don't forget the Salem witch trials, where all those people were executed just because of people's suspicions. I'm sure you can appreciate the fact that in America, we all have the right to worship as we choose, or not to worship at all, for that matter. Even if that worship is an offense to others, there's nothing we can do. From the law enforcement perspective, the line that can't be crossed is when a crime is committed as a part of worship. That's where we can get involved," he said, wagging his index finger for emphasis, "And we can do something about it. But we can't bust someone for shouting 'Hail Satan', or put them in jail for a gathering in the woods."

"But the blood!" Jim protested, "what about that? Obviously they killed some animal to get it - or even ..."

He stopped himself, noticing that a few sets of eyes turned his way at this outburst. He lowered his voice. "Well, who knows where they got it."

"Exactly," Rich replied, keeping his voice low, "We can't bust anyone for worshipping the Devil. But animal cruelty we can prosecute, if we can prove it. And the murder of the girl, obviously. What the hell, we can prosecute for having a fire in a state forest ... Oops - pardon my French, Reverend."

"I didn't know that was French."

"Rich, you haven't told us anything new yet," George said, ignoring Jim's comment. "You said that you had some news to contribute."

"Yeah, I was going to get to that," Rich said. He paused for a moment, looking up at the ceiling as if gathering his thoughts. Jim and George stared at him in anticipation. Finally, Rich began.

"Well a few weeks ago, I busted a young punk for selling roofies outside a high school in my district."

"Selling what?" Jim interrupted, a quizzical look on his face.

"Roofies - Rophynol. You know, the so-called date rape drug. Take too much, and it renders you almost semi-comatose. Anyway, I'd been watching the guy for days on and off, whenever I drove by the school. I could tell he didn't belong there. Finally, I caught him with the goods and a pocketful of money. He was Mr. Tough Guy until I threw the cuffs on him and put him into the back of the cruiser. Before we got to the station, he had a change of heart." Rich stretched out the last three words for emphasis, while holding up his fingers for the 'quote-unquote' sign.

"Turns out, he was willing to snitch in exchange for a memo from me to the county prosecutor. He wasn't so tough after all, at the prospect of doing hard time in the California state men's club."

"So ...," George said expectantly while gesturing with his hand in a rolling motion for Rich to continue, "what did he tell you?"

Rich smiled with satisfaction, and went on. "He gave up his supplier ... or should I say, he gave me everything he knew. Turns out that the supplier has a whole group of dealers that work directly for him. My informant thinks - or thought, that there were at least twenty dealers working various locations. And here's the interesting part," he said, suddenly lowering his voice, and stealing a quick glance to each side. "The supplier is supposedly a Satanist. Not just a gothic or some kind of poser or wannabe, but the real deal. According to this guy, the supplier is part of some kind of organized Satanic grotto. He thinks that they're into other stuff besides drug traffic."

"Like what?"

"Not sure exactly, but once this supplier told my informant about his beliefs when they were both loaded. Anyway, supposedly the focus of their worship is some deity called Anubis, one of the gods of the ancient Egyptians."

Jim suddenly felt a now-familiar chill, like ice water flowing down his spine at the mention of the same name his friend Bjorn had used just a few days before.

"Apparently," Rich continued, "they think this Anubis is actually mentioned in the bible, that he and his followers are known collectively by another name - The Nephalim."

"The Nephalim," Jim repeated, cocking his head and looking toward the ceiling. "Yes, Genesis chapter six mentions that name in a very interesting passage. But it doesn't really say much about who they are, other than they were large and powerful. The Hebrew word 'Nephalim' means *'Fallen Ones'*."

Jim dug into his back pocket and retrieved the small bible that he carried with him at all times, and started eagerly leafing through it. He noticed Rich regarding him with an amused smirk on his face.

"Do you really carry that with you all the time?" Rich asked.

"Sure. Don't you carry a handgun with you all the time?"

"That's my personal weapon."

"So's this."

"Good point. What does it say?"

Jim found the start of Genesis six and started reading. "When men began to increase in number on the Earth and daughters were born to them, the sons of God saw that the daughters of men were beautiful, and they married any of them they chose ... The Nephalim were on the earth in those days - and also afterward - when the sons of God went to the daughters of men and had children by them. They were the heroes of old, men of renown."

"So what happened next?" George asked.

Jim shrugged. "God killed them and everyone else with the flood. They were annihilated. The bible doesn't say anything about the Nephalim after that."

"I don't get it," George said, shaking his head slowly, "What's the significance?"

"The thing is," Rich answered, "they apparently believe these Nephalim are actually Satan's angels - demons, in other words. And they believe that their leader, Anubis, is a powerful demon, second only to Satan himself. They also believe that the bible passage Jim just read shows that he came to earth and procreated with regular women, and produced offspring."

"But why does the passage call them 'the Sons of God'?" George asked, looking perplexed.

"Well ...," Jim started, "some bible scholars believe that they were supernatural beings of some kind - not regular men. I think that much is plausible, anyway. At least one well-known bible teacher suggests that they were demons. But I haven't seen anything that would prove that position to be true. It is true, though, that God created the angels. One third of them rebelled against God, joining themselves to Satan, or Lucifer as he is also known. God cast them out of heaven. So I could see why someone might interpret the passage this way. I don't necessarily agree with that view, myself." Jim stroked his chin as he spoke, looking out the window as he thought out loud.

"Well, that's what they believe, anyway," Rich said. "And they think that this procreation with women resulted in a superior race of people. People who had special powers and abilities."

George appeared to be growing visibly impatient again, playing with his empty paper coffee cup. He gently bounced it off the wood table repeatedly while listening to Rich and Jim. Finally he cut in.

"Wait a minute. Even I know that the flood supposedly killed everyone on Earth except for Noah, his wife, their sons, and their wives. Eight people in all."

"Correct," Jim replied, pointing at him. "So you must have attended Sunday school at least once as a kid. Now that I think about it, the Nephalim are also mentioned again in Numbers chapter thirteen, when Moses sent spies into the promised land. Presumably, if they are not mortal, they didn't die in the flood, and may have begun to reproduce again afterwards. Of course, that's just a theory."

"So, what's the bottom line here?" George asked impatiently.

Now Rich sat forward in his chair and spoke in a low voice as he looked them both in the eye alternatingly.

"The bottom line is, they want to re-create this superior race."

"What for?" Jim asked incredulously.

"Power. To gain control and influence. Think about it - a race of people with supernatural abilities, who's loyalty is to Satan." Rich sat back in his chair and raised his hands up as if in mock surrender. "Not like I actually believe any of this stuff, anyway. But I do believe that these people are capable of doing whatever is necessary to implement their plan, whatever that involves. They are a crime wave in the making, and the law enforcement establishment at large isn't going to do anything about it. The cops will probably just pick up the pieces and react to the crimes, rather than try to deal with it proactively. If they're well organized, we'll never get the leaders, just a few of the foot soldiers."

"And I suppose you just want to do your civic duty by busting them early?" George said with a twinge of sarcasm.

"Something like that. Besides, I don't plan to be just a deputy forever. I'd like to move up at some point. Look, each of us has our reasons for being involved in this - maybe they're just different reasons."

"Speaking of involvement," Jim said, "we should all probably consider just how involved we're willing to get in this thing. It looks like I'm already involved somewhat, considering just what we've done so far." He raised his eyebrows at George. "But what can someone like me do? I mean, you're talking about a crime investigation. I don't have any background in that kind of thing."

"Actually," Rich replied, "you could be a great help to this investigation. Even though your knowledge of Satanism is limited, as you yourself said, you probably have some insight about the spiritual aspects of this group, and what they might do next. Since you are by nature their enemy, I think we can use that to our advantage."

"Well …," Jim said reluctantly, "what's the next step in this?"

"There's one more thing I haven't told you yet," Rich admitted, while gesturing with his left index finger. Again he sat forward in his chair and lowered his voice. "The informant said something about a place in the Mojave Desert – Yermo. This cult has an archaeological dig going there, or something like that. His supplier wasn't really specific about it, but maybe they're looking for remains of these Nephalim. Who knows? But it's a lead, at least. Maybe we should take a road trip out there."

"Yermo?" George asked. "Isn't that just a wide spot in the road on the way to Las Vegas? I think I've seen an exit ramp for Yermo on the I-15."

"Yeah, but it's actually off the road a bit. It's the kind of place that nobody would go to for any conceivable reason. Which is exactly what makes it a great place to hide something."

"Rich, can't we at least get a little more detail from your informant before we go off on a wild goose chase?" Jim asked. "I mean, believe it or not, even a pastor has responsibilities to attend to during the week."

"I wish I could get more information from him …," Rich started to say.

The other two looked at him expectantly. After a moment, he completed his response.

"He's dead. He was found hanging by the neck from a rolled-up sheet the day after he was booked in at the jail. An apparent suicide." Rich paused and looked down at the table. "But I have doubts about that."

Jim felt a chill ripple through his body at this new revelation. This was starting to sound and feel to him like he had walked into an old TV mystery show – but there weren't any cameras around.

He and George just looked at each other. Jim thought he saw a look of interest growing on George's face.

George stepped out the front door of Starbucks and into the cool night air. Pausing at the curb, he took a deep breath and slowly exhaled a visible vapor trail. He turned and walked around toward the parking lot, which was nearly invisible to the street on the left side of the building. Jim and Rich had already left, after talking over the things that they had discovered.

The parking lot was dark, lit only by dim, amber-colored lamps that shed an eerie glow over the sparse assortment of cars that were still there. The moon contributed only a faint illumination to the area, blocked intermittently by thick clouds passing across the autumn sky like a grotesque flock of migrating birds. Strolling out toward his car, George's head was filled with the discussion that the three of them just had, and he was considering the next step that they had agreed on: visiting the archeological site in Yermo.

So deep in thought was he, that George was startled when his military-bred internal alarm went off.

Whoa - what's wrong with this picture? he said to himself, suddenly noticing the two grunge-dressed young men in the parking lot.

George observed that the two strangers were standing about thirty feet apart; equally distant from George's car. One was leaning against a car, taking short, nervous puffs from a cigarette. The other was milling around and fingering a key ring, apparently pretending to look for the right key for a car door.

George's deeply-ingrained martial arts experience had developed a heightened awareness for his surroundings and people's behavior, which told him that these two had no business being here. George continued slowly strolling toward his car, while tacitly observing the two strangers from the corner of his eye. It was too dark to see their features clearly, but they looked to him like the type of young punks that thrive on trouble. One of them had his dark hair pulled back into a ponytail, his tank shirt partially covering a colored tattoo of some kind. The other had short, spiked hair that was bleached white at the tips.

Although he pretended not to notice, George could see that they were both beginning to slowly plot an intercept course as George was approaching the car. The stranger with the ponytail was beyond George's car and moving toward him, and the other punk was circling around behind George.

This is it - Don't let them know you're on to them, he said to himself. Tension clutched his gut tight.

George fished the keys out of his pocket, trying to appear oblivious to the mayhem that he was sure was about to start. He pushed the button on the electronic key fob, which caused his car's taillights to flash once. The car replied with a chirp. Ponytail approached George, who was now standing at the car door. George mentally approximated the distance of the man behind him based on the sound of his footsteps. He guessed that he was about twelve feet away, and closing. Ponytail drew close, and spoke up.

"Hey man, got a light?" he asked as he dug a pack of cigarettes from the belt of his loose jeans.

"Yeah, sure I do," George replied, and he feigned a movement of his right hand up toward his shirt pocket.

Suddenly, without warning, George spun around to his right, leading with his right elbow. His estimate was correct - the punk with the spiked hair was almost right on top of him. George saw a freeze-frame of the startled look appear on the punk's face for a fraction of a second, just before George's elbow struck the attacker's jaw. He connected forcefully, with a sickening thud. He felt the solid impact of his elbow hitting flesh and bone. A spray of blood and teeth came flying out of the attacker's mouth. George knew instinctively that the hollow crunch that came with it was a breaking jawbone.

The whole scene seemed to play out in slow motion. The man's neck jerked back violently as the full force of the blow was delivered to his jaw. George saw the man's eyes shut and a grimace form on his face before he went down. He was sure that his attacker was unconscious before he hit the cold asphalt of the parking lot.

At once, George felt a strong arm wrap around his neck, pulling him backward. He pivoted instinctively to his left slightly, and found the man's crotch with the back of his fist. His attacker instantly jerked forward in pain. George seized the moment, and set his stance, abruptly bowing forward and rolling his shoulders to the right. The perfectly executed shoulder throw swept the attacker off his feet and launched him over George's back. When he finally met the ground, it was on his head and the back of his neck. George could tell by just observing the landing that Ponytail wouldn't be getting up for round two. After holding a ready position for several seconds, George relaxed slightly and moved to get into his car. That's when he did a double take - the tattoo on his attacker's upper arm was now clearly visible. An inverted pentagram in red and black, with a goat's head in the center.

"Who are you?" George shouted at the wounded would-be assailants. "What do you want from me?"

They didn't answer. Again George questioned them, while prodding them with his heel - none too gently.

"Who do you work for?"

Still they remained mute and unresponsive, only grunting in pain as George jabbed them with his heel. They both remained on the pavement, now curled up into fetal positions. Finally George gave up and hopped into his car, knowing full well that he couldn't call the police because of his 'implied liability' as a black-belt holder. He threw his car in gear, and tore out of the parking lot with tires squealing.

CHAPTER 17

Cajon Summit, California

The sun rose above the mountaintops, and the heat waves were already starting to show in little squiggle lines across the surface of the black freeway asphalt of Interstate 15.

George had finished telling Jim and Rich about his altercation the previous night with the two punks. Now he glanced down at the temperature gauge on his car's dashboard, where the needle had risen only slightly above the middle indicator bar. George turned off the air conditioner to avoid overheating going up the long, inclined grade. Even in early October, the desert heat could be brutal – both on cars, and on people.

"Thank God," he said quietly, monitoring the gauge.

"That's the closest thing to a prayer I've heard from you," Jim remarked from the backseat.

George, Jim, and Rich were heading north on I-15 in George's car. They had just cleared the top of Cajon Summit; a long, steep incline that culminates in a high desert plateau, forty-three hundred feet above sea level. As they transitioned back onto level ground, the car began to pick up speed.

George wiped the sweat from his brow with the back of his hand. "Time to cool off," he said, switching the A/C back on. "It's like an oven in here."

"This looks like an ideal place to dump a body," Rich remarked casually, observing the dense growth of chaparral on both sides of the freeway as they passed through the town of Hesperia. "They'd never find it in a million years out here in this thick brush." Then he added with a jovial tone, "Maybe if we don't find anything, we should keep on going to Vegas. I'm off duty until day after tomorrow."

Jim wasn't so sure he was kidding.

"But I suppose," Rich continued, "that a pastor wouldn't set foot in Sin City.

"Actually, I have been to Las Vegas a number of times with my family. It's a pretty good vacation spot, and the kids love it. We usually stay at the giant Egyptian pyramid. It has a nice relaxing atmosphere."

"But what about the other atmosphere - you know; gambling, drinking, prostitution and everything?"

"Sure, there's a lot of excess. But people choose to sin or not sin regardless of where they are. It has a lot more to do with where their heart is at spiritually, rather than where they are physically. But if someone is already inclined to sin, then yes, there are plenty of opportunities of every kind available in Las Vegas."

"You know what?" Rich said, "I think I remember a story in the bible like that. That guy - you know ...," he gestured expectantly with his hand for Jim to help him out. "That nephew of Abraham. What was his name?"

"Lot."

"Yeah, Lot. He chose to move into Sodom and Gomorra. He was a righteous man supposedly, but he was living in the midst of a really sinful place. Then God destroyed the whole city, after getting Lot and his family out. His wife turned back to look longingly at the city after they had left, and she was turned into a pillar of salt." Rich stopped and smiled. "That's a great legend."

"What makes you think it's a legend?" Jim asked.

"Well ... all those stories in the Old Testament are legends, aren't they? Written by ancient authors and passed down from generation to generation." He paused a moment and turned around in his seat to study Jim's face, looking for a glimmer of acknowledgment. "You aren't suggesting that it's a true, literal story are you?"

"I'm not just suggesting it - it is a true story. Jesus himself quoted the Old Testament frequently, including the story of Jonah. That's the one most people stumble over - a man being swallowed whole by a huge fish, then regurgitated alive three days later to become a prophet to the city of Ninevah."

Rich sat silently for several minutes without responding, but didn't turn back to his map. At last he spoke.

"So, then - you believe what the bible says about the Nephalim is actually true?" Rich's tone sounded to Jim more like a statement than a question.

"I believe that the bible is the complete and inerrant Word of God," Jim replied. "In other words, it's inspired by God and there are no errors in it. I don't have any problem believing the story of Lot, or any of the other stories recorded in the bible for that matter. That includes the Nephalim. But as far as who or what they are, that remains something of a mystery. Like I said before, the bible isn't all that clear on their identity."

"Hmm ...," Rich grunted. He turned himself back around to face front.

I guess that's not what he wanted to hear, Jim thought.

He turned back to looking out the window at Palo Verde shrubs, Joshua trees, billboards, and an endless empty desert that greeted his view.

"I thought you said that this place was just a wide spot in the road," Jim said, while George drove them along yet another dirt road that appeared to be leading nowhere.

After passing the army base, they had cruised the whole of Yermo and found nothing except the Calico Ghost Town, and the solar power generating station. That, and the homes of a handful of people who apparently lived out here in the middle of the forbidding Mojave in order to be left alone. Joshua trees stood on weed-covered empty lots, and the dust-filled desert wind sent tumbleweeds bouncing along the streets. Jim saw a singularly large hill that rose up to sky like a huge angry pimple from the stark flatness of the desert floor.

They had ventured out onto several smaller dirt roads, looking for something - although none of them knew exactly what. George fidgeted in his seat and drummed his hands on the steering wheel. Jim figured that George must be sensing the impatience of his companions, or perhaps it was just that he was growing so impatient himself.

"All right," George said, "if we don't find anything in the next ten minutes, we'll head back to the interstate and blow this God-forsaken place."

Jim was tempted to comment on the choice of words George used to describe the place, but found it a hard point to argue based on the spartan, run-down and generally empty appearance of the area. Suddenly, Rich pointed out the window at a small building that took his interest.

"What's that?" he said, with a suspicious twinge in his voice.

George pulled to a stop on the deserted dirt road. About a hundred yards off the road, he saw a small, austere structure sitting by itself. The small building had no road to it, just a worn-down path of two rutted-out tire tracks. While the others squinted at it in the blinding mid-day sun, Rich already pulled his binoculars out of his backpack, and surveyed the structure.

"That's interesting," he said, scanning back and forth with the binoculars.

"What?" George said, expectantly.

"It's too small to be someone's house. And it looks like a relocatable building of some kind."

"Maybe a construction office," Jim offered.

"Oh, really," George replied sarcastically. "Look around. Do you really think anyone would be building out here? I don't see any real estate boom coming to this area."

"Fine," Jim said, "so let's go over and have a look."

George pulled the car around and onto the path, and it bumped along the deeply rutted tire tracks. The car hit a deep indention, which caused the car to lurch hard. Jim's head hit the car's headliner.

"Ow! -hey, take it easy, will you? This isn't an off-road rally!"

"Sorry," George replied curtly, but he continued driving at the same pace. Jim thought he caught the two up front smiling secretly at his expense.

After pulling up alongside the small building, they got out and were again blasted by the dry, hot air. Their shoes scrunched on the sandy soil as they approached the silent structure.

The building had a few dark-tinted windows with blinds tightly drawn, and only one door which was accessed by a short flight of steps. Rich found a loose piece of siding along the bottom, which gave way when he pulled on it. They noticed that there were wheels under the building, which were obscured by wood siding – it was a trailer. A gas powered generator was also sitting behind the panel that Rich had just removed. Nobody seemed to be present as they cautiously tried the door and looked all around the trailer building.

"Seems too small to be someone's house," Jim observed.

"Maybe," George replied, "but who knows? This isn't exactly an upscale neighborhood."

"It looks pretty new," Rich said, while examining the license plate on the lower wood siding. He jotted the number down on a page of a small notebook that he had pulled from his backpack.

"Seems a bit odd, don't you think?" George asked. He continued to stroll the perimeter of the trailer. "If you were so dirt poor to live out here on a piece of empty land, how could you afford a new trailer? And why an office trailer, instead of a mobile home? Doesn't make sense to me."

Jim cocked his head back and sniffed the air, his face contorted with loathing. "What's that smell?" he said.

"I don't know," George replied, grimacing, "but it smells like something rotten."

"Stinks even worse over here," Jim said, approaching the end of the trailer.

"This might even be BLM land," Rich observed, looking around the vast expanse of flat, barren land.

"Government owned, you mean?" Jim asked.

"Yeah. I'd need a more detailed map to be sure, but I think this area we're in is under the control of the Bureau of Land Management."

"Looks like someone is doing some kind of farming, by the look of the ground over there," Jim said, pointing at a football field-sized parcel of ground about a hundred feet from the North-East corner of the trailer; furthest from the dirt road they had just traveled up. Here Jim noticed that a section of ground appeared to have been dug up or cultivated. They started to walk over, and when they got closer, Rich was the first to notice an oddity.

"Strange kind of farming, if you ask me," he said, observing the layout of the area.

The two-acre area had the ground disturbed in numerous places; there were rows of squares about three feet by three feet where the soil had evidently been dug up and replaced. The squares were arranged in a grid pattern, with about six feet between them on each side.

Jim looked at the unusual pattern. "It doesn't look like any kind of archaeological dig I've ever heard of, either."

George had meanwhile gone back to the trailer, where he earlier noticed several shovels and other digging tools stashed under the steps that led up to the door. He returned holding two shovels.

"I'm nobody's archeologist," he said, "But I do know how to dig a hole. Let's see what we can find."

"Some of the areas look fresher than others," Rich noted. "If we're going to dig, let's start with one of those."

"Wait a minute," Jim said, looking around nervously. "Can we do this? I mean, is it legal?"

He looked at Rich for guidance. Rich suddenly stood straight and held his cupped hand to his ear, listening intently. The others went silent and listened too. After a moment, Rich spoke.

"I'm listening, but I don't hear anyone saying that we can't do this," he said, with a sly grin.

George slapped his leg and burst out laughing, then rammed his shovel into the soft earth.

"Allow me," he said, and began digging.

They traded off, rotating the shoveling work until the hole was about three feet deep. Jim's shovel suddenly struck something solid that made a hollow sound as the shovel tip hit it.

"Hey, buried treasure, maybe!" George said gleefully, as they began to expose a large plastic box that appeared to be about one foot by two feet long.

"Let's take it to Vegas!" Rich added. He got down on his hands and knees and slowly pulled the box out of the hole. To Jim, he said, "Here, Reverend, why don't you do the honor?"

Rich set the box on the ground away from the hole, and motioned to the two sealing latches at either end of the box. Jim admitted to himself that he was as excited as a boy about to open a pirate's treasure chest as he wiped the excess dirt from the lid of the opaque, whitish box. Rich and George stood closer as he reached for the latches and snapped them back. He carefully removed the lid, and hung his face over the open box. Immediately, Jim recoiled backwards as if he'd been slapped in the face. He lost his balance and fell into the empty hole they had just dug. Rich jumped over to help him out of the hole, but George looked into the box.

"My God," he declared, turning his head away. His face knotted up with revulsion.

Rich cautiously approached the box and peered over the edge, barely getting close enough to peek in.

"Oh, Lord," he said slowly, surveying the contents. "I wasn't expecting anything like this."

"Who would?" George replied. He moved back up next to Rich and took another quick look.

Laying in the plastic box was were the partially decayed remains of a tiny infant, wrapped in a blue blanket.

"Looks newborn," Rich said in a matter-of-fact businesslike tone. "Probably not more than a few days old. Hasn't been here for long, either."

George turned slowly in a circle, taking in the multitude of square holes surrounding them in the field. The realization hit him harder than any desert storm or flash flood could – each hole would yield the same grisly contents. He was shell-shocked and suddenly at a loss for words. Rich broke George's trance with his verbal observation.

"There must be over a hundred. Maybe one-twenty-five. Are you going to get your video camera?"

"Why bother?" Jim answered for him tightly, "Nobody wants to see something like this on the news."

"Jim, close the lid, will ya?" Rich asked.

But Jim wasn't there. Rich spun around and saw Jim on his hands and knees, puking on the ground.

***

The three were silent as they embarked on the long journey home. Nobody had spoken a word since Rich finished his pay-phone call to the sheriff's dispatcher, from a booth outside of an aging diner they stopped at just before getting on the I-15 Southbound ramp. Jim finally broke the silence.

"I think maybe we should have stayed there until the local sheriff's deputies arrived. Isn't it actually illegal to leave the scene of a crime?"

"Look," Rich answered, "there's nothing of value we could contribute there. I wasn't about to hang around and try to explain why an L.A. Sheriff's deputy is digging around in the San Bernardino Sheriff's backyard. That's why I made an anonymous call to their dispatch line from a pay phone. They would have picked up my cell phone number."

He stopped for a moment and looked out the window, apparently still gathering his thoughts. "Besides, do you have any idea how long we'd be detained at the scene? And the kind of questions they'd be asking?"

"Yeah," George chimed in, "How would you explain what we were doing there?" He straightened up in his seat and spoke in a nerdy nasal-sounding voice. "You see, officer, it was like this - me and my buddies were out here in the desert snipe hunting, when I just fell into this hole. It was only then that I realized I was surrounded by dead babies."

Nobody laughed.

"He's right," Rich said, nodding his head in agreement. "We couldn't tell them the truth - I guarantee that they're not going to accept it. Sometimes the truth is stranger than fiction. They probably would have busted us for trespassing, just on general principle."

Jim pulled on Rich's sleeve. "I thought you said that was federal land!" he protested.

"I said, it *might be* BLM land," Rich replied, with emphasis on the 'might be' part. "Besides, even if it is, they'd probably nail us for littering, loitering, and singing off-key. Cops get agitated when they have a major crime scene on their hands and nobody to blame for it. Believe me, I know. But set your mind at ease, Rev - we didn't violate the law by not staying around."

"After what we've been through," Jim replied, "I'd think you'd be comfortable calling me by name. I do have a name, you know."

They drove on in silence for what seemed to Jim at least fifteen minutes before he finally spoke again.

To Rich, Jim asked, "Could this have been what your informant was talking about? Do you think that the Satanists are responsible for those dead children?"

"I've been thinking about that," Rich replied, "It has to be the place he was talking about, but he probably didn't know the details. The people he reports to – did report to, that is, must refer to this place as an archeological site as a code name. I wish now I'd brought my lock picking set with me so we could have had a look in that trailer."

George suddenly snapped his fingers and pointed at Rich.

"Who do you know in the San Bernardino County Sheriff's office?" he asked abruptly.

"I guess I've got a couple contacts. Why?"

"Wait until tomorrow, then make a few casual inquiries. You know that they're gonna bust the door on the trailer and go through it. Word travels on something like this, so they won't think anything of it when you ask."

Rich looked at the window again and gently bobbed his head from side to side, looking like he was weighing it over.

"Yeah," he said at last, "that might work. I'll look through my Rolodex tomorrow and find one or two guys I can call." Suddenly he slapped his forehead with the palm of his hand, and exclaimed "Ah!"

"What?" Jim and George asked in unison.

"I have an old girlfriend in the San Berdoo department," he said. "Ex-fiancée, actually. But I don't know … I haven't talked to her in a long time. We didn't part on good terms."

They continued to drive on for miles along the flat, deserted highway without speaking.

"I've been thinking," George said at last, pointing his thumb over his shoulder at Jim, who was uncomfortably hunched up behind him. "Your friend Trey -he seemed to know a lot about this kind of stuff. Maybe we should consult him."

"Hmm," Rich mumbled. "Yeah. Why don't you talk to him, Rev - I mean, Jim."

"Maybe I'll do that," Jim answered, and he adjusted himself again in the uncomfortable back seat. *I need to have a long talk with Jasmine when I get home,* he thought to himself. *I'm in way too deep on this thing, and Lord knows where it will end up.*

CHAPTER 18

Westlake Village, California

Jim was dropped off at his car, which had been left in the Starbucks parking lot in Canoga Park while they went to Yermo. Making his way home on the freeway, he watched the last rays of late afternoon sunlight paint a stunning panorama of orange, then pink on the clouds that hovered over the saddleback mountains to the Northwest.

Jim needed to get home. Home was his refuge, a place to be safe and free from the pressures and obligations of his ministry.

Scarcely before he realized it, he found himself on the exit ramp at Westlake Boulevard. Pulling into his garage, he noticed that Jasmine's car was already there.

Jim paused for a moment to gather his thoughts, then stiffly got out of the car and entered the house through the door of the attached garage. His legs were still achy from his long oddesy, crammed into a near-fetal position in the back of George's small car.

Upon opening the door, the smell of frying onions and meat welcomed him like a friendly hug. Jasmine was in the kitchen.

"I'm in here," she called, hearing the door slam shut.

Jim came up behind her at the stove and gave her a hug. He clung to her as if she were a life raft amid a tempestuous sea of trouble. He felt her body stiffen slightly at his touch.

"How was your day, hon?" he asked.

"Interesting," she replied tersely. "I want to tell you about it."

"Okay, but first I need to tell you about what I did today, and some other things that have been happening recently."

Jasmine gulped quietly and turned to face him. She set down the spatula she was holding.

"Come and sit down," Jim said, slowly walking over to the family room couch.

Jasmine turned off the range burner and followed, and sat down on the loveseat directly across from Jim. She sat looking expectantly at him, unconsciously wringing her hands.

"You'll never believe where I've been today," Jim began. "But it all starts with Bjorn Nilsson's visit last week. He told me something after dinner that night that was really disturbing. I didn't really believe it at the time – maybe I just didn't want to believe it. But since then, it's gotten worse."

Jim proceeded to describe to his wife in detail the events that led up to his junket to the small desert town of Yermo this day. As he did, her feelings of shock and horror were manifested in the pained expressions on her otherwise lovely face, a reaction that did not surprise Jim in the least.

"I didn't want to tell you all about what Bjorn said before, because I knew it would upset you," Jim said. "That, and I didn't know for sure how real the threat is. But after what we've uncovered, I knew I had to share it with you."

"I wish you would have told me before," Jasmine replied. "It might have been easier to digest in smaller doses." She shook her head and let out a sigh. "What are we going to do now?" she asked.

"You mean, what am *I* going to do now," he corrected. "I don't want to get you involved in this mess. I'm still trying to figure out what should be done, and who can do it, for that matter."

"Look, Jim. We started this ministry as a team. Don't tell me you want to go solo now. You've always told me how much you need and appreciate my support and help. And this is something that affects God's kingdom here on Earth. I think you need me on this problem as much as you've needed me on anything we've had to deal with in the past - maybe even more."

"Jasmine, this is dangerous ground I'm treading on here," Jim cautioned, gesturing with an upraised hand. "These people - whoever they are, are evil. We already know that they have killed animals and small children. Older children, even, according to Bjorn. And if what Rich and George think is true, they may have even killed a young woman. If I'm going to pursue this, I don't want to be putting you and the kids in any danger. It wouldn't be fair."

"But don't you see?" Jasmine said, cutting him off, "the fact that you and your friends have already learned this much about them already puts us all in danger. If they are as evil as it appears, then you've already shown yourself as a threat. Don't assume for a minute that they aren't aware of what you're doing."

A cold chill of fear shot down Jim's spine, and caused him to involuntarily straighten with the realization that he might have already been made.

We've been checking them out - maybe they've been checking us out, too, he thought.

He tried to not let his fear show, but it was no use to hide it from Jasmine, who could read him like a book.

"All right," Jim said, "let's not freak out here. They're just people, after all. Not normal or decent people, obviously, but they don't have any magic powers that would allow them to see through a crystal ball, or something," he said, trying to sound casual. "They probably don't even know I exist at this point. And I'd like to keep it that way, if possible."

"Maybe it's too late for that, Jim. We should assume that they already know about you. Don't underestimate them. Anything that you plan to do about this from here out, I need to be a part of. It'll be safer for all of us to know what's going on. Promise me."

Jim weighed it over for a few moments. "Okay, but what about the kids?" he asked.

Jasmine nodded. "We should level with them. They're not babies anymore, Jim. They can deal with it. How can we expect to resist and defeat the enemy, if we don't realize he's even there?"

"They already know that there's evil in the world. They know it from the bible, and they've had a chance to see it firsthand, even. Remember that youth group trip they went on to the rescue mission on skid row?"

"But this is a real specific evil," Jasmine said. "Quite honestly, Jim, we could use their prayers, too."

"All right," Jim agreed finally, with a single nod of his head, "we'll talk to them after dinner tonight."

They both sat quietly for some time, facing each other, deep in thought. Finally, Jim broke the silence.

"I'm sorry, hon. I didn't give you a chance to tell me about your day, and that important piece of news you had."

"Ah, yes," Jasmine said, raising her thin blond eyebrows. "Well …," she started, taking a deep breath, "It seems we have another problem, just in case this wasn't enough."

"What could compare with murderous Satanists running around in our midst?" Jim said sarcastically.

"I had an interesting lunch with Barbara today." She paused a moment. "Do you know a woman named Angela Shepherd?"

Jim involuntarily gritted his teeth at the mention of the name. It sounded like trouble.

"Yes, I met her once. She came to the office for a crisis counseling visit. What about her?"

"Well," Jasmine said, fidgeting in her seat, "I learned today from Barb that there is a rumor circulating in the church regarding that visit."

Jim tilted his head with an apprehensive look. "What do you mean?" he asked.

"The rumor is that …," Jasmine started, rotating her hands as if she were treading water.

Jasmine placed her hands in her lap, took a breath to brace herself, and started again. "The story is that you had a … sexual encounter with her in your office." Jasmine used the 'quote - unquote' gesture to underscore the questionable nature of the rumor.

Jim sat in stunned disbelief and his jaw went slack. "What?" he asked numbly.

"I hope you don't really want me to repeat it."

"Who is saying something like this?" Jim said, his voice rising in volume and pitch.

"I don't know for sure. Like I said, I learned about it from Barbara. She thinks that Angela started it. Who knows who's spreading it around."

Jim shook his head. "I knew that woman smelled like trouble." Looking his wife in the eye, he added, "Well, it's obviously not true, and there were other people in the office at the time she was there, anyway. Bev was at her desk the whole time, and Pete was in his office."

"Well, we need to figure out how to put a stop to this rumor. It could be very damaging, false as it is."

As she was speaking, the phone rang. Jim got up, irritated, snatched up the receiver from the kitchen wall, and was greeted by the voice of Scott Corwin, the church council president.

"Scott! How are you? … oh, fine … tonight? Well, I suppose … what's it about? Okay, all right then. See you at seven-thirty."

Jim set the phone back on it's cradle and turned back to Jasmine, who looked at him quizzically.

"What was that about?" she wondered.

"Scott is calling a special church council meeting for tonight," Jim said, scratching his head. "He was pretty vague about the subject. Just said it was a matter of some urgency."

"That doesn't sound good."

"No, not really. And I'm beat, too. I'd rather not go out."

"Well, let me get dinner on the table, then. Garrett is at football practice, and Chelsea is studying at Sharon's house. They can eat when they get home."

***

Scott Corwin gently set the phone back on it's cradle on Pete LeTourneu's desk at the church office.

"You're doing the right thing," Pete said assuringly.

"I hope so," Scott replied. "Considering the circumstances, I don't think we have a whole lot of choice."

"We don't. Okay, now that we have a meeting time confirmed, let's call the other council members and get them down here. I'd help you with the calls, but as church council president, the request should really come from you."

Scott nodded silently and looked at the sad-looking but stunning young woman seated across the desk from him before reluctantly picking up the phone.

CHAPTER 19

Westlake High School: Westlake Village, California

Garrett DiMario left the high school gym locker room after showering off two and a half hours of sweat and grime. Junior Varsity football was proving to be hard work. He often wondered if it was worth the effort of going through the grueling practices just for the promise of some fleeting future glory. He had to admit, there was nothing quite like that winning feeling when his team was victorious - even if he spent most of the game warming the bench.

Garrett wasn't a starter, but he usually got to play a few minutes of each game as a running back - as long as his team was ahead. And run he could, especially when chased by boys who were much larger than his own wiry five foot - eight, one hundred - sixty pound body.

Garrett doggedly dragged himself through the deserted school quad toward his locker, with the purpose of grabbing his social studies book before catching a ride home with a friend. His whole body was sore and achy from practice, and it was an effort just to walk across campus.

He passed through empty hallways that only a couple hours before rang with the sounds of students joyfully leaving their classrooms behind for the day. Turning the corner at the wall which was home to his locker, he was surprised to see a lone female figure standing at an open locker. There was nobody else around. She was bent over, apparently looking for something hidden within the depths of her disorganized locker. She turned and looked at Garrett. He recognized her as Kristi - Something from his social studies class; he couldn't actually recall her last name.

"Hey, Garrett," she said coyly, looking over at him. "What are you doing here this late?"

"Uh, football practice," he replied. "How about you?"

"I just came back to get my math textbook. I forgot it after school, and my dad made me come back to get it," she said, with a pout.

Garrett had never spoken to Kristi - Something before. She was a Gothic, and hung with that peculiar group that dresses only in black. He noticed that she had numerous small rings and studs pierced through her right ear, and a tiny jeweled stud in her nose. Her short cropped, wild jet black hair was a sharp contrast to her milky white skin, which was so pale it looked as if she had never seen the sun. She wore a short black mini-skirt over black fishnet tights with numerous holes that looked like they were purposely torn in them. Her tall black leather boots came up to within about two inches of her knees. Garrett knew that she hadn't worn this outfit to school today - he'd have noticed for sure. Especially intriguing to him was her black mesh top, that gave a fairly clear view of her lacy black bra underneath. Hanging around Kristi's neck was a beaded necklace with a large silver crucifix dangling from it. In spite of her eighties-style Madonna-turned-vampire look, he decided that she was pretty hot - a hot girl who was paying attention to him. In class he had never realized how attractive she really was.

"Yeah - uh, me too," Garrett said. "I need to get my social studies book. You know what that old bag McAllister is like if you skip the homework."

"She's a witch," Kristi said matter-of-factly.

"Yeah."

Kristi turned back to her bottom-row locker and bent over low to find her book, and took several seconds arranging her things. As she did so, her already short skirt hiked up several more inches on her shapely backside, giving Garrett quite a view.

Dang! he thought to himself, evaluating the picture before him.

Too soon, she stood up and slammed her locker shut, then turned back to face Garrett, who stood flummoxed.

"Well, I'll walk over to your locker with you if you want," she said.

"Sure!" Garrett said eagerly. He started walking slowly down the wall of lockers with Kristi at his side. Although he was trying not to look out of the corner of his eye, the serpentine way she moved her hips as she walked reminded him of some of the babes he'd seen on MTV music videos.

Idiot! Think of something to say, he told himself.

"Here's my locker," he said, and he turned to it and proceeded to work on the combination lock. "So, Kristi," he said, still facing the locker, "do you go to any football games?" He lifted the latch and opened his locker.

"Never been to one. Not my thing - the whole jock scene, you know. But it works for you, I guess, so that's cool."

Garrett retrieved his book and closed the door of his upper-row locker, and he suddenly felt Kristi's breath on his neck. He turned to face her again. He was surprised - pleasantly so, to see that she was now standing quite close to him. Garrett looked into her intense, big green eyes that were only inches away from his, offset by the dark, heavy mascara and eyeliner surrounding them.

"Gotta go," she said coquettishly. "My dad's waiting in the car. See you around, Garrett."

She gave him a mischievous smile, then quickly walked off. Garrett watched her go, admiring the wiggle of her lithe form that was tucked into clothes that surely would never pass muster at any private school. When she turned the corner, Garrett exhaled loudly and leaned back against the row of lockers. He gently banged the back of his head against the upper locker, which reverberated with a metallic thunk.

Stupid! he thought to himself. *You didn't even ask for her phone number.* He was actually surprised that a girl like her would even notice him, let alone be flirting like that. *I wonder what she'll be wearing tomorrow.*

After she had turned the corner, Kristi stopped for a moment and pulled a pen out of her small purse. She opened her math textbook to the blank page in the back, and quickly jotted down three numbers: sixteen, thirty-four, and twenty-four. Closing the book, she glanced over her shoulder and went on her way.

CHAPTER 20

Solid Rock Community Church: Westlake Village, California

Jim drove in silence through the darkness over to the church, which was only about five miles from his home. Situated across the freeway in an industrial area, Solid Rock Community Church had freeway visibility, and the benefit of less-expensive property compared to the center of town.

Jim arrived at the church a few minutes before seven-thirty. He pulled his car into a parking stall amongst the small group of cars that were bathed under the amber glow of the sodium vapor lamps.

A light rain started falling from the crisp October sky as Jim briskly crossed the parking lot. As he approached the office trailer, he could hear the sound of voices, some of which were rather strident. Just as he reached for the door handle, he could hear Scott Corwin's distinctive southern drawl say loudly:

"We aren't going to discuss this until he arrives."

At that moment, Jim opened the door to the church office, and stepped inside. He saw an assemblage of people in the conference room, which was just to the right of the entry door. Every eye turned to him, and a pall fell upon the room as if a funeral prayer was about to begin. Jim noticed that most of the church council members were present.

Bill Peters was a heavy equipment operator, and had a body to match. Clad in dirty jeans and a tee-shirt, his bulky frame threatened to snap the folding chair he sat on like a number-two pencil between the fingers of a pro wrestler.

Ron Austin was a local attorney who usually dressed more casually than an attorney is expected to. His neatly-trimmed dark brown hair perfectly matched the style of his button-down collar shirt.

David Frederick, a mortgage banker in his mid-forties who worked out of town was also present. He religiously listened to Pastor Jim's sermon tapes each week during his long commute. He wore his standard uniform of a short-sleeved white dress shirt with a wild patterned tie.

Blake Aanstad, a research & development engineer who worked for a high-tech company, was there too. He had brown hair that was graying even as it was thinning. His company's culture allowed him the freedom to wear almost anything to work, which today happened to be a tropical print shirt and jeans.

And of course, Scott Corwin, a radiologist at the regional medical center, was seated at the head of the table. He exuded the stereotypical physician's demeanor; somewhere between extreme confidence and outright arrogance. Most of Scott's hair was gone, and it was anybody's guess as to whether it was genetic, or a side affect of his profession.

Jim was surprised to see that Pete LeTourneu was also present. Church council meeting typically involved only the senior pastor, and the council members themselves. As laymen who worked out in the 'real world', the council provided balanced feedback and advice to Jim on administrative and even spiritual matters involving the church. In spite of the spirited discussions that often took place during their regular monthly meetings, their support of Pastor Jim had always been unwavering.

Although the church council was collectively imbued with decision making authority through the majority vote process, Jim could never think of a time that they had overruled his wishes. As founder of Solid Rock Community Church, Jim was highly respected and even revered by these men, most of who had been with the church since it's inception, or near enough. Among those seated around the table, Associate Pastor Pete LeTourneu was the newest by far, having started with the church staff only half a year ago.

Scott stood up and offered Jim a strained smile. "Good evening, Pastor," he said. "Sorry for the short notice, but something has been brought to my attention that is serious and needs immediate discussion. Please ...," he said, gesturing to the empty chair at the opposite end of the table, "sit with us."

Jim sat down slowly in the folding chair, even as all eyes remained fastened upon him. A scripture verse instantly popped into his mind: *'Even as a lamb before her shearers is silent, so the Son of Man does not open His mouth.'* Jim had the unpleasant sensation that he was about to be sheared.

He was nervous, but didn't know why. Based on the troubled expressions on the other's faces, he could tell that he was the only one here who didn't know. He felt a drop of sweat trickle from his armpit into his shirt, and suddenly realized that he was perspiring heavily. He noticed that across the table, Scott seemed to be struggling to find the right words to start the meeting. Jim mustered his courage, and took the initiative.

"Well gentlemen," Jim said, "don't keep me in suspense. What exactly are we doing here?"

Scott took the cue to begin the meeting that he appeared to want no part of.

"Pastor DiMario, council members," he began, "the purpose of this meeting is to discuss a serious situation that was brought to my attention just this afternoon. Before I deliver this information to you, I want an agreement from every man here that you will not disclose the topic of discussion of this meeting outside of this room, due to the sensitive nature of the subject."

Scott looked around the table, getting eye contact and an affirmative nod or gesture from each member before continuing on.

"A … complaint was brought to Pastor LeTourneu from a young woman in the congregation," he said. "And Pete in turn brought it to me. I met with the woman in question and Pastor LeTourneu this afternoon, in an effort to get the facts from her position."

Scott paused for a moment, and lowered his eyes away from Jim's intense gaze. The silence in the room felt heavy to Jim - stifling even. The air in the room was quiet and stale, as if all the oxygen had been sucked out of it. Every eye bored into Scott as he fidgeted uncomfortably on his chair. Jim thought that Scott looked like a moth caught under the focused beam of a magnifying glass on a summer's day, who might suddenly start smoldering if he didn't pull away from the focal point. At last he continued.

"This woman allegedly came to see Pastor DiMario for a marriage counseling session …"

Suddenly, the realization hit Jim as hard as a bat swung by home-run legend Sammy Sosa, and he reeled from the impact as the accusatory blow followed through.

Scott continued haltingly, "And she claims that our pastor … behaved in an inappropriate manner toward her. I have a signed affidavit from her here," he said, tapping the notebook in front of him with a long, slender finger.

"What!" Jim exclaimed, rising to his feet, "That's ludicrous!"

"I'll read the affidavit first, then pass it to Pastor Jim for his review," Scott continued calmly, trying to maintain decorum. "Council members, please hold your comments until I am done reading the affidavit."

Jim looked at the others, and reluctantly sat down.

Scott Corwin pulled out a sheet of paper from the notebook, and held it out in front of him. He cleared his throat loudly, tilted his head back slightly to look at the paper through his bifocals, and began.

"She claims that during their session in his office, Pastor DiMario reached out to hug her - apparently as a comforting gesture. But then, she says, he kissed her and placed his hands up her skirt. He also supposedly touched and fondled her …"

Scott's voice seemed to gradually taper off into an ethereal soft echo as Jim sat dumbfounded, riveted to his seat. He could see Scott's mouth moving as he read off the charges in the affidavit to the men who would act as his judge and jury.

Jim fell into a shocked stupor; it seemed as if he was watching the proceedings on television, with the mute button on. He watched as the council members exchanged facial expressions that ran the gamut between amazement, anger, and denial. Some stole furtive glances at Jim, but none looked him in the eye as the detailed charges against him continued to build. His body and mouth felt paralyzed, unable to speak or move.

Jim's thoughts curiously turned to the image of the famous painting of The Last Supper by DaVinci - The disciples at the table engaged in serious deep discussion, striking various animated poses. Jesus Himself, however, was a picture of peace and serenity, as He sat in the midst of them.

Even as Jim felt isolated and separate from the group assembled around the table, he was anything but a picture of serenity. Amongst all of the men in the room, only Pete LeTourneu seemed to Jim to be nonplused by it all. His appearance and facial expressions bore no evidence of emotion all the while. Jim's semi-comatose meditative state was interrupted when he heard Scott say in a suddenly clarion voice:

"Pastor DiMario, you have the floor to respond to these charges that have been made. Please, take as much time as you wish."

Scott gestured with an open hand, palm up, as if he were making an offering to Jim. He passed the affidavit across the table to Jim, who didn't reach to receive it. All eyes now turned and fastened upon Jim expectantly.

Jim's mouth was parched and his tongue clung to the roof of his mouth. Blake Aanstad drew a cup of water from the water cooler next to him and passed it to Jim, who eagerly took the small paper cup and drank greedily. The room was so silent that even the subdued sounds of Jim's drinking were painfully audible. The rain started again, gently drumming on the thin roof of the trailer. At last he set the near-empty cup down solidly on the table, and spoke. In spite of the emotional upset, his voice still had a strong timbre.

"Over the years, I've heard complaints from various people about lots of things. The length of my sermons, the subjects I choose to preach on, the quality of the Sunday School program, you name it. I've even had complaints about the color of the carpet in the sanctuary, and the seats being too uncomfortable. But never, until today, have I heard someone complain that I am immoral. This makes all the other issues seem pretty small by comparison."

Jim tipped the cup up to his lips and drew out the last few satisfying drops of water before continuing. He crumpled the paper cup in his hand and threw it into the trash bin near the door. He couldn't mask from his voice the sound of his irritation and building anger, and he wasn't really trying.

"I'm not going to pretend I'm not offended by this accusation. By the way, where is my accuser? Shouldn't she be here?"

"Actually, Pastor," Pete answered, "she was too intimidated to attend this meeting and face you and the church council. That's why she signed this written affidavit."

Jim looked at him coldly.

"The nature and content of the conversations that I have with people who come to me for advice is confidential," Jim continued. "Nevertheless, since this woman chooses to make false accusations against me, I'll tell you about her visit. Keep in mind …," he said, pointing his right index finger in an arc at those around the table, "you are all bound by Scott's admonition of confidentiality."

All the men around the table nodded eagerly, and continued to listen in rapt attention as Jim told his story.

"Mrs. Shepherd made an appointment with Bev last week. She came in to see me about marital difficulties she was having. She became distraught as she was telling me her troubles. When our session was over, she stood up and hugged me before leaving. I never touched her, as she claims I did."

As Jim was talking, his mind drifted back to that morning in his office. *Were her actions deliberately seductive?* he wondered. The short skirt hiked up high on her thighs while she sat in the chair facing him. The thin white blouse that did little to conceal the firm, unfettered breasts behind it. Her mannerisms and demeanor as a vulnerable woman in need of solid guidance. Intentional or not, all of it added up to a powerfully seductive formula. Jim knew he'd been wise to end the session when he did.

"There were others in the office at that time," Jim added. "Bev was there, and so was Pete," he said, gesturing toward his associate pastor, who was sitting back from the table against a wall.

"So, that's it? That's the whole story?" Scott asked.

"That's it."

"Can you think of any reason why she would say something like this?" Scott raised his hands apologetically, noting Jim's distasteful facial response. "Hey, I believe you, Pastor Jim, I'm just trying to get your full statement, that's all."

"I understand, Scott. But no, I can't think of why she would make these kind of statements, unless she's emotionally disturbed. But I don't know her, really. I never met her before that day, nor have I spoken to her since."

Scott nodded his head thoughtfully, and turned to Pete LeTourneu. "Pastor Pete, you were in your office. Did you notice anything?"

Pete studied his hands for a moment, then looked up and answered.

"Well, no ... not really," he said slowly. "I happened to be at the door of my office when Angela – Mrs. Shepherd, came out. She was buttoning her suit top and straightening herself when she came out the door. She looked quite emotional, and ...," he paused briefly to verify that everyone was looking at him before continuing, "Well, Pastor Jim looked pretty flustered, too."

A few of the men at the table exchanged looks. Scott's face looked flushed, and he nervously shifted in his chair at this latest revelation, his eyes darting back and forth at the other council members.

"Perhaps we should get Bev Hanson in here to get her take on it," Scott said. Then he raised his hand shoulder high and added, "Just as a formality, of course. Until then, if there are no other questions, I move that this meeting come to a close."

"Just a minute," said a voice that pierced the general feeling of agreement in the room like a crack of thunder. It was Pete LeTourneu, who now stood up, looking as if he were about to deliver a sermon. His chair audibly scraped against the floor as he slowly rose and struck a serious pose standing as straight and tall as his five and a half-foot frame would allow. All eyes - including Jim's, now turned to Pete, who gestured with open hands as he started to speak.

"I think we're overlooking something here," Pete began. "When the morality and behavior of our spiritual leader is brought into question, the integrity and image of the church as a whole is brought into question, too."

He gestured widely with his hands as he spoke. He was going into a preaching mode, putting special emphasis on certain words and looking each council member in the eye. "Even if we keep mum about this, a story of this type will surely leak out. We can't control what Angela Shepherd or others in the church talk about."

"That's true," Jim cut in. "Word of this gossip has already gotten back to me."

"Exactly my point!" Pete said, pounding his right fist into his palm. "People are going to hear about it, one way or another. And they're going to expect the church council - you men right here, to take decisive action."

LeTourneu looked around the table, making eye contact with each of the council members, many of whom nodded in agreement. He didn't look at Jim. Convinced that his audience was ready, Pete LeTourneu moved ahead to close the deal.

"A difficult decision needs to be made right now. I believe that the integrity of our leadership is at risk if we don't make the right call." He paused for a moment to add gravity to his next statement. "I move that a vote be taken to temporarily relieve Pastor Jim from his responsibilities, pending the outcome of a thorough investigation."

Immediately the room came alive with animated discussion. Jim felt a stabbing pain in his chest like a knife piercing his heart, and it seemed to him like everyone was talking at once. The indignation Jim suddenly felt made him think of how it must have been for Jesus, when he was put on trial before the Pontius Pilate. The rabble continued to grow louder, then Pete shushed the crowd so that he could continue.

"I know that this move is unprecedented in our church history," he continued, "but it's in the best interest of the church overall. We must be careful to not let the Lord's name be blasphemed because of actions - alleged actions, that is, of one man."

"This is ridiculous!" Bill Peters shouted out in his typical booming voice. "I don't buy it for a minute. I know our pastor better than that – we all do. This woman is a liar!"

More murmuring and loud discussion ensued. Blake Aanstad, who was shifting back and forth in his seat, stood up to get everyone's attention. He waited until the room quieted somewhat.

"I don't think we have a quorum to vote on Pastor Pete's motion, anyway," he said.

"First of all," Scott interrupted, "Pastor Pete can't make a motion, since he's not a council member. We do have a quorum, however, since five out of our group of seven are here. But considering the circumstances, I wouldn't make a decision like this without everyone present, anyway."

Scott's hands were busy as he spoke, nervously crumpling his Styrofoam coffee cup into a geometric shape.

Now David Frederick cleared his throat loudly and spoke up.

"Let's not go off half cocked here," he said, his hands smoothing the waters of some phantom lake. The tension in the room was high, and it was obvious from their appearance that everyone felt it. "I'm not in favor of asking our pastor to step down, even on a temporary basis. But even if he did, who would fill in for him in the meantime?"

More murmuring in the room, and a few eyes glanced over at Pete LeTourneu, who had sat down quietly during this debate. Again, he rose to his feet.

"As Associate Pastor, it would fall to me to cover Pastor Jim's responsibilities during the proposed suspension period," he declared boldly. "You can be sure that I am one hundred percent committed to do everything in my power to uphold the church during this time, and I feel that I'm prepared to step in."

Pete looked around at the skeptical faces fixed on him. "Of course, I'm not as good a preacher as Pastor Jim - we all know that," he said condescendingly. "But the important thing is that the bible continues to be taught, without controversy. And I can do that. Now then - being leaders in this church means being able to make the tough decisions. Who is going to make a motion to vote on this proposal I've brought up?"

All the men around the table began looking at each other, many of them shaking their heads gently, almost imperceptibly. The looks on their faces were like those of men being asked to hold a live rattlesnake. After a few moments of the assembly playing a figurative game of 'hot potato' with Pete's proposal, Scott once again took charge.

"Well, it looks like nobody's interested in pursuing that option. That being the case, I move that we adjourn until we can get Beverly in here to give us her statement, and get the other council members in attendance."

"I second that," Blake said, raising his right hand.

All the others grunted their agreement and raised their hands shoulder high, just long enough to make it official.

"That's it then," Scott said decisively. "Thank you, gentlemen. You'll be hearing from me. And remember," he admonished with a wag of his index finger, "this matter is not to be discussed with anyone outside of this room."

One by one they stood and filtered out quietly, leaving only Jim, Scott, and Pete in the office. Jim remained in his chair, too shell-shocked to move. The room had again grown quiet enough to hear the sound of the rain tapping lightly on the roof. Scott came over and sat down next to Jim.

"Jim, I just want you to know, I don't believe this accusation has any merit. I don't think the others do, either," Scott said, as he tried to build back some of the damage that he knew was dealt to his pastor's ego.

"I don't believe it either," Pete added, sounding disingenuous. He sat down on the other side of Jim. "But for the sake of the church, I do think that you should voluntarily step down for a period of time until this matter is resolved. Everyone will respect you for making that move in protection of the church."

"I disagree, Pete," Scott snapped back, with a tone of annoyance in his voice. "Pastor Jim hasn't done anything wrong, so there's no reason that he should step down."

Pete ignored Scott's remarks, and continued talking into Jim's ear, since his Jim's head remained turned away from Pete.

"I just think you should consider it, Jim," LeTourneu pleaded. "I really think that both you and the church would come out better from all of this if you step aside now. You can always come back to your duties as soon as this blows over."

Jim had been sitting with his back to Pete, shaking his head in short, slight movements. Now he turned to face the associate pastor.

"Blows over?" he repeated. "What's to blow over? Nothing happened, so why make a bigger deal of this than it is?"

"That's good enough for me," Scott said. "Let's drop this and go home. It's a tempest in a teapot, as far as I'm concerned."

Jim stood up and took a deep breath. "I'm out of here," he said angrily. He strode to the door without another word, and out into the rainy night.

CHAPTER 21

Solid Rock Community Church: Westlake Village, CA

Pete LeTourneu found himself sitting alone in the now quiet church office. Only the barely-audible sound of the wall clock punctuated the enveloping silence.

They had just left; the ignorant pastor and his equally dull yes-man, the church council president.

Pete should have known that they would all stand behind their pastor. Their blind loyalty was sickening. But now Pete had played his hand, and lost. His single best chance to meet the goal had met with failure, and The Magus would not be happy about it. But Pete would fashion a new plan, a new strategy. It was a game, after all. One that The Magus took very seriously. His quarry had escaped this time, but his luck wouldn't hold out forever. Sooner or later - preferably sooner, Pete would obtain his goal. He hadn't invested this much of himself for nothing.

Six months of playing nice and kowtowing to the senior pastor and the church council was hard, draining work. But his efforts were sure to pay off in the end. The corrupting of Solid Rock Community Church was a commendable goal, one that was worth the effort. Yes, Pete would formulate a new plan, perhaps a more aggressive strategy. He would consider every option, regardless of who might get hurt - or killed, for that matter. After all, the end justifies the means. Besides, these Christians proclaim that *'To live is Christ, to die is gain'*. What would be the harm in letting some of them gain an early ticket to their final reward?

Pete had always harbored a deep-seated contempt for the weak and the slow. These Christians were both. The obligation to forgive each other was their Achilles heel. They didn't understand that the path to power was made by walking on the backs of their kind, crushing them in the process.

Pete had learned many things in college on his way to earning a master's degree in philosophy. One was that nature favored those who were prepared to take action. Since his training in philosophy and situational ethics had taught him that there is no absolute right or wrong, he realized that the fastest path to success was a straight line of one's own making. It didn't matter who or what got plowed under along the way. Survival of the fittest - that was what nature taught by example, time and time again.

Of course, everything that Pete and his comrades did would be viewed by those judgmental Christians as wrong - not that he cared. Those pious, ignorant fools - if they had any idea how much power is at the disposal of those who follow the

Prince of Darkness, some of them would probably change sides on the spot. The rest of them deserved to be crushed, like sacrificial animals.

Pete had become involved in paganism in college, thanks to a girlfriend who introduced him to her "coven" of friends who fancied themselves to be witches. But he soon found the white majick practices of Wicca were too tame for his liking, especially after he was recruited by a member of the Temple of Osiris, a hard-core satanic grotto.

The man that Pete came to know as *The Magus* was everything the title implies - a powerful wizard who possesses unexplainable supernatural abilities. He was a professor at the university that Pete attended, and Pete was drawn to him immediately. A practitioner of black majick for many years, The Magus slowly groomed Pete for introduction into the Temple of Osiris grotto.

Once part of the temple, Pete soon learned how far he could go with his ambitions, and a group of like-minded people. And the sex was good, too. Their ceremonies usually involved sex acts with the Priestess to release more psychic energy, which could then be focused for their own purposes.

Pete rose in status and leadership responsibility in the grotto, and reaped large sums of money for himself through a variety of illegal enterprises. He ran his own "escort service" for those who desired discreet, intimate female companionship. He provided illicit pharmaceuticals to those weak-willed sub-humans who needed a little something extra to make it through another day of their boring, meaningless existence. In all of these things, he was providing a positive service to humanity. Simply giving customers what they want, who in turn, were willing to pay handsomely for it. There were no victims, just willing participants and customers. By providing well-paying employment to his girls, Pete was stimulating not only his customers' lusts, but the nation's economy as well.

The power that he felt building within him, imbued by the Prince of Darkness, made him grow ever bolder and more confident in what he could do. He knew that nothing could stand between him and his goals - to become a multi-millionaire, and wield power like his mentor.

When he was approached by The Magus for a new challenge, Pete was ready: The formation of a powerful new Satanic organization. Like Pete, The Magus had become disappointed with the lack of power-building activity in their Temple of Osiris grotto. Power building was a progressive process - one had to stretch his powers to the extreme by taking intrepid risks in order to keep advancing. Lucifer favored those who would boldly seize what they wanted. Not unlike Adolph Hitler and countless others before him, The Magus and Pete LeTourneu shared a common desire to grow in power.

With their goals in alignment, LeTourneu and The Magus had moved three years ago to Brazil - a hotbed of occult power and activity. There they continued to increase their occult abilities together, without hindrance from any government or religious leaders. As an added bonus, they both made some big money at the same time. Now at the age of twenty-six, Pete had surpassed his original financial goal; his various numbered bank accounts in Switzerland and Grand Cayman held over five million dollars. Pete needed a new goal. Thanks to The Magus, he now had one.

The formation of an organized crime network was not a new idea. It had been done successfully in the Los Angeles area already. In fact, there were several organized crime rings currently in operation. The Magus chose the San Fernando Valley as his base of operation, and intended to gradually expand northward up into Ventura county. Of course, there were some competitors who took exception to their plans at first. The small-time hoods that tried to resist them soon met with unusually gruesome deaths – even by brutal street standards. The gory details of these heinous killings soon spread amongst the gangs. The level of cruelty dealt out by the Temple of Anubis to it's competitors raised the bar to a level that even the most hard-core gangsters couldn't bear to touch.

It wasn't long before any overt resistance to their activities stopped. The Chinese triads and other Asian gangs were still busy, but they kept mostly to the city. The Crips and Bloods – black gangs that terrorized the inner city areas, steered clear of the Temple of Anubis' business interests. So did the various Mexican gangs. It became known that the San Fernando Valley and points north belonged to the highly feared Temple of Anubis.

Now the Temple expanded to tacitly provide employment for scores of prostitutes, drug dealers, gun smugglers, sports bookies, pornographers, and underground gambling operators. All under the protection - and iron fist of, the Temple of Anubis.

Their particular brand of Satanic worship had imbued them with the power to overcome their competitors, avoid the police, and grow their businesses under the fronts of an import/export establishment, an adoption agency, a dating service, and a video production company. The Magus certainly knew how to take advantage of every power, trick, and benefit that the Prince of Darkness could grant. Such power came at a cost, of course.

Regular sacrifices of innocent flesh was the tithe that Lucifer demanded in exchange for the privileges granted. It was a price that The Magus, Pete, and the others were willing and able to pay. Their ambition to control all organized crime activities in the San Fernando and Conejo Valleys had no limit. Their only hindrance was the restraining power of praying Christians.

Of course, many of the churches in the area were weak and insipid in their teachings - headed by pastors who were concerned primarily with attendance, and the tithe and offering money that came with large numbers of people. These were preachers who told their congregations what they wanted to hear - not what they needed to hear. They typically regaled their people with jokes and clever stories, while eschewing any serious bible teaching. Some were old, established denominations that had grown cold years ago, without anyone noticing.

Pete and The Magus weren't concerned about them. Indeed, Satan had joined the membership rolls of those churches long ago, in a manner of speaking. They posed no threat, no resistance to the activities that the Temple of Anubis was engaged in. They had no prayer power - weak, like the church of Ephasus spoken of in the book of Revelation.

There were, however, a few churches that posed a problem. Some were large, others small, but these were headed by pastors who's passion was for spreading the confounded 'good news' of Jesus Christ. These single-minded pests focused their efforts on winning souls for Christ - telling people that they could have eternal life by trusting in Jesus to take their sins away. They spent time in serious prayer to God, and taught others to do the same. They prayed at church and prayed at home. They prayed while driving their cars, and on their lunch breaks at work. They prayed for all sorts of things - the health of friends and relatives, for the nation's leaders, for their communities.

And that was the problem - all that praying proved to be bad for business.

Even Satan himself, with all the minions of darkness at his disposal, was hindered by these praying Christians. Because when they prayed, God responded.

Something had to be done to eliminate this problem. Burning or bombing the churches was out of the question. That would only make the survivors pray more earnestly, and they would come back stronger than ever. Like a virulent bacterial infection that re-grows more pervasive than before, these Christians would only thrive on that kind of frontal attack. No, an internal attack was the way to go. Like a packet of yeast worked through a lump of bread dough, the sure way to disable the enemy was to sow corruption from within. And the beauty of it was, these trusting, gullible people would never see it coming. So eager to find the good in others, they wouldn't recognize their enemies even when singing with them in church, shoulder to shoulder.

Once these sheep-like believers felt disillusioned in their church and fellow brethren in Christ, their prayer life would dry up. If they thought their life in Christ was like some big self-help program that didn't work any better than the secular ones, they would slowly leave the church and join the swelling ranks of prayer warriors-turned-couch potato. When these former warriors for Christ stopped their incessant praying, the church would be ripe for the taking.

There was no need to become anxious. Solid Rock Community Church would eventually fall into his grip, just like the last church had. Once DiMario was out of the picture, Pete would step in to fill the leadership vacuum. They would thank him for it, too. They'd probably vote him a big raise - not that he needed their chump change. He would have the congregation happy and feeling good about themselves by preaching sermons that would tell the people just what they wanted to hear.

LeTourneu knew that he could even buy books with pre-written sermons, so he wouldn't even have to waste too much time each week. After all, he still had more important duties to attend to at the import/export company.

Next, he would convert the bible study groups into social groups. Keep the people busy with plenty of charitable and social activities. Yes, the change would come. It was coming like a glacier; slow but steady. And the payoff would be worth the effort. The Magus felt certain that Solid Rock was the only thing standing in the way of them spreading their roots deep into the Conejo Valley; Thousand Oaks, Westlake Village, and Newbury Park. Solid Rock Community Church was a light shining in the darkness, and it needed to be snuffed out. After that was accomplished, they would continue to look north to Camarillo, up into Ventura, and Oxnard.

But first things first, Pete thought to himself. He turned out the church office lights and confidently walked out into the deep darkness of the rainy, foreboding night with a satisfied smirk on his face.

CHAPTER 22

Westlake High School: Westlake Village, California

Garrett slipped through the door of his third period math class, just before the late bell resounded with it's shrill beep. He had taken his time getting his books from his locker, in hopes that Kristi might make an appearance. He had to look around for his combination lock anyway, which was missing from his locker door for some unknown reason. Eventually, he gave up and went to class.

Weird, he thought to himself, *I know I closed the hasp and turned the dial on the lock when I left my locker the last time.*

The classroom hummed with the low voices of students talking about the weekend, the upcoming snowboard season, and plans for Halloween activities and parties.

Garrett squeezed between two girls who were blocking the aisle way while talking about some boy, and greeted his friend Eric with a touch of the fists. He quickly found his seat and got his book out as the teacher, Miss Hertz, stood up and moved toward the white board.

"Today we're going to talk about applications for the quadratic equation," Miss Hertz announced, turning around to face the class, thus abruptly bringing Garrett out of his daze.

She had no sooner turned back to the board and started writing out the equation when a knock resounded on the closed door. Garrett saw the broad, rounded face of Mr. Merrill, the boy's Vice Principal, appear in the narrow slit of reinforced glass imbedded into the door panel. In an instant, he saw that face disappear from the slit only to be replaced by a beckoning index finger. Miss Hertz turned to the class with a surprised look pasted on her face. Garrett knew from past observations that Mr. Merrill's presence was usually a harbinger of bad news.

"Um ... start reading on page one-sixty-three," she commanded. "I'll be right back."

She quickly strode over to the door and opened it, revealing a uniformed Hispanic-looking Sheriff's Deputy standing next to Mr. Merrill, who wore his signature crew cut and a polo shirt that was about two sizes too small to cover his protruding gut. They were flanked by Principal Brooks, who looked somewhat out of place in his tailored dress suit. Miss Hertz stepped gingerly out into the hallway, and the door bumped her backside as it shut behind her. Immediately the quiet classroom started buzzing with whispers about nearly everything except algebra.

In only a few seconds, the door opened again, and Miss Hertz stuck her head into the suddenly quiet classroom. The stricken look on her face conveyed bad news. She locked eyes with Garrett.

"Garrett, could you come out here, please?" she said curtly. Then her head retreated back out the door.

A few cat-calls and cute remarks greeted Garrett as he slowly rose on rubbery legs and walked deliberately to the door. A sudden sensation of fear grabbed hold and squeezed him hard, deep down at the intestinal level. He knew he hadn't done anything wrong, but that knowledge didn't deter the dread that formed over him like a welling thunder cloud. He opened the door tentatively and saw the four of them huddled somberly in the middle of the hallway.

To the others, Miss Hertz quietly said, "I just can't believe it."

Just then, Garrett stepped out into the hallway. The solemn looks on their faces as they turned toward him made it clear that they weren't here for a social visit. Mr. Merrill took the initiative.

"Garrett, come with us to the office," he said. "We need to talk."

Garrett reluctantly fell into step with the three men as they marched toward the office, leaving a crestfallen Miss Hertz in the hall. A late straggler on his way to class crossed their path from an intersecting hall. Taking in the scene, he declared:

"Whoa! Dead man walking."

"Don't you have someplace to be right now?" snapped Mr. Merrill.

The straggler responded by picking up his pace and getting out of the way.

To Garrett, the hallway seemed impossibly long as they kept walking. Their footsteps on the linoleum floor grew louder and louder into a cacophony of noise that sounded to him like a herd of cattle being led to the slaughterhouse. Nobody spoke.

At last they reached the office, and Mr. Merrill held the door while the others walked in. The Sheriff's Deputy looked Garrett over all the while.

"In here," Principal Brooks announced, gesturing to a small sterile-looking conference room just inside the large administration building.

There wasn't a bright light shining over Garrett's chair, but there might as well have been, since he already started sweating even before he sat down. The men took their seats, with the principal and vice-principal across the table from Garrett. They were an odd couple sitting there; Brooks looked to Garrett more like an FBI agent than a high school principal, with his neatly trimmed black hair and dark suit. Merrill looked just like a stereotypical football coach, which he had been at one time.

The deputy drew up a chair next to Garrett, thereby blocking any possible hasty exit. Principal Brooks was the first to break the silence.

"Garrett, I'll get right to the point. We received an anonymous tip that you were selling drugs. So we took the liberty of searching your locker."

"What?" Garrett exclaimed, "no way! Somebody must be playing a trick on you - and me. Who said something like that?"

"Like I said, the tip was anonymous. But that doesn't matter at this point, anyway. The fact of the matter is, Deputy Beltran and I went through your locker and … well, I was disappointed with what we found."

As if on cue, Deputy Beltran stood up and grabbed a plastic grocery store bag from the side bench. Beltran dramatically upended the bag, dumping it's contents onto the Formica-covered table with a theatrical flourish.

Garrett stared incredulously at the pile on the table - about a dozen or more snack-sized ziplock bags. Each bag contained a small mass of a green, leafy substance.

Garrett tentatively reached out to pick up one of the bags, and held it cautiously by the edges as if it were an antique photograph. Upon closer inspection, he noticed that each bag contained a small amount of what was undoubtedly marijuana, which was tightly wound around a small wooden stick by a thread.

"What – you think this is mine?" Garrett asked. He dropped the bag, and said, "This wasn't in my locker when I closed it yesterday afternoon, or this morning when I found my lock missing."

Beltran picked up a bag and opened it. He stuck his sizable nose into the bag, upon which he rested on his Pancho Villa mustache. He took a big sniff, continuing his exaggerated act.

"I got to give you credit, kid," he said. "You only sell the best stuff - Thai stick. I don't see this grade of weed every day." His voice carried a tone of smug enthusiasm that made it obvious to Garrett that he enjoyed this kind of interaction - that of a spider to a fly.

"That's not mine," Garrett protested. "That couldn't have come out of my locker."

"But it did," Principal Brooks cut in. "I opened the locker myself with a bolt cutter." Rapping his knuckles on the tabletop, he shook his head and exhaled loudly. "I really wish it wasn't true."

"But I … I've never smoked marijuana before. I've never even seen it before now."

Deputy Beltran chuckled out loud. "Of course not!" he said sarcastically. Then he pulled the back of his chair around to face Garrett and straddled it, drawing his face to within a foot of Garrett's.

"Now listen up good. I'm gonna ask you some questions, and the answers you give me are going to decide if you spend the rest of the day with me and the detectives at the East Valley Sheriff's Station, or go home to your parents."

Holding up his meaty hand in front of Garrett's face, he extended one finger, then another for emphasis as he continued. "There's two things I wanna know right now. I wanna know who you're buying from, and I wanna know who you're selling to. Take your time to think it over before you give me another bogus answer."

Garrett shook his head desperately and held up his hands. "I don't know what to tell you. The dope isn't mine. I don't know where it came from."

"Fine, have it your way. We'll just go for a little ride." Beltran stood up and pushed his chair out of the way, and grabbed Garrett by the arm. "Let's go, cupcake. We've got a date."

"But I haven't done anything," Garrett protested tearfully, as he reluctantly rose from his chair.

"We'll see about that. Maybe your memory will come back after awhile," Beltran said, as he led Garrett to the door. Turning back to the two still seated at the table, he said, "You can let his parents know where he'll be."

Deputy Beltran left with Garrett, and shut the door behind him. Brooks and Merrill looked at each other, and shook their heads.

"I never woulda guessed it from a kid like him," Merrill said. "I guess you just don't know, these days."

"Nope," Principal Brooks agreed, "You just don't."

CHAPTER 23

Starbuck's Coffee: Moorpark, California

Trey Simmons dropped his backpack full of books on the table at the Starbucks coffee house just down the street from the Moorpark College campus. It was a good place to study - and also to check out the female student body that frequented the place.

It was about eight thirty in the evening, and Trey just got out of his religious studies class. As a full-time student who also worked part-time, Trey had a couple night classes in addition to his day classes.

He wanted to get into UCLA, and his grades were good enough to make it. Unfortunately, his funds weren't. His father had died from cancer when Trey was twelve years old, and his mother barely made enough to get by, much less put a son through college. Trey's goal was to save up some money by working part time at a local pizzeria, and get enough scholarships to pull off going to his dream university long enough to get his bachelor's degree, after getting his A.S. at MC.

Trey went up to the counter and ordered a large frappucino. Normally, he didn't have enough spare money to afford such indulgences, but a friend from one of his classes was working that night, and hooked him up with a deep discount.

He took his liquid refreshment, and settled in at his table. He had stopped by the church office earlier in the day to take advantage of Pastor Jim's standing offer to let him borrow books from his personal library.

He was fishing around in his pack for the Post-It flags that he used for page marking, when the door opened, and she walked in.

Trey had never seen her before, and he was sure he would have remembered if he had.

Whoa - hot! he said to himself, trying to appear casual as he observed the tall, slender girl with the short-cropped black hair swagger toward the ordering counter.

She turned her head toward him and gave a little smile as she walked past. Her svelte lower body was tucked into tight black stretch pants that looked like they might have been painted on. Her hips swayed suggestively back and forth as she strutted to the counter, in a manner that reminded Trey of the Victoria's Secret runway models that he saw in the Superbowl commercials back in January.

She ordered her caramel macchiato, and bent over to get her wallet out of her backpack. Her top rode up slightly as she did so, revealing a tattoo of some type on the small of her back.

Must ...not ...stare, he told himself, as he forcefully tore his gaze away from the attractive newcomer.

Out of the corner of his eye, Trey watched tacitly as she received her coffee, and slowly turned toward the door while taking a sip from the cup with her sensuous lips. Trey's table was next to the aisle way, and he looked up as she strutted past. He was surprised to be treated to another smile from the young hottie.

She continued past him, and paused at the condiment stand near the door to grab some napkins and a straw. Not wanting to be too obvious, Trey turned back to his books, trying to resist the powerful urge to peer at her over his shoulder. He unconsciously ran a hand through his spiked brown hair, which was stiff as a scrub brush from the styling gel he lavished upon it.

"They're out of napkins," said a soft, sultry voice.

Trey's ears instantly pricked up as he turned to face the source of the voice, and found himself looking at a tanned, slender waist with a pierced navel, wrapped in a blue top. His eyes shot upward to the buxom chest, and finally to her piercing green eyes. His jaw involuntarily went slack.

"I noticed you had some extra napkins on your table, if you could spare me one?" she said coyly.

Trey pulled himself out of his momentary state of shock to respond. "Yes, absolutely! Take as many as you like."

"Thanks," she said with a grin, taking a napkin from Trey's trembling hand. "Well, it looks like you've got a big load of homework to do."

"Oh, this?" Trey replied, waving casually at the stack of books and papers. "It's just for a research paper I'm working on."

"Hmm. Looks like a lot of work," she said, surveying the books.

She casually picked up the top book on the stack and looked at the title. Trey noticed that even her hands were beautiful, with remarkably long acrylic nails that were perfectly sculpted and painted. Each one was a work of art in it's own right, and some were decorated with flowers that had tiny rhinestones in the middle.

"You must be some kind of philosophy scholar," she commented. "What's your name, anyway?"

"Trey. Trey Simmons. What's yours?"

"Kristi," she replied, flipping her hair back with her right hand.

"Uh, is this your first year at MC?" Trey asked, desperately trying to make conversation.

"Is it that obvious? Do I look too young to be a college student?" she asked. Placing her hands on her prominent hip bones, she struck a challenging pose.

"No, no. You look ...really...uh, good." Trey stammered. "Uh, would you like to sit down?"

Kristi smiled. "I can't stay. I've got homework tonight myself, and it's due tomorrow." She looked toward the door for a moment, then back at Trey. "But I wouldn't mind if you walked me out to my car. It's dark out there," she said, with a subtle smile.

Trey tried not to look as startled as he felt. "Sure, no problem," he replied, without hesitation. "I'll just leave my books and stuff here for a few minutes. That way I won't lose my table."

Kristi nodded and turned toward the door, and Trey stood up and followed. He couldn't believe his good fortune. His eyes - and those of several other male patrons, were indelibly fixed upon this beautiful visitor.

Outside the door, she turned to wait for him to catch up, and they walked to the parking lot behind the store. The lot was bathed in a sentient amber glow, and the cool night air had the crisp feel of autumn. A light breeze carried the pleasant smell of wood burning in the fireplaces of nearby homes. Kristi talked about her U.S. history class, holding Trey in thrall all the while as he happily followed her out to the far end of the lot.

The two men broke the spell when they approached. Trey didn't even notice them until they were nearly on top of him. The one with the ponytail spoke first, as he got up in Trey's face.

"Gimme your wallet, sucka," he said, then he shoved Trey up against a car.

"Leave him alone!" Kristi protested.

Instantly, another assailant grabbed her from behind, locking her in a bear hug. She struggled and pulled against his grip, and tried in vain to grab for his short-cropped blond hair. Trey turned to help her just as the bully with the ponytail landed a hard roundhouse punch squarely on his jaw. Trey felt a shockwave like an eight-point-zero earthquake course through his whole head before the pain even started. His world suddenly shifted into slow motion as he looked up just in time to see the uppercut coming for his nose.

With no time to react, the huge fist tore into his nose, and for a moment, there was a bright flash of light. The smell of his own blood spewing from his broken nose, and the disorientation from his damaged olfactory nerves caused him to reel back. Trey's hand went up automatically to cover his abused face, as he stepped back in retreat. He pulled his hand back to see why it felt wet. His knees suddenly went wobbly at the sight of so much of his own blood. Without warning, a hot searing pain jabbed through his side like a spear. Trey hadn't noticed that the other mugger had let go of the girl, and now laid into Trey's kidney area from behind with powerful jabs.

His upper torso jerked back involuntarily from the abuse coming from behind. The mugger in front evened it out with a hard punch to the stomach. Trey doubled over in pain even as a sudden, hot nausea swept over him like a tropical storm. His legs buckled, and he dropped to his knees. The blows kept coming, and Trey squeezed his eyes shut and tried to curl himself up in the face of the brutal onslaught.

For some strange reason, an image of Jesus being blindfolded and beaten by temple guards flashed through his mind; *Prophesy! - who struck you that time?*

More blows. His body starting to feel numb. Then the lights went out, and his unconscious body fell hard to the ground.

CHAPTER 24

East Valley Sheriff's Station: Simi Valley, California

Deputy Rich Harrison was hanging around at the front desk of the East Valley Sheriff's Station talking to the receptionist when Jim arrived. As soon as he saw Jim bolt through the door with a nervous look on his face, Rich motioned him over to the side.

"I saw your son," Rich said quietly. "A detective has him in one of the interview rooms down the hall."

"How is he?" Jim asked, breathing heavily.

"Pretty scared, by the looks of it. Detective Pagliani is questioning him, and he has a way of bringing out fear in people. I didn't get a chance to talk to Garrett, though."

"Can you take me to him?" Jim implored. Then he added, "I'm really glad you were here when I called."

"Yeah, I'm actually supposed to be out on the street about now," Rich replied, looking at his watch. "C'mon, let's get down there."

Rich started walking briskly down the vacant hall. Jim fell into step behind him. They walked along the shiny linoleum floor for what seemed to Jim like a city block before stopping in front of a nondescript room with a sign that said *Interview room #1*. Jim followed Rich inside, and suddenly found himself in a small, darkened room. The room was bare except for a one-way mirror imbedded in the wall. Jim saw Garrett through the mirror in an adjacent small room, sitting on a metal folding chair across the table from a gruff-looking detective. Jim couldn't hear the conversation between them, but the graying, barrel-chested detective was quite animated. He repeatedly punctuated his remarks to Garrett with his left index finger, poking the fat digit at the boy accusingly. In reply, Garrett raised his hands to shoulder level while shaking his head and answering.

This doesn't look good, Jim thought. *I hope this hasn't been going on long.*

Rich turned to Jim and said, "Good thing you got here ASAP. Let's see if I can break up this little party now."

Rich turned the cold steel knob on the door and went in, closing the door behind him. He had his back to the door, and Jim watched through the mirror as he pointed with his thumb over his shoulder while talking to the detective. The detective looked over into the mirror with a piercing gaze that seemed to Jim as if it could penetrate the one-way glass. He nodded at Rich, then stood up from his chair. The two of them went to the door and came out. The detective looked Jim up and down with a distasteful expression on his face, but said nothing. Jim clenched his teeth nervously under the detective's probing visual evaluation.

He must think I'm some kind of criminal, or a lousy father at the very least.

To Jim, Rich said, "You can go in and see him. I'll be back in a few minutes."

"Thanks," Jim replied, then he stepped into the room.

Garrett jumped to his feet when Jim entered. The look on his face reminded Jim of a drowning man being thrown a life preserver.

"Dad," he said, with tears already starting to form in the corners of his eyes.

Jim strode over and hugged him. "Tell me what happened, son."

Garrett disengaged from his father and looked in his face. "That guy, the detective, is trying to get me to confess to something I didn't even do! And I didn't do anything!" he said, his voice catching with emotion on the last word. "Somebody must have planted dope in my locker."

Jim felt bile rising up from his stomach and his muscles tense, and he looked at the mirror. He imagined the fat detective watching through the mirror, smirking and snickering to himself. He fought down the urge to tear open the door and come down hard on this tormentor of his only son. Instead, he turned his attention back to Garrett.

"Who could have done that?" Jim asked. "You have a lock on your locker, don't you?"

"I did, but it was gone when I stopped by there before class. The cop said they cut it off when they got an anonymous tip."

"The deputy cut it off?"

"No. No, the cop said that Principal Brooks cut it off."

Jim scratched his head and looked away for a moment before turning his eyes back to his son. "Who else has the combination to your lock?" He asked.

"Nobody, dad. I've never given anyone the combination to my lock. I've been trying to think of who could have it, but ...," Garrett shrugged his shoulders. "It has to be somebody who knows how to pick a lock like that."

"That would be tough," Jim said, frowning and shaking his head. "I bought you that lock, and it was a good one."

Garrett looked his father in the eye. "Dad, you believe me, don't you? I didn't have anything to do with this, that's God's honest truth." His eyes looked imploringly at Jim.

"Yes, Garrett," Jim nodded, "I do believe you. You've never given me any reason not to. But we have to deal with the fact that they've found this dope in your locker, and we don't have any other explanation to offer them. But we'll have plenty of time to think about that once we get you out of here."

"What did mom say?" Garrett asked with a wavering tone.

"She doesn't know yet, at least I don't think she does. I came over right away as soon as I got the call."

"She's gonna freak, Dad."

"I know. I'm freaking myself right now."

In the hallway, Rich turned to the detective and they started strolling slowly up the hall. "So, what's the deal, Pagliani? What have you got on the kid?"

"Possession of marijuana for sale," the detective replied smugly. "Kid had a dozen Thai sticks in individual baggies stashed in his locker."

"Did you find anything on him?"

"'Fraid not. The deputy that responded to the tip searched the kid after he found the stash in his locker. He didn't have anything on him."

"How do you figure the possession for sale charge? Or even possession, for that matter?"

"You know the drill, Harrison. Individual packages of dope means intent to sell. You don't even have to catch 'em in the act of making a sale."

"So," Rich said slowly, "I suppose you must have the kid's prints on the bags of dope, then?"

The detective stared back at him without answering, then sighed loudly. "No, but I don't need his prints on the bags, anyway. You must be watching *CSI* again, huh?" Then he gestured at Rich. "So what's your interest in this one, anyway, Harrison? I know it wasn't your bust - it was Beltran who brought him in."

"His father's a friend of mine. Pastor James DiMario."

The detective chuckled derisively. "Figures! Wouldn't be the first PK I've busted, that's for sure."

"PK?"

"Pastor's kid. They're some of the worst, seems like. They rebel against their upbringing, then seem to think that God still oughta be on their side, on account of their father." He nodded his smirking head. "Yeah, I know their type, all right."

"Looks like you're gonna have a hard time selling this to the D.A." Rich said. "He had nothing on him, and you've got no witnesses to testify that he ever sold - or even had any dope in his possession, for that matter."

"What makes you think I've got no witnesses?" the detective challenged.

"'Cause you would have been crowing about it by now if you did," Rich said with a grin. "How long have I seen you in action, Pagliani?"

"Okay, fine. So it's a little weak. But that doesn't mean some witnesses won't come forward once word of this gets out."

Rich gave him a doubtful look. "The only witnesses you're likely to see are Jehovah's Witnesses at your door," he said mockingly.

Rich saw Pagliani's eyes turn narrow, as he stuck his finger in Rich's face. "That's why I'm tryin' to get the kid to plead out," Pagliani said. "I'd rather have a bird in the hand than two in the bush."

"I think this bird's gonna fly away home, and soon," Rich retorted. "You gonna charge him, or not?"

The pudgy detective studied the floor for several seconds. "Not today." He pointed his left index finger at Rich. "But that doesn't mean he's off the hook. As soon as I get one of his classmates to rat him out, I'm gonna drag his scrawny butt back in here and book him."

"Fine."

Rich walked a few steps down the hall, back to the room, with detective Pagliani in tow. Just when Rich reached for the doorknob, Pagliani grabbed his arm.

"Hang on a minute," the detective said. He turned the doorknob and entered the small room first, leaving Rich trailing behind. Garrett and Jim turned to look at the cocky detective swaggering up. He bent down and put the palms of his thick hands on the table in front of Garrett. He lowered his head like a vulture, his eyes boring into Garrett.

"Okay, Garrett," he said menacingly, "I'm gonna give you one more chance to come clean about all this. If you tell me everything now, I can go with just the possession charge - you won't have to do time." He smirked, and added, "And I don't think you'd make it in the big house very long, kid."

Jim's entire body burned with anger and frustration at his inability to stop this disrespectful diatribe from the detective.

Lucky for him he's a cop. Nobody gets away with saying things like this to my family.

With considerable effort, he remained seated. But he fumed with anger, and could feel the veins rising in his reddening face.

"I've already told you everything a dozen times," Garrett pleaded. "There's just nothing else to tell. I didn't have any dope. I never even saw any before today."

Pagliani shook his head and turned it to the right, so the others wouldn't see the defeat etched into it. "Okay, fine," he said. "You can go - for now. Don't leave town until further notice."

Jim started to open his mouth to speak up, but when he looked up at Rich who was standing behind the rotund detective, he saw him shake his head one time. The detective stood upright and turned on his heel, and left the room without another word. The door slammed like a cell door behind him.

CHAPTER 25

DiMario Residence: Westlake Village, California

The atmosphere at the DiMario home was tense during dinner, like a thick storm cloud hanging in the air. Jim and Garrett tried to explain the situation to Jasmine. She couldn't keep herself from interrupting repeatedly.

"Who gave the principal this tip to search Garrett's locker, anyway?" she demanded, while standing at the sink doing the dinner dishes.

Jim noticed that her skin tone was starting to turn slightly pink, a sure indicator that Jasmine was working up to a major emotional blowout.

"I don't know," Garrett replied wearily. He and Jim still sat at the dinner table in the eat-in kitchen. "He said it was an anonymous tip. That's all he said." With his elbows on the table, Garrett buried his head in his hands.

"That's ridiculous," Jasmine said, waving a butter knife before plunging it into the sudsy sink. "What ever happened to our country's constitution? We're supposed to have the right to face our accusers. They can't take action like that just on some anonymous tip."

"They did, Jasmine," Jim replied dryly.

"Well, we could probably sue them for this. It's a violation of privacy, and a violation of our son's civil rights," she said, pointing a dirty fork at Garrett. A wet dish slipped from her other hand as she did so, and it smashed loudly on the tile floor.

"I think it would be tough to make that stand up in court, considering that the locker was loaded with dope," Jim noted, trying hard not to sound sarcastic. He went to the closet and pulled out the dustpan and brush, and started cleaning up the shattered remains of the dish.

"People have sued for less, and won!" Jasmine clasped her arms across her chest and shook her head, frowning. "I just can't imagine someone planting drugs in your locker, Garrett. Why would they do it?"

Jim stroked his chin thoughtfully. It made a faint scrunching sound as he rubbed the five-o'clock-shadow. "You've got an enemy, son," he said decisively.

"Why?" Garrett asked. "Who would do something like that?"

"That's what we need to find out."

"When I do find out, they're a dead man," Garrett asserted, smacking his right fist into his open palm.

Just then, the door opened and Chelsea stepped in from the attached garage. "What's going on?" she asked, reading their concerned expressions and the taut atmosphere in the room.

"Honey, you don't even want to know," Jasmine sighed, shaking her head.

The phone suddenly rang, and Chelsea grabbed for it. "Hello? No, this is her daughter ... Okay, just a minute, please." She covered the receiver and turned to Jasmine. "Mom, it's for you." Reading her mother's sign language, she shrugged her shoulders and quietly mouthed the words, "I don't know who it is."

Jasmine took the phone that Chelsea handed her. "Hello? Yes ... oh, hi, Debbie ... no, no problem. What's wrong? Oh, no, that's terrible! Where is he now? How bad? Well, I'm sure that Jim will want to come see him. He asked for Jim? ... Uh-huh ... Okay, you bet I'll tell him. Bye."

Jasmine put the phone down and turned to face her family with a furrowed brow. They all stared at her, looking as expectant as a father-to-be in a maternity unit waiting room. Jim became apprehensive as he saw the stressed look on his wife's face increase.

"Well?" he asked, with baited breath.

"I can't believe it," she said quietly. "That was Debbie Simmons. Her son Trey was attacked out by the college last night by two muggers." She paused for a moment to compose herself, then continued. "They beat him up pretty bad. He got a front tooth knocked out and a split lip that needed to be stitched up. And a couple broken ribs, too. You know how skinny he is. It's lucky he even survived."

"Lucky?" Jim replied. "Since when do we believe in luck? Thank God he did survive. I should run over and see him. Where's he at?"

"Los Robles Medical Center. But it's getting a bit late for visiting now," Jasmine said, looking at the kitchen clock. It was almost nine-o'clock.

"They'll let me in. They always do," Jim replied, reaching for his keys in the kitchen drawer. "In the meanwhile, Garrett, I want you to think about the events of the last few days. Replay them in your mind. Someone must of had a reason and an opportunity to do this. We've got to find the answers. You're not out of the woods yet."

Chelsea looked at her mother quizzically. "What's Dad talking about?" she asked. She turned back to her father, but Jim was already out the door.

CHAPTER 26

Los Robles Medical Center: Thousand Oaks, California

The oak tree-lined thoroughfare of Lynn Road winds it's way like a serpent past the The Oaks Mall, and toward the North end of town on it's way toward the hospital.

Jim followed the gently curving path mechanically, as if on autopilot. He dwelt upon the circumstances of Garrett's run-in with the law and the repercussions of it, while cruising the familiar route to the hospital.

Jim parked his car in the visitor's lot, and got out into the crisp fall night air. His thoughts were still on his son, rather than the young man he had come here to see, as he methodically headed for the hospital's main entrance.

The massive automatic double doors swung outward to meet him, then Jim walked through and strode up to the reception desk. An elderly volunteer dressed in a pink frock with perfectly coifed white hair answered his query about Trey.

"He's out of intensive care, Reverend," she said, perusing her clipboard. "You can find him in room two-thirteen." Then she added, "We don't let just anybody in here this late to see patients, you know."

"I know," Jim said with a wink. "Thank you."

She smiled and pointed him to the bank of elevators nearby. Jim walked toward them, as his thoughts about Garrett began to close in on him again. He barely detected the faint necrotic hospital smell in the background as he walked the clean polished floor.

When Jim stepped quietly inside the door of the dimly lit hospital room, what he found was worse than he had expected. Trey was in a bed near the window of the twin room, with the head of his bed slightly elevated. The sliding curtain was partially drawn back. He had no neighbor in the adjoining bed to commiserate with.

As Jim approached, he noticed an IV bag on a stand, infusing Trey's left arm. His face was a mess - swollen nearly beyond recognition. Trey's right eye was black and blue and swollen almost shut. His nose looked about twice it's normal width. A nasty gash rose vertically from his swollen upper lip, and had evidently required several stitches to close. His upper and lower arms had angry-looking bruises on them, testifying to the thoroughness of the beating he had endured. He appeared to Jim to be either sleeping or unconscious.

"Probably the best thing for him," Jim murmured under his breath.

Trey stirred and opened his eyes slightly. His face was swollen to the extent that he looked to Jim to be more oriental than anglo, with his eyes barely more than narrow slits.

"Pastor," Trey said dryly, "I hope you're not here to read me last rites."

Jim smiled. "I think you'd have to make a major turn for the worse before you'd qualify for last rites," he replied. "Besides, you're not Catholic, anyway."

Trey grimaced as he tried to move into a more comfortable position on the uncomfortable hospital bed.

"I took a heck of a beating for the few dollars they got," he said, with a twinge of pain evident in his voice. "I feel like I'm gonna die."

"You look like it, too."

"Thanks. I bet the other guys' fists hurt, though."

Trey's half-hearted chuckle was cut short by a sharp jolt of pain from his broken ribs. His face contorted into a mask of suffering, and he inhaled sharply.

Jim suddenly became serious. "Those guys really worked you over good, didn't they?"

"Yeah, and the worst part is, I didn't even get the girl's phone number before they came along."

"What girl?"

"The one I just met there at Starbucks. Kristi - I didn't even get her last name."

Jim stroked his chin. "Tell me exactly what happened."

Trey proceeded to fill him in on the whole sequence of events that led up to his unceremonious admission to the emergency room.

"So ... ," Jim asked, "what happened to Kristi?"

"Don't know. I went down for the count. I asked all the nurses I've seen if she was brought in, but they all said that nobody matching that description is in here. I hate to think what they might have done to her."

"Trey, you said that her car was all the way in the back of the parking lot. Was the place really crowded?"

"No, not too much. There were other people there, sure. But there were plenty of empty parking spots closer in. But, hey - I wasn't complaining. It gave me more time to talk to her."

Jim started turning the pieces of the story around in his mind, seeing if the pieces would fit together naturally. They didn't.

I must be getting paranoid and skeptical in my old age, he thought to himself, as he helped Trey gingerly take some ice chips from a cup into his decimated mouth.

Jim sat quietly watching him struggle with the ice for a few minutes before he finally spoke again.

"Trey, you know that visit we made to the ceremonial site out in the woods a few days ago?" he asked.

"Are you kidding? How could I forget? That picture will stick in my mind for a long time," Trey breathed laboriously. "The majick circle in the clearing, and especially, all that blood."

"Did you do any other research, or tell anyone else about what we found?" Jim asked.

Trey looked thoughtfully out the window at the view of the parking lot for a moment.

"Well, yeah. I did some more digging, and I was gonna tell you guys about what I found out. And, yeah, I did talk about it to a few people. Come to think of it, I even brought up the subject in my philosophy class. So my professor and the whole class heard about it." He tried to smile. "Makes for great conversation, you know." Trey observed the concerned look growing on Jim's face, and his own forced smile faded. "Why, Pastor? Why do you ask?"

"Oh, no reason, really. I was just wondering if anyone knew we were out there."

Trey went silent for a moment before responding. "You mean, like the people who built the site? The Satanists? You think that they know we were out there ..." He suddenly caught on to Jim's drift, and added, "and maybe even know who we are?"

"That's what I'm wondering," Jim replied, nodding solemnly.

Jim observed the countenance of Trey's face transform from curiosity, to concern, and finally, to fear.

"I've got a new friend I'd like you to meet," Jim said, changing the subject. "I bet he can help us put the pieces together." Looking the battered young man up and down, he said, "You won't be going anywhere for awhile, will you?"

Trey managed a smile. "I think I'll chill here awhile. The room service is pretty cool."

"Good. Let's pray, then I'll let you get some rest."

Trey nodded. They bowed their heads. Jim slid his chair close to the bed and prayed for God's healing and protection upon his young friend. He didn't realize how badly Trey would need God's protection.

CHAPTER 27

Far East Imports Co.: Reseda, California

"Idiots! You're idiots, all three of you. Get in here, and shut the door."

The veins on Pete LeTourneu's neck swelled as he bellowed at the two young men and the young woman entering his office.

LeTourneu's large, luxurious office at the Far East Imports headquarters was well-appointed with a dark teakwood desk and matching credenza. Beautiful paintings and art objects - all with oriental themes and style, decorated the walls and the tops of tables and file cabinets. It was late in the evening, and they were the only ones in the building. The blinds on the only window in the office were drawn.

LeTourneu sat back in his high-back leather chair and glowered at them as they discreetly walked across the plastic drop cloth-covered carpet toward his desk. The plastic made a faint scrunching sound under their feet.

"What's with the plastic on the carpet?" asked the young man with the short-cropped blonde hair.

"I'm redecorating," replied LeTourneu. "But don't try to change the subject. I gave you a simple assignment, and you jacked it up," he barked, slicing the air in front of himself with his right hand. "I told you to snuff him, but I hear that he still lives. Why is that?"

"Sir," began the pretty young woman with the short black hair, "I did exactly what you said. I got him outside in the parking lot by himself with nobody around." She turned to the two burly, rough looking men on her left and gestured toward them. "It's them who screwed up," she accused. "They were supposed to take care of him once I delivered him."

The man with the long dark hair tied back in a ponytail raised his hand defensively. As he did, his sleeveless tee shirt slipped back far enough to reveal a tattoo on his muscular shoulder. The tattoo depicted an inverted five-point red star inside of a black circle.

"Hey, we tore him up big time," he said. "I thought he was dead. He might still die, anyway."

"He's out of our way, anyhow," added the other man with the short spiked bleach-blonde hair. He had an identical tattoo on his shoulder, plainly visible with his 'wife beater' shirt on. "He won't be able to cause us any more trouble. We didn't really have to kill him."

"When did you presume to start making decisions for me?" LeTourneu demanded. "If I say he needs to die, then you are to carry out my orders without question." His eyes flared with rebuke.

Pete LeTourneu stood up from his chair and leaned his diminutive frame over his desk as he continued to chastise the blond-haired man.

"This is the second time now that you've failed me, Big-D," he hissed. "And I've noticed that the control of your dealers has started to decay. You're only moving seventy percent of the pot you were moving this time last year, and crank sales are off, too."

Big-D turned his unshaven face toward the floor, the walls - everywhere but LeTourneu's piercing gaze. He started to speak up in his own defense. "It's because the quality has gone down, man. The crank you're giving me now isn't as good as before." His desperate lie lacked a ring of conviction.

"Really! If that's the case, why is Craig here increasing his output?" Pete LeTourneu demanded, pointing at the other man.

The young man with the ponytail turned his head toward his partner and gave a small smirk.

"Has anyone complained to you about the quality of our pot or crank?" LeTourneu asked him.

"No, sir," Craig replied.

Pete turned again to Big-D. "Maybe the quality problem has something to do with somebody cutting the product with mannitol," he said accusingly.

It was a common practice for drug dealers to dilute, or cut methamphetamine 'crank' or cocaine with inert fillers. In doing so, they would get more product to sell, hence, more profit. The only catch was, product quality was diminished by doing so.

"Hey, I don't know what you're talking about, man," Big-D protested. "I just sell what you give me. I haven't stepped on it."

LeTourneu turned his attention momentarily to the young woman. "Kristi," he said, with a gesture of his left hand. On cue, she opened her purse and removed a tiny ziplock bag containing a white powder. She stepped forward reluctantly, and handed it to Pete LeTourneu without a word. He took it, and held it up in front of Big-D, shaking it teasingly.

"I decided a little quality check was in order," LeTourneu said sarcastically.

He produced a chemical analysis kit from his top desk drawer, and opened it. After administering the appropriate number of drops of colored reagents into a test tube, he opened the tiny bag and stuck a little spoon in to get a sample. He then dropped the sample into the test tube. LeTourneu took his time with each step, moving slowly and gradually, so as to savor the discomfort and anxiety that grew on Big-D's face. He slowly swirled the profane mixture of methamphetamine and chemical reagents around in the test tube longer than necessary to mix it up completely. Big-D gulped quietly and was visibly starting to sweat. LeTourneu pulled the color gradient chart from the kit and held it alongside the test tube up to the light. After viewing them for a dramatically long time, he set them down abruptly on his desk and shook his head.

"So, you were too cheap to use mannitol to cut our product with. Instead, you used talcum powder from the drug store," he declared, staring hard enough at Big-D to bore a hole in his head.

Kristi and Craig intuitively started backing away from LeTourneu's desk, moving almost imperceptibly to distance themselves from the accused. Big-D started looking around desperately at his companions, who he now realized had conspired against him.

"Dude, I don't know where she got that stuff, but it didn't come from my dealers," Big-D lied. Then he added, "If one of my guys is doing that, I'll be all over him about it."

As Big-D was blustering, LeTourneu picked up a letter opener from his open desk drawer and secreted it in his right hand, and he casually walked around his desk to confront Big-D face to face. Although Pete LeTourneu was considerably shorter in stature, it was obvious to the others by his agitated body language that Big-D was very much afraid of him.

LeTourneu crossed his arms and looked into Big-D's eyes. "Did you really think that you could get away with it?" he asked.

The only response from Big-D was a desperate shake of his bleach-blonde head.

"I'm going to turn your territory over to Craig," LeTourneu said to his trembling subordinate.

"But ... but what about me?" Big-D asked.

"You," Pete LeTourneu said, as if considering the subject. "You ... are about to retire from the business."

In one sudden fluid motion, LeTourneu unfolded his arms and swung the letter opener in a swift arc. It found its target in the side of Big-D's neck, puncturing his carotid artery as it plowed deeply into its victim. Big-D tensed instantly and swung his arms in a belated attempt to ward off the attack. Streams of crimson blood squirted from his neck at the place that the letter opener handle stuck out of his neck like a flag. His arms flailed around helplessly, unsure whether to pull it out or leave it in. The decision was irrelevant. Big-D sank to his knees on the plastic-covered carpet. The look on his face was one of shock and horror, his right hand helplessly holding the handle of the letter opener.

The spurts of blood started to wane in intensity, and he fell headlong to the floor. His two remaining companions stared in rapt horror at the drama in front of them, unable to believe what their eyes were telling them. They backed themselves even further away.

"Failure is not an option," LeTourneu declared to the two surviving visitors, who stood silently with jaws dropped.

Several thick drops of bright red blood got onto the back of his murderous hand, and he raised it to his lips and licked the blood off.

"Congratulations, Craig," LeTourneu continued brightly. "You've just been promoted. I know you won't disappoint me."

"No, sir, I won't," Craig responded somberly. "I will always be loyal to you."

"Good. We have an understanding then. Sometimes, small sacrifices have to be made in order to keep progress on track. Big-D obviously didn't share my vision. But from now on, you will address me as 'Master'. Is that understood?"

"Yes, Master," Craig and Kristi replied in unison.

"Very good. Now then, Craig, clean up this mess." LeTourneu pointed to the dead man at his feet, with a pool of blood forming around his head. "Roll him up in the plastic, and make sure you don't spill any blood on the carpet. But first, you can help me harvest the remaining blood. No point in letting it go to waste. Pass me that case over there," he said, pointing at the suitcase-sized brushed aluminum hard-sided container sitting in a corner of the room.

Craig complied, and brought the case over to where his boss was now kneeling beside the body of his hapless underling. LeTourneu took the kit and laid it down flat. He deftly pressed the two latch buttons, which opened almost simultaneously with a loud snap.

***

Kristi jerked slightly at the harsh sound. She wondered what her evil boss would use the blood for, and what he might do next. She had never actually seen him kill anyone before, even though she had heard that he had done so on several occasions. There was no turning back now, she knew. Her survival depended on total obedience to her master. And she was a survivor, having lived almost a year on the streets before being taken in by LeTourneu's organization. Sure, they had some weird rituals and practices, but they had clean beds and good food, too. And protection. She didn't have to work on the streets of the San Fernando Valley like the other girls in the group.

Her pretty, young face with the peaches n' cream complexion was framed by luxuriant, shiny black hair, which she sometimes supplemented with extensions or wigs to change her look. These assets, combined with her firm, shapely body made her desirable to the highest paying customers. The fantasy sex acts that she was required to perform for these well-heeled customers, and those she did during the group's black masses were the price she had to pay for being part of a close-knit family. All of her needs were met - except for unconditional love. Pete and his helpers provided her with a large wardrobe of nice clothes that would be the envy of most teenage girls, even those who had a 'normal' family life.

She always had spending money in her purse, but never enough to allow her to put aside very much for her future plans. Sometimes, a very satisfied customer would hand her an extra twenty as a tip, as she was leaving one of the plush hotel rooms that she had become accustomed to in her work.

At age seventeen, Kristi knew that she couldn't stay with Pete's organization forever; it was just a matter of time before she outlived her usefulness, or angered The Magus or Pete LeTourneu in some way. But for now, total obedience was expected and required to keep her relatively pampered position within the group. It was getting harder all the time to go along with everything that Pete wanted, and now, this brutal murder right in front of her face. Kristi tried to push away the realization from her mind that she was within a few feet of a dead man who was just moments ago walking and talking.

***

LeTourneu opened the case and plugged in the portable embalming machine. He never used embalming fluid, of course. He only used the equipment to make a withdrawal, never a deposit. He attached the long cannula needle to the extraction tube of the machine. Then in one swift motion, he buried the needle into his victim's carotid artery. He turned on the switch, and watched the column of sanguine blood move up the extraction tube and into the thick plastic bottle that was inside the case.

Whenever the needle started to suck in air, LeTourneu would simply pull it out and penetrate another target where he knew blood would be pooling; the femoral arteries in the legs, the aorta, the heart, the lower lungs.

Kristi couldn't force herself to watch the macabre spectacle, and turned away to face the door. LeTourneu noticed the look of disgust on her young face.

"Not to worry, dear Kristi," he said cheerfully, "Big-D didn't die in vain. His lifeblood will make up for his failures and greediness. It will be used to strengthen me further, and protect my people - those who are faithful to me. But for those who are not …," he looked down at the corpse at his knees. Big-D's skin was now pale and starting to take on a shade of blue. LeTourneu shook his head gravely. "Tsk, tsk. It's a shame, but these things do have a way of working themselves out."

After exhausting the bulk of the blood in his expired underling's body, LeTourneu closed up the kit. He handed it over to his accomplice, who placed the large plastic bottle of blood on his desk.

"Thank you, Craig," he said, as casually as if his accomplice had just helped him with his coat rather than an exsanguination.

LeTourneu took a container of wet wipes from the top of his desk, and diligently wiped all traces of blood from his hands, the embalming kit, and the plastic bottle of blood.

"Now then, Kristi, he said, "I have something for you and your friend to help me with as well."

The words made her ears tingle, and her body tensed up. She knew somehow that it wouldn't be something as simple as last time.

"First of all, help Craig roll Big-D up in this plastic sheet and put him in the trunk of his car out back. I have a dump location picked out already. Then get back here. I have a career advancement opportunity for you and Angela, and you're going to love it."

Pete LeTourneu walked over to his closet and opened it. He turned around to face Kristi with a big smile on his face, as she looked expectantly at what was in his hands. Hanging from a wooden hanger was a clean, pressed nurse's uniform.

CHAPTER 28

Los Robles Regional Medical Center: Thousand Oaks, California

The attractive young nurse nervously stuck her head in the door of Trey Simmons' hospital room, but he was sleeping too soundly to notice. She heard the faint sound of his deep breathing in a slow, relaxed rhythm.

Thank God, she said to herself.

She had just passed by the nurse's station where the wall clock showed the time of 8:45 P.M.

She had arrived at the start of the shift, introducing herself as Angela Johnson from the temp agency – saying that she was filling in tonight for Carol Blanchard, who was home sick. Although she wore no makeup under her large blue-framed eyeglasses, and the hair of her dark brown wig was up in an untidy bun held in place with a large clip, she still got the attention of the male nurses and the last remaining doctors on the floor.

After getting the roster of patients from the head nurse, she had casually walked down the hall to room two-seventeen.

I can't do this, she said to herself. *Why did I agree to it? But then it's not a matter of agreeing, anyway. I have to do whatever he says – no choice.*

She gently pushed on the metal door lever, and silently entered the darkened room. In the subdued light she could make out the shape of the bed, furniture, and IV stand.

I thought this was a fun acting gig when I started, she thought. *I can't believe it's led to this. But nobody says 'no' to Pete, unless they're tired of living.*

Angela Shepherd quietly padded over to Trey's bed and looked around. No other patients in the room.

Good, she thought.

She took a look out the window; it was quiet outside in the parking lot. Next to the bed was an IV bag on a stand, which infused some solution into the kid's arm.

Perfect.

She slipped her hand into the pocket of her floral-print scrub top and pulled out a syringe. With quivering hands, she carefully pulled off the pink plastic cover, exposing the sharp stainless steel needle.

Angela gingerly approached the IV, and gripped it in her trembling left hand. With the other hand, she brought the tip of the needle to the infusion port at the base of the bag - her target, just as she was told. She hesitated for a moment.

"I hope I'm not interrupting anything," came a booming voice from the door.

The sound caused Angela to jerk her body toward a tall man in a sheriff's uniform standing silhouetted in the doorway.

"No, no, I was just finishing," Angela stammered.

She casually tossed the syringe into the trash container at the foot of Trey's bed, and wiped her hands nervously on her uniform smock. She forced a fake smile at the lawman, but didn't look directly at him.

"Well, I suppose you want to talk to him," she said, and headed toward the door.

Rich Harrison noticed that the nurse didn't make eye contact as he watched her go. Trey stirred slightly at the sound of voices in the room, but didn't wake up. Rich walked over to the bed and looked in the trash can. Then he pulled out a Kleenex from the box on the rolling nightstand. Carefully, he reached in and picked up the full syringe with the needle exposed. Rich looked it over in his hand. Then he noticed the plastic cover lying next to the trash can, and he bent down and picked it up. He cautiously snapped the cover over the needle, then pulled out a Ziplock bag from one of his shirt pockets. He put the syringe in the bag, and put it into the pocket of his uniform shirt. He looked toward the door again. The nurse was gone.

In his twelve years with the Sheriff's department, Rich had developed a sixth sense about certain things. He was pretty good about telling when people were lying to him. Whenever he walked into a situation where something was askance, the back of his neck started to tingle. And it tingled now.

Weird, he thought to himself. *No medical professional throws sharps into a trash can. There are special biohazard collection boxes for them. And a full syringe - whatever this is, she didn't put it into his IV.*

Rich tapped his full pocket thoughtfully. *I'm no Bruce Willis, but most of the nurses flirt a bit, or at least are friendly to cops. She didn't even look at me.*

The sense that he had just stepped into something grew on Rich; more of a feeling in his body than in his mind. Something was out of place here, he knew. He glanced over at Trey who was still sleeping fitfully on his hospital bed.

He'll wait, Rich figured. *He's not going anywhere.*

Rich strode to the door and jerked it open, then stepped out. He looked up and down the hall. Empty. He quickly walked down to the nurse's station.

"'Scuse me," he said to the duty nurse behind the desk who was crouched over a clipboard, "Where is that brunette nurse I saw just a minute ago?"

The nurse looked up and smiled at Rich. "You can flirt with her on her own time, deputy. She's got rounds to make."

"I'm serious," Rich replied tersely, without returning the smile. "Where is she?"

The casual look faded from the nurse's face at once. "She just came by here less than a minute ago," she said, pointing out the direction with her finger, "She was in a big hurry."

"Don't you think that's a bit strange?" Rich asked.

"Not around here," she replied, with a shrug of her shoulders.

Rich trotted down the corridor in the direction the nurse indicated. His chest tightened at the sight of the exit sign about thirty yards ahead. Without warning, a dark-haired nurse stepped out of one of the numerous doors lining the corridor. Rich darted to the side just in time to avoid bowling her over. She jerked her head up and let out a gasp, stopping on a dime. Rich didn't bother to excuse himself.

"Where's the brunette nurse?" Rich demanded.

The flabbergasted nurse sputtered out a reply. "I ... I just saw her run down that way a few seconds ago," she said, nodding her head toward the end of the corridor.

"Go check on the man in room two-seventeen."

Rich broke into a run down the hall as the nurse scooted off in the opposite direction. He came to the end of the corridor and crashed through the door leading to the stairs. Rich guessed she was headed to the parking lot. He took the two flights of steps down to the ground floor two at a time, and burst out of the stairwell on the ground floor like a man on a mission. Startled volunteers, visitors, and doctors reeled back out of his way as he ran down the wide first-floor corridor to the reception desk.

"The young brunette nurse - did you see her?" Rich snapped at the white-haired octogenarian behind the desk.

In reply, the elderly man pointed a crooked finger at the main entry doors. Rich made a beeline for the automatic doors and accidentally slammed into them when they didn't open quickly enough.

When he pushed his way through to the entry Porte Cochere, he saw the nurse next to a car at the curb about forty yards away. She roughly pulled another woman out of the passenger side door. Rich could see that this woman's hands were bound and her mouth covered by duct tape, and she was blindfolded with a piece of towel.

He started to sprint toward the car and shouted at the nurse, "Hey, stop!"

Angela Shepherd didn't stop to look over her shoulder at Rich, but instantly slipped into the passenger seat, leaving the bound, gagged, and blindfolded woman stumbling around at the curb. Her door wasn't even shut all the way when the driver punched the gas on the silver '04 Pontiac Grand Am GT, and tore away from the curb with tires squealing. Rich could barely make out the driver - a dark-haired woman. He couldn't make out the license plate through the smoke that peeled off the spinning tires.

Rich slowed from his dead run as he approached the curb. He touched the blindfolded and gagged woman on the shoulder, and she instantly jerked away from his grasp.

"Sheriff's deputy, ma'am," he said. "You're gonna be okay. It's over. Let me take this tape off you. Just hang on a second." With one hand he snatched the radio mike that was clipped to his shirt lapel, while lowering the woman's blindfold with the other hand. "X-ray nine to base," he barked into the mike.

"Go ahead, X-ray nine."

"All units in the northwest sector of T.O., watch for a Pontiac Grand Am 2004, silver in color. Unknown plate. Last seen going southeast on Janss Road. Wanted for reckless driving and possible kidnapping at this time. Over." Rich released the key on his mike.

"Copy that, X-ray nine," came the reply.

Rich grabbed one corner of the duct tape that held the woman's mouth shut. "This may hurt a bit," he said, ripping the wide, heavy tape off her face.

"Yeow!" she yelped as the tape came off.

"Sorry about that. Let me get your hands. Tell me quick what happened."

"Well, I was coming into work as normal, and ..."

"Why did they have you tied up?" Rich interrupted, while freeing her hands from the thick duct tape. "Who are those two?"

"I ... I don't know. They just jumped me and tied me up. I don't know why, or who they are."

"Are you okay?" Rich asked, scanning her up and down.

She nodded her head yes, and her eyes started to fill with tears.

"C'mon, follow me," Rich commanded. "I'll bet you work in the second floor ward."

"Yes, I ...I do."

Rich walked brazenly back inside the hospital lobby with the tattered nurse in tow, eliciting stares from those who had watched him only moments before blast through those same doors. He gently guided the nurse into the elevator, and pushed the button for floor number two.

"I'm going to have your friends look you over, to make sure you're okay," Rich said.

"Thanks a bunch," she sniffed. "Why didn't you catch them?"

"I didn't make the Olympic track and field team this year," Rich deadpanned. "But not to worry. I sent out the alert. They'll probably get stopped."

The elevator door opened, and Rich saw the nurses gathered around their station in a knot, chatting excitedly. They all looked up at the same time and fell silent when they saw him coming out of the elevator with their disheveled co-worker Carol Blanchard behind him. The head nurse was the first to speak up.

"What's going on?" she asked.

"The young man in two-seventeen - is he okay?" Rich countered.

"Yes," said the dark-haired nurse that Rich had startled in the corridor. "I just checked him. He's fine. He's awake now, too."

"Who's that nurse that bolted out of here?" he asked the head nurse.

"She's a temp. Filling in for Carol here - or so she said," she replied, looking at her bedraggled colleague. She put on the horn-rimmed glasses that were hanging from a gold-colored chain around her neck, and looked down at her clipboard. "Johnson. Angela Johnson. Never saw her before tonight. Why? What did she do?"

Rich gestured with his head at Carol Blanchard. "Kidnapping, for starters. And I'm not sure what else yet."

The other nurses bunched around Carol like bees in a hive, hugging her and asking her twenty questions all at once. Rich reached into his pocket and pulled out the syringe. He started to speak, but could scarcely hear himself above the din of the nurses.

"Ladies!" he bellowed. They fell silent again and turned to him simultaneously. "What is this?" he asked.

One of the nurses punctuated the sudden silence with the obvious. "A syringe," she said. "A full syringe."

Rich opened his mouth to deliver the cutting remark he felt forming on the tip of his tongue. He fought down the urge to dispense it.

"Yes, it is," he said, matter-of-factly. "But what's in it?"

The head nurse boldly stepped forward and took it from his hand. She put on the reading glasses once again, which were hanging on the chain in front of her rotund midsection. She examined the syringe, looking down her nose through the black-framed glasses.

"It's not marked," she said, "so there's no way of knowing what it is. Where did it come from?"

"She tossed it in the trash can when I came in the room," Rich conceded. He immediately kicked himself mentally for revealing potentially significant information.

Hell-O! Investigation one-O-one, he said to himself. *You ask the questions, they give the answers. Not the other way around.*

"I think I know how we can find out what it is," one of the nurses blurted out excitedly. "There's a pathology lab in the basement. They have an FTIR scanner. But the technician is gone for the day."

"What's that?"

"Fourier Transform Infrared Spectroscopy," she said slowly, carefully sounding out the words. "It can tell the chemical composition of almost anything, by means of an infrared spectrograph." She smiled proudly, as the others nodded with admiration.

"Her boyfriend works down there," the head nurse said, eliciting laughs from the others.

Rich looked at the syringe. "Let's get him in here," he said.

"I think I can arrange that," the young nurse said sweetly.

More giggles.

CHAPTER 29

North Ranch, Westlake Village, California

The hand of the Lord was upon me, and He brought me out by the Spirit of the Lord and set me in the middle of a valley; it was full of bones. He led me back and forth among them, and I saw a great many bones on the floor of the valley, bones that were very dry.

He asked me, "Son of man, can these bones live again?"

I said, "O Sovereign Lord, you alone know."

Then He said to me, "Prophesy to these bones ..."

So I prophesied as I was commanded. And as I was prophesying, there was a noise, a rattling sound, and the bones came together, bone to bone. I looked, and tendons and flesh appeared on them and skin covered them, but there was no breath in them.

Then He said to me, "Prophesy to the breath; prophesy, son of man ..."

So I prophesied as He commanded me, and breath entered them; they came to life and stood up on their feet - a vast army.

Ezekiel 37: 1-10

Pete LeTourneu guided his new Jaguar S-class sedan up the long, tree-lined driveway to the large chateau-styled home at the top of the hill. As he crested the top and pulled into the circular driveway, he took a moment to admire the stately home of his leader. Much of it was covered with decorative stone, including the prominent turret that jutted forth from the front of the house, which was capped with a sharp-peaked roof. A large fountain sat at the hub of the large driveway's radius, and the grounds were beautifully landscaped with a wide variety of mature trees and shrubs.

In spite of the opulence of this fine home, Pete LeTourneu knew it was a mere crackerbox compared to what it's owner could actually afford. In the interest of keeping up appearances, it wouldn't be fitting for a university professor to overstep the expectations of those who considered themselves to be his peers.

LeTourneu was met at the door by two burley young men dressed in dark slacks and white shirts. They nodded and motioned for him to follow. They led him back to the sunroom, where The Magus was seated at a table.

The Magus extended his left hand while remaining seated. LeTourneu took his hand and dropped to one knee, and kissed the ring on the Magus' hand. The ring had a black onyx background, with an inverted gold cross on top.

"Sit, Pete," The Magus said, gesturing to the empty chair opposite him at the table. "I haven't seen you in awhile. I'm eager to hear how things are progressing in the northern frontier."

LeTourneu sat as he was bidden, and the Magus waved his hand at the two assistants standing by. One of them nodded and left the room.

The Temple of Anubis had a stranglehold on the San Fernando Valley area for drugs and prostitution, and was eager to expand that dominance to the Conejo Valley - Thousand Oaks and Westlake Village. This was the "northern frontier" that The Magus spoke of.

"So tell me, Pete - what news?" The Magus asked.

LeTourneu took a breath and answered. "Things are going well. I've got Pastor DiMario facing an accusation that will get him removed from his position, if he doesn't resign voluntarily. His son has been busted for marijuana possession. And his young crusader is in the hospital from a serious beating."

"Pete," The Magus replied, shaking his head slowly, "I thought I made it clear that the kid must die. He knows too much about us – he's led them to our ceremonial site."

"Yes, Magus. I sent a team to do just that. They beat him severely, but he somehow survived. Then I sent a second team to finish him, but they were thwarted by police presence at the hospital." Pete looked down at the Italian tile floor as he spoke. "He must have supernatural protection. Otherwise, he'd be dead now."

"Hmm," The Magus intoned solemnly, nodding his gray head. "That's exactly why I need to finish the translation of the Necronomicon - the Book of Dead Names. I paid a big price for my authentic copy, as you know. It was translated into Latin from the original language in the fifteenth century, in Germany. My expert consultants have proven it to be genuine. The only other copies of the Necronomicon verified to be authentic are in the British Museum and in the Bibliothèque Nationale in Paris. I searched for years, and looked at several fake copies of the book before finding this one in the private collection of a certain wealthy industrialist. He wasn't willing to part with it himself, but the trustees of his estate were much more reasonable, after his untimely death."

LeTourneu chuckled quietly. "Who would have guessed that he had that high-risk heart condition? It's amazing what just one injection of digitalis can bring on."

The Magus grinned, the edges of his salt n' pepper Fu-Manchu style mustache rising as he did so. "Not everyone realizes that an offer from me is an offer to continue living - if they comply with my request."

He became thoughtful for a moment before continuing. "Pete, our followers are weak. They don't have the powers that you and I have cultivated over the years. But with the Necronomicon in my possession and translated from the original Latin, we will be able to conjure the spirits of ancient warriors and give them habitation in the bodies of our loyal disciples. They will become unstoppable. They will be able to carry out anything I command them to do; no one will be able to stand in their way. Their meaningless lives will take on new meaning - to serve us well, without failing. Just as the bible says in Ezekiel chapter thirty-seven; they will live again, a vast army, powerful and ready. And loyal only to me."

The dreamy look on the Magus' face faded as he turned back to LeTourneu. "But for now, we need to break the hedge of protection around young Simmons. Did you bring the lifeblood from your former employee?"

"I did."

Good. Let's take it down to the basement and offer it on the altar. We'll conjur a shoggoth daemon to see to this matter. And as for the pastor?" The Magus asked.

"He's as good as out. The church council didn't dump him yet, but it's just a matter of time before the pressure becomes too much."

"You'd better be right. I want him out of our hair as soon as possible. Time is of the essence, you know. What's the date today?"

"October twentieth," LeTourneu said, looking at his watch calendar.

"Samhain is only a week and a half away," The Magus noted. "That's when our ability to mobilize our lord's daemons will be at it's peak. I want Solid Rock Church neutralized by that time, so that their prayers won't hinder our efforts. But it's important that we disgrace DiMario so that his followers will abandon him completely. We don't want them to start praying for him. I'm still confident that the adultery angle is the best plan. After all, the Christian church is the only army that shoots it's wounded."

"Bunch of self-righteous hypocrites," LeTourneu laughed. "For all their talk about love and compassion, they'll soon drop him like a hot potato once his reputation is fully tainted. Nobody will take him seriously after that."

"Any news about that missionary from Brazil?" The Magus asked.

"Ah, yes. I sent him on his way with a special treat - a batch of cookies loaded with enough anthrax spores to infect a small herd of cows. He's probably dead by now."

"You don't know for sure?"

LeTourneu paused, sensing the disappointment in his master's voice. He glanced at the floor before looking up and answering. "I don't have any contacts in Minneapolis. I checked news reports from that region on the Internet. I didn't find anything."

The Magus grimaced and shook his head disapprovingly. "Pete, don't drop the ball again. Our people in Rio warned me about this guy. He's been dogging their steps for quite awhile. He was scheduled for elimination, but he flew out here just before the planned hit. I don't want him showing his face and warning the pastors here, alerting them of our existence. The less they know about us, the better. They won't know how to fight an enemy that they can't see and don't even know exists."

"Yes, Magus. I'll take care of him myself. I'll tell DiMario I need to go visit my family. You can consider Bjorn Nilsson as good as dead, if he isn't already."

"Good, Pete. Do it yourself this time. That way there'll be no screw-ups."

Pete LeTourneu nodded in agreement. "If I have to finish him, I'll bring you a souvenir."

The Magus smiled. "His tongue would be fine," he said. "Now, let's go down to the basement and get down to business."

As he was speaking, one of the young men arrived carrying a platter.

"Ah!" said The Magus, "lunch first. I had them make us a club sandwich. Okay by you?"

"Great - I'm starved. We can wash it down with a sip of blood."

They both laughed as the assistant laid out their lunch before them on the table.

CHAPTER 30

Minneapolis, MN

The late morning sun cast a clearly delineated shadow on the front side of the stately hospital edifice. The shaded area of the porte cochére made a fine segue way for a man to meld back into the great outer world.

Bjorn Nilsson took the obligatory wheelchair ride to the hospital door. Powered by a matronly and graying volunteer, the wheelchair came to a stop just outside the second set of automatic doors, where he was met by his friend, Pastor Dennis Heipler. Bjorn greedily took in a deep breath of the crisp autumn air and slowly exhaled, savoring it's freshness.

Bjorn's formerly athletic and robust body had been racked by severe diarrhea and vomiting for an extended period of time. Only strong drugs brought temporary peace to his tormented gastrointestinal tract. Unable to keep any solid food down, Bjorn had dropped weight rapidly. Now at the end of his fourteen-day ordeal, the minimal body fat he had previously carried around his midsection was gone, as was the original size and strength of his muscles. Only his abdominal muscles looked well-toned, on account of the retching and cramps. His face was gaunt, and he looked older. Most acquaintances wouldn't even recognize the man if he walked right past.

Previously just acquaintances before this visit, Dennis had visited Bjorn in the hospital every day, and even sat vigil at times when Bjorn was sleeping. He had stayed abreast of Bjorn's treatment, too.

Dennis helped him to the car.

"I don't think I've spent that much time indoors in one stretch since college," Bjorn said.

"So, what are your plans now?" asked Dennis, pulling his car out of the parking lot and onto the quiet side street.

"Well, I think I'm going to start up a new weight loss program," Bjorn joked. Lifting up his shirt, he said, "Take a look at this." His ribs were prominently distended from his emaciated torso.

"Whoa!" Dennis exclaimed. "There's a lot of people who would gladly pay a dear price to get those kind of results, I'll bet."

"Yeah, but they wouldn't be willing to pay quite as dearly as I have. I've lost nearly thirty pounds on the anthrax weight loss program, and I wasn't even overweight to begin with."

"We'll soon turn that around. Just look at what my wife's cooking and the weekly potlucks have done for me," said Dennis, as he patted his ample midsection. "You'll be back to normal in no time," he added, with a laugh.

Bjorn smiled, but soon turned serious. "You know, I've been considering this situation and praying about it for a long time, Dennis," he said somberly. "I've got to call Jim DiMario and talk to him about this anthrax poisoning thing. I've gone over it in my mind dozens of times. There's only one place that anthrax could have come from."

"Bjorn, I just can't understand why you didn't share your suspicions with the FBI or the Center for Disease Control. You had the chance when they were here."

"I didn't want to go about it like that. I want to give Jim the chance to deal with it first. I don't want to go around him by informing the authorities of my suspicions."

Dennis was quiet for a moment as he drove along the leaf littered streets. "Do you want to have me in on a conference call, Bjorn?"

Bjorn smiled and shook his head. "You've been so good to me, Dennis. But no, I have to do this on my own. Jim will listen to me. I've known him for so long. He'll know I'm not coming out of left field."

"Are you sure you don't want to stop by the house first - get something to eat?" Dennis asked, as he pulled his car into the church parking lot.

"No. The sooner I do this, the better. My only worry is casting doubt on the reputation of a man who might be innocent of wrongdoing. Pastor LeTourneu said he didn't make the cookies himself, when he gave them to me."

"Well, it'll be Jim's job to figure out what actually happened," Dennis said. "You just have the responsibility of informing him."

He pulled into a parking space and stopped the car. "You're doing the right thing, Bjorn," he said, gently gripping his friend's shoulder.

Bjorn nodded, and opened the car door.

CHAPTER 31

Westlake Village, CA

Jim leaned back in his black leather high-back chair at the church office while talking on the phone to Jasmine. He looked at the clock on his office wall - almost ten thirty in the morning.

"I know, Jasmine," Jim said into the phone receiver. "I'm upset about this thing with Garrett, too. But they have nothing to charge him with, since he didn't actually have any marijuana in his possession."

"But his reputation, Jim," Jasmine replied. "I believe him, and I know you do, too. But we have to get this black mark erased from his record. It'll come back to haunt him later in life if we don't insist on the sheriff expunging it. I don't want this to be an anchor on him his whole life."

"It's not on his record, Jasmine. He doesn't even have a record at all, for that matter. I've already gone over this with Rich - Deputy Harrison. Garrett wasn't actually arrested, so there's no record of any kind against him. He was only brought in for questioning."

Beverly Hanson, the church secretary, hobbled her matronly form through Jim's open office door. "Excuse me, Pastor," she said sweetly, "Bjorn Nilsson is on line two."

Jim's chair squeaked as he sat forward, and he put his hand over the receiver. "Bjorn? Okay, thanks."

Turning his face back to the phone receiver, he said, "I'm going to take this call, Jasmine. I'm sure we'll be talking about this subject for a long time to come. See you tonight. Love you."

He punched the button for line two and shouted, "Bjorn, how the heck are you?"

"Okay, Jim. Surviving. How about you?" came the sober reply.

"I guess I feel about the same right now myself," Jim admitted. "Just surviving. There's a lot going on right now. But you don't sound like your old self. Are you all right?"

"Doing better now. I just got out of the hospital here in Minneapolis. I'm staying with Dennis Heipler. I think you've met him at a conference before. He and his wife have been great to me."

"The hospital?" Jim exclaimed, "what were you doing in the hospital?"

Bjorn proceeded to update Jim on the details and events of the last few weeks that had culminated in his extended stay at St. Paul's Medical Center.

"Bjorn," Jim asked incredulously, "how could you have ingested anthrax spores? That's pretty much unheard of since those September eleventh terrorist scares."

"That's a question that a lot of people have asked," Bjorn replied. "The Center for Disease Control sent out someone from Atlanta - nice lady, by the way. Said she was going to check out the airline food. Never heard anything back from her."

"I've had bad airline food myself," Jim interjected. "But anthrax? This takes the cake!"

"Two FBI agents came by, too. Asked me all kinds of questions about where I'd been, what I'd eaten, even asked me to remember all the things I touched in the twelve hour prior to getting sick."

Jim had a sudden realization. "Geez, Bjorn. I hope you didn't pick it up here."

"Actually, Jim, that's what I wanted to talk to you about. I've thought about all the possibilities as to when and how I could have picked it up. I did some research about anthrax - the CDC lady was real helpful with that."

"And … what do you think?" Jim felt a cloud of uneasiness envelop him as he waited for Bjorn to reply. *I don't think I'm going to like this.* His stomach involuntarily tensed up as he waited for Bjorn's answer.

"Jim, what I'm going to tell you now I didn't tell the FBI or the CDC. I'm pretty sure I know where the anthrax came from. I've turned it over and over in my mind, but there's just one possibility - and I don't like it."

Bjorn's last words carried an ominous tone to Jim. The silence of waiting for the other shoe to drop was worse than whatever was coming next. The few seconds that passed seemed like an eternity to Jim, who was waiting spellbound for the punch line to what he knew was no joke.

"Bjorn, for goodness sake, just tell me - don't leave me hanging."

Jim heard Bjorn exhale into the phone, and then speak. "Jim, when your associate pastor, Pete, came to see me off at the airport after my visit there, he brought me a bag of chocolate chip cookies - the ones that one of your church ladies makes and brings into the office," he said. Bjorn took a labored breath, and continued. "The cookies were delicious - I ate all of them. I was so full after pigging out, I didn't eat anything on the plane. After I found out from the CDC lady how long it takes for gastrointestinal anthrax to take effect, I knew the anthrax spores had to be in the cookies."

Jim's head started to spin as he tried to grasp the implications of what Bjorn had just said. He felt his body starting to sweat a little and tense up in a knot.

"Whoa, wait a minute," Jim said. "You're telling me that Pete met you at the airport to see you off? And he brought you cookies?"

"Yes, he did. He told me that you sent him, and sent your kind regards along with those cookies."

"No, no that's not right," Jim protested. "I didn't send him to see you off that morning. And I didn't give him any cookies. I have no idea where those might have come from. I don't even know how he knew where to find you."

Jim furiously wracked his brain for memories of Bjorn's visit. Suddenly, his mind's focus caught on the staff meeting that morning of Bjorn's departure. He recalled telling everyone in attendance - including Pete, about Bjorn's visit, and that he was on his way to the airport en-route to Minneapolis.

"Bjorn, I mentioned your visit in my weekly staff meeting the morning you left. Pete must have left to meet you shortly after that. I thought he was going to work, since he still holds a second job. I didn't send him to the airport. He never said a word about it to me."

"Jim, I've got to ask you this," Bjorn said with a hesitant note. "How well do you really know your associate pastor? I know he hasn't been with the church for too long, but how much do you really know about him?"

Jim sat forward in his chair, and put his elbows on the desk in front of him. He rested his forehead on his fist. "Look, hold on for a minute, Bjorn. I need to think about this for a minute."

"Of course, Jim. Take your time."

Jim's automatic instinct was to defend Pete. He always closed ranks around his staff members when one of them was criticized for a decision that was made, a policy that someone didn't like, or when somebody felt that they'd been snubbed. But considering who he was talking to right now, and the circumstances he just described, Jim caught his tongue before responding, and held it.

The fact is, Jim thought, *Pete's performance hasn't been up to my expectations. He hasn't really turned out to be the valuable team member I expected and hoped for. Heck, his bible knowledge isn't really sufficient to make him a good bible study leader or a fill-in for me in the pulpit if I go away over a Sunday. Maybe it's more than that,* he speculated, while rubbing his temple.

Lack of bible knowledge can be offset by enthusiasm and a desire to serve, combined with an anointing from God, Jim knew. But he wasn't so sure Pete had any of these things going for him. And then of course, there was the issue of Pete's disloyal handling of the Angela Shepherd situation. Jim might have chalked that up to youthful inexperience; Pete had addressed the problem entirely the wrong way, that was for sure.

Calling a special church council meeting for an allegation like this, then moving to oust me from the pulpit - even on a temporary basis, supposedly. That was inexcusable. That's just not the way we do things, Jim thought, frowning as the unpleasant memory of it ran through his mind.

If he were to be completely honest about it, Jim didn't feel the same about Pete since that incident, which was still open like an angry boil on the skin of the church body. Pete seemed to be making sure it would stay open, too. Far from being a peacemaker, Pete seemed intent on sowing discord, and it was working. Or could it be possible that Jim was just imagining it, disappointed as he was with Pete's betrayal of his senior pastor.

"Are you still there, Jim?" Bjorn's voice in the receiver brought Jim back to the here and now. "What about Pete? I remember you mentioned that he was fairly new to the church."

"Yeah," Jim said numbly. "He's been with us about six months or so."

"Where did he come from?"

"He's from out in the Midwest - a church in Michigan. He was highly praised by that church's senior pastor. I have his letter of recommendation on file."

"Did you ever talk to the pastor of Pete's old church?" Bjorn asked.

"No, not personally. I just have the letter of recommendation. The council and I made him an offer based on that, and the strength of his interview. He sounded great in the interview."

"And now?"

Jim sighed. "He hasn't really met my expectations, Bjorn. He's a young guy, not married. I've cut him some slack because of his age and experience level. But he hasn't become the helper I'd hoped for."

"Do you trust him?"

Jim was stunned by Bjorn's point-blank question. He thought for a moment before automatically answering in the affirmative.

"No," he admitted at last. "No, not really. Fact of the matter is, he's recently given me some cause not to trust him. But are you asking me if I believe he poisoned you with anthrax-laced cookies?"

"Yeah, that's basically what I'm asking," Bjorn replied.

"It's so hard to even fathom that, Bjorn," Jim said, shaking his head. "Is that what you believe?"

"Yes, I do."

Silence. The weight of this accusation felt unbearably heavy to Jim as it seated itself squarely on his shoulders. He shifted his weight forward in his chair under the load. A tempest of conflict began to form in his mind as he tried to reconcile the apparent foolishness of what had been said with the integrity of the person who was saying it, combined with Pete's observed behavior.

It's too much to fathom, Jim thought. *It's crazy. Or does it make perfect sense?*

"Bjorn, why would Pete do something like this?" Jim asked his friend. "What would his motivation be - assuming for the moment that he actually did it?"

"I've had plenty of time to turn that question over in my mind too, Jim," Bjorn replied. He took a breath that Jim could hear three thousand miles away. "Do you remember what we talked about when I was out there?"

"Are you kidding? The satanic cult you uncovered in Brazil - how could I forget?"

"Did you happen to mention it at your staff meeting the morning I left?"

Bjorn's question hit Jim like a bowling ball in the stomach. He felt suddenly ill as a cold sweat flooded over his body, both mind and body reeling from the sudden realization. He couldn't believe the implication - didn't want to believe it. Yet there it hung, right in front of his face – as ugly and repulsive as a pile of roadkill.

"Yes," Jim intoned. "Yes, I did mention it, as a matter of fact." He paused for a moment before continuing his admission. "Pete heard from me that you were headed to the airport, and I told the staff that you warned me about a satanic group." Jim's tone was like that of one speaking into a confessional booth, rather than into the phone. "What was the name?"

"The Temple of Anubis."

"Right. So then …, " Jim said. He didn't like where this conversation was going, but he knew he couldn't turn it around. Like a man riding on a runaway train, he knew a wreck was imminent, but there was nothing he could do to prevent it. "Are you suggesting, Bjorn, that Pete is in some way involved with this satanic group?"

"As crazy as that sounds, Jim, I don't have a better explanation - or any other explanation at all, for that matter," Bjorn said. "Like I told you that night, my sources said that they were establishing themselves in Southern California."

Jim thought he heard an apologetic ring to his friend's comments. Bjorn was, after all, dropping a bombshell on Jim's lap. But he was doing it as gently as possible.

"But Bjorn, how could this even be possible?" Jim pleaded. "It's true I don't have much history with Pete, but he comes from the Midwest."

"Are you sure?"

"He's already worked at another church as an associate pastor."

"Are you sure?"

The inflections in Bjorn's voice changed, and now sounded to Jim more like a prosecuting attorney questioning a defense witness.

"I thought I was sure of a lot of things before you called, Bjorn," Jim answered, "but now I can add Pete to the list of things I'm unsure of."

"I'm sorry Jim. Really, I am."

"So am I. I'm sorry for what happened to you." Jim shook his head and slapped his sweaty forehead with the palm of his left hand. "Oh, Bjorn," he said doggedly, "we were so eager to find a new associate pastor. My workload had increased with the church growth of the past year, and we didn't have any local candidates. We just weren't selective enough. I guess it's kind of like that story in the book of Acts, where the eleven apostles chose a replacement for Judas by drawing lots. God's anointing wasn't on that guy - he's never mentioned in the bible again after that. I can't even remember his name."

"Neither can I."

Jim allowed himself a brief chuckle at that. "My point exactly. But now, I've got to do something. But what can I do? I can't just up and fire my associate pastor on suspicion of being a Satanist."

"You're going to have to make the call on what to do, Jim. Pray about it, talk to your closest advisors."

"Pete is taking a few days off," Jim said. "He has a family emergency - or so he said. He's going to see his ailing father in Michigan. He'll be gone at least three days."

"That will give you enough time to put a plan together, Jim," Bjorn suggested. "Whatever you decide to do, Jim, I know it'll be the right thing. I have faith in you to do the right thing."

"Thanks for the vote of confidence, Bjorn. I'm glad you still trust in me. I'm not even sure my own church council does, at this point. But you're right - I will do the right thing, once I've figured out what that is."

Jim grunted in frustration. "Sometimes doing the right thing is the hard way to go."

"I know," Bjorn replied, "But don't forget - God is still on the throne."

"Yes, He is. I always remind my people of that fact when they're going through hard times. So, are you going to be at the Heipler's for awhile?"

"Yeah. Until I get my strength back, or until they kick me out - whichever comes first."

"Okay, Bjorn. Let's keep in touch. We'll have more to talk about soon, no doubt."

"Be careful, Jim."

Jim set the phone down in it's cradle and stared straight ahead at the wall. His stomach had started to burn during the conversation with Bjorn, and now a pulsing headache was getting underway, too.

With his elbows on the desk, he rested his chin on his fists, surveying the wall in front of him. The numerous plaques and speaker awards covering the wall testified to Jim's involvement in community and church activities. He had a number of pictures as well; him with his golfing buddies out on the links, a picture from the recent pastor's convention in Colorado Springs, even a picture of Jim shaking hands with President Bush, whom he had met as Governor Bush way back when.

Hmm, he thought, *Pete doesn't have any personal pictures in his office of any friends or relatives, as I recall. No awards or plaques, either, except the one from the seminary he attended.*

He shifted back in his leather chair and let it envelop him in it's worn-in comfort. His eyes shifted over to his bookcase, stuffed full of commentaries on the bible, study guides, books that focused on different areas of ministry, and several bibles.

Pete doesn't have much in the way of books either, come to think of it. Of course, it takes time to build up a personal library. Still ...I don't think I've ever seen an old bible in his hands. Just the new one he carries around.

Who is this guy on my church staff, anyway? Jim wondered. *Gotta find out more about him somehow. Maybe it's high time to check out that letter of recommendation.*

Jim pushed himself up from his chair, which squeaked in protest. He casually walked across the hall and over to Pete's empty office, and went inside. Stepping through the open doorway, it seemed strangely cold to Jim. It was almost if the office was uninhabited - no personality. There was just one picture on Pete's desk, of a couple who looked to be in their late fifties.

Must be his parents, Jim surmised, picking up the rosewood frame and studying the picture.

The more Jim looked at the picture, the more something didn't feel right. It was a casual shot of a graying, yet vibrant-looking couple standing smiling on a boat dock, yet it looked professionally done. The picture looked a little too good, a bit too clean. Jim pulled the back off the picture frame and took the photo out. He felt the paper between his fingers and held it up to the light, and confirmed what his instincts had told him - it wasn't a photograph at all, but a picture cut out from a magazine. The printing on the back confirmed it.

Jim set the picture and it's frame back down on the desk, and rubbed his face with both hands.

Why would somebody put a phony picture into a frame and set it on their desk? Maybe Pete's parents are famous for something, and got their picture in some magazine. Or, maybe, these aren't his parents at all.

This presumption led to many more disturbing questions that started to swirl around in Jim's mind.

Maybe I don't know him at all. Maybe he really is here to hurt the church - and me. Oh, Lord, what am I going to do when he gets back?

On Pete's desk lay the bible that Jim recognized as the one that the associate pastor carried around. He casually picked up the small black book with the pages edged in gold. The cover bore the title, in small gold letters: *The Holy Scriptures, Universal World Translation.* Jim immediately recognized it as the adulterated bible translation that was published exclusively by the *Messengers of Elohiem.* No bible-believing Christian would use this bible, Jim knew, because it contained numerous changes in wording that were specially designed by this pseudo-Christian cult to minimize and lower the position of Jesus as the Son of God. A non-believer might not notice the difference, but a Christian pastor, on the other hand …

Is it possible that Pete doesn't know the difference? Jim wondered. *Or could he actually be with the Messengers of Elohiem?*

Jim quickly set the book back down on the desk exactly where he had found it.

He stuck his head out of the door of Pete's office and looked up and down the hall. Empty. All the other staff members were at their own desks or elsewhere around the church grounds. He closed the door quietly, walked back over to Pete's desk, and tried the drawers. Locked.

No problem, he thought, whistling a few notes.

Jim opened the door quietly and strode across the hall to his office, and opened the second drawer of his own oak credenza. Reaching in, he pulled out a large metal ring that was hung thick with keys.

There's not a lock in this place that I can't get into, Jim said to himself, with a sly grin.

Casually walking back out his door, he stopped and smiled at Bev Hanson, who was passing by in the hallway going to her desk. He waited for her to pass, then went into Pete's office again. He shut the door behind him and started hunting for a match of lock and key that would perhaps yield more incriminating evidence about Pete. He tried the keys on the ring, one by one - those that looked to be about the right size. He was nervous and excited all at once, like a kid sneaking a cigarette behind the barn. Excited to hunt for evidence to use against his associate pastor, and fearful of what he might find. His stomach tingled like it did when he was at the starting line of a 5K race.

Traitorous, that's what Pete is. Even if he isn't a Satanist, he's disloyal and ineffectual - a poor excuse for a pastor. Got to discover his plan and put a stop to it. Or maybe I should just trust God to sort it out. He's never let me down before. Like Bjorn said, God's still on the throne. But I would be a bad steward of His church if I didn't take action when it was needed.

Thoughts swirled in his head, pro and con. Just then, he found the matching key. The desk responded with a dull *thunk* as the metal bars inside pulled away from the latch. Jim took a deep breath and licked his parched lips. Then he slowly pulled open the top desk drawer.

Inside the drawer was a small wooden figure, in the shape of a man.

CHAPTER 32

Los Robles Regional Medical Center: Thousand Oaks, California

The clock on the wall at the nurses' station ticked past two o'clock in the morning, and things were pretty quiet. Most of the nurses on duty were huddled around the central station area, chit-chatting about the upcoming Tupperware party that one of them had scheduled. Most of the patients were asleep, and were therefore in a low-maintenance mode.

Trey was asleep too - barely. He tossed and turned like a ship riding the waves of a tempestuous sea, trying to get comfortable on his bed in the cool, dimly lit room.

Trey's mother had stayed most of the day, but went home hours ago to get some rest herself. But after she went home, she had felt compelled to pray for her son's safety, and stayed up late doing so.

The pain medications were of little comfort to Trey. Nor was the armed guard posted outside his door. The latter was compliments of Deputy Rich Harrison, who had spent considerable time interviewing the exhausted youth the day before, until Trey was drained.

Frightening nightmares coursed through Trey's restless mind, and manifested themselves in his body - heart rate high, rapid breathing, cold sweat oozing out of pores all over. His eyes darted back and forth under closed eyelids, desperately seeking sanctuary from the monster that was chasing him in his night terror.

Suddenly jarring himself awake, his legs and arms thrashed wildly about him. Overcome by a sense of dread and raw fear - so strong it didn't seem possible, he was near a state of panic. Sitting up in bed, he frantically scanned the dark room. He saw nobody. Nothing, no reason for his terror. The input from his eyes didn't calm his anxiety, however. Something was wrong, he was sure of it.

Danger. I'm in danger here, he knew.

The air in the dank room was oppressive, and it was hard to breathe.

"Hey!" Trey shouted, straining his gaunt lungs.

His abdominal muscles protested the small amount of work required of them to sit up and yell, and his mouth hurt as he opened wounds anew with his shouting.

The door to his room burst open and the security guard rushed in. He flipped the light switch on, suddenly flooding the room with brilliant light.

"Wha' is it?" demanded the pudgy Filipino rent-a-cop, "wha's wrong?"

Trey looked around the room frantically with eyes wide. "There's somebody in here - I think there's somebody in here," he gasped.

The guard searched around the room with his large black aluminum flashlight positioned atop his shoulder. With the keys on his belt jangling as he walked, he looked in the closet, and in the bathroom. He soon came out of the bathroom with a smirk painted across his round face.

"So," he said casually, "wha' dis intruder look like?"

"He was ... he – well," Trey stammered, "I don't know what he looked like, exactly."

Robocop let out a guttural, "Hr-umph. You got a nightmare, buddy. Der's nobody in dis room but us."

"But ... it was so real. I felt someone in here, and he - or it, was attacking me," Trey replied breathlessly.

His heart rate began to go down gradually, and he started to calm himself. The sheer terror of what he had felt was unlike anything he had ever experienced before.

A young nurse bolted into Trey's hospital room and looked at the guard.

"What's going on here?" she asked.

"Nothin'," the guard replied dismissively, with a quick shrug of the shoulders. "Kid had bad dream, dat's all."

The nurse looked at the state of Trey - drenched in sweat, his hair matted down to his forehead and face. She quickly came over to the bed and began to mop his brow with the bed sheet.

"Look at you," she said, while wiping him down, "You're completely saturated with sweat. You didn't have a fever before ... I better check you now."

She reached into her pocket and pulled out her infrared thermometer, snapped a fresh plastic cone on it, and unceremoniously stuck the cone into his ear.

Turning her head to the security guard, she said, "You can go now. Do me a favor and get one of the other nurses to come in here. I'm going to need some help."

The guard did as he was told, turning on his heel to leave. He marched out the door.

"We're going to get you into a dry gown and change your bedclothes," she said. The digital thermometer beeped, and she pulled it back out of Trey's ear and looked at the screen. "Ninety-nine point one. Not bad. If you did have a fever, it looks like it broke."

Another nurse breezed into the room, older and a bit heavier than the first. The first nurse told her, "Bed change and fresh gown." Turning to Trey again, she admonished him with mock irritation, "You're making extra work for us, mister." She helped him sit up and swing his legs over the edge of the bed.

"Lucky you," added the second nurse, "I'll bet it's not everyday you get your clothes removed by two women."

The two shared a laugh at Trey's expense, who stood up off the bed with the first nurse holding his arm.

"Look," Trey said, "I can do it myself. Just give me the gown, and I'll go into the bathroom and change."

"Suit yourself," said the second nurse, handing the gown to Trey. "but you're giving up bragging rights."

Trey came out of the bathroom after changing his gown and washing his haggard face in the sink. He saw that the second nurse was gone, and the first nurse was waiting to help him back into bed.

"Feel any better now?" she asked.

Trey expected a twinge of sarcasm, but he decided that she sounded genuinely concerned.

"Yeah," he replied. "A lot better."

"Sometimes it helps just to get cleaned up," she said. "Don't ask me why."

She helped him back into bed and tried to get him comfortable. "Okay," she said, "you're all set. I'll pour you a fresh cup of water and put in on the tray here. And here's the call button in case you need anything. I'm pinning it to your pillow, okay?"

Trey noticed the tiny gold cross that dangled from a dainty chain around her neck as she hovered over him.

"Thanks," Trey replied. "I'll be fine now, I'm sure. Sorry to bother you."

The nurse smiled, showing a set of straight, white teeth. "No bother at all," she said. "They actually pay me for this kind of service."

She patted him on the shoulder, then turned away and walked to the door, switching off the light as she slipped out of the room.

Trey pulled the spartan sheet and blanket up under his chin and tried to get comfortable. From the physical standpoint, he was definitely more comfortable now, but those same feelings of uneasiness crept back in, and started growing again.

***

It stood in a dark corner of the room, having an affinity for the darkness. Equally invisible in the dim light of the room as it was in bright light, the entity's presence was still somehow evident to it's intended victim.

Large - over seven feet tall and covered with thick black hair, the Shoggoth daemon existed outside the three-dimensional world that all humans see and experience. It would have stayed there, in forced exile, in it's appointed place of incarceration – the Outer Darkness. But it had been summoned by a human having the knowledge and skills to do it - someone who knew the incantations well, and used them effectively. Although invisible to humans, with their limited vision, it was no less real, no less menacing. It absorbed light like a galactic black hole, yet exuded a stench of decay that could even carry over into the mortal realm, to those who were spiritually discerning.

It pulled back it's thin dark purple lips in a sardonic smile that exposed two rows of sharp, pointed teeth that pierced the dark like slivers of steel. Stringy threads of thick saliva drooled from it's repulsive maw. The red, lidless eyes fell upon the lad on the hospital bed, who shifted restlessly between the sheets. Yes - he sensed the presence of evil. There was no comfort to be found for the young man in the Shoggoth's presence.

Most people had been unaware of it's coming until it was much too late. Over the centuries, it had been called to visitation upon many an unsuspecting victim. More often than not, it's victim was the very one who called it out from the Outer Darkness. The possession of the Necronomicon was a dangerous thing to all but the most experienced and learned Magi. Many had fallen victim to his or her own incantations, used incorrectly. To the creature, the taste of human blood was equally invigorating, regardless of who it came from.

It would take it's time; no hurry. Tormenting it's victim was part of the intent. The daemon would continue to gradually make it's presence known - to the intended victim only. It would make itself partially visible for a brief instant here and there; just long enough to evoke sheer terror and make the victim wonder if he was losing his mind. The result of these teases was always intense fear; even from brave rulers and military leaders.

The Shoggoth had already seen the terror on this young man's face, and it took pleasure from his fear. How much more so when it would finally take solid form in the three-dimensional realm, just before seizing him by the throat with it's long, sharp teeth. There would be no time for him to cry out then; his larynx would be torn out in one quick, decisive move. The demonic entity would then take it's time feeding on his blood, puncturing the carotid arteries one at a time and sucking up the pulsing crimson fountain.

It had free will once, long ago. Free to choose it's leader. It could have stayed loyal to God, but a challenger rose up in opposition to God's absolute sovereignty. This challenger was both beautiful and powerful, the most dazzling to look at of all the angels. Lucifer promised freedom; freedom from God's rules and requirements for His angels. So compelling was Lucifer's promise and his countenance as a leader, that a third of all the angels followed him in rebellion against God. How could they have thought that they could somehow force God to allow Lucifer to sit on a throne equal to His? How could they have failed to see that Lucifer was entirely corrupt and evil beyond measure?

But they had made their decision, the die was cast. After their failed rebellion, Lucifer and the angels who favored him were cast out of Heaven and onto the Earth - into the dimension of Outer Darkness. There, they were destined to follow the direction of their Chosen One, who soon showed the full extent of his evil nature. The main object of his hatred was mankind, simply because God favored them. Over time, separated from God by countless ages, the angels of darkness grew more and more like their master, both in their hearts and in appearance. Once beautiful to behold like Lucifer himself, their appearance began to change, once cast into the Outer Darkness. These rogue angels took on uniquely grotesque forms, and became as ugly as they had previously been beautiful.

They emulated Lucifer in their behavior, too. They had incited wars, encouraged murder and rape, and whispered in the ears of those who were considering aborting their unborn children. They flattered and puffed up those who sought to rule and plunder the masses, and they never failed to justify those who pilfered and extorted money from others. Human nature was corrupt in itself, but the dark angels offered plenty of encouragement.

With the fresh, crisp bed sheet pulled up under his chin, Trey lay on his back in the stiff bed, not feeling much like sleep. His legs and arms twitched involuntarily, and he couldn't bear to close his eyes. His heart pumped more rapidly than it should, he could feel it - could even hear it's dull thud in his eardrums. He breathed deeply, but it was more like the breath of a marathon runner trying to oxygenate his muscles than the breathing pattern of deep relaxation. He felt the hair on his arms standing up, and gooseflesh prickled his limbs.

The sense of dread - it came back to him again. It was as if he'd just stepped between two rival gangs that were about to cut loose on each other with guns blazing. But no person - or gang, for that matter, had ever evoked such deep-seated fear in him before. In fact, Trey would have been more comfortable standing on a street corner in south-central LA between the Crips and the Bloods than he was right now.

Maybe it was the fact that he couldn't see anything in the room that could frighten him that chilled him all the more. Looking around the darkened room, he warily regarded the deeply shadowed shapes of side tables, IV stands, visitor's chairs, and other furnishings that were spread out menacingly around the room.

This is crazy, he thought. *There's nobody in here. Maybe it's that post-traumatic stress disorder thing that shrinks talk about.*

Just then, Trey saw a dark shape appear in his peripheral vision on the left side of his bed. He gasped and wheeled over to the left. Nothing there.

Lord, now I'm hallucinating.

Silence in the room, except for the throbbing of blood pumping up into his head. A glint of metal on his right. Trey jerked his head to the side quick enough to hurt his neck. For one instant he saw it - a dark hairy thing, bigger than a man, with red eyes and a huge, gaping mouth; then it was gone.

My God, that wasn't my imagination that time.

Trey's skin tingled with sweat and his heart threatened to burst forth from his chest. Wide awake, he knew this was no nightmare. He sat bolt upright in bed, pushing himself with hands and heels back toward the head of the bed. His eyes darted back and forth around the room.

The dark figure appeared abruptly at the foot of his bed. Solid. Large. Real.

The huge lidless red eyes bored into Trey and it exposed it's rows of fang-like teeth. To Trey, the beast looked like a picture from one of the moldering ancient tomes on Satanism and demonology he had dug out of the county library archives. Horrified, Trey called upon the only self-defense method he knew.

"In the n...name of Jesus Christ of Nazareth, I command you to be gone," Trey blurted out, as forcefully as he could muster.

The wicked smile painted across the face of the hideous beast diminished at the mention of The Name.

Although terrified, Trey pressed further. "In the name of Jesus, I rebuke you, unclean spirit."

As he watched, the visage of the Shoggoth began to become fuzzy, less defined. Trey barely noticed the warm light starting to illuminate the room, ever so slightly.

To the left of the creature, a rip in space appeared as if the giant zipper of some invisible garment was being opened. A hand came through the rip. It was like that of a man, only larger, having a gold or bronze color to it. It gripped itself to the arm of the repugnant beast. The Shoggoth let out a horrible cry, as smoke came from the site where the mysterious hand was latched on. A sizzling sound accompanied the smoke, like a steak slapped onto a hot barbecue grill. The sulfurous, acrid stench of the smoke reached Trey's nose, and nearly made him retch.

The hand pulled the creature's arm into the rip. The sound of the growling and hisses of protest made Trey's blood run cold. In a matter of moments, the beast's head was pulled into the rip, haloed by the bright golden light emanating from the unknown source. The head was soon followed by the rest of the detestable, hair covered body, which was inexplicably sucked into the glowing slit that looked to Trey to be no larger than three feet in length. As quickly as the horrifying vision appeared, it was gone. The rip sealed itself up just as quickly, the golden light disappearing. The room was just as it was before, except for the smell. Almost as if nothing had happened - but it had.

Trey sat paralyzed on his bed; not moving, not knowing what to do. He wasn't dreaming, not hallucinating - he was sure of that. The caustic whiff of the creature's singed hair and flesh still hung heavy in the air like a toxic cloud. What Trey had just seen and experienced was real, but his mind couldn't come to terms with what his senses told him.

His abdominal muscles now reminded him of the beating he had taken. He wanted to get up and kneel at his bedside to pray, but couldn't manage to convince his limbs to work in unison. So he prayed as he was - sitting up uncomfortably in bed.

"Lord Jesus," he prayed, "Bind Satan and his demons. Deliver me from evil. Protect me from those who would do me harm, I pray."

He sank back heavily on his bed and stretched out his aching body, then took a deep breath. He felt his heart rate gradually starting to come down, along with his anxiety level. Utterly exhausted from the ordeal he had just experienced, Trey fell into a deep sleep, and didn't shift for the rest of the night.

Unseen and unknown to Trey, the confrontation that started in his room was far from over. In another dimension of time-space, the Shoggoth angrily prepared to square off against the one who had pulled it away from finishing the business it had been called to perform.

The angel facing it was tall, though somewhat shorter than the beast. Clad in a brilliant white vestment that draped over one shoulder of his muscular frame, his skin was a rich deep gold tone that had a warm glow to it. A mantle of white hair was capped by a wreath of ivy.

With his left hand, the angel traced a vertical line beside himself, starting at the floor and ending at shoulder height. As he did so, another rip in space opened up, following the path of his finger. No light emanated from this rip - the space beyond was black as the inside of a deep cavern.

The Shoggoth looked disdainfully at his adversary, then at the rip. It's face formed into a deep scowl, and it spoke.

"You can't make me go there," he hissed, challenging the angel who stood unruffled before him. "You did not call me forth from the Outer Darkness, and I will not go back."

The creature lunged at it's antagonist, who silently raised his two hands to shoulder height, palms facing the enemy. Only an inch or two away from the angel, the Shoggoth plowed headlong into an invisible wall. It pawed at the angel repeatedly with it's huge hands, claws inaudibly scraping the unseen barrier. Like some grotesque mime gone bad, it flailed high and low against the force field protecting the angelic entity, who stood unmoved and unshaken.

"What is your name?" the angel demanded.

The Shoggoth wailed and unleashed a string of obscenities, fouling the thick air with it's visible yellow, putrid breath. It slammed it's head against the translucent barrier, which twinkled with golden flecks with each repeated impact.

"Your name!"

"I am Bezalel, Prince of Tyre," shouted the beast, straining against the barrier. "You cannot make me go!"

Even as the creature struggled to give it's answer, the angel was effortlessly pressing the wall back against his nemesis, and maneuvering Bezalel toward the rip.

"May God rebuke you," the angel said. His words had such force, that Bezalel reeled back from the barrier as if it were electrified.

The angel lowered his hands, and the demon cut loose with another monologue of curses harsh enough to make any sailor cringe. Unfazed, the angel stepped forward and raised his right hand.

"In the name of Jesus Christ, whom I serve, I order you back to the pit."

"No!" screamed Bezalel, with a bone-rattling cry so shrill and loud that it might have peeled paint off the walls in the mortal dimension.

The angelic being pressed the palm of his golden hand forward at the beast, which stumbled back from the force directed at it. The eyes of the infernal creature flared now more with fear than rage.

"Wait!" it begged, "don't do it. What if I promise to serve God, rather than Lucifer? Would you still cast me into the Abyss?"

"You cast your lot long ago," the angel replied, without malice. "A brier bush cannot begin producing figs."

He took another step forward, and pushed again with the palm of his right hand. "Be gone."

The Shoggoth stumbled back into the opening, spreading the sides of the rip wider. A look of horror pasted across it's already hideous face, desperately clawing at the sides of the rip in a remiss effort to remain in the current dimension. With a final shove from the angel, Bezalel tumbled back and downward, screaming and writhing in anguish as it's hairy bulk disappeared into the utter darkness.

The angel watched impassively as the Shoggoth vanished from sight, it's screams and wails mixing with the other ungodly sounds emanating from the Outer Darkness. Then he stepped back and sealed the rip with his finger, in the same manner as he had opened it.

He looked across the room into the three-dimensional world at the young man lying curled up on the bed. Sleeping peacefully, oblivious to what had just transpired. But well aware of the fact that God had his back covered.

CHAPTER 33

Simmons Residence: Westlake Village, California

The weather outside had turned cold, and a late afternoon wind blew a few dry leaves through the door as it shut behind the last member to arrive for a hastily-called meeting. Trey had just been discharged from the hospital the afternoon before, and brought home by his mother. With considerable pleas and convincing on his part, she had gone back to work at her receptionist job at the real estate office that morning. Trey had shared his harrowing experience of the night before his release with Pastor Jim before the others arrived, but didn't intend mention it to the others, who were now showing up.

Last to arrive was Rich Harrison. He wore a black v-neck T-shirt that stretched against his muscled torso. He ambled into the modest entryway, and into the spartan living room of Trey's house, waving at Jim, George, and Trey.

"Thanks for coming, Rich," Jim said as he rose to greet him. "I know it's short notice."

"Not a problem. I'm working tonight, instead of day shift. They like to rotate us around, since there's more action at night."

"That figures," Jim commented. "Those who do evil prefer the cover of darkness."

Rich took a seat on the well-worn brown couch next to George, who nodded and shook his hand.

Trey, still recovering from his beating, was sprawled out on the loveseat, which faced the couch. Jim sat back down on the blue La-Z-Boy chair that completed the unmatching ensemble of furniture.

"How you doin', man?" Rich asked Trey with a smile. "Looks like you survived, after all."

"Yeah, I'm surviving - barely. But don't tell my mom that. I've been trying to convince her that I feel fine." Trey shrugged his shoulders. "She really can't afford to take the time off to wait on me. She doesn't make that much as it is."

"We've got a lot to catch up on," Jim said, "and I hardly know where to start. Thanks for having us over, Trey. I appreciate you opening your home."

"No problemo, Pastor. I'm just glad Rich didn't show up in his squad car. It wouldn't help my rep. You know how people talk."

Jim laughed derisively. "Don't even get me started on that subject."

Rich took the initiative to get to the point. "Okay, George, why don't you start by telling everyone what you found out after we left you out in the desert, knee-deep in dead babies?"

He caught himself, and raised his left hand while shaking his head. "Hey, I'm sorry. I don't mean to sound flippant about something as horrible as that."

"Yeah. Anyway, to answer your question," George replied, "I got an exclusive on the six- o'clock report that night."

He playfully licked his right index finger, and pretended to chalk one up for himself on an imaginary scoreboard.

"Besides that, I found out that there were eighty-six dead infants buried in identical plastic boxes."

"Eighty-six!" Jim shouted. "Oh, Lord, that's worse than I ever would have imagined. Eighty-six children dead, never to experience the joys and trials of growing up, or to be the joy of their parents. It's a travesty – it's … it's horrible."

George continued. "They were in different states of decay, but here's the kicker." He sat forward on the edge of his seat and made sure he had everyone's attention before continuing. "They were all newborn infants, not aborted late-term fetuses like I had figured at first. To be honest, I was thinking we'd come across the dump zone for an illegal abortion mill. You know - the kind that does late-term and partial-birth abortions. But that's not the case. The autopsies indicated that some of them were as much as six months old at the time of death."

He paused for a moment to let his audience digest this unseemly revelation. Jim started to move his mouth, but couldn't get the words out quick enough before George went on.

"But that's not all," George added. He gestured toward Rich, who took the cue.

"I was able to get more information a couple days after our visit," Rich said. "It turns out that all of these babies were killed the same way - a clean stab wound to the heart. Apparently by the same or similar weapon; a narrow-bladed knife or dagger of some kind, very sharp, according to the skin and tissue condition around the wound – on those victims that weren't too badly decomposed."

"And there was another wound, too, common to all of them." Rich glanced back and forth at the others who had drawn near him in a huddle. "They also had a slice through the carotid artery on the side of their necks, and hardly any blood left in the bodies. They were bled out."

He gestured with his index finger across the side of his neck.

All present exchanged looks that ran the gamut from shock, to disgust, to knowing acceptance.

"How did they get the blood out?" Trey wondered. "I know from my anatomy class that once the heart stops beating, the blood will just stop flowing and pool where it is. It doesn't just flow out by itself."

"Good question," Rich said. "The answer is – I don't know, and I don't think the coroner does, either."

"There must be some record of these missing children," Jim interjected. "They must have had parents, who would have filed missing children reports. Surely it must be possible to find out who these children are, and who they belong to. How could all these missing children fall below the radar of the authorities? Eighty-six missing children must have made big news, but I don't recall hearing about it."

"They didn't all go missing at the same time, that's the thing," Rich replied. "It looks like it happened one at a time, judging by the state of decay. And yes, I agree there should be reports of missing children on file. I don't see how they could have all come from this same geographical area without the press having a field day."

Rich continued on.

"My ex-fiancé, Rhonda, over at the San Bernardino Sheriff's Department gave me the details. It was the talk of the office; good gossip material, I guess. I think she has a boyfriend who works in the coroner's office over there. They really had a project on their hands, apparently."

Rich paused a moment to wring his hands and study the worn green carpet at his feet. "After exhuming all of the bodies, they examined each one to determine age, sex, cause of death, race, everything. There were boys and girls, white, hispanic, black. Asian too, of undetermined extraction. Besides the cause of death that George already told about, and the fairly close age range, the other common denominator was the method of disposal. Very consistent. Same kind of plastic box; not something you'd get at Wal-Mart, but something special. You all saw one - except Trey, of course."

"I remember seeing the box," Jim acknowledged solemnly. "But I was paying more attention to the contents."

"It comes from a specialty manufacturer," Rich continued. "A supplier of plastic ware and lab materials to the medical and scientific industries. Not something you could just buy off the shelf. So there's a lead there. I just need to get in there to the coroner's office to get the details on the box. But that's a problem."

"Why?" George asked. "I thought you could get in anywhere. Official business and all."

Rich shook his head. "They're really trying to keep it quiet. I already went down there - in uniform, even. They told me I needed written authorization to the coroner from my supervisor before they'd consider letting me in. They usually only do that for celebrity corpses."

"Can't you get authorization?" Jim asked.

"Are you kidding?" Rich snorted. "I can't let my lieutenant know that I'm even looking at this case."

"Why not?" asked Trey. "Isn't your job all about crime fighting?"

"Oh, naïve young man!" Rich shot back. "Sure, it's all about crime fighting, but I'm supposed to be only good for keeping the peace out on the streets. I'm a patrol deputy. This stuff is the domain of homicide detectives. But even at that, since there's no obvious link to L.A. County, not even a detective from our jurisdiction would be allowed to touch it anyway."

George stroked his chin thoughtfully, with his elbows on his knees. "There's a way around the access problem," he declared. The others looked at him expectantly, but he said, "I don't know what it is yet. But I didn't get to where I am now in the news business by being a wallflower. I'll figure something out. I usually find the most ignorant person in an organization, then throw a carefully crafted load of bull at them." To the stares aimed at him, he replied, "Hey, these stories don't just come to you, you know. You've got to grab the bull by the horns."

"Have you tried dumpster diving?" asked Trey. "They can't keep those boxes forever. Think how much space they must be taking up."

"The kid's right," Rich said. "They'll probably keep one or two for evidence, but if they're all the same like Rhonda said, the rest may get dumped. We need to be there when that happens."

"I think I can arrange for that," George said. "I'll just go down there and find a local kid or bum that wants to make a few extra bucks."

He looked at Rich, who nodded in agreement.

"Oh, one other thing, Rich added offhandedly. "That fake nurse who visited Trey last night had a syringe full of sodium cyanide."

"What?!" the others exclaimed in unison.

"Yep. Deadly stuff. Had it analyzed in the lab at the hospital. Couldn't catch her before she got away. It's a good thing I came along when I did. I can't imagine who'd want the kid dead, but somebody sure does."

The group sat in stunned silence for a few moments before George spoke up.

"Unbelievable," he said, shaking his head. "Jim, do you have any news for us?"

Jim hesitated. He knew better than to share any personal information about his staff members or congregants with outsiders. But desperate times called for desperate measures. He took a deep cleansing breath.

"Yeah," he admitted. "I've got a major problem at church right now, and I'm having a hard time dealing with it."

The room took on the dead silence of a confessional booth as Jim tried to frame up the next statement carefully.

"My associate pastor - Pete LeTourneu. I've got some major concerns about him."

"Pastor Pete?" Trey blurted, "What's up with him?"

Jim proceeded to lay out his concerns, starting with the first warning from Bjorn, to the poisoning incident, and the Angela Shepherd debacle. He finished up with his suspicious observations of the associate pastor's office furnishings.

"Look, I've got a higher degree of suspicion about people than the average guy," Rich asserted, "but I've got to ask myself - why would a Satanist infiltrate a church, as you seem to be suggesting?"

Trey cut in before Jim could answer. "First of all, I can't believe Pastor Pete would be into Satanism. Or that he would try to kill Pastor Nilsson. But I gotta say, Solid Rock is a prime target for different religious groups to evangelize in. It's a big church, easy to get lost in."

"But that's exactly what I don't want," Jim answered back. "I want everyone to have the chance to get plugged into a bible study or small group, and get involved in a ministry they're suited for. I'm trying my best to keep people from feeling lost in our church, in spite of it's size."

"I know, I know, Pastor," Trey replied, "but let me finish what I was saying. I'm just saying that it's possible to come and go every week and still remain anonymous, that's all. After all, can you honestly say that you personally know everybody that comes to church?"

"No, of course not. Not anymore. We've got over three thousand people coming to church each weekend. How could I know them all?"

"That's my point," said Trey. He winced in pain as he sat up from his semi-reclining position. "You remember that time last year when I warned you about that couple - the ones who were into the Christian Identity Movement?"

"Oh, yeah," Jim said. His chiseled face grimaced at the memory. "They were the ones who believed that white people of European descent are the true nation of Israel. The old 'Ten Lost Tribes' theology. They started inviting people from church over to their house for bible studies, and pushing their beliefs that the Jews and blacks are responsible for most of the world's woes. Yeah, I remember, all right. Once I found out about it, I went over to confront them on it; it ended up that I asked them to leave the church."

"So what does that have to do with Satanists?" George asked impatiently.

"What I'm saying," Trey replied slowly, for emphasis, "is that if cult groups are looking to infiltrate the church, why wouldn't Satanists do the same thing?"

"Doesn't seem likely to me," George said, his mouth forming a tight scowl. "How would they get people to turn away from God and serve Satan?"

"They wouldn't," Trey said, shooting him a gesture with his index finger. "They would only have to disrupt the work of the church."

Jim nodded, but the others looked back at Trey blankly.

"What you guys don't get, is that Solid Rock is a major force for God's kingdom in this valley," Trey said. "People are coming to Christ and getting saved. They're learning the bible. Getting solid teaching." He gestured at Jim, who preened at the remark. "They're praying - for their families, their community. For their political leaders and teachers. I can't think of a better group for Satanists to try to ruin."

"You're right," Jim said. "And the best way to sow corruption and discord is from within."

George shrugged his shoulders. "I'm still not sure what their motivation would be. Hey, don't get me wrong - I love a good conspiracy theory as much as the next guy. Maybe more. And I suppose that Satanists would be natural enemies to Christians; Kinda like cats and dogs. But what would they hope to accomplish?"

"Maybe you're a threat to them," Rich proposed. "Maybe something you're doing at church, or even your very existence, for that matter, is hindering them in some way."

"Well, I would hope so," Jim answered. "I would be a lousy pastor otherwise. The work of God's church pushes back the darkness in the ...,"

George cut him off at the pass before Jim could get his expository underway. "You mean, they have some secret agenda? A plan, a criminal activity of some sort? And the church - or Jim in particular, is standing in the way of it?"

"We already know they're killing babies," Rich answered. "And that murder of the teenage runaway less than two weeks ago had satanic undertones, although I can't link the two crimes - not yet. Who knows what else they may be doing?"

Trey spoke up. "I think these crimes are a means to an end. I'm sayin' maybe they're killing these innocent children for their blood. Rich said that they'd been bled out. And that girl – somebody said ... I think Rich told me when I was in the hospital; she was a virgin. It's no accident that they chose these victims. They've been very selective. They're using the blood of innocents to strengthen them for something in particular. And with *Samhain* only a week away, they've got to be building up to something."

"So-when?" George asked perplexedly.

"Samhain," Trey repeated, sounding it out. "It's the occult holiday that falls on Halloween. Didn't I tell you guys about this already? It's the day that occult powers are at their highest, supposedly. Whatever they're up to, I bet they'll leave a trail of bodies until then."

Rich nodded. "We'd better kick it up a notch if we're going to stop them. But first we need to find out who they are." He absently scratched the side of his face. "So we've got to track down every lead we've got. Everything that looks suspicious or strange. George is going to follow up on the plastic box."

He looked over at George, who acknowledged with a thumbs-up.

"Jim," Rich continued, "I want a little information from you, then we'll spend some stakeout time together." To Jim's perplexed look, Rich answered, "I want to know your son's locker number at school, and the combination to his lock."

Jim's mouth started to open, but Rich plowed on. "And this woman - Angela Whatever. I want to know more about her. Giving you the benefit of the doubt, Rev, I'd like to check her out." His face formed a wry grin. "No pun intended," he added. "And as for your associate pastor ... give me everything you've got on him."

Rich looked over at Trey. "Maybe the two of us can check his closet for any skeletons."

Trey smiled, cracking the scab on his lip. "Ouch ... sounds like fun, Rich. In the meanwhile, I'll spend some quality time on line. If there's anything to be found out about the Temple of Anubis, I can find it."

Jim felt like the mood in the room was elevating now, as a new sense of direction and an action plan was being laid out.

"Let's just see if their devil is big enough to protect them from us," Rich boasted. "We'll find them. And when I nail 'em, may God have mercy, 'cause I sure won't."

CHAPTER 34

Minneapolis, MN

Pete LeTourneu cruised down Cedar Avenue South in his rented Ford Taurus, glancing from time to time at the Minneapolis street map he held in his right hand.

He passed over a narrow bridge that spanned Lake Nokomis, one of the ten-thousand lakes in the state. The windshield wipers lazily wiped away the few light flakes of snow that slowly drifted down from a windless sky. The light was still dim in the early morning atmosphere, the glow of the rising sun having made it's appearance only a short time ago.

LeTourneu made a left, and pulled into a residential development just off the main drag. He slowly crept down streets full of small generic brick houses, most of which had steps going up to screened-in porches in front. A few cars were pulling out of their driveways, leaving long white vapor trails in the frigid air from their exhaust pipes as they ambled out to work. One car owner was vigorously scraping ice off the windshield of his car that had been left out overnight.

Pete glanced at the address written on the piece of paper that sat on the phonebook in the passenger seat, then picked it up for a closer look. Slowing down, he scanned the house numbers, gliding by the homes of peace-loving and unsuspecting people like a malevolent wraith. He smiled as he spied the house he was looking for, and continued to drive past. LeTourneu turned the Taurus around in a tight U-turn at the end of the street.

He pulled up several houses away in front of another cookie-cutter brick house, trying to position the car in an inconspicuous spot, away from the front door or windows. He shut off the engine and looked around. There was nobody on the street now, except for the ice-scraper down at the opposite end of the block. No dogs barking, nobody looking out windows.

Good.

LeTourneu adjusted his seat so that he was reclining well back. He could see just barely over the top of the hood. He put down the piece of paper with the address on it, and grabbed a small pair of binoculars from the glove box, setting them on his lap. Then he picked up a stainless steel thermos that he had bought and filled with coffee at one of the ubiquitous Starbucks establishments near his hotel. He poured himself a cup and settled in to wait.

Within thirty minutes of his arrival in the neighborhood, Pastor Dennis and Laura Heipler came out of the front door of the squat, nondescript brick house down the street. LeTourneu lifted the binoculars to his eyes and watched the man raise the old, wobbling garage door and walk into the garage, while the woman waited outside. Moments later, Pete observed a plume of exhaust hitting the frigid atmosphere, which soon became a white gaseous cloud. About a minute later, a late-model American-made car came into view through Pete's binoculars as it backed out of the garage and down the driveway. On cue, the woman closed the garage door, then opened the passenger door of the car and got in. As the car reversed and backed into the street facing Pete's direction, he laughed to himself at the sight of the electrical plug that was protruding from the grille of the car.

Idiots, he thought. *Who in their right mind would live in a place that could freeze your engine block overnight if you didn't have an electric heater for it? They deserve what's coming to them, every one of these losers.*

Pete slid down in the seat and set his binoculars aside. The Heipler's car slunk down the street like a tired creature trying to wake itself up, but Pete was already invisible to others below the line of the windshield. He stayed in that position for a minute after he heard the car go past, then sat up. Reaching into the glovebox, Pete found a pair of latex surgical gloves and stretched them over his cold hands. He then reached into the back seat and picked up his soft-sided leather briefcase, which completed the look of a businessman or door-to-door solicitor.

"Ladies and gentlemen, it's show time," he said to himself, under his breath.

Picking up the pair of black leather gloves in the seat next to him, he pulled them on over the latex gloves. He opened the door, and set his feet on the cold pavement. An expected chill hit him as he stood up and gently shut the car door behind him. Taking a last look around, Pete walked casually down the sidewalk with briefcase in hand.

His eyes moved relentlessly back and forth as he walked, scanning for any trouble. With his free hand, he buttoned his long overcoat. He gradually approached the target house, and took a furtive glance over his shoulder before walking up the entry path and up the steps.

LeTourneu pulled aside the screen door on the porch, thanking his dark lord for the cover that the porch provided from inquisitive eyes. Stepping quickly into the subdued light of the porch, he immediately set down his briefcase. He pulled off the leather gloves, exposing his latex covered hands. Quickly reaching into his suit pocket, he retrieved a lock-pick set and put it to work. He manipulated the two steel picks with such skill and experience that the lock yielded in just a few seconds - and he was in.

The air inside was warm and humid, and smelled of fried sausage and eggs. Pete took a deep breath. He closed the door silently behind himself.

So nice of these sheep to not bother installing a deadbolt, he thought. *They think they're completely safe.*

His reverie was interrupted by a voice coming from the direction of the kitchen.

"Did you forget something?" the voice called out.

LeTourneu reached down and deftly unplugged the phone jack connected to the phone on the entry table.

"Yes, I'm afraid I did," he answered back.

Almost immediately, the thin figure of Bjorn Nilsson appeared in the kitchen doorway. Bjorn looked at the unexpected visitor, then registered who he was. The change in his facial expression was amusing to Pete - from curiosity, to realization, to fear. Of all the people he'd put out of their misery over the years, Pete LeTourneu never ceased to be entertained by the dumbfounded looks on the faces of those who were about to die.

"So," Bjorn said slowly, "you've come to finish what you started. Then I was right." He crossed his arms defiantly.

"Very inconvenient of you, Reverend," Pete said, stretching out the last word. "You were supposed to be dead by the time you landed here."

"Must be the Viking blood. We don't give up easily."

"Neither do I."

Bjorn started surveying the front room of the house, as they remained at opposite ends. "I hope you won't mind if I put up a fight," he said defiantly.

"That would be fun, but I'll make it easy for you," Pete replied. He bent down to retrieve something from his briefcase. That was the moment Bjorn needed.

May Laura forgive me, he thought, quickly snatching Mrs. Heipler's silver teapot from it's matching tray on the cart.

He hurled it like a minor-league pitcher at the intruder. The pitch was a bit high and right, but it clipped LeTourneu's head, causing him to cry out and raise his hands in a tardy attempt to defend himself.

"Son of a …!" he cursed. Blood flowed between his fingers, as he pressed them against his smarting head. "All right, I'm not playing around with you!"

LeTourneu reached again into the briefcase, and pulled out the Glock 9mm pistol he had purchased in a downtown alleyway the night before. His other hand found the mating silencer in his coat pocket. He hadn't assembled the deadly pair before, because it wouldn't easily fit into his briefcase. He started to screw the silencer onto the weapon, keeping a hairy eye on Bjorn all the while.

Bjorn quickly ran over to the adjoining dining room and grabbed one of the chairs from the dining room table, then came charging at his adversary with it. The four legs of the chair protruded like the jousting lances of some medieval knight. LeTourneu wasn't quite quick enough screwing the silencer into the gun's barrel. With a final lunge, Bjorn pinned Pete up against the closed entry door, between the chair's legs. As he tumbled back against the entry door, Pete dropped the pistol and silencer on the wood parquet floor, and they clanged and spun on the hard surface. He cocked his leg back and braced it against the door, then pushed off at an angle against the chair.

Bjorn spun in his stocking-clad feet on the hard floor, and the chair flew from his grip. Losing his balance, he fell down on his chest.

Immediately, LeTourneu was on top of him. He jerked Bjorn onto his back, straddling him. He bent down and grabbed Bjorn's throat in his small but powerful hands, and squeezed down hard. Bjorn wasn't done yet, though. Pete dropped to his knees to apply even more choke force to his victim, but Bjorn managed to bring a well-timed shin up into LeTourneu's crotch at just the right moment. Pete's face turned red and instantly sweaty with the pain and nausea. He rolled off of Bjorn, curling up into a fetal position.

Bjorn struggled to get a breath, now that the hands of his enemy were off his throat. His own hands instinctively came up to tend the abused area, and he continued to gasp. He sat up, and saw to his horror that LeTourneu had already managed to crawl back to the spot where he had dropped his pistol and silencer, and was putting the two together. Bjorn got to his feet quickly, but Pete was quicker. Still on the floor, Pete spun around and pointed the pistol at Bjorn, stopping him in his tracks.

"Nice try, preacher man. But the game's up."

Bjorn knew he couldn't cross the eight foot distance to get at his nemesis in time. He resignedly raised his hands before his enemy.

"Any last words?" LeTourneu asked sarcastically.

Bjorn paused, then lifted his eyes and hands toward the ceiling. "Father," he said, "into your hands, I commit my spirit."

Then he dove at LeTourneu.

The sound was so quiet coming out of the muzzle of the gun, it didn't match the powerful impact of the bullet as it struck Bjorn squarely in his upper chest. He continued in his forward dive, but now without focus. The hollow-point bullet that entered through his chest exited out the back of his emaciated torso, leaving an exit wound the size of an apple. Bjorn was already dead as he fell on Pete's legs.

LeTourneu took a deep breath and let out a roar of excitement. He was exhilarated by the thrill of the hunt, and the final decisive moment of the kill. His crotch still hurt terribly, but the adrenaline coursing through his body offset the pain quite effectively. He stood and raised his arms above his head, the pistol held high in his left hand. He stomped his foot forcefully down on the head of his adversary, like a victorious big-game hunter.

Enraptured by the moment, Pete held his pose and let out a deep guttural grunt. He breathed and exhaled deeply, his skin prickly with sweat. He stood over his conquest for several enjoyable moments, drinking in the exhilarating sensation.

Satisfied at last that he had savored the experience enough, LeTourneu shifted from his conquering position, and went back to his briefcase. He removed the case that concealed the specially-designed ceremonial dagger, and snapped it open. The tool inside had a straight blade made of industrial grade ceramic, sharp as a razor. The blade was mounted in a handle made of high-impact Nylon, with an obsidian hilt. This non-metallic weapon was undetectable by X-rays that scanned luggage at the airport. He figured that he probably could have even slipped it into his carry-on bag, but didn't want to chance it.

LeTourneu returned to his fallen prey, and hovered over him for another long moment of gloating. Then he rolled Bjorn over onto his back. He put his forearm under Bjorn's neck and pulled it upward. He fell onto his victim's neck like a wild animal, biting viciously into it. LeTourneu greedily lapped up as much blood as he could from the wound he had just created, grunting and laughing to himself all the while. The flow was limited, since there was no heart pumping it through the coarse gash in the neck.

After Pete had satiated himself with the blood of his victim, he went to work on his tongue, grasping it with his gloved right hand, and bringing the dagger to bear with his left. It took only moments for Pete to sever his prize loose from his victim's mouth. He set the dagger down on the floor and slipped the bloody tongue into a Ziplock bag, which he produced from his pants pocket. Wiping his bloodied hands on Bjorn's shirt, he deftly placed the bagged tongue into two more layers of Ziplock bags, expelling any excess air in the bag as he did so.

Pete put the tongue into his briefcase, then turned to survey the room. Working quickly, he carefully overturned more chairs, broke a lamp, then went into the master bedroom to root around through the drawers.

Not like they have anything I want, he thought, *But I might as well make it look good.*

He pulled out the dresser drawers and dumped the contents on the floor. He found a fat envelope among the clothes in the Heipler's dresser drawer that was marked 'School lunches'. He opened it and found it stuffed with one-dollar bills.

Oh, boy. Coffee money.

He stuffed the bills in his pocket and dropped the envelope on the floor, and continued to quickly sift through the room.

I wonder how old their kids are, Pete thought. *Oh well, no time for that, anyway. Gotta finish up and get out of this rat trap.*

He left the master bedroom and went into the adjoining bedroom, which appeared to be the domain of a young teenage or pre-teen girl. Pete went to work going through the dresser drawers.

She would have been perfect, he mused, looking at the framed picture of the girl on the dresser. *I should've done my homework better, I guess. Wonder what time school gets out?*

A knock on the front door startled Pete out of his daydream. His head jerked up and he held perfectly still. The knock came again, accompanied by a female voice from the outside. "Pastor Dennis? Laura? … Everything okay?"

Pete quickly evaluated the options: more carnage, or flight. In a split-second decision, he chose the latter. He quietly tiptoed back to the front door and grabbed his briefcase, then headed to the back of the house. Opening the back kitchen door slightly, he stuck his head out and looked around. Clear. He dashed out the back and across the back yard to the alley behind the row of houses. Once in the alley, he walked briskly down to the end of the street, occasionally looking behind him.

Must've been too noisy. Forgot that these sheep up here are more nosy than back in Cali. If I'd had to waste the neighbor, it would have been Nilsson's fault for putting up a fight. He smiled to himself. *But that did add to the fun.*

LeTourneu couldn't help but chuckle to himself as he turned the corner onto the street, got into his car, and drove off.

CHAPTER 35

Solid Rock Community Church: Westlake Village, California

Jim impatiently tapped his fingers on his car's steering wheel. Seated next to him, Rich Harrison fidgeted with his binoculars, occasionally raising them to his eyes. Rich was in uniform, but his squad car sat unoccupied and obscured from view behind the handball court at the most distant part of the church parking lot.

Jim was parked next to the handball court; a location that afforded them an unobstructed, although distant view of the front of the church sanctuary on the small hill about two hundred yards away. It was Wednesday morning, and the sun was starting to burn off the marine layer that had previously enveloped the area in fog.

They waited.

"What time did you say this coffee-klatch wraps up?" Rich asked, looking at his watch. He lifted the binoculars up for the umpteenth time.

"Eleven o-clock," Jim replied. "At least, that's when their bible study officially ends. Some of them stay awhile longer, though. Some of the ladies - my wife included, like to chat it up until there's nobody left to talk to."

"Yeah, women like to talk - don't I know it," Rich said. He paused for a moment, then added, "That's how it was with my ex-fiancé Rhonda, at the San Berdoo Sheriff's Department. She used to talk all the time. Said I didn't communicate with her enough. She always wanted to talk about everything. She wanted to know what I was thinking and feeling all the time. Shoot, I used to tell her that she did enough talking for the both of us." He turned his face away toward the window.

"So what happened?"

"I don't know. We just kind of drifted apart, then broke up. It's kinda like that song by Trisha Yearwood - *'For reasons I've forgotten now, we brought love to an end. Ain't it funny how the little things seemed so big back then'.*" He looked at Jim. "But I guess your not much into country music, are you, Rev?"

"No, not really. But I do understand how people can drift apart because of lack of communication."

"But what I'm saying is, she wanted to talk even when there wasn't anything in particular to talk about. I talk when I've got something to say, not just to make small talk."

Jim looked up through the windshield, then nudged Rich.

"Here they come," he said.

Rich grabbed the binoculars, and raised them to his eyes. Jim pulled a second set out of Rich's duffel bag, and did the same. The church sanctuary came into view, with a few women starting to trickle out.

"Jasmine said she'd try to be near her when she comes out the door," Jim said, "and since you just met my wife at dinner last night, you should spot her right off. I only met the woman once, so I'm not one hundred percent sure I'd recognize her from this distance."

The pair continued apprising the throng of women exiting the women's bible study. A couple dozen women filtered out, most of them in no apparent hurry. Then Jim saw her.

"There's Jasmine, in the blue dress," Jim said.

"Got her."

Trailing behind Jasmine DiMario and her friend Barbara was a group of three younger women who were talking amongst themselves. The one with light brown hair was wearing a smartly-tailored skirt suit in burgundy with black trim.

"Okay, that's her in the burgundy," Jim said excitedly. "That's Angela Shepherd."

"Got her. Wow - what a babe!" Rich exclaimed. "I think I'm gonna like this assignment."

Jim's cell phone rang, making him jump high enough to bump his head on the car's headliner. He pulled the phone off his belt, and saw Jasmine's cell phone number displayed as he flipped it open. He pushed the green button and answered.

"Hi," he said.

"Hi. Do you see us?" Jasmine said coyly.

"We see. Rich is on it from here."

Jim turned his binoculars back to where his wife was walking. He saw a wicked smile on her face as she spoke to him from two hundred yards away.

"Okay," she replied in a musical voice, "We'll see you this afternoon then."

"Sounds good. Have a nice lunch. I love you."

"We will. Love you, too. Bye bye."

Jim pushed the red button on his phone and set it down.

"I think Jasmine is enjoying her role in this caper," he said. "You heard last night what her friend was able to find out about Angela."

"Yeah, not much solid," Rich pointed out. "Supposedly she's new in town. Married, no kids. But no home address, no work address or employer name or phone number. Nobody has met her husband. But that's okay. I'll find out plenty, believe you me."

Rich opened Jim's car door and got out. "Time to go to work," he said cheerfully. He shut the door, and walked over to his hidden car.

***

Rich had been following Angela's white Mustang GT for several miles on the freeway, keeping a good distance. He was thankful that she had gotten on the Southbound 101 freeway. Since Westlake Village straddles the border between Los Angeles and Ventura counties, she was leading him deeper into his own jurisdiction.

By the time they were hip deep in San Fernando Valley traffic, Rich wondered where she might be going.

Somebody who lives this far south probably wouldn't choose a church so far away, he figured.

He decided to make his move, since he was nearing the end of his patience. Rich pulled up behind the Mustang, and called in the plates. He flicked on the red and blue lights, and the driver soon pulled over.

Rich got out and walked over to the passenger side of the sporty car to avoid the freeway traffic. He tapped lightly on the dark tinted window. It rolled down like a veil, revealing the beautiful woman behind it. She smiled sweetly at Rich.

"Did I do something wrong?" she asked innocently.

"Good afternoon, Miss," Rich said, returning the smile. "Can I see your driver's license and registration, please?"

"Sure thing," she replied.

As she dug into her purse, Rich took it all in. The skirt hiked way up her thighs, higher than it would be under normal circumstances. Her legs were shapely and tan. She looked to him like a woman who spent a lot of time in the gym, and at the beach or tanning salon, for that matter.

This show must be for my benefit, he figured. *She doesn't want a citation. Smart girl.*

"Here's my license, and I'll get the registration for you," she said, holding her license between perfectly manicured fingers.

She reached over to the glove box and opened it up, taking her time finding the registration card - and giving Rich a good view of her bountiful cleavage at the same time. Rich noticed that the top button of her outfit was undone, which enhanced the viewing of her womanly features and the lacy black brassiere that contained them. He was sure that the button hadn't been undone earlier when he had seen her at church through the binoculars.

Oh, yeah, she's good, he thought.

"Here it is," she said at last, looking up at him.

Rich adjusted his gaze to her face, and took the registration from her. The name on the license and registration was Angela Fredericks, and the address was in West Hollywood. It was then he noticed that the wedding ring was also gone.

"Okay, Miss Fredericks, I'll be right back."

He went to his squad car, and quickly jotted down the driver's license number and address from the registration card.

Fredericks, eh? Rich thought. *She seems to have difficulty remembering her own last name.*

After Rich walked away from her car, Angela Fredericks' smile faded instantly when the face recognition suddenly hit her like a freight train.

Oh, my God – it's that cop from the hospital, she thought to herself. *I knew I recognized him from somewhere. I don't think he recognizes me, though. Of course not; I was in disguise when he saw me, and it was dark in the hospital room anyway.*

Her smile gradually returned. *He has no idea who I am. Otherwise he would have said something. Don't freak out, you're cool,* she told herself.

Rich came right back to his seductively smiling customer.

"The reason I pulled you over is because your right brake light isn't working," he said. "I'm not going to give you a citation, but you should get it taken care of soon."

"Well thanks for letting me know," she purred, "I'll get it fixed right away. My car is still under warranty. The guys at the dealership have been real helpful to me."

"I'll bet. So, is this your current address in West Hollywood?"

"Yes, officer, it is."

"Good. I know where that is," Rich ventured.

Well, here goes nothing, he thought to himself. "Can I pick you up there tonight?" he asked boldly.

She smiled again, and looked at his name badge. "Make it seven-thirty. And I like Italian food, Officer Harrison."

"You must have read my mind. And it's Rich."

"Well, I'll see you then, Rich." She put her sunglasses on and peered at him over the top. "Bye, bye."

She fired up the engine and started rolling up the side window. Rich was leaning on it, and he pulled his hands away. She gave him a last wink over the top of her sunglasses, then pulled away from the shoulder with the pedal to the metal. The engine of her potent car transferred excessive horsepower to the ground, and she was gone amidst squealing tires and smoke.

Rich knew that it was taboo to date someone he had pulled over, but he figured that desperate times call for desperate measures.

She probably won't even be there when I show up anyway, he reasoned. *Just looking to flirt her way out of a ticket. Happens all the time – and it usually works.*

"Well, well, Angela Fredericks," Rich muttered as he walked back to his car, "can't wait to get to know ya."

He opened the door and sat down. *The things I do in the name of law and order,* he thought.

CHAPTER 36

Plastec Industries: City of Industry, California

George got out of his car in the parking lot and took a deep breath of brisk morning air.

Here we go, he thought.

He shut the car door behind himself, then took a look at his reflection in the glass. The fake mustache was a nice touch for the occasion, he figured. After adjusting his tie and the black-framed, minimal power drug store eyeglasses once more, he got his briefcase and the plastic box from the car's trunk.

Yesterday, he had picked up the box in San Bernardino from a gangly teenage skateboarder who had been checking the dumpsters outside the county coroner's office. A pair of twenties were paid to the youth, who sped off to squander his windfall.

He had carefully examined the familiar-looking plastic box on all sides before finding what he was looking for. The manufacturer information was molded into the bottom of the box as he had suspected, along with a symbol that looked something like a round clock face with arrows pointing at numbers, indicating the date of manufacture.

Jackpot, he'd thought to himself.

After driving home, he did the late night Internet search that led him to this company's parking lot.

Now, steeling himself for his upcoming role, he strode boldly up to the front entrance of the nondescript concrete tilt-up building and pulled back the massive etched glass door. He stepped out of the cool morning air and into the formal, opulent environs in the lobby of Plastec Industries. George swaggered across the expanse of black and tan marble, which was laid out in alternating slabs like a huge chessboard. Approaching the monumental marble front desk, a young blonde receptionist looked up from the newspaper help wanted ads spread out before her, and smiled.

"Good morning, sir. How can I help you?" she sung in a sweet melody borne of practice.

"George Markovitz of Innovative Medical Supply, here to see your quality control manager, Mr. Taylor," George replied. Before she could ask the obvious follow-up question, he answered it for her. "I have an appointment."

"One moment, please." She punched the appropriate buttons on her PBX switchboard, and informed the other party that he had a visitor. "He'll be right with you," she said. "You can have a seat over there if you like."

She gestured toward a plush sofa grouping in the corner of the expansive lobby. George didn't have long to wait.

Bill Taylor was a big man. When he pushed through the pair of glass doors on the inside of the lobby, George feared they might come off their hinges. He walked up to George smiling widely, and extended his hand.

"Bill Taylor. Pleased to meet ya," he said with a slight southern drawl.

"George Markovitz," George said, taking the meaty hand and squeezing it. "Thanks for seeing me on short notice. Here's my card."

George disengaged from the big man's grip, and proffered the business card he had designed and printed from his computer the night before.

"My pleasure," Taylor replied jovially, taking the card and sticking it in his pants pocket. "You mentioned on the phone that you wanted to learn about our quality system before you decide to do business with us. I'll tell you all about it while I show you around."

Taylor showed George the factory floor where dozens of injection molding machines and rotational molding machines were perpetually turning out industrial plasticware. A platoon of expediters armed with large carts periodically loaded and took away the products being produced on each machine. Quality control inspectors carefully examined various parts under illuminated magnifiers, and measured critical dimensions with digital calipers.

"As you can see, we take quality very seriously here at Plastec," Bill Taylor said proudly, as he surveyed his kingdom. "Every lot of product is sampled by our inspectors before it is approved to go to the finished goods warehouse."

George watched the gowned workers move purposefully around the gleaming linoleum floor.

"Is your company ISO 9001 certified?" he asked.

"Yes, sir-ee we are," Taylor proudly acknowledged.

"What I'm looking for as a purchasing manager is a company that has a robust quality system in place," George said, delivering his rehearsed lines using terminology he'd learned the night before. "Our customers want traceability and documented quality in the products they buy from us."

"We've got a solid, documented quality system," Taylor said. "All of our product lots have full traceability through our electronic lot history record archive."

He eyed the box that George had in his hand. "I see you've already got a sample of one of our products. Is that one that you're interested in handling?" he asked.

"Yes, it is." George held the now-sanitized box up with both hands to show his host. "You want to impress me?" George asked, issuing an understated challenge, "Show me the cradle-to-grave history of this box I'm holding right here."

Bill Taylor took the box from George and held it in his chunky hands, looking it over.

"Can do," he said, with a smile. "Follow me."

He walked over to one of the computer terminals on the production floor, with George in tow. Sitting down, the chair creaked in protest at his weight. Taylor logged in and began working the internal archive system for several minutes as George looked on. Finally, he snapped his fingers in victory and pointed at the computer screen.

"Here we go," he said triumphantly. Turning to his guest, Taylor pointed at one of the Hispanic men on the production floor. "That box of yours was made by Carlos over there, on that machine he's standing in front of, on August second of last year."

He looked back at the screen. "Then it went through inspection, and was sent to finished goods. It was sold to Far East Imports on August twentieth, and shipped the next day."

Taylor gloated over the wealth of information he held at his disposal. "I could even run a shipping trace and find out who received it, and when."

"I'll call your bluff," George answered. "Go ahead and run it."

Bill Taylor turned back to the screen and proceeded to work the keys with remarkable speed. He found the shipping company's web site, and entered the tracking number. A moment later, he rotated in his chair back to face George, smiling broadly.

"It was signed for by Peter Duchamp on August twenty-second, at ten-fifteen in the morning."

George smiled back. "Well, I'm impressed, I must admit. But just out of curiosity, why do you suppose an import company would buy these kind of boxes?"

"Who knows? People think up all kinds of new uses for our products. They've bought quite a few of this same box, so it doesn't much matter to me what they do with them. You could talk to our sales department - they might know."

If only you knew what somebody is using them for, George thought.

George managed a chuckle. "Naw – doesn't really matter," he said. "By the way, what shipping carrier do you use to get the order there so quick?"

"Oh, just standard UPS, in this case. The customer is in Reseda. And if they'd wanted it sooner, we could have even couriered it over there for same-day delivery. It's just across town."

George nodded, then slapped his own thighs and stood up.

"Well I think I've seen everything I need to. And I thank you for the tour, Mr. Taylor."

"Bill, please," Taylor said, latching on to George's extended hand. "My pleasure. I look forward to your first order."

"I'm impressed with your operation overall, and you're obviously really service oriented. You'll be hearing from me," George said, as they strolled down the linoleum path back to the lobby, with the plastic box under his arm.

Taylor exchanged pleasantries with George at the glass inner doors, flushed with pride all the while. As George pushed through the door, the receptionist looked up, but continued her apparently personal conversation in hushed tones on her telephone headset without missing a beat. George headed out the door into the mid-morning sunlight, with a broad smile across his face.

CHAPTER 37

Solid Rock Community Church: Westlake Village, California

Jim returned to the church office with a spring in his step this bright, sunny morning after seeing Rich off in the lower church parking lot. At last, he was optimistic about taking some positive action about the accusation that dogged him like a monkey on his back.

He entered the church office door with a smile on his face, and passed the receptionist's desk as he started toward his office.

"You look cheerful this morning," observed Bev Hansen, who's ample body filled the swivel chair at her desk in the front entry of the outer office.

"I am," Jim answered. "Why wouldn't I be? It's a beautiful day outside. I feel good, in spite of current circumstances."

She raised a cupped hand next to her mouth. "Let's go into your office," she whispered. Bev got up and led the way down the hall to Jim's office and he followed her in, shutting the door behind him. She turned to him, with an anxious look pasted across her face.

"This is hard for me to say …," she said, wringing her arthritis-ravaged hands. "But it needs to be said."

Jim looked on as Bev set her resolve to let it out.

"I've never felt good about Pastor Pete," she blurted out. "There's something about him that doesn't feel right - more than that, even. From the first time he came here, I've had a nagging, uncomfortable sense about him. I don't think he's a Christian believer, for one thing. And besides that, the Spirit of God is telling me that he doesn't belong here."

Jim turned his eyes away from her and sat down heavily in his leather chair behind his desk. He motioned for her to sit as well. Jim said nothing for about a minute, and Bev knew enough to let him alone to digest her revelation.

She finally broke the silence, adding to her remarks a conciliatory comment. "I know it must be hard for you to imagine something like this …," she started.

Jim raised his hand and cut her off in midstream. "It's not that hard for me to imagine - now. I wish it weren't true, but I've become suspicious of Pete recently myself," Jim confessed. "I want to figure out what he's up to, and why he's here."

He suddenly raised a finger as a light bulb went on in his head.

"And I'll start by finding out more about where he came from."

Jim opened the file drawer in his desk and fingered through the tabs decorating the tops of olive-green hanging folders filed therein. He grabbed the one marked 'Pete LeTourneu' and pulled it out. Leafing through the few papers inside, he pulled out the resume he was looking for, and set the rest of the file down. Jim scanned down the page until he found the information he wanted, then reached for the phone.

"Do you want me to leave?" asked Bev.

"No - please stay," Jim replied, as he punched the speaker phone button. "In fact, I'd like you to listen in."

The phone emitted the ubiquitous dull dial tone, and Jim punched in the long-distance string of numbers. By the fourth ring, Jim was expecting an answering machine to pick up. He knew from experience that some smaller churches didn't have the luxury of a receptionist keeping regular office hours. Then someone picked up.

"Good morning, Tri-Valley Bible Church," a sweet female voice answered.

"More like, 'good afternoon' out in your neck of the woods, isn't it?" Jim replied jovially.

"Oh, of course," she replied. "I wasn't looking at the time. How may I help you?"

"This is Pastor Jim DiMario, calling for Pastor Ellis."

"Let me see if Reverend Ellis is available," she replied. "Please hold."

Jim and Bev were transferred to a collection of hymns, a-la-muzak. After several minutes, the phone was finally picked up again.

"Frank Ellis speaking," announced a deep male voice.

"Reverend Ellis," Jim said, "This is Jim DiMario. I'm the senior pastor at Solid Rock Community Church, out here in Southern California."

"Well, good morning, pastor," the man said warmly. The female voice mumbled something in the background. "Good afternoon, that is," he added quickly. "You know how time flies when you're busy."

"Don't I know it," Jim chuckled. "I won't take much of your time today. I'm just doing a routine follow-up on Pete LeTourneu. We hired him recently as an associate pastor, and I wanted to get your feedback on him."

"Ah, Pete. Well, I was sorry to see him go, that's for sure. But it's not for me to hold someone back from a calling. He considered working for your church to be a great opportunity."

"Uh-huh. What exactly were his responsibilities at your church?"

"Oh, a bit of everything. He was my right hand man. We have a small staff here, so it was just Pete and myself doing most everything. I always counted on him for helping support all the ministries. And he can preach a good sermon, too. I don't know if he's had the chance to speak at your church yet, but he's certainly competent to do so."

"Well, I'll definitely keep that in mind," Jim replied, grimacing at the thought. Bev showed her own feelings by slowly shaking her head.

"So, were there any shortcomings I should be aware of?" Jim asked.

"No, nothing at all," came the reply. "I think you're lucky to get him. He's a good man."

"Okay," Jim replied, sensing that the end of the conversation was at hand. "Well, I thank you for your time, Reverend Ellis."

"No problem. Glad I could help."

"Bye, now. God bless."

"Likewise."

Reverend Ellis hung up, and Jim's speakerphone again reverberated with the dial tone. He punched the button, then sank back into his chair.

Bev shook her head, frowning. "Wrong, wrong, wrong," she muttered. She stood up as quickly as her arthritis would allow, and started toward the door, still shaking her head. "Doesn't feel right," she said.

Bev opened the door. "I'll be up front," she said, ambling out. She shut the door behind her.

This is crazy, Jim thought, *Instead of answers, all I get is more questions.*

***

The Magus set the phone down on the desk of his stately home office. He continued staring at it thoughtfully, stroking his gray moustache for a time. He turned to the lingerie-clad young woman standing next to him, who had a nervous expression etched on her face.

"Good thing you got that call," he said. Her expression softened into one of relief. "Where's Pete now?" he demanded.

"On his way back from Minneapolis," she replied. Then she added, "He might have already arrived at the airport."

"Find out, and tell him to get over here," The Magus barked. "And check the bug in DiMario's office. Start rolling tape on it twenty-four-seven using voice activation mode on the tape recorder. Have one of the guys trade off with you monitoring for any talk related to Pete or his Angela - or anything else of interest."

He stared out the window of his luxurious home. "It's time to kick it up a notch."

***

Mid afternoon found Jim still in his office, working on his sermon for the following Sunday. He wasn't getting far with it, since he couldn't stop thinking about how adamant Bev had been earlier about Pete LeTourneu and Angela Shepherd.

When the phone on Jim's desk rang, it didn't really break his concentration on the sermon, just his pre-occupation on the subject of Pete LeTourneu. It was Bev Hansen.

"I'm sorry to bother you, Pastor. I know you told me to hold your calls," she said apologetically, "but there's a man on the phone - Pastor Dennis Heipler. He says it's urgent."

"Okay, I'll take it," Jim said.

"Oh, by the way," she added, "I checked the church directory for a Tri-Valley Bible Church in Michigan. There's no listing. I thought you should know."

"Well, it's possible that some of the smaller churches might not be listed in the directory," Jim theorized out loud. "Why don't you look up that town on the Internet? Livonia, wasn't it? Most towns and cities have at least one official webpage these days."

"Good idea, Pastor."

"Okay, I'll take that call now."

He pushed line two on his phone, where the tiny red light was blinking. "Jim DiMario speaking."

"Pastor DiMario," answered a strong tenor voice, "this is Dennis Heipler, in Minneapolis. We met a few years back at the association conference."

"Yes, of course, Dennis, I remember. I was glad to hear that our friend, Bjorn, was staying with you."

"That's why I'm calling you today, Pastor," Dennis replied. His voice sounded serious in Jim's receiver.

A sensation of uneasiness abruptly swept over him. "Please, call me Jim." Then he added, "What's wrong?"

"Okay, Jim," Dennis answered, "I'll tell you." After a brief pause, he added, "Look, even after all my years in the ministry, Jim, there's just no easy way to do this, so I'll just say it. Bjorn is dead – he was murdered."

"What?!" The response came out of Jim's mouth without thinking - a reaction to the unthinkable, rather than a question. He jerked bolt upright, his back straight as a soldier.

"It happened just yesterday afternoon."

"But ... but, I thought Bjorn was doing better now!" Jim protested vehemently, "In fact, last time I talked to him, just the other day, he said he was on the road to recovery. Did he take a sudden turn for the worse, or what?"

"No, Jim. That would be bad enough. There was a home invasion robbery at my house. It happened sometime after my wife and I left for the church office, and Bjorn was there by himself."

"This is ... unbelievable," Jim sputtered, his mind reeling at the gravity of the news. "Your house was targeted by armed robbers?"

"That's what the police are saying," Dennis replied. "But I don't have much worth taking, and my neighborhood isn't exactly ... upscale, if you know what I mean."

"So, you don't agree with the police?"

"There were ... circumstances, that the police don't want me to discuss publicly at this time." He took an audible breath that Jim could easily hear through the phone line. "Laura and I found him in the house. I know we'll never forget the sight of him if we live to be a hundred."

Jim didn't know what to say, and was too stunned to speak anyway. "Oh, Dennis ..., " he murmured at last.

"Look, Jim. I know you and Bjorn were close. Will you come out for the funeral? I'm arranging it for Friday. I want you to be a pallbearer, if you can make it. His friends from Brazil probably won't be able to come, and it would mean a lot to all of us if you could do it."

Dennis paused to wait for a response from Jim which wasn't immediately forthcoming. "I'll talk to you then in more detail," he continued. "I'm really troubled about this, and not only because of Bjorn's loss. Some of the things he told me in our private conversations … well, we'll talk then."

"Yeah, yeah, Dennis," Jim answered absently, "of course I'll come. I'll make travel arrangements. See you before Friday."

"Thanks, Jim. Call me when you know your arrival time. I can pick you up at the airport of you want."

"Okay - I'll let you know on that. See you then."

Jim hung up the phone and slumped back in his chair. He stared at the wall for a few minutes. Then he sat up and reached for the speed-dial button on his phone that called home. But he diverted his finger at the last moment, and punched Bev's extension instead.

"Yes, Pastor?" she answered.

"Book me on a flight to Minneapolis," he said tersely, "make it Wednesday or Thursday."

"All right," Bev replied. Then she added, "Is everything all right?"

"No - no it's not," Jim answered. "On second thought, make it two tickets. I hope to have company."

CHAPTER 38

Minneapolis, MN

The journey to Minneapolis seemed to Jim interminably long, especially since he knew what awaited him at the end destination.

As the Boeing 737 started it's final approach into Minneapolis / Saint Paul International Airport, Jim looked over at his companion on this trip. Jim was glad that Rich had made himself available on short notice to participate on this journey.

Jim's attention was diverted by the aircraft's noticeable deceleration. He gently elbowed Rich, who protested with a snort.

"We're almost there," Jim said.

Rich opened his eyes slightly, and peered at Jim through slits. "Already?" he asked.

"Already! You've been sleeping most of the way," Jim replied.

Rich started to stretch his stiff body in the coach-class seat that uncomfortably restrained his long legs.

"Hey, I've got to be able to get sleep when I can, with the hours I keep," he said.

Minding the 'Fasten seat belts' sign, the two straightened their seat backs and prepared for the landing.

Upon arriving at the airport, Jim and Rich rented a car and headed over to the Heipler's home.

"By the way," Jim asked offhandedly while driving, "what did you find out about Angela Shepherd?"

"Ah, Angela. Well, she lives in West Hollywood, so it seems a bit odd that she would be coming to your church. Plus, it also appears that she's not married, after all."

"Really? Are you sure?"

"Well," said Rich with a grin, "it would be pretty inappropriate for her to go out with me for dinner if she was married."

"What the - no way!" Jim retorted incredulously.

"True. I'm supposed to pick her up at her place Saturday night, so we better get back on time. I don't want to disappoint her."

Jim stared at him slack-jawed. "I can't believe this. You pulled her over then?" He shook his head. "And instead of a ticket, she got a date!"

Rich smiled like the cat who ate the canary. "Yep. And she was quite cooperative, I must say. Not to mention pretty, but you already knew that. We'll see how cooperative she is when I drop the bomb on her. But I'll give her a nice Italian dinner first, though."

"I can't believe you, Rich! You must have ice water running through your veins."

"Hey, didn't you say you wanted to find out what the deal was with her? I've already found out a couple fishy things. I'll find out what else drops out, and maybe I'll even have some fun doing it."

Jim just shook his head, but he couldn't hide the thin smile that formed on his lips.

It was late in the afternoon when they arrived at the house. They were greeted at the door by Laura Heipler, who was wearing an apron and rubber gloves. Dennis came to the door and embraced Jim. He was introduced to Rich, and Dennis embraced him as well, much to the deputy's chagrin.

They were led into the family room of the small house, where the Hiepler's early-teen daughter, Sarah, was watching TV. She stood up and smiled welcomingly at the newcomers, as the pastor's daughter had on hundreds of other occasions. Then she turned down the volume a bit and sat back down.

"I was planning on having you for dinner," Laura said, as she peeled off the rubber gloves, "Let me check on it. I hope meat loaf is okay with you fellas."

"Sounds great to me," Jim answered.

"You betcha," echoed Rich.

Jim shot him a look. *Oh, man,* he thought, *I hope he's not going to be a wise guy with his Midwest stereotype talk.*

Laura padded off to the kitchen as the men sat down on the two couches that were arranged in an L-shape. Sarah went back to watching her show on the Disney channel; something about twin sisters competing in basketball.

Jim noticed the pail by the front door, and the damp area surrounding it. Rich noticed it, too. He'd also noticed the faint smell of pine-sol in the air when they walked in.

"I bet that's where you found him," Rich said.

Dennis nodded. "Yeah, Laura has scrubbed that area about a dozen times now. I guess it's some kind of therapy for her. She's got to keep herself busy.

"So, how are you doing, then?" Jim asked.

Dennis pursed his lips and sat forward on the couch next to Sarah. "I'm just thankful that our next-door neighbor called me at the church office. She said she'd heard some noises at the house. When I called, there was no answer, and I knew Bjorn wasn't going anywhere in his condition."

He paused for a moment and studied the worn taupe carpet at his feet before continuing his story. "So we came home early to see if everything was all right."

Dennis' eyes started to mist up. "Obviously, it wasn't. But if we hadn't come home when we did, Sarah would have found him when she got home from school."

He put his arm around his daughter and gently hugged her. She responded by putting her head on dad's shoulder.

"We kept Sarah outside when she got home from school, then sent her over to her friend's house down the street," Dennis continued. "Then we called the police. Next thing we knew, the place was crawling with cops, detectives, and crime scene investigators."

"Can you describe what the scene looked like, and what kind of wounds the victim had?" Rich asked.

Dennis gave him a funny look, but Jim quickly spoke up.

"I should have mentioned to you, Dennis, Rich is a sheriff's deputy - and a friend," Jim said. "I asked him to come along to see what we could find out."

Rich looked over at him with a wry face.

Dennis nodded. "Sure," he said, "I'll tell you everything I know. But later." He motioned with his eyes toward Sarah.

"Of course," Rich replied, taking the hint. "Maybe you can give me the name and number of the lead detective who came out. I'd like to stop by and pay him a visit."

"Sure thing. I've got his card."

Laura appeared in the doorway. "Dinner's about ready," she announced.

After an enjoyable dinner of the tastiest meatloaf he could remember, along with roast potatoes and asparagus, Rich made a call to the Minneapolis detective who had supervised the crime scene.

"He's still at the office," Rich announced as he put the phone down. "Let's see how far professional courtesy goes up here."

The ride was only about ten minutes, since the Heipler's house was in one of the older neighborhoods in town, not far from the civic center. They pulled into the parking garage of the police station, which shielded cars from the worst of the inevitable winter storms to come. They took the elevator upstairs and met Detective Ellis, who turned out to be fairly accommodating after Rich identified himself.

"So, what's your interest in all this?" Detective Ellis asked of Rich. "You're not so short of crime down in L.A. that you needed to come up here to find some, are ya?"

"Not hardly," Rich laughed. "This one's more personal. The victim was a close friend of my buddy, the reverend here."

The detective nodded at Jim.

"So, what can you tell me about the killing?" Rich ventured.

"Well, it was pretty bloody, ya know." He stopped and looked at Jim again. "You up for hearin' the details?" he asked.

Jim replied with a silent nod.

"The vic took two nine-millimeter rounds to the chest, point blank. But not before puttin' up a fight. There were signs of a struggle. The perp got a little bit of money - not much at all, really. A hundred bucks, tops. Nothin' else in the house was missing."

"But you're thinking home invasion style robbery?" Rich asked.

"Maybe," Ellis emphasized by drawing out the word. "Might have been a burglary gone bad. The victim surprises him by being home. They fight, he gets popped. Usually a home invasion involves a small crew of robbers, not just one. There's nothin' to suggest that there was more than one."

Detective Ellis took a sip of his coffee. "No prints, either. We dusted the house good - nothin'." Another sip. "It's kinda weird. The people didn't have anything that would bring in a crew of robbers - at least nothin' that I could find. Maybe the guy just got into the wrong house. The victim was in the wrong place at the wrong time. Still, there was one strange thing that I haven't figured out at all."

The detective gently blew into his Styrofoam cup.

"Which is?" Jim asked impatiently.

Ellis lifted his Mona Lisa smile up from the cup. "The perp cut the victim's tongue out," he said.

"What!?" Jim bellowed.

"Cut it clean out. At first I figured it was a revenge thing, like maybe the vic's connected to organized crime somehow. But then I find out the poor guy's a missionary, staying at the home of a pastor. Doesn't make sense, unless it's a mistaken identity thing, ya know."

"This is unbelievable," Jim lamented, "it just keeps getting worse."

"Anything else?" Rich asked calmly.

"Yeah. The tongue was gone, but he left the knife. And it's somethin' special. Definitely custom. The blade's not even metal. Never seen anything like it in my life."

"Can I see it? And the body?" Rich asked.

Ellis shrugged his shoulders. "Why not? I'll take you down to evidence, then I'll call ahead to the morgue for ya." He looked at Jim again. "But take my advice," he said to Rich, "look at the body yourself. Let him wait outside." He indicated at Jim with his chin.

Rich nodded in agreement. "Yeah, no doubt."

The evidence cage was located down in the basement of the building, an area tucked away off the beaten path of the normally busy criminal justice center. Rich and Jim flanked Detective Ellis as he walked up to a square hole in the cage that had a narrow Formica desk top imbedded about waist level. A bell sat on the desk top, and Ellis immediately rang it. Jim heard the feeble shuffling of feet long before an ancient, short man with white hair and large ears arrived behind the cage desk.

"Yeah?" The octogenarian demanded.

"The knife from the Nilsson killing," Ellis said. "I brought it in a couple days ago."

The man said nothing, and shuffled off.

Probably a retired cop who got tired of TV and golf, Jim figured.

Soon the white-haired man shuffled back with a Tupperware box in his hand. He plopped it on the desk, and thrust a tattered brown clipboard at Ellis, who signed it without comment.

The detective turned to his guests and opened the lid, while they craned their necks to look inside at the knife, which was sealed inside a Ziplock bag. Ellis took the knife out of the box and removed it from the bag. The white ceramic blade shone like a huge fang in the subdued light of the basement. He offered it up to Rich.

"It's already been dusted and checked out by the lab," Ellis said. "It's clean. No prints at all, and there was just the victim's blood, which they've cleaned off." He looked at the expression of distaste on Jim's face. "Told ya it was somethin' special. Never saw a knife quite like it."

"Me either. It's more like a dagger," Rich noted, observing the sharp double edge of the six-inch long milky blade as he turned it around in his hands. "I'd like to take a picture of it, for future reference."

"Sure, no problem. I figured you might."

Rich pulled his small digital camera from a jacket pocket. "Just hold it in your hands there," he told Ellis. Rich lifted the camera to his eye and took several photos of the knife.

"It really is a beautiful knife," Jim said. "And very unusual, as you said. It must have been expensive. Why would the killer leave it behind?"

"Don't know for sure," Ellis replied. "Could have been deliberate, but I don't think so. The neighbor came knocking at the front door because she heard some noise. She might have caused the perp to make a quick retreat. We know he left out the back door. Foot prints show that he came in the front door, which is kinda weird, especially since the pastor and his wife are sure they locked the door before they left the house."

After returning the knife to Evidence, Detective Ellis walked them over to the morgue, which was connected to the police department building by an enclosed skywalk.

"I suppose you'll be wanting some time with the body then," Ellis said to Rich. "Good timing on your part. I was about to sign off on the release to the funeral home. They've called me about three times today, already. I just haven't gotten to it yet. Don't know what they're moaning about; it only takes four hours at the most to prepare a body for burial."

He extended his hand to Rich, who shook it. He repeated the gesture with Jim. "I'll leave ya then. Gotta get home at some point tonight, or I'll be goin' hungry - again."

"I hear you," Rich replied. "Thanks for everything, we appreciate it. We'll probably be heading home tomorrow night. Can I call you if I have any questions?"

"Sure, sure." Ellis fumbled around in his pocket and finally produced a business card. "Here's my cell number," he said, jotting it down on his card.

He handed it to Rich, who thanked him again. Ellis turned and started walking off, then turned back toward them.

"Remember what I said," he admonished with a smile, pointing at Jim. "leave this one outside."

He turned and continued on his way.

To Rich, Jim said, "I'm not nearly as faint of heart as he might think. I've spent more time in hospitals and hospice care homes than most people." He sighed, "But that's the least favorite part of my job, to be honest."

"I believe you, Jim. But in this case, I think he's right. You don't want to see this."

Jim hesitated a few seconds, then nodded in agreement.

***

Being in the presence of dead bodies was not a new experience for Rich, but it was one he'd never grown comfortable with.

The medical examiner pulled a slab out from the massive human refrigerator built into the wall. On it, the lifeless body of Bjorn Nilsson lay, obscured by a blue paper sheet, except for his head. Rich got a pair of latex gloves out of the supply cabinet, and snapped them on. Turning back to face the body, Rich was careful to look only at areas on the body that he was interested in. He didn't want to see the body as that of a man who had been brutally murdered. It was easier to put on a scientific mindset, looking for damage and clues on an object, rather than a person.

The mouth was partially open, and beyond those pale blue lips was a dark hole. Rich carefully pulled the jaw open. The rigor mortis resisted his effort, and he had to use more force than expected. He moved the bright halogen examination light directly over the gaping mouth.

No tongue, just like the detective said, he thought.

A gruesome mask of coagulated blood marked the place where the tongue had been excised. Rich moved his eyes downward, and saw purplish-maroon marks around the neck - and a ghastly wound on one side of the neck, at the carotid artery.

Whoa - what caused that, I wonder? He looked closer, and saw a faint arcing pattern of purplish marks surrounding the wound. *What the - those are teeth marks. This sick creep did more than biting, though. Looks like he actually chewed on the victim's neck.*

He pulled back the sheet, uncovering the site where two bullet holes had torn into the chest. They were about half an inch in diameter.

They'll probably be big on the exit side, unless he used fully jacketed bullets, he thought.

"Let's roll him on his side for a minute," Rich said.

When they did, Rich saw two ugly exit wounds on Bjorn's back about the size of small apples, which confirmed his suspicion of hollow-point bullets. They rolled him back over onto his back.

Rich noticed some stippling from gunpowder burns around the holes. *Must have been point blank. And the choke marks. I wonder if he was killed first, then brutalized, or if he caught the guy without the gun in his hand, and fought for his life. If they had their hands on each other, maybe there'll be some evidence.*

Rich took a closer look at something on one of the deceased's hands that caught his attention.

What's this? he thought. A little trace of red on the finger tips of the right hand, specifically.

Rich tentatively took hold of the right hand and started to lift it. The arm resisted his effort; stiff like a two-by-four. The examiner eyed Rich curiously all the while, but said nothing. Rich moved the light as close as possible, while keeping his grip on the recalcitrant wrist at the same time. He carefully examined the fingers for several seconds.

"Take a look at this," Rich said, pointing at the hand. "There's a little blood on his fingertips. Go get us a tweezer and a specimen dish," he ordered. "And a couple cotton swabs," he added, as the examiner scurried off.

Hopefully this guy doesn't realize I'm not with the Minneapolis P.D. Rich thought to himself.

The medical examiner took Rich's instruction without question, immediately locating the items Rich asked for, and held them out to him.

"What do you see?" the bookish young man asked.

Rich took the specimen dish.

"It looks like there's a tiny bit of tissue under the fingernail of the middle finger. Do you see it?" Rich asked.

The examiner drew close with his thick eyeglasses to the finger that Rich indicated.

"Yeah."

From under one of the corpse's fingernails, the medical examiner carefully extracted a tiny bolus of material, with two fine hairs sticking out of it.

"What's this?" asked the M.E.

"Hair and skin from the killer, probably."

"Whoa, good catch. The chief medical examiner didn't find that earlier. How did you know?"

"I didn't. Just a hunch. The detective said he put up a fight."

Rich held the petri sample dish, while the examiner delicately placed the specimen into it.

"Got to cover all the bases," Rich added. "Sometimes you get lucky."

He took the dish and pressed the round plastic lid on. "Can you make sure the Chief Medical Examiner and Detective Ellis get this?"

"Yeah, you betcha," the young man replied. "I'll hang onto it until he comes in tomorrow morning."

He smiled to himself, evidently gloating about having a leg up on his boss.

"Thanks. And get some good close-up pictures of that wound on the neck. Those are teeth marks, and I want to record the pattern for when we get a suspect. Swab it for a saliva residue, too. The killer must have left some DNA in there."

Rich ungloved himself and disposed of the latex in the biohazard container, as the investigator looked at the neck wound with fresh eyes. Then Rich left the chilly room. He met Jim in the hall outside.

"Find anything?" Jim asked.

Rich grimaced and nodded his head.

"Oh, yeah."

CHAPTER 39

Mount Olympus Funeral Home: Minneapolis, Minnesota

The turnout for Bjorn Nilsson's funeral the following afternoon was even better than Jim had expected. Dennis Heipler had originally planned to have it at his church, but it soon became apparent that a change of venue was needed.

The response to the e-mails that Dennis and Jim had sent out days earlier was overwhelming. A small contingent from Brazil were able to make it. Most of Dennis' congregation came, as did a number of parishioners from nearby churches.

There were a few curiosity seekers in the assembly, too, since Bjorn's murder had received media coverage. But the biggest surprise was the number of pastors and regular people who had flown in on short notice from cities and small towns in a number of different states. In all, the funeral home was packed with hundreds of mourners.

Jim and Rich had arrived early, and took a place in the front row – a position that made Rich more than a little self conscious. Rich turned around in his pew up front, where he had been sitting quietly next to Jim for about twenty minutes. He saw the throng that continued to pour into the already-packed sanctuary, and mumbled a truncated expletive.

"Holy …," he muttered to himself.

"What?" asked Jim.

"Look at all these people. I had no idea that this funeral would draw so many people," Rich whispered excitedly. "You'd think he was a movie star, instead of just a missionary."

"I'm not surprised, really," Jim whispered back, looking around. "I have no doubt that Bjorn was dearer to God than a hundred movie stars."

He paused for a moment, then added, "I can guarantee that he had more positive impact on the world than all movie stars combined, more than the movie industry in general."

Dennis Heipler stood up and introduced Jim, who came up to the lectern to give the invocation.

Immediately after speaking, Jim walked down to join the other five pall bearers at the back of the chapel, and they wheeled in the gleaming enameled metal coffin. Again, everyone stood, and a prayer was offered by Jim when they reached the foot of the podium. That was followed by a sermon from Dennis.

The funeral service ended, and a large number of those who had attended drove or walked the short distance to the cemetery site for the brief graveside internment ceremony. Brief, since it was quite chilly in the late afternoon air.

Man, Rich thought, clutching his coat around himself, *If it doesn't snow, it's passing up a good chance. If he'd died much later in the year, they'd have to wait for the spring thaw to bury him.*

Pursuant to a few words of solace from Pastor Dennis, Bjorn's coffin was lowered slowly into the yawning abyss that had been torn out of the cold earth. The same backhoe that had dug the hole stood by silently in wait to fill in behind the coffin, like an uncaring vulture waiting for it's chance to pick over a carcass.

When it was over, most of the mourners left right away. A few who Dennis and Laura invited over followed them back home in their cars.

***

Rich had insisted on stopping for coffee on the way, so the bulk of the people attending the wake at the Heipler's home were already there when Jim and Rich arrived. After they entered and took off their coats, a twenty-something couple with a young boy came over to greet them.

"Hi, I'm Glen Aarsvold," the man said, extending his hand first to Rich, who shook it, then to Jim. "And this is my wife, Joanie."

She smiled at both of them, then brought her son forward, who had been standing beside his mom. "This is our son, Joseph," she said, patting his shoulder gently. "We live just down the street a ways."

"Hello, young man," Rich said to the boy, who looked to be about seven years old.

"Hello, sir," he replied seriously.

To Jim, the father said, "We really appreciated your remarks this morning about Reverend Nilsson. I can tell by the way you spoke that he was important to you."

"Yes," Jim acknowledged, "he was a special man, that's for sure. I have a lot of wonderful memories of him."

"We met him a couple times while he was staying here at the Heipler's," Joanie added. "He had some great stories to tell about Brazil, and his experiences there. And he played with Joseph, too."

"It's terrible that something like this would happen to a man of his character," Glen remarked. "He had so much to give."

"He should have stayed away from strangers," Joseph declared.

"Joseph!" His mother scolded.

Rich's ears perked up. "What do you mean, Joseph?" he asked. He got down on one knee to face the serious looking dark-haired boy.

"Mom and Dad always tell me to stay away from strangers," Joseph replied. "Pastor Nilsson should have stayed away from the stranger, too."

"What stranger?" Rich asked. "Did you see a stranger that day?"

The boy nodded his head. "Um-hum. That was the day I was home sick. The man parked across the street from our house." He pointed in the general direction of the Aarsvold's home.

"There was a stranger in your neighborhood that day?" Rich asked, nearly drooling at the mouth in excitement. However, he managed to hold himself in check so as not to scare the boy. He tried to remain casual in his tone as he asked questions. "So, do you remember what he looked like?"

A nod.

"And what his car looked like?"

Another nod.

"Joseph," his father asked, "why didn't you tell us this before?"

The boy was quiet for a moment, then answered simply, "You and Mommy never asked me."

Rich stood up and faced the boy's parents. "Can we go to another room where we can talk about this more privately?"

The parents exchanged a skeptical glance, but Jim spoke up. "Rich is a sheriff's deputy out where we live. It sounds like Joseph might have seen something important."

"Okay," Glen Aarsvold said. "We can go back into one of the bedrooms." He motioned toward the back of the house. "I don't think that Dennis and Laura would mind."

He took his son's hand and walked to the master bedroom, and the others followed. He sat Joseph down on the end of the bed, and Rich pulled a small stool out from under the vanity table and sat down, facing the lad.

"So, Joseph," Rich said as he tried to make his large frame comfortable on the petite stool. "Why don't you tell me everything that happened that day - Tuesday morning?"

"Well," the boy began, pressing an index finger against his cheek, "I was bored just laying in bed. So I was playing with my telescope by the window, looking at stuff. Then a car stopped across the street."

Rich, Jim, and both parents watched and listened in rapt attention as the boy slowly continued.

"The man sat in the car for a long time. I watched him through my old telescope."

"The low-power one," his mother chimed in. "He got a new, more powerful telescope for his birthday."

"Could you tell what the car looked like?" Rich asked.

"Ford Taurus, dark red color," Joseph answered, without hesitation. "New, or almost new."

Rich raised an eyebrow and looked at the boy's father.

"He knows his cars," Dad replied to the non-verbal question. "He loves cars."

"Okay," Rich said calmly. "Tell me more."

"Well, he sat real low in his car, like he was taking a nap. Then I saw Mr. and Mrs. Heipler go past in their car. A minute or so after that, the stranger got out and walked down the sidewalk."

"Then what?" Rich eagerly prodded.

Jim, who was standing behind Rich, tapped him on the shoulder. "He's telling you," he said, trying to give a hint. "Let him tell you."

The boy went on, feeding off of Rich's enthusiasm. "I kept watching him through my telescope. He kept looking all around while he walked, then he went up to Mr. and Mrs. Heipler's house." The boy stopped his story. "That's all," he happily announced, shrugging his shoulders.

"Okay, that's real good, Joseph," Rich said. "Did you see the stranger come back to his car?"

"No. I went back to bed after that. When I got up later and looked outside, the stranger's car was gone."

"All right. Let's try to remember what the stranger looked like. Was he white, black, brown ..."

"He was white."

"Okay. Do you remember how tall he was?"

"Not as tall as you," Joseph replied. "Not as tall as my dad, either. Or Pastor DiMario. He wasn't really very tall."

"I'm five foot-eleven," the father offered.

"I've got about half an inch on you," Jim answered.

Joseph looked at his mom. "He was only about as tall as Mom," he said, giggling.

"Okay," Rich concluded, "So he was maybe five foot-six or so, let's say. What about hair color?"

"Black hair."

"Any beard or mustache?"

"Nope."

"Do you remember what he was wearing?" Rich pressed.

".A dark suit, like the pastors wear."

Rich continued writing in his notepad, summarizing the details. "All right, Joseph," he said, looking the boy in the eye. "Do you think you'd recognize this man if you saw him again?"

The boy thought a moment. "Yep," he replied. "You have a picture of him?"

"No," Rich admitted, "but we might a bit later on."

"Today?"

"No, Joseph. Probably not today." Rich looked up at the father. "But I'd like to get your contact information, just in case."

After Rich jotted down the information from Glen Aarsvold, he stood up and stretched. "Thank you very much, young man," he said to Joseph. "You've been a lot of help. I'll let you all go back out and join the others now. We'll be right out."

He shook hands with the father and mother, then the boy. "Thanks again," Rich said, as the family walked out of the bedroom.

"This is great!" Rich exclaimed, after they had closed the door behind them. "We've got an eyewitness, and possibly some DNA. If the police can find a good suspect, he can be positively identified, and they'll get a solid conviction."

"This is exactly why I wanted you to come along," Jim exulted. "All they've got to do now is find the guy."

Rich laughed. "Yeah, easier said than done. But the kid did say it was a late model Taurus. There's a lot of those in the rental fleets."

"True," Jim answered. "But haven't you noticed that there's a lot more American-made cars out here than there are back home?"

"Yeah, I have. But it's still worth checking out. I'll call Ellis later today and see if he's game."

"How about right now?"

Rich looked at Jim's serious face. "Sure. Right now is good," he replied.

They parted company and left the bedroom like football players leaving a huddle. Rich went straight out the door to his rental car, while Jim went to the living room and mingled with the other guests.

CHAPTER 40

The Magus' Residence: North Ranch, Westlake Village, California

Pete LeTourneu guided his car to the base of the long serpentine driveway that ascended to the Magus' secluded hilltop estate. He wondered about the reason for his summons. He had the church matter in hand. He'd just returned victorious from his trip to Minnesota. He was vibrant, more powerful than ever, with the blood of his pathetic victim still fresh on his lips. And he had a trophy for his master.

He'd already decided that he wouldn't mention the fact that the ceremonial dagger was lost on his mission.

It doesn't really matter, he figured. *It doesn't have my prints on it, and we have a couple more just like it, anyway.*

It was a lovely California day, especially for this late in the fall, and the afternoon sky was clear and sunny. The gate at the bottom of the drive opened for him spontaneously, since he had already passed the visual inspection of the security cameras stationed at the gate. He drove to the top, and entered the circular driveway in front of the palatial home. The center of the driveway featured a massive fountain, from which streams of water flowed from the mouths of stone lions. Pete looked forward to the day when he could live in an opulent estate like this. He already had the money - he just couldn't use it. Not yet.

He parked his despised '95 Pontiac Grand Am at the head of the circular drive. How he hated his 'working man's car', but he couldn't afford to be spotted at church or around town in the new Jaguar.

He got out of the car, and nodded at the burly sentry posted near the front door. The stern-faced guard glared at him, then motioned with his chin at the door. Pete smiled, taking pleasure in the knowledge that he could have the arrogant guard killed at a moment's notice, just for looking at him disrespectfully. Pete pressed the doorbell, and heard the electric latch on the door release, allowing him entry.

Upon entering the expansive foyer, he was greeted by the Magus' personal assistant - a beautiful raven-haired young woman dressed smartly in a short black dress and high heels. Pete didn't know her name; wasn't privileged to know. He assumed she'd come up the ranks of the girls working the streets in one of the other territories governed by the Temple, to get to this coveted position.

"The Magus will see you now," she said curtly, without a smile.

She turned and walked toward the rear of the house with Pete in tow. The air was electric with lively talking and activity. For a moment, he imagined that he might have taken a wrong turn and entered the Playboy mansion by mistake. He observed that there were a number of young men and women present in the house as he passed through the various rooms of the estate. Some wore dressy attire, whereas others were wearing exotic lingerie or pajamas. A pair of pretty young women surveyed Pete up and down as he swaggered past, following his guide toward the back of the house. He met their gaze as he continued slowly by. He didn't know who they worked for, but it mattered little. He knew that he could have either of them for the asking, if he wanted to. None of his fellow leaders would refuse him, since he was second in temple rank only to The Magus himself.

They passed through a pair of French doors that opened onto the garden-like setting of the pool area. Now Pete felt as if he'd just walked into Sodom and Gomorrah; he saw several completely nude young women swimming in the pool, walking around, and waiting on the Magus. Pete's master appeared to be evaluating these girls, determining their worthiness to enter a higher level of service to the Temple of Anubis. Pete took in the scene with interest, making a mental note of the few he liked the best, for potential candidates to be a priestess. Since the temple ceremonies often included sex as part of the buildup to summon Anubis and his familiar daemons, it seemed only reasonable to Pete to choose the participants wisely.

Pete stepped forward across the huge expanse of imported flagstone toward the Magus' bar table, as his escort returned to the house. The grounds of the pool area were beautifully manicured, with specimen-sized plants and trees. The huge disappearing-edge swimming pool, lined with boulders along the rim, overlooked a panoramic view of the valley below, and even afforded a glimpse of the Pacific Ocean on the clearest days.

The Magus looked up from the long-haired buxom Hispanic girl who was attending him with drinks and hors d'ourves, and beckoned to Pete. Pete stopped at The Magus' chair, and sank to one knee. He kissed the ring that was proffered on The Magus' outstretched hand, the ring with the inverted cross set in black onyx.

"Well, Pete," The Magus said heartily, "what do you have for me?"

He rubbed his hands together expectantly, then dismissed the nude girl with a short wave of his hand. At that moment, another equally beautiful bare girl arrived with a tray, and set a martini in front of Pete's chair at the table.

"Your drink, sir," she said, and started to turn to leave.

Pete caught her arm, and asked, "What's your name, and who do you work for?"

She smiled and answered, "I'm Jennifer, and I'm working for Angelo over in Sylmar."

"Well, isn't Angelo the lucky one?" He winked and pointed his finger at her. "I'm going to remember you. But how did you know I like a dry martini?"

"It's my job to know," she said slyly. She smiled again, then left them.

Pete smirked, and sat down in a bar chair next to his master. "Just as I promised," he boasted, and reached into his jacket pocket to produce a small plastic container. He presented it to The Magus as if it were a cherished gift from Tiffany's.

The Magus returned the smile and took the box, and popped the lid open. He looked inside and smiled even wider, the corners of his moustache rising. He broke out in a laugh.

"Excellent, my friend," he said, pulling out a blood-sodden Ziplock bag from the dry ice-packed box. He examined the tongue carefully, and nodded in approval. "This will do well for us, my young friend. A worthy sacrifice for our Lord Anubis. He will look favorably on this offering of blood from our enemy."

"Yes," Pete agreed, "plus, we won't have to worry about Nilsson bothering us anymore. This helps our brothers in Brazil as much as it does us."

"Indeed. Well done." The Magus returned the grisly remnant to it's box. "So, everything went smoothly, then?"

"Without a hitch," Pete replied proudly.

"Good. It's about time." The Magus set the box on the table before him, then changed to a more serious tone. "Now we have a more serious issue to discuss," he said.

The arrogant smile faded from LeTourneu's face, as the Magus continued. "I had a nice chat with your Pastor DiMario yesterday."

Pete looked perplexed, but his master continued on. "He called to check on your references. After six months, he calls only now." He leaned forward toward Pete, looking him in the eye. "He's on to you, Pete, or at least suspicious."

LeTourneu frowned. "What did he say to you?"

"Just doing a routine check, he said. But why now, all of a sudden?"

"Did he believe my cover?" Pete probed.

"Yes, I think he did. But I'm not comfortable about him inquiring now. He must know something."

"Since when are we about comfort?" Pete asked. "Our Lord Anubis favors the bold. So does nature, for that matter."

"Indeed," The Magus agreed, "that's why it's time for another bold move."

LeTourneu looked at him expectantly, grinning like a teenager about to pull a stunt at school.

"You've been in place at Solid Rock Church long enough," The Magus declared. "Your girl and that hired actress of yours have been setting the stage, too. It's time for the endgame. And I've got a plan to take DiMario's mind off of you."

"Speak, Magus," Pete prompted. "I am ready."

"You told me at one time that DiMario's daughter was a pretty one."

"Yes. Chelsea is seventeen, long blonde hair down her back. Green eyes - real pretty."

"Nice figure?"

"Yeah, real nice."

The Magus nodded sagely, while Pete waited for the other shoe to drop.

"She would be a perfect addition to our soft-core porn web site," The Magus said at last.

"Hah! There's no way we could get her to do it," Pete protested. "She's a straight arrow. Probably still a virgin."

"I didn't say she'd volunteer for the job," The Magus said with a smile, "but after she's in our control, the right combination of drugs and coercion will get her to drop her clothes and pose for our photographers. Of course, you will promise her that she will be allowed to go free when we have what we want. Afterwards, you'll direct the church's attention to the web site pictures. They will condemn her, and her father will be publicly disgraced. You can paint her as a rebellious teen who ran away from her oppressive and incompetent parents. Your pious church people will flock to the site to see the pictures out of depraved curiosity, even while condemning her and her parents. We'll even get some new business out of it, since they have to pay to log on!"

"Bunch of hypocrites," Pete laughed. "But seriously, it'll be a tough job to get her to cooperate, if she's anything like her dad."

"That's why I'm putting you in charge of it, Pete. You know how to make young girls do what they don't want to do. You've had plenty of experience at it, eh?"

"Yes, but then she'll be able to identify me, and then ...," Pete stopped in mid-sentence as he saw the grin forming on his master's face.

"Not to worry about that, Pete. She won't be going home after we're done with her. Her blood will be just what we need for our celebration of Samhain."

"That's only three days away," Pete observed, stroking his chin.

"That's right. So you better make plans right away." The Magus took a deep drink of his martini, and set the empty glass back down on the table. Across the pool, Pete noticed that one of the buff-bare girls responded immediately, going behind the bar to prepare another martini for the man who held her survival and well-being in his hands.

"The sacrifice you just brought is worthy and pleasing to Anubis," The Magus continued, "But by providing him a live sacrifice of a virginal pastor's daughter - our enemy's daughter at that, our lord will grant our every desire. This is what we've waited for, Pete. I have the *Necronomicon*. I have the ability to summon dark spirits to do my bidding. The vortex of occult power is building up, and will peak in three days. We will call on Lord Anubis to imbue our followers with the same mind and power that we have and enjoy."

"Look around my home," The Magus boasted, waving his arm around. "These people who serve us now do so because we provide satisfaction for their needs, and they have nowhere else to go to get what we give them. But soon, they will be indwelt with a familiar spirit, a daemon like I have. Anubis has been with me for so many years now. He's taken care of me, defeated my enemies, granted me wealth beyond imagination. Our people will soon serve us not for money, but out of loyalty to Anubis, or another familiar daemon who will be with them forever. They won't be mere employees, they will be partners in our mission. And what is that mission, Pete?"

"To obtain great power and wealth, to put our enemies under our feet, and to live as gods," he repeated back automatically.

"Who can stop us?" his master asked rhetorically.

"Nobody can stop us," Pete replied, from rote memory. "Those who try, will die."

CHAPTER 41

Westlake High School: Westlake Village, California

The Friday night football game was a varsity match. The Junior Varsity team had played earlier in the afternoon, but the players were required to attend all Varsity home games. Coach insisted that the younger players watch and support the varsity team, and learn from the "Big Boys".

Garrett had already showered up and dressed, and was dutifully observing and evaluating the plays as he sat with his buddy and teammate, Lance, watching the game from the bleachers. Chelsea was there, too, with some of her friends.

Before half time, the large coke she was drinking had taken it's toll on Chelsea's system.

"Want to go to the restroom with me?" she asked her friend, Katie.

"Sure."

The two got up and slowly made their way down through the maze of students, parents, and other spectators sitting on the backless aluminum bleachers. They headed away from the din and hubris of Panther Stadium toward the school buildings, where they knew at least one of the girl's restrooms would be open. The autumn night was crisp, but not uncomfortably cold as they walked a moonlit path away from the noise and bright lights of the gridiron. The pleasant scent of wood fires burning in home fireplaces wafted through the night air; it was a nice evening to be outside.

The Panthers were ahead by twelve in the second quarter and had possession of the ball, so it was a good time to go. There were only a few other people milling around on the path coming from the school buildings, which were set quite a distance from the sports field.

A portly security guard was standing by the gate that led to the school buildings. He finished off his cigarette and flicked the butt into the bushes as the girls walked past.

When Chelsea and her friend came out of the restroom several minutes later, she noticed that the security guard wasn't there. There were a few guys hanging around, though - older looking guys, dressed in dark clothes. They hadn't been there earlier. For some reason, Chelsea sensed that something in this picture was suddenly askance. Her skin involuntarily raised up in gooseflesh, and she felt a chill. She looked at Katie, who met her gaze with a look of concern in her eyes.

I don't like the look of this, Chelsea thought. *This isn't right.*

The two slowly walked down the dim path, silent now in contrast to the animated chat they had shared only moments earlier. Chelsea turned to her friend and whispered.

"Who are these guys?"

"Don't know," came the muffled reply, "they don't look like they go here."

The three strangers were hanging around on opposite sides of the path that the girls were walking on. One was smoking a cigarette, while the other two were trying to look casual. Chelsea knew that they couldn't be waiting for their dates; the girl's restroom had been vacant except for them.

As Chelsea started to turn to Katie again to whisper, she caught a glimpse out of the corner of her eye of another dark figure silently walking the path behind them, not thirty feet away. The other three were looming ahead and on either side of the path, only fifteen or so feet ahead. A sensation of sudden, utter panic gripped Chelsea's heart, and she knew with every fiber of her being that they were in trouble.

A voice in her head said *RUN.* She parroted the one-word command to Katie, who was already prepared to act.

"Run!"

The two girls immediately broke into a sprint as suddenly as if their feet had been positioned in starting blocks on a track.

On cue, the three dark-dressed men closed in on the path to choke off their escape route. One who was closest to Chelsea reached for her, but she swung her small Roxy purse like a medieval mace. The blow caught him in the face, and he reeled back instantly. The purse wasn't heavy enough to deliver a finishing blow; it only stunned her attacker momentarily. Chelsea didn't break stride, but fled down the path at a dead run.

Katie dodged off the path with the skill of a varsity tight end, and around the ogre blocking her path. He made a grab for her as she blew past, but his meaty paw slipped off. The third man was not easily fooled, though. He caught Chelsea and squeezed her in a hard bear hug. She let out a scream as the air was forced out of her lungs by the powerful arms of her attacker. She couldn't draw in another breath, but the man clapped his hand around her mouth. The fourth man outran Katie after about thirty feet and tackled her, roughly knocking her down in the damp grass. Her breath was knocked out of her - she couldn't catch a breath. The man got up and cruelly snatched her up from the ground.

His face was black, but even through her fear-filled eyes, Katie noticed in the dim light that he didn't have the features of a black man.

"This one!" shouted the attacker holding Chelsea.

One of the other two grabbed Chelsea's arm, while the third quickly put a hypodermic injection gun against her skin and pushed the button.

Chelsea hardly felt the pop of the needle as it delivered it's load under her skin. She struggled to free herself, and managed to bite the finger that oppressed her mouth. Her attacker swore, and she screamed - loudly.

Chelsea heard the roar of the crowd in the distance, and knew that her cry was futile - nobody would hear her.

The man who'd been bitten pulled back his thick arm to strike her, but the other grabbed his accomplice, restraining him.

"No marks, idiot!" he commanded. To the man holding Katie, he said, "Forget that one."

The last thing Katie remembered until several minutes later was the sight of the looming fist, and the taste of her own blood.

The Panthers corner back had just sacked the wide receiver of the cross-town rival Lancers, thereby preventing a first down. The fans in the stands got to their feet in appreciation of the strong defensive play.

Even while the cheers and the shouting rang in his ears, an odd sensation came over Garrett DiMario. The numbers on the scoreboard and the action on the field before him conspired to declare that all was well, but he sensed that something, somewhere was amiss. The feeling grew as the crowd sat down, the moment of glory subsiding.

What could be wrong at a time like this? Garrett wondered.

Yet the nagging sensation continued, and Garrett became as edgy as a dog just before an earthquake. Something, somehow, was wrong in his world, but he had no idea what or why.

His friend Lance looked over and apparently noticed the change in Garrett's countenance.

"What's up, dog?" he asked. "What's the matter with you? You don't look so good."

Garrett shook his head slowly. "Don't know. But somethin's not right."

He had no way of knowing that the cause of his disconcertment was standing immediately to his left. Unseen to everyone at the raucous football game, an angel was present, standing at Garrett's shoulder. Stunningly beautiful in his own dimension of time-space, he wore vestments of white and gold that offset his muscular dark glossy skin - skin that glowed with the depth and richness of burnished bronze. He reached out and gently touched his finger to Garrett's ear.

He who has ears to hear, let him hear.

This angel knew Garrett well; knew him better than even his friends and family did. He had been with Garrett on many occasions throughout his life, including many times when Garrett thought he was all alone. He had protected him from danger time after time - circumstances that many people would attribute to luck.

Tonight, in the bleachers, Garrett was keenly aware of the angel's presence, though he didn't realize what it was. When the angelic being touched his ear, he heard it - his sister's voice calling out for help. There it was, clear as the siren's call in his ear; there was no mistaking it. He looked around him on both sides. Apparently, nobody else heard it, since everyone was engaged in watching the action on the field.

"Did you hear that?" he asked Lance.

"What, dude?"

Garrett got to his feet, unsure of where the voice came from. "Come on," he said.

He headed out of the aisle, edging his way sideways past the knees of the other fans who were seated on the bleachers, then moving nimbly down the steps. Lance watched Garrett go, then got up and followed after him.

Garrett was drawn almost involuntarily down the path that went past the bleachers, then snaked it's way through the grassy area to the school buildings. His pace increased as he headed away from the clamor of the field and into the dim nether region between field and buildings.

"Dude, what's your tizzle?" Lance called out to him, trying to catch up to the rapidly marching Garrett.

"I swear I heard my sister calling me," Garrett called over his shoulder, without breaking stride.

"So what, G? Let her come and find you."

"No - something's wrong, I can feel it."

Just then, Garrett's eyes were able to discern several dark figures about seventy-five yards up ahead. They were moving toward the parking lot. But one of them - the smaller one, wasn't moving naturally. Even in the late evening pall, he was able to see that much.

"Chelsea!" he called out.

Immediately, the figures froze.

"Garrett, hel -"

Chelsea's cry was cut short by a cruel hand clapped across her face. But it was enough to confirm her brother's fears.

Garrett and Lance broke into a run. The figures ahead split up, and Garrett saw three of them moving more quickly toward the parking lot, while the other two were coming directly at them on an intercept course. It didn't take long to cover the distance between them, thanks to his coach's training program. Garrett could do the fifty-yard dash in about six seconds flat, and that's how far it was before he and Lance came face to face with two larger and older men.

Weighing in at only about one-hundred-sixty pounds soaking wet, Garrett knew better than to try tackling the dark hulk that loomed before him. Not slowing a bit from his full sprint speed, Garrett gave his nemesis the straight-arm treatment, just as he dodged off the trail at the last instant. The attacker got a piece of Garrett's sleeve, throwing him off balance enough to make him fall. He rolled up immediately to face the large man, who lunged at him. Without thinking, Garrett kicked a game-winning field goal into the man's solar plexus. The attacker's dark features contorted in pain, and he dropped to his knees.

Lance, meanwhile, plowed low into his opponent's midsection with a very direct approach. Being quite a bit larger than Garrett, the tackle was effective at putting the bigger man abruptly on his back. The attacker rolled up and punched Lance hard in the face. Lance fell back down, having just risen to his feet after the sacking. He took another blow to the side of the head, then another to the ribs before he could defend himself. Then the onslaught stopped as suddenly as it started.

Garrett closed the few feet between himself and Lance's antagonist in a leap. The man's back was to Garrett, which proved fortuitous. Garrett landed like a monkey on his back, wrapping his right arm around the man's throat. He pulled back and squeezed hard. The attacker's hands desperately clawed at Garrett's arm that was hooked like a vise around his neck. Garrett felt the man's legs wobble and quake as he latched on even tighter to Lance's tormentor, burying his knees into the man's ribs. Lance got up and plowed a solid punch into the man's belly, and that was the icing on the cake.

Garrett released his death grip and jumped free just as the big man fell. They turned their attention to the other attacker, who was now trying to get up. A few assorted kicks to the midsection and head were sufficient to change his plans.

The boys let out a guttural victory yell, and slapped a high-five, but their celebration was short-lived. Looking over at the parking lot, the remaining two attackers were shoving Chelsea into the side door of a van that was parked at the curb's edge.

Garrett and Lance set off again at full speed, although they were thoroughly winded. They watched helplessly as one of the men rushed around to the driver's door of the van and got in. Before they could reach the lot, Garrett saw the van pull away from the curb with tires squealing, and speed out of the lot. No license plate.

In a matter of moments, their victory came full circle and was swallowed up in defeat. Garrett's sister was gone. The two stopped at the edge of the parking lot, hands on thighs, gasping for breath. Garrett finally caught his breath, and spoke.

"Let's find out who these guys are, and why they took my sister," he said.

"Yeah, we'll beat it out of them right now," Lance replied, punching his open palm.

They turned around and saw before them an empty field. The two men in black were gone. They rushed back to where the confrontation had taken place only moments before. Nothing.

"Quick, gimme your celly," Garrett panted.

Lance dug into the front pocket of his sagging, loose-fit jeans and found the phone, and gave it to his friend.

Garrett punched in nine-one-one, and put the phone to his ear.

This time, it was Lance that heard the voice cry out first. He jerked his head in the general direction of the source. It was faint and weak sounding, and seemed to be coming from over near the gate by the school buildings.

"Help me!"

CHAPTER 42

Los Angeles International Airport (LAX): Los Angeles, California

Saturday morning at LAX seemed to Jim somewhat less of a madhouse than on a typical weekday. As Jim waited for his suitcase at the luggage carousel, he noticed a number of tanned vacationers coming back from somewhere evidently hot and tropical. Rich noticed them, too. They looked entirely too relaxed in their sandals, shorts, and ostentatious, loosely-buttoned camp shirts.

"Man, I'd rather be coming back from wherever they were," Rich said. "Come to think of it, I'd rather be going there now."

"I'm with you," Jim answered, "this was definitely not a pleasure trip."

"At least Detective Ellis said he'd follow up with the kid, and check the rental car logs," Rich said. "He seems pretty straight up. And he was real interested in the bite mark, and the skin and hair specimen I found on Bj ... uh, the deceased."

"Yeah, that was a good find," Jim agreed.

"I'll call him, too," Rich continued. "Honestly, it probably helps to have some outside pressure from LASD. If Ellis solves this one, he knows it'll be a feather in his cap."

Jim grimaced and shook his head. "So much killing. I'd never have expected it in Minnesota. The Christian influence there is strong."

"Sure, Jim. But Minneapolis is a big city. All big cities have homicides, and every other type of crime you can name. Probably a bunch you can't name, too. Don't you ever watch COPS on TV?"

Rich started singing the theme song, acapella and off-key. "Bad boys, bad boys, watcha' gonna do, watcha' gonna do when they come for you?"

"Okay, okay, spare me the torment," Jim begged. "I get the point."

"My point is, there's evil everywhere," Rich explained. "I'd be standing in the unemployment line if that weren't true. I know that the Christian influence does a lot of good, I'll grant you that. There's a lot of good people like yourself in the church, doing the right things, living right and clean. I respect that."

"It's not just a bunch of people trying to live right, Rich. It's the power of God at work, changing people from the heart outward. The word of God gets into them, takes root, and grows. The result is lives changed for the better. Without God working in us, we'd just be a social club or fraternal organization."

"You mean like the Elks or Rotary Club?"

"Exactly," Jim replied.

Rich was silent for a spell, and Jim could see that he was thinking it through. At length, he spoke again.

"So, how does God change people, then?" Rich asked.

"The first step is acknowledging that you're a sinner, and can't make it on your own. That's a big step that a lot of people can't make. Some people come to Christ only when they're faced with a huge crisis in their life, one that they can't fix or deal with. For them, their self-pride has to be broken before they can trust in God."

Just then, the garment bags that the two were waiting for came along on the carousel. They paused to grab them off the moving mechanism, then they started walking toward the baggage claim exit.

"Yeah, but a person would need to clean up their life before they become a Christian, wouldn't they?" Rich asked.

"No," Jim answered, shaking his head. "God invites everyone to come to Him as they are. Then, if they are serious about turning their life over to His lordship, they'll let God clean them up by doing His work in them. We can't wait until we're good enough, because we would never be good enough to merit God's favor."

Rich said nothing, but walked quietly beside Jim up the ramp that led to the first-floor exit to the street.

As they got to the top of the ramp and turned the corner, they saw a multitude of people; other traveler's friends, family members, lovers, all eagerly waiting on the outside of the roped-off security area for their loved ones to disembark. Among the eager faces, one registered in Jim's vision; a face that he didn't expect to see - Jasmine. She wasn't smiling. Her brow was deeply furrowed, and she looked to Jim as if she were in pain, wringing her hands and her lower jaw trembling slightly.

Jasmine - what in the world is she doing here?, he wondered.

Jasmine caught sight of Jim and locked him in her solemn gaze. She quickly slipped under the barrier rope and lunged at her husband, eliciting a disapproving look from the Asian security guard standing watch.

Jasmine engaged him in a tight hug as if she hadn't seen him in weeks. Although she'd put on a brave front up until this moment, she finally lost it and began to weep uncontrollably. Jim felt her warm tears slide down his cheek, and he held her close as she trembled in his arms.

He was, on one hand, glad to see her, yet shaken by her unexpected appearance and uncharacteristic emotional breakdown. He had a dozen questions to ask her all at once, but he sensed that they would all have to take a back seat to comforting her here and now.

It took a few minutes for Jim to calm Jasmine down enough for her to explain to him that Chelsea had been abducted the previous night, that Garrett and Lance had witnessed it and fought the abductors, that the police had been called and been out to the house, and that there were no leads so far.

"I tried to call you at the Heipler's house," Jasmine said, "But they said that you'd just left for the airport, by way of the police station. I spent last night praying, crying, and calling some friends. Barb came over right away. I couldn't bear to wait for you to drive home from the airport, since you didn't know what happened."

Curious spectators turned their heads to see the hysterical woman babbling at the two concerned-looking men. The three of them walked out to the parking lot while Jasmine told them everything that had happened, including the fact that Chelsea's friend Katie had been beaten, and that a school security guard was found bound and gagged not far from where Garrett and Lance had found Katie.

After they got to the parking lot, Rich promised to find out who was working on the case, and to make sure the right things were being done.

"Let me call George in on this, too," Rich said to them. "If this abduction gets publicity, people will be watching for her. It'll put pressure on the captain to put more resources on it, too. Maybe even the FBI. I can make sure an Amber alert gets issued, too."

"Yes, do it - do everything you can," Jasmine pleaded. "We need all the help we can get."

"I agree," Jim added. "Let's see what George can do for us. Maybe someone out there saw something, or knows someone who did."

To Jasmine, Jim asked, "Where's Garrett now?"

"At home, in case someone calls. We should go home first, before doing anything else."

"Okay, let's go then."

Jasmine and Jim took turns hugging Rich, who was evidently unaccustomed to such treatment. He remained stiff and unresponsive to their show of affection. He drove back by himself, and Jim rode home with Jasmine.

For Jim and Jasmine, the drive home from the airport was interspersed with periods of talking, praying out loud, and silence. It seemed to Jim to take much longer than the typical hour drive. He repeatedly looked at Jasmine's cell phone on the dashboard, willing it to ring. But it didn't.

When they finally arrived home, they found Garrett, Lance, and Katie waiting for them, along with Ron the music pastor, and Blake Aanstad. Barbara met them at the front door.

"Any news?" Jim asked, dispensing with the formal greetings as he followed Barbara to the family room.

"Nothing," Garrett replied. His answer was confirmed by the dejected looks and slack body language of the assembly, all of whom were slumped on the couch and chairs. The TV was on, tuned to a local news station with the volume off. Garrett got up from the couch and hugged his dad, burying his own face in the elder's shoulder.

"We tried, Dad," Garrett said forlornly. "We tried to stop them, but there were four big guys, and we were too late."

"I know you did everything you could, Son," Jim answered. "You too, Lance."

Lance, who sat on the couch hanging his head, continued to avert his eyes as he replied, "Not good enough."

"Hey, look," Jim said, "you guys took action. You went through bigger guys to go after Chelsea. You've got nothing to be ashamed of."

"The police detectives were here," Barbara said. She gestured toward the teenagers. "All three of them gave an eyewitness account, along with the unusual details."

"Like what?" Jim asked.

"Like the fact that they were trying to look black, but they really weren't," Katie answered. To Jim's puzzled expression, she added, "The one who grabbed me … his face was black, but I could tell he had the features of a white man. I remember clawing at his face. When I came to and Garrett and Lance found me, I noticed some black stuff on my hand when I got into the light."

"Probably the kind of stuff we put under our eyes before a game," Garrett theorized. "Or maybe the camouflage makeup that soldiers wear."

After a period of comparing notes and commiseration, Jim decided to go down to the church office.

"I'm coming, too," Jasmine said.

"Me, too," Garrett said, standing up again. "I can't sit around here doing nothing."

"Somebody's got to stay around here in case the kidnappers call," Jim said.

"I'll stay," Barbara volunteered. "You go do what you need to do. I'll call you if anything comes up."

The DiMario's agreed, and headed out the door with Ron and Blake in tow. Katie and Lance stayed behind with Barbara.

Better if I get the news first, if it's bad, Barbara thought, with her face drawn tight. *At least I can break it to them gently.*

CHAPTER 43

Far East Imports: Reseda, California

Chelsea was aware of voices and activity swirling around her in the darkness, but she couldn't move or even make her eyes open. She saw occasional flashes of light behind her closed eyelids, and the jumble of voices was starting to become discernible. One voice even sounded familiar, but she couldn't focus enough to identify it. She didn't know where she was, or why she was in this strange condition. Chelsea lost her tenuous grip on the edge of consciousness, and slipped back down into the inky black depths.

Chelsea felt someone shaking her gently, and speaking her name.

"Chelsea, wake up honey," the voice said.

With considerable effort, Chelsea managed to pry open her eyelids. Her dilated pupils were immediately assaulted by bright light. She closed her eyelids down so tight that they were mere slits, barely enough to see through.

"Wakey, wakey," the voice said. "Can you sit up?"

Chelsea looked up, and saw that the voice was coming from a girl about her own age, with auburn hair and a pretty face. Another girl was beside her, blonde and equally pretty. They both wore heavy makeup on their young faces. They smiled at Chelsea, but their smiles seemed strangely cut off at the eyes; there was no sparkle of life in their seemingly cold eyes. She felt hands on her arms gently lifting her up, until she was in a sitting position. Suddenly dizzy, she reeled as if she were sitting at the rim of the Grand Canyon, looking down. She felt herself toppling over the edge.

"Whoa, easy, girl," the blonde said. "Are you okay? You must have had way too much to drink."

Chelsea looked around at the two girls and blinked her squinting eyes. Her head was throbbing now, and she felt strangely numb. She was sitting on the end of a bed in what appeared to be a large studio apartment. "Where am I?" she asked.

"Hey, that's a classic line," laughed the redhead. "You're at our apartment, don't you remember? We took you home after the party where we met you." The two girls looked at each other, and smiled.

"I suppose you're gonna tell us now you don't remember our names, either," the blonde said.

"I don't," Chelsea admitted.

"I told you she was way gone," the blonde said to her friend. To Chelsea, she said, "I'm Aimee, and this is Rachel."

Chelsea's head was pounding, her stomach was queasy, and her throat felt like sandpaper. She hadn't felt this bad since she'd had a particularly harsh case of the flu last winter.

"Want something to drink?" asked Aimee, the blonde.

"Yeah. Some water, please."

Rachel returned in a moment with a glass of water and gave it to Chelsea, who greedily gulped it down. Surprisingly, she started to feel a little better right away, but she was still fatigued and logy.

The two girls went over to the kitchen area and talked in whispers, while Chelsea finished the large glass of water. She raised her head, and noticed the two girls talking furtively, frequently looking over at her. It seemed to Chelsea that she was being examined like a bug under a magnifying glass.

She wracked her tender brain about how she could have got here to this strange place. *The last thing I can remember was being at the football game – then, nothing. I wonder where Katie is? She was with me at the football game. Why isn't she here now?*

Her headache subsided, and she started feeling a warm sensation inside. She got up from the bed and staggered on wobbly legs over to where Aimee and Rachel were, using the wall to bear her up along the way. She felt strangely woozy, but otherwise all right.

"Good, at least you're up," Aimee said.

"I don't feel so good," Chelsea said. She held her own forehead, as if by doing so she could steady herself.

"No duh!" Rachel said. "You don't look so good, either - no offense."

She brushed Chelsea's tangled long blonde tresses back from her face. Chelsea experienced a momentary revulsion at the girl's touch that was out of character for her.

"I think I'll take a shower and get cleaned up," Rachel added. She smiled at Chelsea, then walked over to the adjacent doorway, and disappeared.

"How about a snack?" Aimee suggested.

She went to the refrigerator took out a plate of smoked salmon. Then she got some crackers out of a cabinet. Chelsea noticed that there was nothing else in the refrigerator or cabinet.

"Mmm - I love this stuff," Aimee said, taking a mouthful.

"Aimee, what time is it? How long have I been here?" Chelsea asked.

"It's late, but hey, we're always up late anyway. You're welcome to stay."

Rachel soon appeared again at the doorway, this time completely bare. She toweled off her long auburn hair, then wrapped the towel around her hair like a turban. Besides a smile, it was the only thing she was wearing.

Chelsea was startled. She didn't know anybody who walked around in the nude, outside of the locker room.

"Ah, it feels good to get cleaned up," Rachel said. "You look like you could use some hot water yourself, Chelsea. It would do you good, I bet."

"Me, too," Aimee said.

She unzipped her skirt and let it drop, then took her tailored shirt off. Next, she undid her bra and removed it.

"I'm next," Aimee said. "Then the shower is all yours."

Chelsea replied, "Um ... I think I'll just sit here for awhile, and then I'll go home. Where exactly are we?"

"Reseda," Aimee replied.

"But how did I get here?"

"Like I said, we brought you home from the party. You were totally out of it. We did you a favor, believe me. There were some guys there who would have taken advantage of you. I don't know how you got to the party, or who you came with."

"Relax, Chelsea," Rachel added, walking over to the kitchen. "You're among friends. No worries, we'll take care of you."

"Will you take me home?" Chelsea asked.

"Sure. In awhile," Rachel answered. "But for now, just take it easy. You wouldn't want your parents to see you in this condition, anyway."

In spite of the strange physical sensations of relaxation that were coursing through her body, Chelsea was anything but relaxed. Her senses were on high alert, even dulled as they were.

These girls seemed nice enough, Chelsea figured, but there was something terribly wrong with this situation. Chelsea didn't drink or take drugs, and she never blacked out, waking up to find herself in a strange place, hours later. And she didn't feel normal, either. Her body was loose, fluid. Her brain warned her that it was wrong for her to be here, and she was uncomfortable with this place and the girls' precocious behavior.

Behind the two-way mirror on the wall facing Chelsea, the paunchy middle-aged photographer waited patiently in his hidden position in the underground film studio. He'd already been briefed on the situation, and figured it might take awhile to get the video and digital pictures he was looking for. The lighting in the room was set.

It was a familiar scene to him and countless girls who had performed here long before Aimee and Rachel. Occasionally, he had repainted the place, re-decorated and changed things around to make it look different. But in his films and pictures, nobody was really looking at the apartment, anyway. He'd never had to use the two-way mirror before - that was new. A special accommodation for the new star. He eagerly accepted it as a new challenge, a fresh voyeuristic twist on his work.

Yes, it might take awhile, but that was okay. The payoff would be worth it in the end. And according to his boss, failure was not an option. He would have to come up with some good pictures and video, no matter what. Nobody was leaving this underground set until he got what he needed.

***

George Tanaka pulled his car up in front of the nondescript storefront on Sepulveda Blvd. He got out and fed the parking meter, then walked up to the door. Set between a pawn shop on one side and a Christian Science Reading Room on the other, this wasn't an area that invited a lot of foot traffic from furniture shoppers.

A generic-sounding electronic chime rang in his ears as he pushed through the door into a poorly-lit showroom filled with credenzas, beds, and other furnishings featuring a common oriental design. A dank moldy smell filled the room and George's nostrils, seeming to emanate from the myriad of Chinese, Filipino, and Japanese furnishings displayed therein. Other than the furniture and the close environment, he was alone in the showroom.

Pete LeTourneu's eyes jumped immediately to the video monitor when he heard the chime go off. Visitors and potential customers were few in his import showroom, which was exactly the way he liked it. Fewer customers meant fewer disruptions, and fewer meaningless exchanges with people. He kept the lights low for just this reason. The lack of window displays further reduced any incentive for shoppers to come in off the street. Some business was required to maintain the air of legitimacy, of course. Actual furniture sales to real customers made the laundering of illicit drug and prostitution money all the easier.

Pete viewed the man coming through the door with interest. He looked like a well-to-do gentleman, judging by his apparel. He wore beige dress pants and a black knit shirt. A heavy gold chain adorned his neck, and he wore a fine watch on his left wrist. No wedding ring. Probably divorced, or maybe gay. He looked vaguely familiar – a minor ex-celebrity perhaps. There were plenty of them about in the greater L.A. area, after all, living on the modest remains of their once-significant fortunes. Pete broke his gaze from the array of monitors, all of which showed a different view of his guest. He got up from his chair and went out to meet him.

"Good afternoon, how can I help you today?" the short, well-dressed man said to George as he approached from the rear of the store.

"Just looking to see what you have in oriental bedroom furnishings," George replied.

"Well, take a look around," Pete LeTourneu said. "As you can see, we have quite a selection." He looked George up and down. "Anything in particular you're interested in?" he asked.

"A bedroom set. Something in black lacquer; from the Philippines, maybe."

"We have a couple sets over there," Pete said, gesturing toward the far wall.

George strolled over to look. "Hmm – not exactly what I had in mind. Do you carry anything else besides furniture?" he asked, "Like decor items or artworks?"

"No," LeTourneu replied, "just furniture. We're wholesalers, primarily. I sell some pieces to customers who walk in, like yourself. But mostly, we sell to interior designers and such."

"I see," George replied blandly, as he continued to survey the furnishings. He surreptitiously scanned the room for large plastic boxes, or anything else suspicious.

Hmm … furniture's a bit dusty, he thought. *He's not trying very hard to sell.*

He gradually worked his way closer to the door that Pete had come out of.

"Got anything else in the back?" he asked.

Not waiting for an answer, he went for the door, but Pete immediately jumped forward and put his hand on the doorknob an instant before George.

"Just my office back there - no furniture," he said. "What you see is everything I've got right now."

George nodded. "Okay, well, nothing really takes my fancy here," he said, "maybe I'll check back another time."

"All right. Thanks for stopping in today."

George slowly made his way toward the door, continuing his feigned browsing act.

"All right, then," he called to Pete, who was still standing by the door to his office.

Pete waved. "Bye, now. Thanks for coming in."

George walked out, and let the chiming door swing shut behind him. He casually walked out to his car and got in.

That guy's got to be the worst salesman in the world, or else he wanted to get rid of me, he thought. *He sure didn't want me to look behind that door.*

Pete LeTourneu watched through the dark-tinted glass of the shop front as the visitor got into his car. It had taken him a few minutes to figure out who the familiar-looking man was.

How in the world did he find me? he wondered. *What's his game? He's probably just fishing, but now he knows about the store, and he knows what I look like.*

The pang of fear that initially accompanied his realization was soon replaced with excitement, anticipation.

The Magus is right. It is coming to a head. Endgame.

LeTourneu stood rooted in the same spot for a long time, mulling over the enticing possibilities for the newsman's demise. It would have to be fun. It would have to be bloody. And it would have to be soon.

CHAPTER 44

West Hollywood, California

R ich left the East Valley Sheriff's Station after talking with the detective who was assigned to the Chelsea DiMario abduction case. They got the Amber Alert issued.

A bit late, but still worth doing, Rich figured.

He was able to use his pull to get two more investigators on the case. He also called the FBI and spoke to a field agent he'd met once, who said he would ask his superiors if he could get involved.

Convinced that the department was doing everything it could to find Chelsea, Rich headed home for a quick shower and change of clothes. It was Saturday evening, and he still had a date.

***

Rich pulled up in front of Angela Shepherd's apartment building, and turned the engine off. It was an upscale, nicely landscaped complex with underground parking located in the heart of this hotbed of homosexuality called West Hollywood. Although his heart was heavy with recent events, he had been looking forward to this date, and not entirely for information reasons only. Rich hadn't dated anyone since his breakup with Rhonda, the San Bernardino Sheriff's dispatcher, and he still missed her terribly.

Rich found Angela's building within the complex, and walked up the stairs to her apartment. When she opened the door to his knock, he was not disappointed.

Angela stood in the doorway, looking even more stunning than when he'd seen her the first time. Her angelic form was ringed by the soft light emanating from her apartment, which enhanced the overall ethereal effect. Her long brown hair was smooth and shiny, looking as if she had just stepped out of a shampoo commercial. Her makeup was impeccably applied to her beautiful face, which in fact needed no artificial enhancement. Angela's womanly body was artfully wrapped in a low-cut short black dress that clung tightly to her perfect curves.

Rich was awestruck as he feasted his widening eyes upon her. He sucked in a short breath before greeting her with a returned smile.

"Hi, Rich. You're right on time," she said. "Good thing - I don't like being made to wait."

"Wow," Rich uttered, "you look … incredible!"

Angela smiled all the more. "Thank you," she said sweetly, while putting in her second earring. "You clean up pretty good yourself, for a cop."

She stepped forward and gave him a peck on the cheek. The smell of her cologne and the warm touch of her lips on his cheek was intoxicating to him.

"Let's go, I'm starving," she said. "I didn't eat all day, since I know the place you're taking me to is good."

Rich followed her, dumbstruck, down the walkway and then down the stairs, which she carefully negotiated on impossibly high stiletto heels. Rich would have followed her anywhere at that point - off a cliff, through a minefield - it didn't matter. He was enthralled by the gorgeous creature in front of him.

In the time it took to drive to the Il Fornaio restaurant and get a table, Rich learned that Angela Shepherd was just as taken with herself as he was with her. She spoke incessantly of her past modeling career (she was now "over the hill" at age twenty-six), the TV commercials she had been in, and the music video she strutted her stuff in, with the rapper who always wore the Band-Aid on his cheek.

Heads turned all around the restaurant as Angela sashayed to their assigned table, with Rich bringing up the rear. She finished off her first glass of merlot before her chicken divan arrived, and Rich was more than happy to order her another. Angela was more than happy to continue talking about herself, with only the slightest prompts from Rich. She continued throughout dinner, pausing long enough to chew small bites of her dinner.

After they finished and the plates were cleared away, Rich ordered them each a tiramisu for dessert, and cappuccinos.

"Have you done any more serious roles, or just the commercials and music video?" Rich asked.

"Oh, sure," Angela replied, between nibbles of the sweet dessert, "I had the lead role in *Grease* when I was in high school. And I had a significant speaking part in *The Wizard of Oz* in junior college. I went to Moorpark College in Ventura County."

She took a sip of cappuccino. "And I have another role going right now, but I can't discuss it."

Another sip.

Rich saw the opening present itself, and he went for it. "You know, Angela," he said, sliding forward on his chair and putting his elbows solidly on the table, "that's exactly the role I want to talk to you about."

Angela pulled back from her cappuccino, her top lip painted with foam. The rest of her face was painted with curiosity.

"You see," Rich continued, "you're causing a lot of trouble for a lot of good people. Especially Pastor James DiMario and his family."

Angela's eyes suddenly grew wide, and the look of smug curiosity turned to a mask of fear. Rich saw the color drain out of her flawless face.

"What … I don't know what you're talking about," she said casually.

"Sure you do. We both know what you're doing - there's no point in denying it. What I want to know is why, and who's paying you to do it."

"Look, this is … I don't want to talk about this. I think I'm going to leave." She started to get up from her chair.

Rich grabbed her wrist and held it. "Sit down," he commanded in his best authoritative tone.

Several people sitting at nearby tables in the classy restaurant looked over. Reluctantly, Angela did as she was told.

Rich lowered his voice. "I don't think it would look good to your probation officer if he found out you were involved in a scam to slander a public figure."

To her surprised expression, Rich added, "Yes, I know about that cocaine arrest, and that you pled out to a possession charge. The wrong kind of news would violate your parole."

"But I haven't committed any crime," Angela whispered in protest.

"Are you sure about that? You filed a false report with the church board of elders, you acted to cause harm to other individuals. I think that qualifies for a mayhem charge, or conspiracy. Not to mention potential lawsuits for libel."

Rich looked at her. Her confident beauty and poise was slipping away fast, and she was starting to tremble.

My God, she thought. *I hope he doesn't know it was me at the hospital. No, he would have said something by now. Gotta just keep cool.*

"You didn't spend much time in the Twin Towers central jail downtown - you got off with a light sentence for ratting out your smuggling boss," Rich continued, pushing the needle in deeper. "If you go back in, it'll be for a long time."

Angela was visibly shaken, and started to whimper. "I can't go back there," she pleaded, "I just can't. You don't know what it's like." Tears started to fill her baby blue eyes.

"Then you're going to have to come clean with everything. I want to know who hired you, and why, and what your plan is," Rich demanded, stabbing the table with his finger as he spoke.

"You don't understand," she sobbed, "you just don't cross a guy like this. I think he's Mafia." She dabbed her eyes with the edge of her cloth napkin. "I ... I don't know what he would do to me if he found out I told you anything about it."

"He won't find out, Angela. At least not until it's too late for him to do anything."

Angela decided to change her tactics, since the tears weren't working. "Look," she said with a forced smile, "why don't we go back to my place? You can sleep with me tonight, and we'll just forget about all of this, okay? You'd like that, wouldn't you, Rich?"

She fixed him with a look so disarming, so seductive, that he allowed his mind to consider the possibility for a moment - only a moment.

"I've got a better idea, Angela. You tell me everything I want to know, and we can both walk away on friendly terms. I'll forget about calling your probation officer, and you can go back to life as usual."

Angela still looked hesitant, and didn't answer.

"So," Rich said, "did you have many friends in jail? I bet there are a lot of nice women in there who would love to take a pretty thing like you under their wing."

Angela shuddered at the thought. She raised her palm up as if she could somehow physically hold back the reality of Rich's implied threat. Then she finally answered.

"Okay, okay," she said. She sat forward in her chair and spoke to Rich in a voice that was just above a whisper. "The guy who hired me for this job - his name is Pete. I don't know his last name, I swear it."

"All right," Rich prompted, "what exactly did he tell you to do?"

"Well," she said, "it really is an acting part. I'm playing the role of one of Pastor DiMario's parishioners. My instructions were to get him in a compromised position. I figured it would be easy. But it didn't work out like I planned. I threw myself at him, but he wouldn't go for it."

"Much to his credit," Rich observed.

"A thousand other guys would have."

"No doubt. So what happened then?"

"When I came out of his office, I made it look like I was fixing myself up, like we'd just gotten out of a clinch. I made sure everyone in the office saw it."

"I'm sure you made a fine spectacle," Rich said, his voice dripping sarcasm. "Then what?"

"I dropped some clues at the women's bible study - those women ate it up like candy." She chuckled to herself. "Then I went to the church board president with my complaint that Pastor DiMario had taken advantage of me."

"And who at the church did you approach first?" Rich inquired, taking a bite of his tiramisu.

"That was the easy part," Angela smiled. Her smirk was like that of one gossip telling juicy details to another. "The guy who hired me - Pete. He's the associate pastor."

Rich dropped his fork, and it clanged against the fine china plate. A few people looked over.

"What?" he demanded.

"That's right," Angela answered. "But I know that he's more than just an associate pastor. He's involved in other stuff, too - illegal stuff. I don't know any details about that, but like I said, I think he's Mafia."

Rich tried to digest this incredible revelation, which sat on his stomach heavier than the Italian dinner he'd just finished. If what Angela was telling him was true, he figured, then probably neither Jim nor Angela were safe.

How dangerous is this guy? he wondered. *How did he get on the church staff? Why would he want to? He might be smearing his boss in order to take over his position, but why? There couldn't be that much of a financial incentive.*

"All right," Rich said, trying to remain calm, "how did you meet this guy Pete, and how did he offer you the job?"

Angela took a deep breath and slowly let it out. "Well," she began, "he saw my composite and liked my pictures, then he got my home phone number somehow. It's unlisted, and he didn't go through my agent; he called me directly. I guess that should have been a warning."

"What's a composite?"

"It's a page-sized sheet that has some pictures of me, along with my name, measurements, and agency representation. It's like a calling card for models and actors, so casting directors can see what you look like."

"Okay," Rich said, "go on."

"Anyway," Angela continued, "at first I though he was a crank when he called me, or just trying to get ... well, you know."

Rich nodded.

"But then, after talking to him for awhile, he seemed legit. So I agreed to meet him - in a public place, of course."

"Of course," Rich echoed.

Angela smiled at the memory. "He was real interested in my career," she recounted. "He offered me a new challenge that he said would stretch and grow my acting abilities to the maximum. He called it 'Industrial Improvisation'. Sounded good at the time." She let out a dreamy sigh.

Rich motioned with his hand for her to continue. It seemed to him that she was starting to actually enjoy herself a little, seeing as how she was talking about herself again.

"Pete explained the project to me; he had it all planned out. He made Pastor DiMario out to be a greedy, corrupt religious leader who needed to be brought down. By the time Pete was done telling me the details, I felt like it would be a public service for me to do it."

"I hope you realize by now that it's a lie," Rich interjected.

"Yeah," Angela acknowledged, "I kinda figured that out." To Rich's condemning look, she added, "Hey, by then it was too late to stop. I couldn't turn on Pete. It could be ... dangerous."

"Yeah, plus the money."

"Well, yeah. He's been paying me a thousand bucks a week - cash. That's really helped to get me through this dry period, when I'm between legitimate acting jobs."

"Of course," Rich rationalized. "A girl's got expenses."

"For sure," Angela answered back, unaware that she was being mocked. "New Mustang GT's don't grow on trees, you know. I've got bills to pay." Then she added, "But, see, that's how I figure he's Mafia, or some kind of crime baron. Who can throw around that kind of money?"

"Yeah," Rich agreed, "not an associate pastor."

They both sat quietly for awhile. Angela broke the ice after a few minutes.

"So what am I supposed to do now?"

"Keep attending the church for now," Rich replied. "But keep your head down and your mouth shut about Pastor Jim - no more lies, understand?"

Angela nodded.

"You can keep collecting your paycheck - for now," Rich said. "We don't want to let on that anything has changed. I'll figure out what to do next."

Angela smiled.

"But I'll be watching you like a hawk," he added.

"Most men do," she retorted, "in case you didn't notice."

"I have noticed," Rich admitted. "Just make sure you don't tell anyone we had this conversation. I'll make sure the D.A. knows you helped with this investigation. I'm sure you'll get immunity from prosecution."

Angela looked a little nervous again. "All this over smearing the pastor?" she asked.

"I think there's a lot more to it than that. Your role in this is only part of his plan, I'm sure. I still have to figure out the rest."

"Well, good luck," Angela said coldly. She stood up. "Thanks for dinner, Rich. You've been a barrel of laughs."

She turned on her heel and headed toward the door. She stopped after a few steps and turned back to Rich.

"Aren't you at least going to give me cab fare?" she asked, with a pout.

CHAPTER 45

Westlake Village, California

R ich headed home from the restaurant after paying the bill and Angela Shepherd's cab fare.

That was money well spent, he figured. *Sixty bucks for dinner, and another twenty to avoid driving her home. Wait 'till Jim finds out about this - he's gonna flip.*

He was just reaching for his cell phone when it rang and gave him a start.

"Harrison here," he said into the tiny flip phone.

"Hey Rich, this is Jeff MacKinnon in Forensics."

"Yeah, Jeff. Whassup?"

"That fingerprint you left with me a week or so ago; I finally got around to working on it."

"So soon?" Rich asked sarcastically.

"Hey, you said it was an off the record deal, right."

"Yeah, yeah. So what did you find out?"

"It belongs to a runaway from Akron, Ohio ... name is ... Kristi Hawkins. Reported missing about a year and a half ago."

"No kidding? You got a description, or maybe a photo?"

"I've got both. Where do you want them sent?"

Rich gave his home FAX number to Jeff, then thought better of it. He had Jeff FAX the information directly to Jim's house, to save him the trip home. After thanking Jeff for his help, he hung up and got on the Northbound 101 freeway entrance. He keyed in Jim's cell phone number and held the phone up to the side of his head.

"Jim, this is Rich," he said into the phone. "Where are you?"

"Back at home," came the reply. "Why?"

"Sit tight. I'm coming over. And you won't believe what I've got to tell you."

"If it's not good news about Chelsea, I'm not all that interested," Jim said.

"It's not about Chelsea, but you'll be interested anyway - I guarantee it. Take a look at your FAX machine while I'm on the way. I'll explain when I get there."

Rich clicked off, and maintained a steady speed of eighty-five as he guided his black Mitsubishi Eclipse GT up the Ventura freeway.

***

It was getting late when Rich arrived at the DiMario's, but everyone was still up. Jim met him at the door and showed him into the kitchen, where Garrett and Jasmine were standing around eating snacks and watching the news on the small TV that was mounted under one of the kitchen cabinets.

Rich noticed that they all looked drained, yet on edge. Jasmine's eyes were red and puffy, as if she'd been crying. There weren't any dinner dishes or lingering aromas in the kitchen.

Rich sat down in the family room. The DiMario's took his cue and joined him.

"So, Rich," Jim said as he sat down beside him, "what do you know?"

"I just finished my first date with Angela Shepherd," Rich said, smiling, "I don't expect a second, but it was well worth it."

"We're glad you had a nice time with the bimbo," Jasmine remarked. "Did you get her husband's blessing?"

Rich smiled at her sarcasm. "No husband," he said. "Nothing is as it seems with her."

"I could have told you that much," Jasmine quipped. "I've seen enough of her to know she's playing some kind of game."

"Oh, she is," Rich acknowledged. "More like, she's acting a game."

To the three curious stares pointed at him, he added, "She's a struggling actress," he said, moving his fingers in the quote-unquote sign. "Lives down in West Hollywierd. Been in a few bit parts - commercials, swimsuit calendars, a music video. That kind of thing."

"And?" Jim prompted.

"And - this was her latest role."

All three stared at him, as clueless as a lamb being led to the slaughter.

"Jim - she was hired to set you up," Rich continued.

He sat patiently for a moment, waiting for the lights to come on. Rich knew Jim well enough by now to know that he was intelligent, and he suspected the same was true for his wife and son. Street smart - no. It took awhile for it to sink in. One by one, Rich saw the glimmer of understanding in their eyes.

"Why?" Jim asked incredulously, "Who would hire an actress to do something like that?"

"Somebody who wants your job, for starters," Rich replied.

"Who? You ... you know who hired her?" Jim asked. His brow furrowed deeply. The DiMarios all leaned forward in their seats expectantly, their eyes fastened upon Rich.

"I'm glad you're all sitting down," Rich answered. He paused long enough to feel the tension in the room build. "It's Pete, your associate pastor."

Jasmine threw up her hands and let them drop in her lap. She fell back in her seat as if she'd been kicked in the chest by a mule. "I knew it!" she exclaimed.

Garrett's fists balled up involuntarily. "I never trusted that guy," he growled. "Can't trust a pastor who has less bible knowledge than the average kid."

Jim nodded his head slowly in grave acknowledgment. "I've had concerns about Pete, but this goes way beyond what I suspected." He slapped his open hands on his knees and shook his head. "And to think his former pastor gave him a good reference." He shook his head again, and jarred loose a memory.

"Hey," he said, wagging his index finger in the air, "Beverly said that she couldn't find a listing for that church in the directory."

"What's the name and number?" Rich asked.

"I don't remember, but I've got that info in my desk," Jim replied.

"I'm gonna kill him!" Garrett declared.

"Me first," said Jasmine.

Jim looked at his wife and son.

"Well, he deserves it," Garrett added.

"Garrett," Rich said, changing the subject. "Did you look at the FAX I sent over awhile ago?"

"What FAX?"

Rich looked at Jim. "Don't you people talk to each other?" he asked.

To Garrett, he added, "The prints I took off your locker; they belong to a runaway from Ohio, of all things. I wanted to see if you recognize her."

Jasmine got up. "I'll go check the machine upstairs," she said. "We've all be down here for hours, watching the news."

They watched her go with anticipation. Jim sighed and shook his head yet again.

"I just can't believe that Pete LeTourneu hired an actress to smear my reputation, he said. "Not that I trust him, because I don't - not anymore. This is like something out of a movie."

"I'd like to know where he's getting the money to pay her with," Rich said. "A thou a week isn't chump change."

"A ... thousand dollars? ... a week?" Jim stammered.

"He's gotta be selling dope or something," Garrett said. "Nobody's got that kind of money to throw down."

"Selling dope," Rich echoed, thinking out loud. "Like thai sticks, for example?"

Jim and Garrett both locked their eyes on Rich, then each other as they put the implication together.

They were silent for a moment, then Garrett said, "Do you think?"

"Maybe," Rich replied.

"Well," Jim said, "He couldn't be skimming from the church offering. That's taken care of by two lay staff people who count it together - Pete doesn't have access to it."

"How about the church bank accounts?" Rich asked.

"No. I have our financial controller audit the records twice a year."

"Didn't you say before that LeTourneu had only been with your church for about half a year?"

Presently, Jasmine bounded down the stairs with the papers from the FAX machine. She gave them to Rich, who immediately turned them over to Garrett. He looked at the grainy photo and squinted.

"Well, she does look familiar, but ... whoa - no way! I can't believe it's her," Garrett exclaimed, a light bulb going on in his head. Without lifting his eyes from the photo, he added, "She looks kind of different now, but it's her - Kristi, from my social studies class."

"You're sure?" Rich prompted.

"Yeah," Garrett replied. He finally raised his eyes and looked at Rich. "But how could this be her? She's been in my class for a couple months now, since the start of the school year."

"So she goes by her real name? Kristi Hawkins?" Rich probed.

"No. Not Hawkins. It's Kristi …" Garrett squinted and grimaced as he thought. "Sims. That's her name - Kristi Sims." After a beat, he added, "You think she planted that dope in my locker?"

"Does she have any legitimate business in your locker?" Rich asked.

"No way. I don't even know her, really. I haven't given my combination out to anyone, including her."

"So we've got two good questions here," Rich summarized. "What's a runaway doing attending school a few thousand miles away from home? And why would she plant marijuana in your locker?"

"How did she get enrolled in school here in the first place?" Jasmine added. "She would need documentation - proof of residence. Probably a transcript from her old school. Believe me, you don't get into the Westlake Village Unified School District just by showing up on the first day of school."

"Another good question," Rich replied. "Runaways don't have access to that kind of fake documentation - unless …"

"Unless she's working for a crime organization, like the mafia," Jim said, finishing the thought. "But those kind of people aren't real big supporters of education, are they?"

For several moments, nobody spoke. All minds were running at full throttle, trying to process the different possibilities and scenarios.

"I think we should ask her," Rich said, snapping his fingers. To Garrett, he asked, "Do you know where she lives, or where she hangs out?"

"No, I have no clue where she lives, but she must have some kind of home. She's got lots of clothes and she always looks fly – good, I mean. I saw her after school one day, and she said her father brought her to pick up one of her books from her locker so she could do her homework. That was the day before the cops came for me, and took me to the police station."

Garrett thought some more, and added, "I've seen her at the Whataburger on Thousand Oaks Boulevard a couple times."

Rich nodded. "Cool - I know a parolee who works there. I bet he'd be willing to cooperate just to keep his nose clean."

Jim had been fidgeting during the whole conversation, and was now out of patience.

"Look," he said, "This is interesting news, but it's not going to help get my daughter back. That's the focus right now - nothing else matters. The detective dropped the marijuana charge against Garrett, anyway."

"But look at this pattern of events, Jim," Rich reasoned. "Adverse events, all of which have no natural cause or explanation, and are directed at your family. We've got to consider the possibility that they're related somehow."

Jasmine, who had been standing all this time after coming downstairs, finally sat down next to her husband. Rich stood up and started pacing back and forth, thinking.

"We know now that one of your 'adverse events' is caused by Pete LeTourneu, with his hired bimbo," Jasmine said. "You were obviously dead wrong about him, Jim. An allegation of drug dealing against our son would smear your reputation almost as much as an allegation of sexual misconduct."

She turned to Rich. "Or, as we say in the ministry, a 'moral failure'".

She looked at Jim again. "And according to what Rich has just shown us, this runaway has been in Garrett's locker - she had to be the one who planted the drugs. So who put her up to that, I wonder?"

"We need to find her," Garrett said. "If she wasn't a girl, I'd slap her around 'till she gave a full confession."

"You won't need to," Rich said, pacing slowly back and forth on the carpeted family room floor. "I can bring her in for questioning. Then we'll turn her over to her parents in Ohio."

Jim sat with his elbows on his knees, visibly wrestling with the big question.

"But why would Pete do it?" he said, emphasizing the 'why'. "He's worked in the office, he sees what I do everyday. How could he possibly covet my job enough to do this? It doesn't make any sense."

"Maybe he wants more than your job," Jasmine speculated. "Maybe his goal is to ruin the church."

After a long pause, Rich spoke again.

"Who is this Pete LeTourneu, anyway? Where does he really come from? What is he about? What motivates him?" He looked around at the troubled faces on the couch. "I don't know, either, but I can promise you one thing – I'm gonna find out."

CHAPTER 46

Regal Cutlery Shop: Van Nuys, California

George was hopeful as he walked up to the large knife and cutlery shop on Van Nuys Boulevard.

He had e-mailed the picture he got from Rich of the ceramic-bladed knife that was found at the Bjorn Nilsson murder scene to several custom knife makers around the country, but got only a few responses. Thankfully, the closest one sounded promising.

A knife maker in Van Nuys said it looked like one of his.

George entered the specialty shop with a plan in mind. He would simply play himself; a top television news reporter who had the power to give a small business the kind of exposure that no amount of money could buy. He had already called and talked to the proprietor about coming by, and he'd seemed eager for George to come in.

The proprietor of the store looked up as George walked in, and smiled. It was hard for George to tell that the man was smiling, since his haggard face was covered with a bushy black beard, which was seasoned with gray for a salt-and-pepper look. He had a soiled red bandanna wrapped around his hair, which fell in a long braid down his back. The man wore a sleeveless denim shirt, which showed an array of colorful tattoos covering his meaty arms.

George walked up to the man and introduced himself.

Standing up to greet George, the man replied, "I'm Buzzard." He took George's outstretched hand. "Pleased to meet ya."

Buzzard looked around toward the front door and realized that George had come alone. "No camera crew?" he asked. His eyes narrowed into a disappointed look.

"Not today," George answered, "I wanted to check your place out first. We usually only feature businesses that are really unusual or special."

"Well, you come to the right place," Buzzard replied. "I'm both of those things. Let me show you some of my work."

He proceeded to open the showcase, and laid out several custom knives on the velvet mats on top of the case. He picked up each one to show George, all the while lovingly describing it's features and the work that went into it. His enthusiasm was like that of a proud father showing off pictures of his children.

After Buzzard had gone through the details of each knife, he looked George in the eye and said, "And now I'll get what you came to see."

He stepped through a beaded curtain into the back room, and returned a few moments later with a wooden box about twelve inches in length. He also had a handful of pictures, and he set everything down on the counter. He placed both of his hands on the counter and leaned slightly toward George. Even though there was nobody else in the store, he spoke discreetly, as if he was telling a secret.

"There's not many knife makers that would even dare to try ceramic blades. It's a whole nother animal," he said. "There's even less who are good at it. 'Specially with a large blade. You're lookin' at one of 'em."

With a dramatic flair, Buzzard slowly opened the lid of the wooden box and carefully removed the object inside, which was swaddled in a suede pouch. He let the contents slide slowly out of the pouch and onto the black velvet pad on the counter top. George's eyes lit up when he recognized it as an exact duplicate of the knife in the picture Rich had sent him. Buzzard took in the look on George's face, and smiled.

"This job was a challenge," he said. "The customer was real specific about what he wanted. Funny thing was, he wanted three of these daggers made, all identical. I started by making five blades. Lost one in the process of grinding it. I kept the last one for myself."

"Wow," George heard himself say, "that's really something."

He gazed with interest at the remarkable dagger. The double-edged blade was long and slightly tapered - and sharp. The color of the pointed blade reminded him of an elephant's tusk. The tang of the blade was ensconced in a black nylon handle, with a shiny black finger guard separating the two.

"The finger guard's obsidian," Buzzard continued, his voice flushed with pride. "The customer didn't want any metal in the dagger at all. Do you have any idea how hard obsidian is to work with?" he asked George. "It's basically volcanic glass. I swear, the finger guards were as hard to make as the blades."

Buzzard went on describing in detail the type of ceramic that was used for the blade, how it was formed into shape, the firing methods he used to harden it, sharpening of the double-edged blade, and much more information than George cared to know. A lot of the technical detail went in one ear and out the other, until Buzzard hit on one salient peculiarity.

"It's a custom design," he said, "but the customer wanted the shape and size to be based approximately on this dagger here."

He bent down and unlocked a drawer at the base of the display case. When he rose, he had another dagger in hand, which he placed on the velvet pad next to the custom dagger. George noticed immediately that it was very similar in size and shape to the custom dagger, except that it was a single-edge blade, and was shaped accordingly at the tip. Instead of coming to a symmetrical point, the sharp edge came up to form a radius at the blade's point. The blade was steel, and was set in a black handle. But what really got his attention was the emblem on the handle - a swastika embedded in the center of a red and white diamond shape, and the German words *Blut und Ehre!* etched on the blade.

Blood and Honor, George recalled silently, drawing upon his rusty high-school German.

"It's a Hitler Youth dagger," Buzzard said. "Genuine. Very rare these days, although some replicas are floating around. A beautiful piece of work.." He sighed, "I'm not much worried about what people think of me and the way I look," he said. "But I keep this piece out of sight these days. I've had some pretty extreme reactions from customers who have seen it. There was this one Jewish lawyer who came in - hoo, boy - did he ever go off!"

"Yeah, I'll bet," George replied, nodding his head. "But I'm curious about the customer for the ceramic blade dagger," he added, setting the hook. "With the amount of work you put into this knife and the other three, it's got to be expensive."

"It is."

"But three of them? That's a lot of money."

"Yep. He was willing to pay the price. Paid in cash, too."

Yeah, I'm sure he did, George thought. To Buzzard, he said, "Doesn't it seem strange that he would want three of the same custom dagger, though?"

"Yeah. Most people want just one, especially if it's custom. That's the whole point. I figure maybe this guy was giving them for gifts, or something. I'm not complaining, though," he said, giving George a nudge, "I make more profit on the second and third one, anyway."

George decided it was time to reach for the brass ring. "Can you tell me who the customer was, just out of curiosity?" he asked.

Buzzard fixed him with a suspicious look. "Not on your life," he replied.

The look on Buzzard's face told George that this interview was over.

After George left the knife shop, he wasted no time sharing his news with Rich, who was at the sheriff's station. Rich immediately got on the phone to Detective Ellis in Minneapolis.

"This is a good break," Ellis' voice boomed through the phone. "If there are only four knives like this in existence, and the same guy bought three, I shouldn't have a problem getting a subpoena."

"You get it, I'll serve it," Rich promised.

"Sounds good to me. But if you nail the perp first, don't forget the fact that you've got a standing extradition agreement with the Land 'o Lakes."

"You guys got the death penalty up there?" Rich asked.

"Nope. Our former pro-wrestler-turned-governor didn't have the huevos for it."

"Too bad," Rich replied. "Finding the buyer isn't the end of the line, but it's a big step in the right direction."

"Hey, you did good, deputy. You'd make a good detective."

"Tell it to my captain; but do me a favor and wait until this is a done deal. I'm runnin' this down in my spare time, and I'm not supposed to have any spare time, you know?"

"You betcha."

"All right, Ellis. You've got my FAX number," Rich said. "I'll be waitin' to hear from you."

"Okay, real good now," Ellis concluded.

Detective Ellis hung up, and Rich did the same. He looked around the bullpen to see if anyone was watching him. If anyone was, they would have wondered why an irrepressible grin was pasted across his face.

***

A frown was buried under Buzzard's coal pile of a beard, but Rich didn't expect him to be a happy camper.

"All I need is a look at your records for this transaction," Rich said, after presenting the subpoena.

"Okay," Buzzard replied, "got to follow the law - can't nobody fault me for that." He retrieved his black-covered ledger from the back office and paged through it. "I could tell you the name without even looking it up," he said. He turned the book around to face Rich and tapped his finger at the entry.

"But you wouldn't have without the subpoena," Rich countered.

Buzzard shook his head. "Got to protect the integrity of my business. Some of my customers are big on privacy."

Rich looked down at the ledger entry at the tip of Buzzard's finger, and read it silently. *Description: Dagger, ceramic blade, double edge, no metal, 3 each @ $895 each.* His eyes continued over to the customer entry, and his eyes grew wide. *Aldon Brehm.*

Rich glanced quickly over both shoulders as soon as the words fell from his lips in a whisper.

"*The* Aldon Brehm? The candidate for County Supervisor?"

Buzzard nodded. "Yep. The guy's got money, I guess. Paid in cash, too. Seemed like a nice guy."

Rich stood dazed for a moment. "Does he know that you've got an extra dagger?" he asked.

"Nope," Buzzard replied. "Like I told the reporter, these people pay top dollar for custom knives. They don't want to ever see a duplicate in somebody else's hands."

"Right," Rich said. "I need a photocopy of this page, and I want to take a couple pictures of that extra dagger of yours."

"Your the boss," Buzzard said, bending down to unlock the drawer at the bottom of the display case. "Hey, you ain't gonna tell 'im I've got one, are you?"

"Oh, no," Rich said with a smile. "We'll let him find that out in court."

CHAPTER 47

Trey Simmons' Residence: Westlake Village, California

Trey adjusted his sagging jeans after getting up from the couch to answer the door. He let George in, and motioned for him to follow him back to his bedroom.

"So, what's the story?" George asked. "Why couldn't you just tell me over the phone who the number belongs to?"

"Because you probably wouldn't believe me without seeing it for yourself," Trey replied. "And I wanted you to get an understanding of how hard this person was trying to hide his identity."

Trey sat down at the small computer desk in his bedroom. George looked around the room, which seemed smaller than it was because of the clutter. Several articles of dirty clothing were casually discarded here and there, and the bed was unmade.

"This isn't the first time I've traced a phone number," Trey said. "It's usually pretty easy, once you know how to do it. But this one …," he said, patting a small pile of papers on his desk. "This one was a real challenge."

He smiled and let out a laugh. "You have no idea how hard and how deep I had to dig to get here." He picked up a page from the desk and shook it at George for emphasis. George reached out for it, but Trey put it back down; he wasn't ready to drop the bomb just yet.

"The first trace took me to a PBX system at a large company in Michigan. That company's TRUNK line had been set up to route the call to another number, and so on. They have a DID, a Direct Inward Dial phone system, so somebody on the inside had to have set it up to do the transfer - unless the person who set this up was good enough to do it remotely. But that would be tough. Once I realized what I was up against, I called in for reinforcements."

"From who?" George wondered.

"A friend of mine, who will remain nameless. He's a phone phreak."

"A what?"

"A phone phreak. He's basically like a computer hacker, except he's into telephony - telephone systems. Some of what he does is technically illegal."

George looked at him skeptically.

"Okay," Trey admitted, "it's pretty much all illegal. He can basically get into a company's phone system remotely and make toll calls at will, without being detected." He took a deep breath. "I'm glad I'm talking to you about this, instead of Pastor Jim. I know he wouldn't approve of what I did here."

"The end justifies the means," George offered.

"Not according to the bible," Trey retorted. "But, in this case, nobody's getting hurt by what we did. I'm trying to help Pastor Jim."

"I know you are, Trey. We all are. Fact is, it's a good thing we're helping him. Somebody's got to do the heavy lifting."

"I've got his back, whatever it takes," Trey said. "I owe him big time. It's because of him that I found Christ."

"I didn't know he was lost," George joked.

"He isn't - I was. But now I'm found, like the hymn says."

George looked puzzled, so Trey got back on track.

"Anyway, with the help of my friend, we traced the number back to the point of origin. It went through four different servers before we found the final destination address. There's a limit to how many times you can relay the call, because it has to ring once at each location. I bet if Pastor Jim could remember, the phone rang at least four times before somebody answered."

George stared at him with a glazed-over look.

"So," Trey continued, "then I tracked the address that the final destination phone number is assigned to, through DMV records to see who lives there."

"I didn't think that people could access that kind of information from the DMV," George said. As soon as the words passed his lips, he felt foolish for saying it.

"People can't - I can," Trey replied, stating the obvious.

"Okay, Trey. Stop teasing me - what's the bottom line?"

"Bottom line? The destination phone number is connected to an address in the North Ranch area of Westlake Village, only a few miles from here."

"No kidding? That's a high end area."

"Duh! An entry-level home there is way over two mil."

"So, the name is?" George inquired.

"Drum roll, please," Trey said, as he reached back and picked up the page off his desk. He passed it to George with a flourish.

"Aldon Brehm is the owner of that house," Trey said. "I tried to drive by there this morning, but it turns out that it's up at the top of a hill. There's a long driveway from the street, with a gate at the bottom. Security cameras, too. Can't get near the place."

George considered this unexpected news for a moment. "You're sure about this?" he asked.

Trey cocked his head and gave him a look. "Please," he said, "give me some credit here."

Wow, George thought. *Aldon Brehm, the college professor and would-be politician. I was going to interview him a couple weeks ago. Why would somebody like him be pulling a stunt like this? What's could possibly be in it for him?*

"So," Trey said, shattering George's thought pattern, "this is the number that Rich gave you? Where did it come from?"

"It's supposed to be the phone number of Pete LeTourneu's previous church," George replied. "You know this LeTourneu character?"

"Sure. He was brought in as the youth pastor earlier this year, but that didn't last long. I don't think Pastor Jim was happy with the direction the youth group was going, so Pastor Pete got moved into an associate pastor position. I think he's in charge of facilities now."

George nodded.

"That's probably the best place for him," Trey continued. "He wasn't much of a spiritual leader to the youth of the church."

Trey looked around his unkempt room. He got up and walked over to a shelf and picked up a picture.

"This is him," he said pointing to a small man standing in the front of a group of young people.

Several of the teenagers in the picture towered over Pete LeTourneu, George noticed.

George took the picture from Trey and looked it over. Much to his surprise, he recognized the face. It took a moment for him to do the mental match-up, but he soon realized where he'd seen it before - the import furniture store.

"This is Pete LeTourneu, the associate pastor?" he asked, incredulous.

"Yeah, why?"

"It seems he's moonlighting - he's got another job."

"Yeah?" Trey responded. "Well, that's not too big a surprise. I know he only works part time at the church, and he probably doesn't earn all that much."

"That may be, Trey. But I'll tell you what is a surprise; the import business he's working for is a big buyer of the same plastic boxes that we found at that infant burial site in Yermo."

"Shut up!" Trey exclaimed.

"I'm serious. The manufacturing company only makes and sells about three hundred of that particular size and type of box each year. Far East Imports bought about two hundred of them in the past year. That's two-thirds of the total annual sales of that particular box. And there were about one hundred and seventy five children buried at that site in Yermo."

"A hundred and seventy-four, to be exact," Trey corrected. "And you're right, they were children, not fetuses or unviable newborns. Real children, who were born into this world for a purpose, and didn't deserve to be killed. Which reminds me, did you find anything out about the cause of death?"

"Nope. The San Bernardino Sheriff's Department has a news blackout on that. Nobody's talking about it at all. I need to see if Rich can get anything out of his ex-girlfriend on that."

Trey thought for a minute. "I'll bet if we could get the date of manufacture on all those boxes, we could check against the records at the manufacturer, and see if those same boxes were sold to Far East Imports."

"Yeah, that's a good idea," George replied. "The problem is actually getting the manufacturing information from all those boxes."

"You got a box before. Maybe you could check that same source."

"Ah, it's probably no use. I paid a kid for one box, that's all I needed."

"How much?" Trey asked.

"Forty bucks," George said.

Trey laughed. "Dude, if you paid a kid forty bucks for one box, I can guarantee that word got around the 'hood about it. If the coroner's office dumped all the boxes after their investigation, I'll bet some kid's got all of them stashed somewhere. Maybe a group of kids."

George looked skeptical, but Trey added, "Hey, if they were worth something once, then they have value to the people who find them. And we're about to prove it." He gestured at George and asked, "How much cash you got?"

"Not enough to pay forty dollars a box!" George declared. "I can't afford that much evidence."

"Look," Trey said, "for a story like this, I'd think your boss could cough up some dinero. You're a big-honcho reporter - get us some informant money, and we'll go shopping in beautiful downtown San Berdoo."

George thought about it for a moment. "Okay," he agreed. He nodded his head, and stood up. "Let me call Rich first, though. I want to make sure he can get a subpoena for the box manufacturer's records before I go to the trouble of hunting down all the boxes. I don't want a garage full of disgusting coffins, and the general manager on my back."

"Yeah, call Rich. You can tell him about the phone number thing, too. Maybe he can get a search warrant for Aldon Brehm's mansion."

George jerked his head back and laughed. "Sure thing," he said, "Maybe he can find a judge who's ready to retire."

"But I've got a solid trace," Trey said.

"Which you obtained illegally. And it doesn't prove illegal activity on his part, except maybe an FCC violation. We're going to need a lot more than that to get a search warrant."

Trey's disappointment was evident in his frown.

"Hey, this isn't TV, you know," George added. "But *if* we do get more boxes, and *if* they were bought by Far East Imports, we shouldn't have any problem getting a search warrant for their records and premises." He thought about it a minute, and said, "I bet Rich will tell us if there's a jurisdiction issue. Probably the detectives in his precinct will want to jump in and ace him out of the investigation."

"Why?" Trey asked.

"Because he's just a patrol deputy, of course."

"But the goal is to catch the people who killed these children, and put them in prison."

George laughed and said, "You are young, aren't you?"

To Trey's cold stare, George waved his hands in front of him, as if to erase his comment, and added, "Look, I know that our goal is to solve this and get justice for those children. Not to mention finding and exposing this satanic cult, if there even is one."

"There is," Trey interjected. "That's a factoid."

"Okay. But you've got to understand, the detectives in Rich's department and the San Bernardino Sheriff's Department are both going to want to take credit for the bust, when and if it happens. They'll do everything to make sure the little guy doesn't get the credit. Believe me, I know how these people operate."

"How do you know?"

"Because I was one of the little guys once," George explained. "You wouldn't believe how many times my work got scooped by a more senior reporter, or by some anchorman who was busy getting his nails manicured or being fitted for a new suit while I was out busting my hump to get the story. I finally got smart and learned how to hide my investigative work until I was ready to present it to the boss. That's when I finally started to move up in the news business, and that's where our friend Rich is right now."

"You're not saying that Rich is doing this just for his own personal gain, are you?"

"Of course not. But we've got to help him get his due - he's hungry, and a bust like this would really help him out."

"I suppose it would help you out, too," Trey said sarcastically.

"You're right," George admitted. "That's a side benefit to exposing corruption and evil - which I'm pretty good at, by the way." He gestured at Trey's computer. "Just like you're good at what you do."

"Yeah, well, there aren't many job opportunities out there for computer hackers," Trey said.

"But there are opportunities for people with your skills. Just keep going to college and get your degree; otherwise, nobody will give you a chance to show what you can do."

"Yeah, well that's a problem. Can't get a bachelor's degree from the community college, and my mom can barely get by on what she makes, let alone pay for my college tuition."

"Just keep doing what you're doing," George counseled. "Your break will come. Just make sure you recognize it when it does."

"Maybe."

"Meanwhile," George said, rising to his feet, "It's time for me to go beg and plead for informant money."

"What do you think your chances are?" asked Trey.

"Not to worry," said George. He started toward the door, then turned at the doorjamb and faced Trey. "I'm pretty good at begging, too."

CHAPTER 48

Far East Imports: Reseda, California

Garrett and Jim sat in their car at the end of an alleyway that ran behind Sherman Way in Reseda. Jim had decided he needed to find out what Pete LeTourneu was up to, and Garrett wanted to help.

Several stores with cheap imported furniture populated this stretch of Sherman Way. Just a couple blocks down was the Horse Trader's pawn shop, one of the largest and oldest around. Adding to the sordid environment were an assortment of sex shops, massage parlors, dry cleaners, and a never-ending parade of strange characters, the likes of which Garrett had never seen in his protected middle-class bubble.

Then there were the Hispanic gang-member types who haunted the front of a low-income apartment building that was set back from the street. With their bandanna headbands pulled down low, nearly covering their eyes, white T-shirts and sagging pants, chained wallets, and tattoos, they laid down a menacing shadow across the pavement as they walked along with a practiced strut.

Garrett had made a mental note as they drove past that he wouldn't want to run across a group of them in a dark alley - which was exactly where they were right now.

The DiMarios were situated in their parked car so that they could see the back door of Far East Imports about fifty yards down the alley. Pete LeTourneu's Grand Am was nowhere to be seen, but they knew he was in the store, since Garrett had made a call to the store with his cell phone when they arrived, then hug up when LeTourneu answered.

They were playing the waiting game now, hoping that LeTourneu would come out soon.

What had seemed exciting to Garrett at first soon became boring, since there was nothing to do but sit around and think. His mind went back to that night when Chelsea was taken.

If only I'd gotten up a minute earlier, he thought to himself. *Even if I'd run out toward the parking lot quicker, we might not be in this position we're in right now. Maybe I should have grabbed a couple more of my buddies before heading down that dark path.*

He went over and over the events in his mind's eye, thinking of a dozen ways he could have acted differently to prevent his sister from being taken. Monday morning quarterbacking, that's what his coach called it. But these stakes were so much higher than any football game ever was.

Garrett wondered if his dad was thinking about Chelsea, too. He turned and looked at his father. Jim suddenly seemed old and tired to Garrett, and he had never looked that way before. Garrett realized from seeing the years added to Jim's face just how stressed and concerned his dad really was.

Neither of them wanted to talk about the fear that was causing their stomachs to grind twenty-four-seven - the very real possibility that Chelsea wouldn't be coming home - ever.

Garrett's saw motion in his peripheral vision, and looked up to see the back door of Far East Imports open. Garrett poked his dad, who then looked up in time to see Pete LeTourneu emerge from the open door. He was carrying something; two large plastic boxes.

"Oh, my ...," Jim started to say.

He snatched the binoculars from Garrett and whipped them up to his eyes. The magnified image confirmed what Jim already knew - these were the same kind of boxes that had been found at the Yermo burial site.

"Are they ...," Garrett started to ask.

Jim nodded, still looking through the binoculars. He continued to watch as Pete LeTourneu walked up to the rear of a new-looking black Jaguar S-type sedan. The trunk popped open as he fumbled with the transmitter key chain in his hand. LeTourneu put the boxes into the trunk, then slammed the lid shut. His ferret-like eyes surveyed the surrounding area as he walked around the car, then he eased himself into the driver's seat and started the engine.

So engrossed in surveillance was Jim, that he didn't even notice until now the distinct mechanical click of the shutter of Garrett's camera. He had the two-hundred millimeter zoom lens mounted on it, which was his Christmas present from last year.

"He's moving, Dad," Garrett said, "get ready to follow him."

Jim quickly put the binoculars down on his lap and turned the ignition key. His engine sprang to life, even as LeTourneu's Jaguar was backing out of the parking spot about fifty yards away. Garrett and Jim both slunk down in their seats, but Garrett still managed to get a picture of the back of the Jag as it pulled away. When it reached the end of the alleyway, Jim sat up and slowly headed down the alley after him. The Jag made a left turn onto the street, and Jim sped up to avoid losing sight of him.

It was late afternoon by now, and twilight was rapidly approaching. Jim avoided turning on his headlights as long as he dared, trying to be discreet in his shadowing of the Jag.

Garrett gave frequent and unsolicited instructions to his dad on when to hang back, when to accelerate, and so on. Jim stayed behind the Jaguar as far as he could without losing it, in his effort to make sure that LeTourneu wasn't aware of their presence.

Pete LeTourneu led them on a trip across The Valley to Canoga Park - about six miles. They drove westbound along Sherman way, then made a left on Tampa, crossed under the 101 freeway, then a right on Ventura Boulevard.

Here the environment was decidedly more upscale than where they has just been a short time before. Expensive furniture showrooms, an art supply store, and a name brand mattress shop dotted the street, reflecting their bright neon and incandescent lights off of Jim's windshield as they passed.

The DiMario's observed the Jaguar pull into an alleyway behind the seventeen-hundred block of Ventura Boulevard. Jim shut off his headlights as he crept past the entrance to the alley, and pulled over to the curb. Garrett saw LeTourneu's car pull into a parking space about a hundred feet up the alley as they drove past.

Jim and Garrett both quietly hopped out of the car, and squeezed themselves close to a block wall that separated the alley from a residential area behind it. Garrett had his camera with the telephoto lens at the ready, and Jim held the binoculars. Like a pair of secret agents, they simultaneously lifted the optics to their eyes even as they stood sequestered in the deep shadows of dusk next to the wall.

When LeTourneu disembarked from the car, he was talking on his cell phone. He snapped it shut as they watched, then opened the trunk. As if on cue, the rear door of a shop opened, and a female figure appeared, silhouetted in the growing shadows from the light inside the door. She came out and walked up to Pete LeTourneu and embraced him. They held each other for a moment, then LeTourneu retrieved the two boxes from the trunk. He then walked to the back door and went in, followed by the woman.

The deep shadows of evening darkened the alleyway, and it was increasingly difficult to see any detail. But when the woman approached the door, the light of the single incandescent lamp cast a slight illumination across her, long enough for Garrett to snap a picture. Long enough for him to recognize the face, too.

"What the fizz?" he whispered to himself quietly after the woman had closed the door behind her. He leaned over to Jim and spoke quietly into his ear. "Dad, do you know who that is?"

"No - should I?"

"I can't believe it," Garrett continued. "I mean, she looks different with her hair down, and dressed in casual clothes. But it's her, I'm sure of it."

"Who?"

"Mrs. McAllister, my social studies teacher. The one I've told you about."

It took Jim a moment to identify her name with the denial of Chelsea's bible study group, and the adamant evolutionary teaching in Garrett's classroom. He clearly recalled Garrett telling about her utter lack of tolerance for the alternate creationist viewpoint.

"Well, now. Don't they make a lovely couple," Jim said scornfully. "Come on, let's go around front and figure out what store front that door belongs to."

Jim and Garrett went back to the car long enough to drop off the camera and binoculars, figuring that it would be hard to look casual walking down the busy Ventura Boulevard with them. Then they walked out to the street and strolled slowly along, mentally counting off the number of doors to match those they'd seen in the alleyway.

When they got to the sixth shop, they slowed and looked at the door as they sauntered by. *Saint Martha Adoption Agency*, it read. They kept moving past the mirror-tinted window, unsure if anyone inside could see them.

Jim noticed that there was a Starbucks Coffee a few doors down, across the street. They decided to get coffee, then take up a strategic position in the alleyway behind the office to see where their quarry might go when they came out. Jim couldn't wait to see what would happen next. He would soon be sorry when he found out.

CHAPTER 49

Saint Martha's Adoption Agency: Canoga Park, California

The comfortable offices of Saint Martha's Adoption Agency were empty and quiet, except for Roberta McAllister and Pete LeTourneu. They sat together on a leather couch in one of the cozy consultation rooms, which was professionally painted, furnished, and decorated in such a way as to induce young mothers-to-be to relax and feel safe.

He brought her up to date on The Magus' plans for the Samhain black mass. The news was not well-received.

"But I've already got a girl who's ready to give birth any day now," McAllister pouted. "She's already signed the adoption papers, so everything's in place. As usual, she's been told that a Canadian couple is going to adopt her child, and raise it as their own - a lovely, happy family." She put a thick layer of sarcasm on the last part of her statement. "I thought that was why you were bringing the boxes over."

"No, I just want to get them out of my place. I had an unexpected visitor," LeTourneu said. "No problem, though. I just don't want anything sitting around that might arouse suspicion."

"You worry too much, Pete," McAllister said. She reached up and gently smoothed the hair on the side of his head. "As if anyone would connect these plastic boxes with the ones recovered by the cops from Yermo." She took a breath and added, "I'm still mad about that. If I find out who tipped off the police, I'll cut his tongue out and feed it to my Dobermans."

"Why waste it?" Pete countered. "I turned over the tongue of that missionary, Nilsson, to The Magus recently. We already used it for a ceremony. We conjured a Shoggoth to deal with the Simmons kid."

"And you didn't call me to share the fun?" McAllister chided. "You naughty boy."

"The fun was in killing that sheep Nilsson. But not to worry. Soon we'll have something much better to sacrifice - the virgin daughter of our enemy. The Magus has decided that she will be our key to reaching the next level of power when she is sacrificed on the Most Unholy day. That's why we want you to hold off on doing the baby."

Roberta McAllister looked disappointed, but Pete added, "We'll still use it, of course - later. For now we want to focus on making the most of Samhain."

"Fine, but what am I supposed to do with the baby meanwhile?" she asked.

"We're probably looking at only a week or two," LeTourneu answered. "Maybe I could get one of my girls to take care of it until we're ready for the first post-Samhain ceremony. It would get her off the street for awhile. They'd probably fight over the chance to do it."

***

Outside on the street, Jim and Garrett headed back toward their car to wait. This time they stayed on the opposite side of the street from the 'adoption agency', to avoid being seen. When they got back to the car, Garrett decided to go into the alley to get a good look at the Jaguar that LeTourneu had been driving, since he wasn't sure if he got a clear picture of the license plate.

"All right," Jim agreed, "but make it quick. We don't know how long Pete is going to be in there. If he comes out and sees you, he'll know we're onto him."

***

There was one who secretly watched and listened to the DiMario's from the top of the roof. He wasn't trying to hide; even if they looked directly up at him, he couldn't be seen. He didn't have a physical body - only a spirit body.

Sekhmet was Pete LeTourneu's familiar spirit, and he leered down at the DiMario's through odious yellow eyes. His appearance in the spirit dimension was something akin to a detestable reptile. He had the mouth of a crocodile, and the teeth to go with it. The festering boils that were his eyes were set on either side of his long, narrow head. Sekhmet's body was shaped like a large lizard, except that the arms and legs were much longer, more like those of a mammal. The dark brownish - gray color of his body was covered with reptilian scales that occasionally glimmered when he moved. He stood upright like a man, but at about half the size. His thick tail provided an extra degree of support and balance for his loathsome body.

Sekhmet stayed close to Pete LeTourneu; indeed, he was assigned to do just that. They shared many of the same goals, but not all. Pete LeTourneu considered it a hallmark of his skill and prowess as a practitioner of the left-handed path to have his own familiar spirit. Sekhmet allowed him to think that way, although the truth of the matter was altogether opposite - Sekhmet had LeTourneu as his operative, rather than the other way around. Much of LeTourneu's success he owed to Sekhmet, who protected him from harm, and frequently arranged circumstances to fall in Pete's favor - like now.

Sekhmet visually scanned the long alleyway up and down. Seeing nothing, he employed his other senses, flicking his nefarious long tongue back and forth through the crisp night air. He caught the scent and taste of what he was looking for, and made a move. The daemon jumped down from the top of the building in a single leap, and landed like a feather on the pavement below, inasmuch as he had no mass.

Sekhmet scampered down the alleyway and darted behind a large trash dumpster that was about fifty feet further down from where LeTourneu's Jaguar was parked. There, laying curled up between the dumpster and the concrete wall of the strip mall's backside, was a homeless man.

Sekhmet knelt down beside the sleeping man and began whispering in his ear. After a few moments, the vagrant began to stir, uncomfortably twitching his beard-covered face. He lifted a dirty, callused hand and swatted at the source of the disturbance, as if a bug were tormenting him. His hand passed without resistance through Sekhmet, who continued whispering suggestions and accusations in his conscript's ear. This was a skill that Sekhmet excelled at - controlling the dreams of unsuspecting people.

The homeless man abruptly sat up and looked around. An empty bottle of supermarket-brand whiskey rolled off his lap and clinked onto the asphalt. He rose stiffly to his feet and staggered out from behind the trash dumpster. Then he saw Garrett kneeling behind the Jaguar, writing on a note pad. That's when he came unglued.

***

Garrett heard footfalls on the alleyway pavement, and looked up from his kneeling position behind the car. He was startled to see a wild-looking man coming directly at him, spouting curses. Immediately, Garrett jumped to his feet and faced the stranger, unsure about what to do. The intruder closed the distance between them, staggering and swearing all the while. The man's savage appearance and crazy behavior frightened Garrett much more than the black-faced attackers had only a few nights before. He'd never encountered anyone like this before, and didn't know what to expect. The attacker screamed at him like a lunatic as he came near.

"Stupid punk! I'm gonna teach you to mess with somebody's car," he shouted.

Garrett put his hands up in front of himself to try warding the menacing figure off.

"Whoa, Dude!," he said. "I'm not doing anything to this car. Look, I'm just writing down the license plate number."

Garrett waved the pen and pad to show proof. The vagrant attacker apparently didn't notice or didn't care. He drew even closer to Garrett, and shouted, "I'm gonna kill you."

His fetid breath reached Garrett's nose as he ranted. Then he lunged low at Garrett.

Garrett instinctively spun out of the line of attack and shoved his attacker's right shoulder down, sending him to the ground. Instantly the aggressor was back on his feet again, swinging a rough fist at Garrett's face. Garrett was able to block the first swing, but more came after it in a fusillade of punches and curses. One punch landed on Garrett's nose, and it felt as if fireworks went off directly in front of his face. The sharp pain was matched with the disorienting effect of ten thousand nerve endings being smashed.

Garrett remained standing, but pulled his arms up around his head in a desperate defense, like a boxer on the ropes. More blows came that glanced off Garrett's defending arms. Then, as quickly as the attack started, the blows stopped.

***

Jim knew trouble coming when he saw it. As soon as he saw the vagrant make a run for Garrett, Jim's legs started moving, too.

Garrett had been about fifty feet away from where Jim was standing secluded next to the block wall at the end of the alleyway. Jim couldn't run fast enough to cross the distance before the aggressor launched an unprovoked attack on Garrett. The crazy-looking vagrant was pummeling Garrett with such focus and power that he apparently didn't notice Jim coming at him from the side at full sprint. Jim bent forward and plunged into the man's side with his right shoulder - hard. He heard a distinct crack that he knew had to be the ribs of his son's adversary breaking under the sudden force.

The man fell back and let out a blood-curdling scream as he went down. Jim landed on top of him in a heap, unharmed. He scrambled to his feet and turned to his son. Garrett's nose was bleeding profusely, and Jim saw the crimson trail flowing down Garrett's face and marking his shirt. Garrett tried to wipe it away, but only succeeded in smearing the blood around his face. But their attacker wasn't done just yet.

"I am the servant of Sekhmet!" the man yelled, in a surprisingly strong voice.

Jim spun around to see him rise to his feet, seemingly unfazed by the bone-crushing drubbing he'd just received.

Impossible, Jim thought, *I know that had to do some damage.*

"I will destroy the enemies of my master," the vagrant shouted. A string of spittle oozed from the corner of his mouth, and caught in his stubble of beard. He lunged anew at Jim and Garrett with fists flying.

Standing side by side, Garrett blocked the left fist while Jim parried the right. The blows kept coming and coming, their attacker's eyes blazing with rage, his breath hot and acrid as a wild animal. His strength and endurance seemed superhuman to Jim; he was sure that not even a pro boxer could press an attack with this kind of prolonged intensity.

Jim knew he had no choice.

Drawing on his years-old self defense training, he saw the opening he needed, and went for it. With precise timing, he struck the man in the throat with the edge of his hand.

The vagrant's wild eyes suddenly got wider, taking on the appearance of a wounded animal. His mouth fell open to cry out, but no sound issued forth. The furious attack ended abruptly with the attacker's hands coming up to his own throat, as if he could undo the trauma dealt by Jim's hand.

Jim and Garrett watched as the man's face changed from a mask of fury to one of pain and anguish. His eyes grew wide like a pair of fried eggs on a griddle. He tried desperately to breath in, his mouth forming a grotesque "O", a fish caught on an angler's hook. Like a fish out of water, he couldn't fill his lungs with air, thanks to the well-placed blow. His face turned red, growing deeper in color with each passing second. Soon, his eyes lost focus and he dropped to his knees, then slumped forward in a prone position at the DiMario's feet.

Both Garrett and Jim jumped back instinctively as their attacker lurched forward onto his face. They regarded him cautiously for a moment, then Jim bent down to check his carotid pulse.

"Watch out, Dad," Garrett cautioned. "He might be faking."

"I'm watching," replied Jim. He carefully rolled the man's limp body over onto his back.

Jim felt a strong pulse, but he was concerned about the man's airway. His concern was short-lived, when the man coughed deeply, but remained unconscious.

"Dad, let's get out of here," Garrett said, his voice tight with urgency.

Jim recognized a good idea when he heard one, and needed no further prompting. He stood up and grabbed Garrett's arm, pulling him away from the scene.

"Let's go," he said, "I don't even want to try explaining this to the police."

They took a few steps, then broke into a run back to their car.

As he watched the scene unfold below him from his rooftop perch, Sekhmet sneered and spat in disgust. His thick tail whipped angrily back and forth as he saw his enemies make their break to freedom.

No matter. Their time will come. Their protection can't last forever. They'll slip up, and then they'll be in my hands. Soon enough they will see that their fate will be much worse than merely being beaten up.

CHAPTER 50

The Magus' Residence: Westlake Village, California

Inside the walls of the palatial Tudor-style estate home, three figures gathered around a large mahogany desk in The Magus' private study. Pete LeTourneu, Roberta McAllister, and The Magus himself convened to discuss the next steps of his plan.

"So, Pete," The Magus said, starting the meeting, "I assume you've briefed Bobbi on the latest plan for Samhain."

"Yes, we talked about it a bit," LeTourneu replied, "But there's nothing like hearing it from you directly, My Lord."

"Indeed," The Magus continued. "I wanted to get both of you together to go over the details, since the time is close at hand, and the two of you are my right and left hand. There's no room for error. Both of you will need to coordinate with your people everything that needs to take place between then and now, so that there will be no screw-ups."

"Bobbi," he said, looking at McAllister. She involuntarily jerked to attention when he spoke her name. "I know you already went to a lot of trouble to make sure we had a sacrifice of innocent blood for the unholy day. But now we have something better, and I'll need your help with her."

"You know what is best, My Master," McAllister replied. "Tell me what you want me to do."

"The DiMario girl will be our blood sacrifice for the Samhain black mass," The Magus said. "But she's been difficult. An important part of my plan is to get some good nude photos of her. The more graphic, the better. We can post these on our web sites to portray her as a rebellious teen, an aspiring porn actress, like that rich heiress from the hotel chain. Then, she will disgrace her father and her whole family. When her dead body is found, nobody will be very surprised."

Both LeTourneu and McAllister nodded in agreement.

"But, like I said, she's been a real problem," The Magus continued. "Pete has had two of his girls working on her since we picked her up a few days ago. She's non-compliant. They couldn't get her to take her clothes off - not even to take a shower or to sleep."

"I tried it the nice way," Pete said, "but as I've said, Magus, we can certainly force the issue. I can get my guys to go in and take care of her. I'll even lead the way."

"Ah, Pete," The Magus smiled, "I know you don't want to admit defeat. And, your plan was acceptable, I'll grant you that. But now we'll give Bobbi a chance to work her charms on her. She's charmed plenty of foolish young girls out of their offspring; let's see if she can get the DiMario girl to pose for us willingly."

McAllister beamed. "I can do it, I'm sure of it," she said. "Just let me work with her a bit." She looked toward the door. "So, she's here, at your house?"

"Yes," The Magus replied. "Once I saw that Pete was getting nowhere fast, I had her brought over here. She's down in the basement."

"No more Mr. Nice Guy," LeTourneu added, with a laugh. "She knows for sure now that she's not among friends."

"Yes, yes," McAllister said. "We'll try my personal version of the old 'Good Cop - Bad Cop' routine. Just have your photographer ready. She'll break once I've had a chance to work with her."

"I hope so," commented The Magus, "otherwise, I'll let Pete have his way with her." Then he added with a smirk, "But I'd rather have her smiling for her pictures."

"Let's make a sporting bet," LeTourneu proposed. "If you fail, Bobbi, you can serve as the altar for the Samhain black mass."

LeTourneu was referring to the procedure for black mass, which involved placing a nude woman upon a black, cloth-draped table set up as an altar. Such ceremonies often culminated in sex acts between the participants and the 'priestess' of the group. This was intended to raise the level of energy of the black mass, thereby invoking more dark spiritual power. It also served to insult God by twisting worship practices of the Christian church into something perverse.

"And if I succeed," Roberta McAllister countered, "my prize will be to shave your head, and drain eight ounces of your blood for my own purposes."

LeTourneu frowned as he considered this proposal for a moment, realizing that she was trying to draw off some of his power in order to strengthen her own position.

"Done," he agreed at last.

"Very well," The Magus concluded with a smile. "I like to see a little competition between you two. Now then, Bobbi, get started with your assignment. Time is running down. And I will not accept failure on this matter."

Basement of The Magus' Residence: Westlake Village, California

Chelsea DiMario shivered against the chill as she sat huddled in the corner of the dark, cold concrete room.

She still wore the same jeans and hooded pullover sweatshirt that she had on the night she was taken from the school football game. Chelsea felt quite grungy, as she wasn't able to brush her hair or teeth. Her captors had been more than willing to let her shower, but she had a bad feeling about disrobing around these people. Chelsea hadn't been fed or given anything to drink in a long time. Her stomach growled from time to time, and her mouth was dry like a desert. She ran her tongue over her chapped lips for the hundredth time.

Bare incandescent lights hanging from the ceiling provided dim illumination to her bleak surroundings. There was only one door to this chamber, and Chelsea had already discovered that it was locked.

She had been brought to this place blindfolded and bound with handcuffs by two men. She had no idea where she was, but knew the trip lasted about forty minutes.

Chelsea sat uncomfortably on the cold, hard floor. No windows, no furniture, no nothing. She noticed an assortment of exposed pipes that ran along the length of the empty chamber about seven feet above the floor. The floor was plain and bare, except for some dark brownish-maroon colored stains under the pipes in the middle of the room. The single door was set above the level of the floor, with wooden steps leading up to it. Her rear end was cold; indeed, it had turned numb after sitting here for over an hour.

Chelsea rubbed her wrists, which still smarted from the handcuffs. She realized that she had stopped shivering, even though this concrete dungeon was frigid inside. Quiet, except for the occasional sound of water flowing through the pipes overhead.

The angel wrapped his stalwart wings around Chelsea, enveloping her in a feathered embrace that was warmer than any earthly blanket. Warm enough to transcend the barrier between the different dimensions that the two of them occupied.

This was a powerful angel, a seraph. He did not resemble a human being, but instead had three sets of wings and the face of a creature dissimilar to anything seen on Earth. Unlike his opponents in the spirit dimension, he was singularly beautiful and awesome to behold. The seraph radiated a glory and power that reflected the attributes of his creator. He had been dispatched to this time and place for a special purpose; to protect a beloved child of God from the evil entities that were also present, even in this same grim basement.

At the far end of the basement, three unclean spirits hovered, waiting for the opportunity to work on the girl. One spirit specialized in discouragement, another in fear. The third daemon was a master of lies. They were black in color, and were shrouded by what seemed like a black cloud of flies. The daemon of lies had short, stubby, featherless wings that flapped rapidly as he held his stationary position. The others didn't have wings, yet were able to hover and fly at will. All were experienced at influencing the minds and attitudes of many unsuspecting people for eons past. Their influence usually led to certain actions on the part of their targeted victims, which were always destructive to themselves and others.

They waited like hungry vultures eagerly anticipating the death of their next meal, fuming that their work was being delayed. But they dared not even approach the girl while she was being protected, knowing full well that the seraphim had the ability to send them to the Lake of Fire with one touch of his powerful wings.

So they would wait. There were many more unclean spirits like them present in the house, and there was strength in numbers. The fact that a seraph had been dispatched to attend this girl, rather than one of the protecting angels, made them want her all the more. The presence of one of God's most mighty angelic beings indicated that this girl was especially important, for some reason.

They waited. The greater the value of the prize, the greater the reward would be.

Chelsea woke with a start, and lifted her head off the concrete to see what the sound was.

She hadn't realized that she'd drifted off to sleep until a strange sound disturbed the silence of the chamber. She pulled herself up onto her hands and knees and looked around in the gloom, her senses on alert.

Chelsea heard another sound, which she recognized as the door latch opening. She saw the door open about halfway, and a wedge of light entered the dim chamber from whatever lay behind the door. A partially silhouetted figure was roughly thrust onto the landing at the top of the steps by an arm belonging to someone unseen behind the door. Chelsea realized that the newcomer was a woman from the outlines of her hair and dress. The woman steadied herself against the railing at the top of the steps, and the door slammed shut behind her. Then Chelsea recognized the sound of a deadbolt being latched from the outside; she realized that this was the sound that woke her up.

The woman started to carefully make her way down the wooden steps, and Chelsea squinted in the subdued light to try to see who it was. She heard familiar-sounding hollow footfalls resounding on the steps. Chelsea rose to her feet in anticipation. She didn't know what this new person might want with her. The woman stopped at the foot of the steps and turned toward her.

"Chelsea?" a familiar-sounding voice spoke in a tone just above a whisper. "Is that you?"

"Yes," Chelsea answered. Her brain quickly ran through the voice association. "Mrs. McAllister?" she asked.

The woman walked quickly across the floor of the expansive basement, her heels making a *pok, pok, pok* sound as she covered the sixty feet from the base of the steps.

"Oh, Chelsea," Roberta McAllister said, as she rushed up and hugged her, "Thank God you're all right."

"Yeah, I'm all right," Chelsea replied. "Where am I, and what are you doing here?"

McAllister released her embrace, but kept a hand on Chelsea's shoulder. "They called me at school," she whispered conspiratorially. "Your kidnappers."

Chelsea stared at her face, waiting for more.

"I suppose they found out somehow that I've been an advisor to girls in trouble," McAllister continued. "You're not far away from home. I can't say more than that," she said, looking around the room. "They might have this place bugged."

Then she added, "They brought me here with a blindfold over my eyes. I don't know where we are, just that it isn't far from the school."

"I hope you had the police follow the car that brought you here," Chelsea said hopefully.

"No, Chelsea. There was no time to call the police, and the kidnappers said that they'd kill you if I tipped anyone off. There's nobody else coming."

McAllister let that sink in for a moment, then said, "They're pornographers, Chelsea. That's why they picked you up. They want to use you for some pictures, that's all. Once they have what they want, they'll let you go."

A strange sensation suddenly came over Chelsea as she listened to McAllister talk. She couldn't quite put her finger on it, but the sensation told her that there was something wrong with this situation.

"But why would they do that?" Chelsea asked. "Why would they kidnap me, when there are plenty of girls around who are willing to pose nude for money?"

"They said that you had a particular look that they wanted," replied McAllister. "Look, it doesn't matter. The important thing is to get you out of here safely. And the best way to do that is to cooperate."

"I can't do that," Chelsea protested loudly. "I'm not going to pose for them. Besides, who knows what they might do if I give them what they want."

"Listen, Chelsea," McAllister said, "these are dangerous men. They told me that if you had cooperated earlier, you'd be back at home right now - with your family, safe. Now that they've gone to the trouble of kidnapping you, they aren't going to let you go until you give them what they want."

McAllister looked into Chelsea's eyes. She expected to see fear, like a scared puppy, but instead saw suspicion. What she couldn't see was the seraph at Chelsea's shoulder, towering over her. Nor did she see the spirit of deceit, watching over her own shoulder, coaching her with suggestions whispered in her ear.

"Do you have a cell phone?'" Chelsea whispered.

"No. They took it from me before I came down here."

Chelsea thought for a moment. "If you listen to the road sounds and remember the turns when they take you back, you might be able to pinpoint this location," she suggested. "Then you can tell my dad. He'll find a way to get to me, if he knows where to look. He knows a sheriff's deputy who could help."

"I know he does," McAllister replied, "but I'm hoping to take you back with me, Chelsea. That's what you want, isn't it? You don't want to stay with these terrible people, do you?"

"Of course not. But they can't hold me here forever. They'll have to let me go eventually. And if can give some tips on where to look for me, the police or my dad will find me."

McAllister gripped Chelsea's shoulders and drew her own face near to her. "You don't get it, do you?" she said, with an irritated tone infiltrating her voice. "You are in serious danger here. These people are not to be messed with. We don't know what they might do to you. By the time the police or your father find you, you could be dead."

Chelsea heard in McAllister's voice a cold tone, one that seemed familiar with talking about death and killing. She had heard from others at school that Mrs. McAllister had been involved in handing out condoms to whatever students wanted them, then arrange for secret adoptions of their unwanted babies when the condom use failed. There had been rumors that several girls had had their babies adopted with her help.

Somehow, this teacher didn't seem to Chelsea to be humanitarian in any way, much less pro-life. It was strange. On one hand, giving out condoms, encouraging teenage sex. On the other hand, counseling girls away from abortion of their unborn, and helping to facilitate clandestine adoptions. It seemed contradictory somehow.

She suddenly recalled the time just a few weeks ago in the principal's office, when this same woman had treated her so scornfully. Clearly, this teacher wasn't a Christian - far from it, in fact. She recognized that same hardness creeping back into McAllister's features now, which had only moments ago seemed concerned and compassionate.

"Look," McAllister said, "time's running out here. You don't have the luxury of holding onto your precious virtue. We're talking life or death here. Just do what needs to be done, then we'll be on our way home."

Chelsea drew back from Roberta McAllister's grip. "You seem even more eager than I am to get out of here," she said.

"Of course I'm eager to get out of here. Look at this terrible place. I'm really sticking my neck out to help you. So help me help you." McAllister pointed her twin index fingers back and forth between herself and Chelsea to emphasize her point.

"If you really want to help me," Chelsea retorted, "you should do like I said - remember the sounds, the turns, the speed, how long it takes to get back. Then tell my dad so he can find me."

Before she was even finished speaking, Chelsea could see McAllister's face reddening, and the pressure building up within her.

"Fine," McAllister hissed, "have it your way. But I can't be responsible for the outcome. I tried to help."

She stood up abruptly and turned on her heel. The sounds of her shoes on the concrete floor rang out a faster tempo than when she had come in. She arrived at the stairs and dashed up them quickly. When she had reached the top of the landing, she rapped twice on the door loudly.

Turning to Chelsea, she yelled down, "You're a fool, Chelsea. Make it easy on yourself."

Then the deadbolt unlatched, and the door opened. The slice of light invaded the room, along with a burly man. The man reached for her arm, but she pushed him away.

"Move!" McAllister barked.

The man stepped back and let her pass. Then the door shut, and the sound of the sliding bolt falling into place seemed to seal Chelsea's fate.

Chelsea thought about the attitude change Mrs. McAllister showed from the time she came in to the time she left. She thought about the way she had addressed the guard at the door, the commanding tone she had used with him. She wondered why the kidnappers would contact someone like her in the first place.

And how did she know that Dad knows a sheriff's deputy? she wondered.

Rather than being comforted by her former teacher's visit, the sense of dread that Chelsea had started to experience upon being brought to this dreary place was deepening even further. She assumed a kneeling position and lowered her head to pray, hands folded in front of her.

So, Lord, maybe this is it. I pray again that you would rescue me from this place and from my captors. But if that's not to be ... I'm ready to meet you. I'm so glad now that I stayed close to you all these years, when so many of my friends lost their way. Sometimes, I felt like I wanted to get lost with them. Thank you for watching over me and guiding my steps. Please watch over my parents and brother, and help them get through this, and whatever is to come. Amen.

The ache and cold in her knees told her it was time to shift position again. She lay down uncomfortably on her side, and eventually drifted off to sleep in the dim gloom of her private dungeon, feeling warm and somehow safer after her teacher's departure.

The seraph had not abandoned her.

CHAPTER 51

Downtown San Bernardino

George smiled to himself and patted the fat roll of cash in his shirt pocket. As he drove into the town center of San Bernardino, he fondly recalled the conversation he'd had an hour earlier with his boss, the general manager of KNLA TV.

"I've got to be out of my ever-lovin' mind to turn you loose with five-hundred bucks from petty cash," the general manager had shouted at George. "You'd better come up with a darn good story for that kind of dough."

With these kind words of encouragement, he'd sent George on his way - with the money. George had picked up Trey along the way, in hopes that he could help translate once they got downtown.

Trey had seemed eager for the adventure at first, but now as they took the exit ramp off the freeway and headed into the gritty downtown area, George thought he seemed a bit nervous.

Trey watched the graffiti-covered walls go by and swallowed hard. An interesting clientele of characters seemed to be just hanging around for no apparent reason on street corners, bus benches, and sidewalks. One guy sported long, dirty dreadlocks that looked as if they had formed spontaneously, rather than by design. Another young man had his hair in cornrows, and wore baggy shorts that sunk down to the middle of his calves. Still another was shaved bald, with several tattoos visible under his 'wife beater' shirt, and across the back of his bare scalp.

It seemed weird to Trey to be introduced into an environment where he was now the minority. He'd never felt like this before; strangely conspicuous and out of place, as they pulled into a parking place on the side of the street near the coroner's office. It seemed to him as if they were the only white faces in the neighborhood. For the first time, he could imagine what it must have been like for those few non-white kids who attended their first days at the Westlake Village schools.

They got out of the car and went around to the alleyway in back of the building. George located a set of bins that were behind the coroner's office, and they took a look inside. Nothing - just the usual trash can liners stuffed with the refuse of the previous day's office trash. They continued walking down the alleyway looking in the dumpsters that were lined up like sentries along the back wall of the sprawling county center building.

Trying unsuccessfully to look inconspicuous, they lifted the lids on each large bin, peering inside to scan the gloomy depths. They were almost at the end of the alleyway when they heard footsteps.

Trey pulled his head out of the bin and saw two young black men approaching. They both wore basketball jerseys; one with the yellow and purple colors of the L.A. Lakers, the other displaying the white and red of the L.A. Clippers. Both had white T-shirts under their jerseys. One of the young men wore a white headband with a baseball cap pulled over it, with the brim turned partially sideways. An ostentatious gold medallion hung from a thick chain around his neck. The other guy had a "grille" - several silver teeth in the front of his mouth that gleamed when he opened his mouth to speak.

"Whas' up, cracker?" the one with silver teeth challenged.

George turned away from the trash dumpster he was looking in and swaggered up to the two youths. He stared into the eyes of the one who had spoken first.

"We're looking for something," he said to them.

"I could see dat, fool," replied the one with the medallion. The other one laughed.

Trey stepped up next to George, emboldened by his friend's unflappable presence.

"Lookin' for somebody that can give us the four-one-one on what we're lookin' for," Trey said.

"What 'chu lookin' fo?" the one with the silver teeth asked. "We can git 'chu whateva' you need – fo da right price."

"We're lookin' for boxes," Trey said, without hesitation. "Plastic boxes - clear plastic." The two youths squinted and curled their lip in a scornful expression that was probably well-rehearsed.

"Special boxes," Trey added, "about this big." He motioned with his hands the approximate dimensions.

Silver Teeth's expression suddenly lit up, and he turned to his partner.

"Yeah, yeah. I know da boxes you be talkin 'bout," he said. "They dirty, stinky too."

His friend nodded his head knowingly.

"We can hook you up wit' dose boxes, but 'chu gotta pay a gwap," Medallion said.

"How many you got?" Trey asked.

The two youths looked at each other. "Gotta check," Medallion said.

"You do that," George replied. He reached into his pocket to get his pen and pad. Both of the youths flinched and drew back as he did so, as if they expected to see something else in George's hand as he drew it out. "Here's my cell number," he said, jotting down the number. "Get back to us right away, okay?"

Silver Teeth looked George over warily. "You a cop?" he asked.

"No," George replied, "I'm a reporter."

Medallion smiled and nodded at his friend. "Dat's where we seen him," he said. To George, he said, "Better you follow us over in yo' car. Der's too many to carry."

Several minutes later, George and Trey sat parked on the street in a residential neighborhood of aging, unkempt homes. Trey noticed that most of the houses had iron bars on the windows and steel security doors. Many had chain link fences around the perimeter of the property, that bulged out and sagged along the bottom from age and neglect. Weeds and long grass wove a tangled web into the bottom of the fence lines. The faded and peeling paint that decorated most houses was accented by front yards entirely devoid of landscaping, save for an old tree here and there.

The barking of a few stray dogs wandering the street was the only sound that Trey heard. Apparently, most residents didn't rise this early from their previous nocturnal activities. Trey checked his watch; it was a quarter to ten in the morning.

An object suddenly thumped down on the hood of the car, causing Trey to jump sharply enough to nearly cause a whiplash. The black cat paused only long enough to look at Trey and George through the windshield, then it hopped off the car and ran across the street. It bounded over the low fence of one house and found a familiar crack under the front porch to wiggle through, just as a stray dog came into view, trotting along the sidewalk.

Trey felt the hair on the back of his neck stand up. He lowered his window a bit to catch a breath of fresh air, but as he breathed in, it didn't seem that fresh. The unmistakable scent of dried urine in the background assailed his nostrils. It was mixed with other unrecognizable smells to create a decidedly undesirable pong.

Trey unconsciously clenched his jaw back and forth, as he scanned the sidewalks and street. He looked over at George, who seemed as cool as a glass of iced tea. Sitting with his driver's seat reclined part way, George's body and face were slack, as if he were about to drift off to sleep under a palm tree on a warm Hawaiian beach, without a care in the world. Trey could feel his own body sweating, although it wasn't hot. His palms were clammy and itchy, and his left foot tapped involuntarily against the car floor. Trey took a deep breath and bowed his head to pray silently for a moment. Then he lifted his eyes to George.

"Aren't you nervous?" Trey asked, with his lips pulled tight.

"Nah. These punks aren't armed. If they were, they would have flashed the hardware already. The young ones always do - makes 'em feel macho."

"I can't even imagine the kinds of people you must deal with, George. You've probably seen it all in your work."

"Hah!" George chuckled, "Just when I think I've seen it all, I come across something unbelievable. That's what got me started on this Satanism story in the first place, but I had no idea where it would lead. I guess I've become immune to the dark side of humanity over the years. Things - and people, aren't always what they seem to be. That's what keeps it interesting."

George took in a deep breath and pursed his lips as he blew out. "Speaking of which," he said, "I want to find out everything we can about Aldon Brehm. I've got a feeling that he's not what he seems to be."

"Maybe I can help dig up some dirt on him," Trey offered.

"I'm real good at digging up dirt, Kiddo," George said. "Just ask some of the people and organizations I've exposed over the years. But you've got skills and connections that I don't. I'm sure you could help."

Trey smiled. "If there's any skeletons in his closet, we'll find 'em."

George looked up and tapped Trey on the leg. He pointed up the street to some figures walking towards them. "It's showtime," he said.

The local youths were coming back towards George's car - accompanied by two more young men.

"I don't like the looks of this," Trey said.

"Don't show any fear," George cautioned, "they can smell it. C'mon, let's get out."

George opened his door and got out to meet Silver Teeth and company. Trey followed suit.

"'Sup?" Trey said with a nod.

"We got fifteen of da boxes you want," Medallion said. "You can have 'em fo' fifty each."

"No way, man!" George protested. "Do I have 'Stupid' stamped on my forehead?"

"You paid forty fo' one box befoe," Medallion said, his voice rising. "Now you back again, so it must be worth sumpthin'."

George recognized one of the other youths as the kid he'd bought the original box from.

Trey looked around and shrugged. "They ain't worth nothin' to anybody else," he countered. "Quantity discount - we can pay up to twenty a box for all of 'em."

"You crazy!" Medallion shouted.

He and the others of his crew started to move around with agitated gyrations, pacing around the blacktop without going anywhere. Medallion twisted his neck around to crack it, and bounced lightly on his feet.

He rubbed his nose with his thumb, and said, "How 'bout we just beat the money out a ya?"

He stepped up to George and stared him down. George stepped back, and reached into his jacket pocket. He kept his hand hidden there.

"How about you back off," George said. "You'll live longer."

Medallion turned his eyes to George's hand that was buried in his pocket. George maintained his piercing stare. Medallion blinked first, and stepped back a couple steps.

"We'll pay twenty a box, take it or leave it," George declared. "That's three hundred bucks more than you've got now."

The four youths looked around and made furtive signals and expressions to each other.

"I don't see any other buyers lining up," Trey said.

"Deal," Silver Teeth said finally. He glanced around in both directions. "Show me da money."

"I've got the cash," George said. "Show me the boxes."

Silver Teeth turned and pointed at the house they had come out of.

"Pull up in front," he said.

They were just finishing loading the last box into the back of George's SUV, when Silver Teeth looked up and motioned with his chin at a group of six young punks walking up the street in their direction.

"Y'all betta bug outta here," he said, "Dats some tough dudes comin' dis way. They aint so nice as us."

The others grunted knowingly, and Trey and George didn't wait around for any further explanations. The money changed hands, and they got in the car.

Five minutes later, George and Trey were headed onto the southbound Interstate Two-Fifteen entrance ramp, with the back of George's SUV stacked with the gruesome sepulchers.

"All right," George said, "mission accomplished. Now get Rich on the phone and tell him we've got the boxes so he can get a subpoena for the manufacturer. Then let's go back to your house and we'll see what you can find out about Aldon Brehm."

CHAPTER 52

East Valley Sheriff's Station: Thousand Oaks, California

R ich Harrison impatiently drummed his fingertips on the wood laminate computer desk, which echoed back a hollow, deep tone.

He was seated at one of several computer workstations that the sheriff's station made available for any of the deputies or detectives to use. He stared intently at the computer screen, willing it to give him an answer to his message. Fidgeting around in his swivel chair in the open computer area of the sprawling Sheriff's station, Rich pushed back with his legs until the chair balanced precariously on its rear legs.

He had sent publicity photos of Aldon Brehm and the youth group picture of Pete LeTourneu by e-mail to Detective Bruce Ellis in Minneapolis, and was eager for a reply.

Now he was playing the waiting game; it was a game he didn't like. It was up to Detective Ellis in Minneapolis to follow through, and Rich had every reason to believe that he would. Ellis had promised to present the pictures - along with about a dozen 'test' pictures, to the boy who had seen a man going into the Heipler's house that bloody day. The man he saw was likely to be the murderer of Bjorn Nilsson.

Now, several hours after sending the pictures, Rich checked his e-mail for a reply. Nothing. He had about twenty minutes left on his lunch break, and was about to get up and forage among the vending machines that lined the break room for something to chow down on. Just as he scooted his chair back, his cell phone rang.

He snatched the phone off his overloaded utility belt and put it up to his ear.

"Harrison," he said hastily.

"Rich?" the voice answered. "Bruce Ellis here. Are you ready for this?"

"What do you think?" Rich shot back.

"I've got good news and bad news; first, the bad news - the kid didn't I.D. Aldon Brehm. Not surprising. But now, the good news. He *did* make a positive I.D. on LeTourneu. Didn't even hesitate - he pointed him out among the dozen pictures of other cons that met the general physical description."

"That's great!" Rich said excitedly. "But do you think an eight-year-old kid's testimony and I.D. will hold up in court?"

"In this case, absolutely. Turns out that the kid's a genius. He's got a higher IQ than ninety-five percent of the adult population. He's credible, and his parents are cooperative."

"Excellent. So you can get an arrest warrant, then?"

"I can, but hold on, 'cause it gets even better." After a dramatic pause, Ellis continued. "I did a lot of leg work on this, just so you know. I went to all the major car rental agencies and got them to I.D. everybody that had a dark-colored Ford Taurus rented that day."

"And?" Rich prompted.

"Jackpot. The kid was right. Turns out that Hertz has video surveillance at their rental counter at the airport. Guess who shows up to rent a car for one day only?"

"Gee, let me guess. Pete LeTourneu?"

"Bingo," replied Ellis. "Only his name isn't LeTourneu - it's Durgin. Peter Durgin."

"I'm not surprised a weasel like him has an alias," Rich said. "But now we don't know for sure what his real name is. I'll run Pete Durgin for wants and priors. Nothing came up under LeTourneu."

"I'll run it under Durgin here, too," Ellis replied. "He used a California driver's license with that name."

"Okay," Rich said. "As soon as you find out something one way or the other, you're going to get a warrant, right?"

"Right."

"Good. I want to have it in my hand at the right time. And that time is coming soon, I'm sure of that."

"Okay," Ellis said. "Hang tight, and keep your phone on you. You'll be hearing from me."

Rich said his goodbyes, and pressed the END button. He set his phone down on the desk in front of him, and proceeded to log off the computer. Before he could get up and head for the valley of junk food, his phone played it's familiar melody again.

"Rich Harrison here," he said.

"Rich," George's voice sounded jubilant through the airwaves. "We've got something for you."

"Who's 'we', Kemosabe?" Rich asked, recognizing his voice.

"Trey is with me. We just picked up fifteen boxes that came from the Yermo burial site. I'm gonna hand the phone over to Trey so he can read off the serial numbers to you."

"Okay," Rich said, grabbing a notepad. He proceeded to quickly transcribe the numbers that Trey rattled off. Trey then passed the phone back to George, who drove one-handed while talking.

"Got what you need?" George asked.

"Yep. I'll pay a visit to Plastec Industries and see if I can find out who bought them."

"Aren't you going to get a subpoena to serve them?" George asked.

Rich gritted his teeth. "Nah. That would be tough for me to get. I'm gonna try to get the info without a subpoena. The judge might wonder why a patrol cop is on this, instead of a detective. He might want to call my watch commander, who would then make me turn over everything we've got so far on Brehm and LeTourneu - Durgin, that is, to our detectives."

"Who's Durgin?"

Rich took a few minutes to fill him in on the recent information from Detective Ellis in Minneapolis.

"Pass this info on to Jim," Rich said. "The Reverend needs to watch his back, now more than ever. This Durgin character is dangerous. We already knew he was a troublemaker for the DiMario's, but now it looks like he's a murderer, too."

"Incredible! I'll let him know," George promised. "But can't you just bust him now? What if he does something else?"

"Can't pick him up now," Rich replied. "But he'll soon be wanted in Minnesota for a capital crime, and believe me, I'll be more than happy to pick him up as soon as the warrant is issued. Until then, Jim and his family need protection. Unfortunately, I don't have the authority to assign an officer to baby-sit them, and I can't do it myself. We'll have to think of something else."

"I don't know why Durgin killed the missionary," Rich added, "but he sure went out of his way to do it. Nilsson was Jim's friend, and he had a lot of other friends and admirer's, too. I know - I was at his funeral. People came out from Brazil and all over the states, for crying out loud. I've never seen anything like it. We've already seen how far he was willing to go to discredit Jim, and now, murder one. There's no telling what this Durgin is capable of."

"All right," George replied resignedly, "I'll talk to Jim, and we'll think of something. Talk to you later."

George hung up, and Rich sat with his chin resting on his fists, staring at the blank computer screen for a long time.

How am I going to pull this off? he wondered. *If the Plastec Company doesn't cooperate, I'm sunk. I should go in plain clothes; let them assume I'm a detective. I'll probably have more clout that way. Ellis won't be able to get a search warrant or subpoena for Plastec, since the Yermo crime has no connection to the Minnesota murder - Or does it?*

Rich stroked his chin thoughtfully. *If they're clean, they should give me anything I want to see. If not, well ... I guess I'll have to cross that bridge when I get to it.*

Rich picked up his notepad and pen, then got up from the desk. He looked toward the break room, then at his watch. Frowning, he shoved the pen and pad into one of his shirt pockets, and ducked into the break room where he bought a packet of chocolate covered mini donuts from the vending machine. Then he walked out the rear door to his patrol car.

Detective time's over for now, Rich thought. *Time for the street cop to get back on the beat.*

Rich had been cruising his beat for less than an hour when a call came over his radio.

"Alpha Bravo thirteen, you copy?" a deep masculine voice said.

Rich grabbed the microphone off the dash and spoke into it. "Alpha Bravo Thirteen, go ahead."

"This is Victor Fox-trot twenty-three," the familiar voice said. Rich recognized it as that of his friend Eric. "Meet me on 452-6741."

"Roger that," Rich replied, wondering why Eric wanted to talk privately, rather than over the airwaves.

Rich pulled over into a nearby parking lot and used his own cell phone to call his friend's cell phone.

"Hey," Deputy Eric Vincent said, "I've been trying to reach you."

"What's up?"

"That hot babe you went out with a few nights ago - remember you told me about her?"

"Yeah?" Rich replied.

"What was her name?"

"Angela Shepherd. Why? I'm not giving you her phone number," Rich joked. "I wouldn't do that to a friend."

There was a brief pause before Eric answered. "She's dead, Rich. The word came over the air about a homicide in West Hollywood. At first, I figured it was probably just another gay jealousy killing, you know? We get those over there from time to time. But then I heard the victim's name, and I thought I recognized it."

The news landed a blow on Rich as if he'd just been kicked in the chest by a karate black belt.

"What … happened?" he stammered.

"I called up one of the guys who's on the scene. I know him, and I had his cell number. Turns out she was found by a friend who has her apartment keys. She was naked, on her bed, strangled."

Eric Vincent didn't hear a response on the phone, so he added, "I'm sorry, man. I just thought you'd want to know."

"Yeah, thanks," Rich said absently, before hanging up. He got his friend's message loud and clear.

It would only be a matter of time before the detectives, and probably Internal Affairs came around to ask some questions - questions that he wasn't keen to answer.

CHAPTER 53

DiMario Residence: Westlake Village, California

It was a hard phone call for Jim DiMario to make, but he knew he had to do it. His hand rested on the phone in his home office, where it had sat for several minutes.

Should I tell them everything?, he wondered to himself. *Would they even believe me if I did tell them everything? It'll sound crazy - but it's all true.*

Reluctantly, he picked up the receiver and dialed the phone number on the card that was open on his Rolodex. It was Blake Aanstad's work number, the church council president. Blake answered on the second ring, and Jim identified himself.

"Pastor Jim," Blake's voice resounded through the line, "how are you and the family holding up?"

"Okay. As well as could be expected, under the circumstances," Jim replied.

"Well, I've been praying for you every day," Blake said. "And especially for Chelsea."

"Thanks, Blake. I appreciate that." Jim paused for a moment. "Blake, I need to call an emergency church council meeting for tonight, at my house. I know it's short notice, but if you could contact the others and get them to come, that would be great."

"Why, yes, of course, Jim. I'm at work, but I'll send out an e-mail right now. I don't know if ..."

"Tell them that it's urgent, and they need to be here. My apologies if anyone needs to break a prior engagement, but it can't wait any longer."

"Okay, Jim," Blake answered, his words laced with a concerned tone. "Is anything wrong - other than the obvious, of course?"

"Yes. There's a great deal that's wrong, and I need to share it with you all and get your input."

"All right," Blake replied. "I'll arrange for the meeting to start at seven-thirty. That should give everyone time to get home first. Will you be inviting the pastoral staff?"

"Yes. Everyone except Pete LeTourneu."

Blake was silent for a few seconds. "All right, Jim. We'll see you at seven-thirty at your house."

"Good," Jasmine said, as she walked into the home office. "I'll make sure to have some coffee and dessert for the meeting. It may be a long one."

"Yeah," Jim replied, nodding his head slowly. "I'm sure it will be."

"It's about time," Jasmine said. She wiped her tears with the kitchen towel she had in her hand. "Honestly, I'll never understand you men. I think you should have brought the church council in on this a long time ago. They're in your corner, Jim. We started this church, and most of the council members have been with us for years."

She gravitated over to his desk and leaned against the edge.

"I know, I know," Jim admitted, "and you're right, as usual. At first, I thought the Angela Shepherd thing would blow over once it became obvious that it had no truth to it. I never would have expected that gossip would spread through the church like it has."

"I did," Jasmine interjected. "I know what women are like. Sure, everybody professes to follow the teachings of Christ in all things, and a lot of people really do try. But the fact is, we're all human. And that kind of scandal is impossible for some people to keep to themselves."

"And I sure didn't expect that my associate pastor was a power-seeking betraying liar, and maybe even a murderer," Jim added.

"I told you I never felt right about him, Jim. But I couldn't have guessed just how evil he really is."

Jim wrapped his arm around her hips and pulled her in close, while he remained seated in his desk chair.

"I really need to consult with you more often," he said.

"You really should," Jasmine said, with a smile. "There actually is such a thing as women's intuition you know, and it's closely related to the biblical gift of discernment."

"Sometimes people do let us down, Jim," Jasmine continued. "But they care, too. You can't be like Atlas, carrying the whole world on your shoulders. Even Atlas had Hercules to help him. You need to give other people a chance to come alongside and help you - help us. You've always had a hard time giving ministry responsibilities away, too, but you know you have to do it. You're only one man. You've got to let your trusted people share the burden with us. Believe me, they're up to it."

"How did you get so smart?" Jim asked.

"It's the company I keep," Jasmine replied, smiling.

**

Seven-thirty found all eight church council members and the church staff gathered in the DiMario's living room. Jim had brought out folding chairs and the dining room chairs to accommodate the group.

After everyone sat down, Jim himself sat before them, and Blake called the meeting to order. After the group settled down, he turned it over to Jim.

Jim took a deep breath before beginning. "I've got plenty to share with you tonight. A lot of things have happened since we met last, and even before we met that time that I'll be talking about. You will have questions, I'm sure of that. But please try to hold out until the end of this story before asking them."

Jim looked around the room to get eye contact with all present before continuing. One by one, the assembly acknowledged with nods and verbal affirmation that they were eager to listen.

"The information I'm going to share with you must not leave this room - not for the time being, anyway," Jim said. "The reason why will become apparent as I go along."

Jim could feel the pressure building up in the room as he gave his mysterious introduction. It seemed as if they were watching someone blowing up a balloon higher and higher, waiting for it to burst. Every eye was fastened upon him, and the silence in the room was as complete as the inside of an underground cavern.

Jim sat forward in his chair, and began his story from the beginning with his find of the slaughtered cat on the jogging trail. Every face listened with rapt attention. All present seemed to lean forward as well, as if they could somehow extract the story from their pastor quicker or in more detail by doing so. Jim continued the story to include the discovery of the bloody ceremonial site in the hills above Lake Sherwood, the find of the infant corpses in Yermo, the violent attack and beating of Trey Simmons and the murder attempt that followed, and the attempted assault of George.

Jim went on to describe to the group the visit at his office from the young woman Angela Shepherd, and the subsequent discovery that she was a hired actress. When Jim dropped the bomb of whom she was hired by, his listeners broke into spontaneous loud exclamations and sidebar discussions.

A few stood up, apparently uncomfortable to sit on this revelation. Some expressed disbelief that their associate pastor could actually do something so diabolical; others contended loudly that Jim wouldn't say it if he didn't have proof. All agreed that they wanted to hear more.

And Jim gave them more than they could have imagined. He told them about the murder of Bjorn Nilsson, and the connection of the murder weapon to Aldon Brehm. When he added the fact that Pete LeTourneu was proven to be in Minneapolis on the day of the murder, rather than Detroit as he claimed, and that he had been I.D.'d by a witness, the room erupted again in outcries of shock and disbelief.

"This is inconceivable!" one council member shouted.

"It's incredible news, that's true," Blake Aanstad said, "but it's not impossible. Let's let Pastor Jim finish."

"We should act now to expel that rotten scum Pete LeTourneu," one council member declared.

"Is he connected to this Satanic group?" asked another.

Jim stood up and raised his hands to quiet the group. "Those are good questions and issues to discuss," he said. "First of all, although I would love to, we can't fire him just yet."

Several voices immediately began murmuring, but Jim increased his volume and forged on.

"We've got to give him enough rope to hang himself with," Jim said. "We still don't know why he would kill my dear friend Bjorn Nilsson, or why he's gone to such lengths to discredit me. We can't let him know we're on to him yet. I don't know who kidnapped my daughter, but considering everything that's gone on ..."

"He's going to burn in hell for all eternity for what he's done!" one council member blurted out. "He couldn't possibly be saved. He fooled us all."

"Yes, he did fool us all," Jim replied. "Everyone except Jasmine, apparently. But now we've all got to keep our collective eye on him. And I need to ask for your help."

"What took you so long?" Blake asked. "We're here for you - tell us what you need, and we'll do it." He turned to the others and said, "Am I right?"

Several in the assembly replied with "Absolutely", "Here, here", and "Amen!"

"First of all," Jim said, "I need protection for my family. Not only prayer, but physical protection, too. We know that Pete LeTourneu means harm to me and my family, that much is clear. But now that he's killed a man who was my friend, I can't be sure that he wouldn't do the same to me or my family. Of course, all of you know that my daughter, Chelsea, was kidnapped, and we haven't heard anything. No ransom demands, nothing."

"Yes," Blake said, "we can set up twenty-four hour protection for you. I don't know how yet, but I'll figure out a way to do that. Don't worry about it, Jim. Just leave it to us. We'll find a way."

In the background, the phone rang. Jim could hear Jasmine pick it up, and have a brief conversation with someone in a low voice. Moments later, she appeared at the edge of the living room.

"Excuse me, gentlemen," she said.

Jasmine walked up next to Jim, and whispered something in his ear. Jim's eyes grew wide, and he gasped audibly. "Go ahead and share it with the others," he said.

Jasmine turned to the group. "That was our friend with the sheriff's department. He just got off his shift, and wanted to let us know that ..."

Jasmine's eyes grew misty and she choked up on the next sentence. "... that Angela Shepherd – Angela Haskell, actually, was murdered in her apartment, early this morning or possibly last night."

Another collective gasp went through the room and Jasmine continued. "There's more. It looks like Pete LeTourneu's name is an alias. His real name - or maybe just another alias, is Peter Durgin."

Several council members shook their heads in disbelief, and the grumbling started again.

"Is your son here?" Blake asked.

"Yes," Jasmine replied. "Why?"

"Why don't you bring him in here?" Blake answered. "I want to lay hands on the three of you and pray for your protection. After that, we'll wrap this meeting up and do what we need to do to arrange protection. I'll need a daily schedule from each of you that details your activities."

"Okay," Jim said, "we can do that."

Jasmine went out to get Garrett, and all present rose to stand in a circle. Jasmine and Garrett returned presently, and the group closed in to place their hands upon the trio, or on the back or shoulder of someone who was touching a DiMario. As Blake Aanstad began his prayer of blessing and protection, it seemed ironic to Jim that he would be on the receiving end of such a prayer. He was always the one who prayed for others, calling upon God to bless and protect different people for different reasons.

So overwhelming were the heartfelt words that poured out from Blake, and the affirmation of the others, with "Yes, Lord" and "Amen" being heard around the circle, that Jim began to weep freely. All of the burdens that he'd been carrying on his own, the fear for his daughter, the uncertainty about the charges made against him, his heartache over his lost friend; finally he shrugged the load off his own shoulders, and lay it all at the foot of the cross.

Why did I ever think I could handle this all myself? he wondered. *This is all God's problem, not mine. And now that I've shared it with these friends, they're going to shoulder some of the burden, too.*

By the time Blake got to the end of his prayer, Jim realized that being prayed for had never felt so good as it did right now.

CHAPTER 54

East Valley Sheriff's Station: Simi Valley, California

The morning shift roll call was just breaking up when Rich heard his watch commander call his name.

"Harrison," his boss barked, "get in here." He motioned to his office, and turned to go inside.

When Rich followed him through the door, he noticed that there were two plainclothes cops sitting in the only two extra chairs in the office.

These guys aren't dressed good enough to be Internal Affairs, and they didn't look like Feds, Rich figured, quickly sizing them up.

The barrel-chested watch commander sat down behind his desk in the cluttered small office, his desk nameplate prominently displayed at the edge of the desk - *'Mac Evans, Watch Commander'*. Rich was the only one left standing, and he felt like he was the odd man out in some warped game of musical chairs.

"Shut the door, Rich," Evans said. Motioning at the two strangers, he added, "These two detectives are from LAPD Hollywood Division. They want to ask you a few questions about a murder case they're working."

Neither detective stood or extended their hand to Rich.

"Okay," Rich said, "shoot - no pun intended."

He eased the door shut, and stood uncomfortably by it.

The two didn't return his smile, apparently not amused by Rich's jest.

"We understand you knew the deceased," said the detective with the shaved head and camel hair sport coat. "Angela Haskell."

Rich nodded. "I heard about it yesterday," he replied. He could feel three pairs of eyes upon him, studying every nuance of every move, every tone and inflection in his voice. "I didn't know her very well; I only went out with her once."

"How did you meet her?" asked the rotund detective with the garish clip-on necktie and rumpled suit.

"Traffic stop," Rich answered.

Both detectives turned to each other, and the chubby one raised an eyebrow.

"I see - and did you offer her leniency on a traffic violation in exchange for … anything?" the portly one probed.

Rich could feel his blood pressure starting to rise, and actually heard the blood pumping in his eardrums. "No," he said coldly, "I didn't. Why do you ask?"

"Just covering all the bases," Portly said casually. "Would you be willing to take a lie detector test while we ask you some questions?"

"Do you have reason to think that I'm lying?" Rich countered.

"No, but if you have nothing to hide, you shouldn't mind ..."

"If you insult my personal integrity?" Rich interjected, cutting him off. He started to walk over to where the detective was sitting. "Look, if you want to call me a liar, why don't you do it when we're both off duty. Then there wouldn't be anything to stop me from punching you in the nose."

Rich stopped only about two feet from his accuser and towered over him, staring him down. Mac Evans got up from his seat and moved over to them.

"Hey, now, let's calm down here," Evans said. "Nobody's making accusations here."

"Sure sounds like it to me," Rich said.

The shaved-headed detective with a five o'clock shadow all around his head went on the offensive.

"Is there some reason why your name and phone number would be written on a note beside her bed?" he demanded.

"No," Rich said, turning to him. "No reason I can think of. I haven't talked to her since our one and only date."

"And when was that?" Bald Head asked.

"Saturday night."

"Last Saturday night? Four days ago?" Portly asked.

"That's right," Rich replied.

"Did you have sex with her?"

"No."

"Did she invite you in to her apartment?"

"No."

"Did you have an argument with her at the restaurant you had dinner at?"

Rich suddenly realized that the detectives must have talked to a witness at the restaurant, who saw Angela Shepherd get up and walk out in a huff.

"No, not an argument, really," he said, choosing his words carefully. "We did have an animated discussion, though. She got mad and left."

"What did you fight about?" Bald Head probed.

"I already told you that we didn't fight," Rich replied, trying to keep his cool. "We were talking about her acting gigs. She apparently thought I was downgrading the quality of her roles."

"So she got up and left," Portly summarized. "What happened then?"

"I gave her cab fare to get home before she left. Then I finished my dessert, and left. The tiramisu is really good there."

"Gave her cab fare, huh? What a gentleman," Bald Head said.

"Was that a question?" Rich asked tersely.

"Let's stick to the facts here," Evans warned. He slowly returned to his chair behind the desk and sat back down.

"Of course," Portly replied. Turning back to Rich again, he asked, "So, where did you go after that?"

"A friend's house, up in Westlake Village."

"So you've got a friend who'll give you an alibi for last night?"

"Three, actually. As if I needed an alibi." Rich said.

"It would help," Bald Head said. "You want to give me their names and contact info?"

"You want to charge me with something first?"

Bald Head turned to the watch commander with raised hands. "I'm not getting much cooperation here," he said curtly. "Can you do something about this?"

"We're always willing to cooperate with LAPD, of course," Mac Evans replied with feigned sincerity. "But Deputy Harrison is right - he doesn't have to prove his innocence to you. He's given you the answers to your questions." He stood up from his chair. "Will there be anything else, gentlemen?"

The two detectives looked at each other, then Portly replied, "Not at this time." To Rich, he added, "We may have more questions for you later. I'll advise you not to leave town."

"Oh, please," Rich replied, "you guys must be watching too many reruns of *Dragnet*."

Without another word, the LAPD detectives opened the door and walked out, and shut it behind them. Rich watched them go, his eyes boring a hole in their backs as they left the office area.

Rich turned to his supervisor. "Thanks for backing me up there," he said.

"No problem. I don't appreciate them coming down here to throw out random accusations at one of mine," Mac Evans replied. "I've known you for a long time now, Rich. You're a good cop. You'll make a good sergeant, too, before long."

"Thanks, Mac."

"But, I know you well enough to notice that you've got somethin' going on the side," Mac said.

Rich let the statement hang in the air without reply.

Mac Evans was a large black man, about fiftyish, with short hair that was starting to speckle with gray. He was a bit overweight, but had a powerfully heavy build rather than flabby-heavy. He'd been in the department since the Earth was young, and was working well past his minimum twenty for retirement. Rich figured him to be the kind of guy who wouldn't know what to do with himself after a week of retirement.

"You've been working on somethin', I know that much," Mac continued. "Your work hasn't suffered for it, though, so I haven't brought it up before. You've been taking days off at a moment's notice, requesting beat changes, working on the computer whenever you get a few spare minutes. I'm not blind, Rich, and I'm not dumb, either. I've been working with you, so be straight with me."

Mac sat down in his chair. He folded his arms and leaned back, waiting. Rich could tell that he wasn't going to let him off the hook until he fessed up. Mac motioned to a chair, and Rich took the clue and sat. He tried to quickly formulate a plan to give his supervisor enough, but not too much.

"Yeah, you're right, Mac," Rich began. "I am working on something - on my own time. It's an investigation. It's best if I don't tell you too much."

"Okay," Mac replied cautiously, "tell me enough to give me a clue and make me feel good, but not enough to keep me from using plausible deniability."

"Remember that thing that came up in the desert a couple weeks ago? The dead infant graveyard?"

"Yeah?"

"The case I'm working on involves that, and a lot more."

Mac sat forward in his chair and looked Rich in the eye. "That's not our jurisdiction, Rich," he said warily. "That's SBSD - you know that."

"I know, I know. But I'm not stepping on any toes there." Rich tried a different tack. "You know those cat mutilations that come up in Westlake Village now and then, up by county line?"

"Yeah?"

"You'd like to get those solved, wouldn't you?"

"You know I would," Mac replied, fighting back a grin.

"That's part of this, too," Rich said. "And don't worry, I'm not going to make you look bad."

"So, what do you know about this Angela Haskell killing?"

"More than I told them," Rich admitted. "But I did answer their questions honestly. She's part of the overall investigation. When I get to the bottom of this, I won't be surprised if we get her killer, along with a bunch of other pond scum."

"I wouldn't mind coming out on top, for a change," Mac said. "I've always said there's more to being a patrol cop than writing traffic citations and breaking up marital disputes. But we can't withhold any pertinent information from LAPD, you know that."

"Of course not," Rich replied, straight-faced. "I gave them what they need, for now. They need to look elsewhere for a suspect."

"How long is this investigation going to run?" Mac asked.

"The pieces are starting to come together. And when it's over, it's gonna be a big bust," Rich said.

He sat forward in his chair and looked his boss in the eye. "Mac, I need you to support me on this. You know I wouldn't do anything to hurt the department, and I'm on to something really big here."

"All right, Rich. As far as I'm concerned, your only crime is extreme enthusiasm to put the bad guys away. Just keep it low key, and for cripe's sake, don't let our own detectives find out what you're doing. I'd really catch hell for that. I'll try to keep LAPD off your back, but I can't appear to be uncooperative."

Mac sat back in his chair again and linked his fingers behind his head. "So," he said, "Do you need any help on this? Not like I could offer any official help, anyway. But I'd at least like to know that you're not in over your head."

"I've got some help. A detective up in Minneapolis, and a news reporter."

"Watch out for that one," Mac warned, pointing his finger at Rich. "You know the news media can't be trusted. Some of those guys - and gals for that matter, would sell their own mother for a hot story."

"I know," Rich replied. "But I think this guy is signed on to the plan of putting the bad guys away. He won't jump the gun - he wants the whole story when we get to the end, and it'll be an exclusive for him. He's not dumb enough to blow it for us."

At least I hope not, Rich thought. *I better not mention to Mac that my other partners are a church pastor and a teenage computer hacker.*

"All right," Mac said. "Just watch yourself. I've got your back on my end." He stood up and motioned to the door. "Now get out of here and bring me some bad guys."

CHAPTER 55

Simmons Residence: Westlake Village, California

George pulled up in front of Trey's house as the calm of twilight was settling upon the neighborhood. It had been breezy and cool today, but for a brief half hour or so between late afternoon and nightfall, the brown and amber leaves that littered the street didn't stir.

George got out of the car carefully, holding the cup carrier loaded with goods from the local Starbucks. Trey's instructions had been clear - bring strong coffee, and lots of it. George was happy to oblige, expecting a good payoff of information.

He knocked on the door, and was greeted by Debbie Simmons, Trey's mom. She looked surprisingly young for having a son Trey's age, George thought. Her brown hair was shoulder length, and was formed into a contemporary style, with a jagged part on one side.

"You must be George," she said. "Of course you are - I've seen you on TV often enough. But you look different on TV."

"Let me guess - I'm shorter in person," George joked.

"No, no, it's not that," she said, smiling, "Come in. Trey's back in his room." She stepped aside and waved him in.

"Thanks, Mrs. Simmons. I'll try not to spoil his appetite for dinner with these pastries and coffee."

"Are you kidding? He can eat everything you've got there and still put away twice as much as either of us. By the way, I'm planning on having you stay for dinner."

"Thanks, Mrs. Simm ...," George started.

"Debbie," she corrected. "We're having pot roast and baked potatoes. If you're one of those vegetarians or vegans, you're out of luck."

"Hey, that sounds great - smells great, too. I don't get home-cooked meals much these days."

"No problem. I'll be able to brag to my friends that I hosted a TV celebrity." She motioned toward the hallway. "Trey's room is at the end of the hall. You can go back, if you like. Dinner will be ready in about ten minutes."

George nodded, and headed down the hall to Trey's lair. The door was open, and he found the young man huddled in front of his computer, illuminated in the dim light of the room only by the glow of the computer monitor reflecting off his determined face. He glanced up momentarily when George filled the doorway.

"Hey," Trey said, looking back down at his screen. "I thought I heard you come in."

"I come with fuel for your search," George said, offering up the coffee and pastries.

"Sweet," Trey replied. He looked at the selection of four cups on the tray and quickly deciphered the coded markings on the side of each. "Café mocha, extra hot, extra shot," he recited, pulling one cup out of the cardboard carrier. "Thanks."

He took a long sip, then set the cup down on the desk in front of him.

"Ah, that's da bomb," he said. "Still hot, too - thanks."

Leaning back in his chair, he interlaced his fingers and stretched his arms out in front of himself, eliciting multiple cracking sounds from his knuckles in the process.

"Well," he said at last, "I've already got enough to know that Brehm's dirty, and I expect to get more." He smiled at George with a look of self satisfaction.

"What did you find out?" George asked, taking a cup of his own.

"Have a seat, and I'll tell you," Trey said.

George complied, clearing a spot for himself on the cluttered bed. Trey pivoted around in his swivel chair to face him.

"After my first scan, I found four e-mail addresses that belong to Mr. Aldon Brehm," he said. "Three of them are official, business types; one for his campaign for county supervisor, one for his office at the college. But one is his personal e-mail address. I sent him an e-mail from one of my own addresses that I don't use much; I've got about eight addresses myself."

"You sent him a message?" George asked, his voice rising slightly in alarm.

"Relax. I made it look like spam in the content, but I put in a subject line that I hoped he might go for, and he did."

George raised his hands and gave a curious look.

"I put the word *Anubis* in the subject line," Trey announced.

George was flabbergasted, and he stood up and demanded, "Why would you do that? We don't want him to know we're onto him."

"To get him to open the message," Trey replied. "I embedded a keystroke-logging program into the message as a Trojan Horse."

"What does that mean?" George asked, with evident frustration. He outstretched his hands in front of himself as if he expected to receive the meaning of it all on a silver tray.

"It means that my little application will record everything he writes on his computer, and send me a report every hour of what he's written, what e-mail he's received, and what he's sent. It'll also give me his personal address book. He won't know that I'm monitoring him, because the reports will automatically be erased from his *sent items* folder as soon as his computer sends them."

George sat back down on the edge of the bed, and scratched his head. "Sounds like some kind of computer virus," he said.

Trey shrugged. "Yeah, that's basically what it is."

"You know how to write computer viruses?" George asked incredulously.

"Sure," Trey replied matter-of-factly. "But I like to call them applications. *Virus* has such a negative ring to it." In response to George's look of shock, Trey added, "Hey, I've never sent anyone a destructive virus. I'm totally against that."

"Why would anyone do that?" George asked. "I can't understand what would motivate anyone to do such a thing."

"To show the world that they can. It's a power trip. Most people who write Trojan code never actually send it. They just show it off to their friends."

George shook his head in disbelief. "But won't Brehm be able to trace it back, find out who sent it to him?"

Trey smiled. "No way," he replied smugly. "I added a feature that makes it look like someone in his personal address book sent it. As soon as it hits his inbox - boom! It randomly picks an address from his address book and sticks it in the sender's line. The return address is changed in a fraction of a second. So even if he was watching closely when the message arrived, he'd never see the real sender - me."

"What if he has anti-virus software?"

"Doesn't matter. Those applications protect only from known viruses. Mine is brand new."

George again shook his head slowly from side to side. "Incredible," he said. "But what if he replies to your message?"

"Wouldn't that be interesting?"

George thought about that a moment, then changed the subject. "You said that you already found out some info about Brehm."

"Oh, yeah," Trey answered, turning back to some sheets of paper on his desk. "Let me show you."

He picked up a few sheets and looked over them, then handed them to George.

"He's pretty well off for a college professor," Trey said. "Here's a list of his real estate holdings - his *personal* real estate holdings, I should say."

George looked over the list and raised an eyebrow. Trey continued to download his findings to George. "He's got that phat crib over in North Ranch, we knew that already. But he's also the owner of a few other fine properties, too."

"Phat?"

"Yeah, you know, luxurious, fancy - phat."

"Okay. But there's nothing illegal about having a *phat* house," George countered, using his fingers in the 'quote - unquote' sign. "This is the land of opportunity, you know."

"True. But the North Ranch place is worth about three mil, and he has a place in Laguna Beach, on the water. That one's worth about five mil. Then there's his mountain crib up in Big Bear - we're not talking a cabin here, either. It's a three-thousand square foot custom log home at the base of the Snow Summit ski resort. Same neighborhood as that boxer, Oscar De La Hoya."

Trey paused a moment to take a sip of his coffee. "I wouldn't mind coming home to a place like that after a hard day of snow boarding. He bought it last year for about nine-hundred large. It's worth more now, of course." He sat back and sipped some more.

"How do you know about all those houses?" George asked.

"Public records," Trey replied between sips. "You just have to know how to search. Once I got the addresses, then I got into the county assessor's records through a back door using the county clerk's web site." He paused and raised a finger. "That part isn't public record," he said with a sly smile.

"After I got the assessed value for each property, I got onto the realtor's multiple listing service site to get more details. And then ...," another sip. "You'd be surprised at how helpful some realtors can be in estimating current values of homes if they think you're interested in buying." He laughed, "I'll probably be getting follow-up calls for weeks."

"You told them that you were a buyer?" George asked.

"Of course not!" Trey replied with simulated offense. "I told them that I'm *interested* in these properties, which is true. They might assume I'm a buyer." He let out a self-satisfied chuckle.

George grinned and pointed a finger at Trey. "I'm gonna tell your pastor on you!" he said.

"Sure, in about five years from now, okay?"

George nodded in agreement, then Trey added, "But there's more, and this is the best part. He's a principal partner in a corporation that owns more properties - lots more."

"What kind of corporation?" George asked.

"I don't know yet. It's called TOA International, Inc. Want to know the other partner's names?"

"I'm all ears."

"One of 'em's a familiar name - Peter Durgin."

"Huh!," George replied, with a jaded grin. "Small world, isn't it?"

"Yep. The other names I don't recognize; Roberta McAllister, Jack Nelson, and Gilberto Pimental."

George just shrugged at the names. "So, what do they own, and what's their business?"

"Well," Trey said, "it looks like TOA International is a shell corporation of some kind - a holding company that runs a bunch of other businesses. I don't mind telling you that I really had to dig to find the names of the partners. They're clearly trying to remain invisible."

"How do you know about shell corporations and stuff like that?"

"Macro Economics 101."

"What kind of businesses do they have?"

"I thought you'd never ask. One of them is Far East Imports, as you might have guessed. They also operate Saint Martha's Adoption Agency in Woodland Hills, and Pyramid Entertainment Enterprises in Chatsworth. It's a porn video distributor, I already found that out. I don't know if they actually film their own porn movies, or just distribute them."

George nodded. "West San Fernando Valley actually is the pornography capitol of the whole country," he said. "I read that somewhere."

Trey handed some papers over to George as he was talking, then finished off his café mocha. He sat the empty cup down on his computer desk.

"They also run a drug rehab center down in Van Nuys, and a teen center in Burbank," he added.

"A bunch of saints, except for the porn business," George remarked with heavy sarcasm. "I think I'll need to visit all these businesses, with a hidden camera and a wire." He smiled to himself. "It makes for must-see TV."

"Sounds like as much fun as our trip to beautiful downtown San Bernardino," Trey said. "But first let me tell you about their land holdings."

"There's more?" George asked, genuinely surprised. He straightened up into an erect sitting position on the end of the bed, his hands on his knees.

"Oh, yeah. They own some industrial buildings all across the Southland," Trey said, while scanning and flipping through the pages in his hand. "City of Commerce, Norwalk, Carson - a bunch of others. But they own 'unimproved' properties, too."

"Meaning vacant land," George acknowledged.

"Right. And guess where one of these vacant lots happens to be?" Trey grinned and winked.

"You don't mean ..."

"Yermo!" Trey blurted. "Nine and a half acres of land out in the middle of nowhere."

"The same land as the burial site?" George asked in wonderment.

"Dunno. The county records just have the legal description of the property. Lot so and so of tract whatever, that kind of thing. No street address."

"But we should be able to find out from an assessor's map, right?" George stated, more than asked.

"Sure. I just haven't got that far yet."

"Well, you've got plenty of coffee now," George prompted.

"Dude, man does not live on coffee alone; I need food, too. And I've got classes in the morning."

George frowned. "All right, what can I do to help? This is important stuff you're onto here. I really want you to follow it up."

"Well," Trey said, trying to suppress a sly grin, "I could be more effective if I had a Blackberry."

"What? I'll get you a whole crate of blackberries."

Trey gave George the look that all-knowing teenagers frequently give to their older counterparts; a patented, smug blend of exasperation, condescension, and impatience.

"I'm talking about the wireless communication device that's called a Blackberry, he said, slowly sounding out the words as if George wouldn't understand. "It's a combination cell phone and PDA, that has wireless e-mail connectivity."

"Don't you have a cell phone now?" George asked.

Trey held up his empty hands. "Nope – can't afford it."

"So, if you had one of these things, you could send and receive e-mail from anywhere, go on the internet, and make calls, too?"

"Yep," Trey said with a smile.

"Consider it done," George said. "We'll go out after dinner to the nearest big box store and hook you up."

"All right!" Trey exclaimed.

Trey's mother appeared in the doorway. "Speaking of dinner, we're ready. Come sit up to the table." She turned and left.

"Okay," Trey and George said in unison.

They both got up, and Trey stopped George before going out the door.

"Why would a business corporation own vacant land in a place like Yermo?" he asked.

George shook his head. "One thing's for sure, it's not for the investment potential."

"No kidding. But it sure is a great place to hide stuff."

CHAPTER 56

Whataburger Restaurant: Thousand Oaks, California

R ich drove his Crown Victoria police interceptor as fast as he could, with lights and siren blazing. The cell phone call from Garrett DiMario had been brief - *"She's here"*.

As he got off the 101 freeway at Moorpark Road, he turned off the lights and siren, and quickly punched Garrett's cell number into his own phone, and held it up to his ear.

"Almost there," he said when Garrett answered. "Tell me where she is exactly."

"She's inside the Whataburger, sitting at a table with two guys," Garrett replied. "I don't know who they are - they don't go to my school, and they look too old anyway. She has black hair in a short bob cut, with short trimmed bangs, and she's wearing all black - including a short black mini-skirt."

Rich smiled to himself. *Sure, he would notice that*, he thought. "Ten-four," he replied, forgetting momentarily that he was speaking into a cell phone, rather than his police radio. "I'll come right in and take her into custody. Then I'll bring her to the church, like we planned. Make sure you and your dad and mom are there. I'm putting my neck on the line to take her over there, instead of the Sheriff's station; it's against policy."

"We don't want you to get in trouble, Rich. But we need to find out why she planted that dope in my locker. I know it's not as important as finding my sister, but we've got the opportunity now."

"Right," Rich replied. "Don't take off until I've got her in the car. I want you to be a witness, just in case."

"Gotcha. My buddy Austin's here with me – we're sitting at a table outside," Garrett replied. Then he snapped his phone shut.

Rich drove up Thousand Oaks Boulevard, and turned into the burger joint's parking lot. He parked in back, and when he opened his car door, he caught the inviting whiff of burgers on the broiler. He wished for a moment that he had time to enjoy one of the big burgers - the best in town, with sliced jalapenos on top. He decided that's how he'd play it - a hungry cop coming in for a late lunch.

Rich approached the door and saw Garrett, and acknowledged him with a quick nod. He walked in the door casually, and played his eyes across the menu above the ordering area. He could sense the girl and her two male companions looking over at him, but he didn't look their way.

A friendly high school-age girl waited patiently for Rich behind the counter. There weren't any other customers in front of him.

"May I help you, officer?" she asked sweetly.

"I'm still deciding," Rich replied. He continued to scan the menu board until he noticed out of the corner of his eye that his target and the other diners were now ignoring him. Then he made his move.

Rich turned abruptly and walked into the dining area where the trio were seated, eating french fries and drinking their cokes. They were talking and laughing, until he strode up to where Kristi Sims was sitting. She looked up at the large, muscular cop, and the smile quickly faded from her face.

"Kristi Hawkins of Akron, Ohio," Rich said, "I'm taking you into custody for being a runaway. Get up."

An expression of shock and astonishment came across her face, which she tried to quickly cover up with a well-rehearsed look of aloof hardness.

"I don't know what you're talking about," she said, averting her eyes from his intrusive stare. "My name is Kristi Sims, and I've never even been to Ohio."

Her denial was well-practiced, but unconvincing to Rich, who dealt with liars routinely. On a scale of one to ten, he mentally ranked her charade at a five.

"Hey, I'll even show you my I.D.," she added, digging into her purse. She opened her wallet, which Rich noticed was stuffed with a lot of cash for a teenager. With trembling hands, she pulled out the California driver's license that bore her false identity. "See?" she said, thrusting it at him.

Rich took the driver's license and looked it over thoroughly. "This is a real good forgery," he said, "one of the best I've seen."

By now, every eye in the place was trained on the drama unfolding in the midst of afternoon consumption.

"Get up," Rich repeated, "And put your hands behind your back."

Kristi reluctantly complied, and Rich fastened his handcuffs around her slender wrists.

"Dude, this is bogus," said the scruffy-looking young man with tousled hair and black jacket who was seated at her table.

"Yeah, you can't do this," added the other, an asian punk with a thin goatee, shaved head, and a colored tattoo on his neck.

"I can, and I am," Rich stated, matter-of-factly.

With that, he escorted her out of the dining area and out the door, with his right hand firmly clamped around her left arm.

As they left, the shaggy young man seated at the table turned to his companion.

"We can't let this happen," he whispered fervently. "We've got to do something!"

"I know," replied the asian youth with the tattoo and goatee on his chin. "How could that cop find out who she is?"

"Who cares?" replied the other. "If she gets taken in, we'll catch the heat for it. Do you want to explain this to The Master?"

"Hell, no! We've got to put a stop to this. I didn't see any other cops, did you?"

The other guy shook his shaggy head silently. Then they both got up and casually walked to the door.

From his vantage point at the outdoor table closest to the street, Garrett DiMario watched the activity inside the restaurant, with his friend Austin by his side. He didn't like what he was seeing.

"Dude, check it out," Garrett said, elbowing Austin.

Austin looked up from the last remains of his French fries to see that the two creeps that had been sitting with Kristi Hawkins were now exiting the side door, and moving toward the rear of the building where Rich's patrol car was parked.

"Uh, oh," Austin said, "this doesn't look good."

"C'mon," said Garrett.

They got up quickly, and followed the two.

Rich unlocked his patrol car's door, while keeping a grip on the vigorously protesting Kristi. In his peripheral vision, he noticed them - the two companions of his prisoner, coming his way. There was nobody else in the parking lot behind the burger joint.

Rich quickly got the rear door open, and unceremoniously shoved Kristi into the back of the car, and slammed the door shut. He turned to face the two young punks, who approached menacingly. Rich noticed the glint of metal in the hand of the one with the goatee, then looked and saw something in the hand of the other one, too.

The first one flipped his wrist suddenly, exposing a six inch-long blade. He flipped it open and closed teasingly - a *Balisong* butterfly knife. The two came to a stop about three feet from where Rich was standing, just outside his striking radius.

"Let her go, pig," the one with the goatee demanded. "Let her go, or we'll cut you up."

The guy with the long shaggy hair also tried to flip his knife around, while staring at Rich, but he was clearly less accomplished at knife handling than his cohort. Rich sized them up, his martial arts experience dictating that he take out the strong one first.

Goatee took a step forward and raised the tip of his knife up toward Rich. Rich raised his right hand up, palm open. His left hand stealthily moved to the handle of his PR-24 baton.

"Hey, let's take it easy here," Rich said. He stared his assailant in the eye. "Do you have any idea how much trouble you can get into by pulling a knife on a peace officer?"

"Looks like you're the one in trouble here," taunted the shaggy-haired one.

For one instant, Goatee averted his focus away from Rich to shoot a gloating smile at his accomplice. That was all the time Rich needed. In one fluid motion, his left hand that cupped the handle of the baton shot forward, pulling the side-handled weapon out of the ring on his belt. His arm reached the end of it's extension, and he let go of the baton handle. It found it's mark, slamming into the nose of the knife-wielding punk in front of him. Goatee didn't see it coming until one millisecond before impact.

Blood sprayed from his nose, and the knife flew out of his hand simultaneously as a result of Rich's split-second move. Goatee fell back onto the asphalt, stunned and hurt. Rich sidestepped to his right and pivoted left, his hand coming to his sidearm. He expected an attack from the other punk, but instead of an attack, Shaggy-Hair lurched forward spastically, his head snapping back hard enough to incur a whiplash injury. He slammed belly-first into Rich's patrol car, like a rag doll being cast about by a careless child.

It was only then that Rich realized that his tormentor's mode of propulsion was Garrett DiMario, who plowed into the guy's lower back with a big head of steam. Immediately, a fusillade of blows fell upon Shaggy-Hair's head, neck, and back from Garrett's friend, Austin.

Rich stepped back and watched as the attacker's body twitched and jerked, with Austin's fists and elbows repeatedly lacing into him. After several hits, the guy was down for the count. By the time Garrett straightened up, he found nothing left to hit.

Rich smiled at the two panting teenagers. "Nice work, guys. Thanks for the help," he said.

Not like I needed help, he thought to himself.

Rich opened his door and got on the police radio to get backup.

Twenty minutes later, the two punks were sitting, cuffed, in the back of a second deputy's car. Garrett and Austin had given their statements, and were ready to roll. Before they headed to Austin's car, Garrett glanced over at the two thugs in the back of the car. Goatee's nose was red and swollen, with dried blood around his face. The other guy's left eye was nearly shut from the swelling incurred by Austin's well-placed punches.

He also looked over at Kristi, who had been sitting in the back of Rich's police cruiser during the whole incident She looked to him like a caged animal - nervousness marking her pretty face. She looked at Garrett and shouted a curse, which was muffled by the rolled-up window.

You'll be singing a different tune pretty soon, I'll bet, Garrett thought to himself.

He gave Austin a high-five, and they walked off to his car.

CHAPTER 57

Solid Rock Community Church: Westlake Village, California

Pressing down on the accelerator of his police cruiser, Rich kept his eyes focused on the road. His prisoner in the back seat had been quiet until now, but as the squad car merged onto the freeway, she spoke up.

"This isn't the way to the Sheriff's station," she said. "Where are we going?"

"Oh, so you've been to the cop shop before, then?" Rich asked.

Kristi Hawkins-Sims was silent for a moment before answering. "No, I've never been there," she said. "Other people have told me about where it is."

"You're technically telling the truth, Kristi. But you have been a guest of our brothers to the south, haven't you?"

Rich adjusted his rear-view mirror to assess the look on her face as he dropped this information bomb. She didn't answer his question. Rich had one eye on her stunned reflection in the mirror, and the other eye on the road.

"Got picked up for prostitution by the LAPD down in Van Nuys under your assumed name, didn't you? Almost two years ago. What have you been doing since then?" Rich probed.

"That was a mistake," Kristi protested from the back seat. "I wasn't hooking, I was just hanging around with my friends."

"Oh, okay," Rich replied sarcastically. "And then some 'friends' bailed you out and got an attorney to defend you. You didn't get convicted, thanks to your high-priced shylock."

"That's right!" Kristi shot back, "not guilty, like I said."

"Yep, somebody invested quite a bit of dough to get you off the hook. I understand Irving Cohen charges about two bills an hour for his services."

Rich watched the mirror as her countenance of contempt shifted to a deer-in-the-headlights look.

"'Course, if the police had really done their homework," he pressed, "they would have figured out that you were a fifteen year-old runaway from a family in the Midwest. Then things would have turned out a bit differently, wouldn't they?"

"That's not true," Kristi countered. "I showed you my I.D. I was eighteen then, and I'm twenty years old now."

"Wow! That's pretty old to be attending high school," Rich chided. "You must be the oldest tenth-grader Westlake High has ever seen."

Rich was playing her like a fish hooked on an angler's lure. But unlike the fish, there was no chance of Kristi getting off the hook this time, and they both knew it.

"Okay, so I got held back a couple years," Kristi ventured. "I've had some problems in school - big deal."

"Boy, don't I know it. For one thing, you just appeared at Westlake High School at the start of this semester with a transcript from Royal High in Simi Valley."

"That's right."

"Problem is, you never went there. There is no official transcript or record of you attending there." Rich took a deep breath and let it out. "You just don't seem to exist, Kristi Sims – Hawkins, that is. You're a ghost."

"Their record keeping must be bad at that school."

"Maybe so," Rich replied, setting the hook deeper. "I'm sure some of your teachers will remember you. Not to mention your counselor, and all your old friends. You know, all those friends whose pictures are in the class yearbook - the same yearbook that you're not in."

Kristi didn't reply. When she finally did speak, she changed the direction of the conversation.

"You didn't answer me before," she said. "Where are you taking me?"

"I know a pastor who has worked with runaways," Rich replied. "I'm sure he'd be willing to help you transition to the next step."

"What next step?"

"Reuniting with your parents."

Kristi didn't answer. In his rear view mirror, Rich took a peek at the girl who's face now looked pale and sick.

"I want to see my lawyer!" she blurted out suddenly.

"Ha! You don't get a lawyer. You're an underage runaway. But we can ask your parents if they'd like to retain legal counsel to represent you."

Kristi slumped back in the hard plastic rear seat resignedly. There was nothing left - no further lies to try. For the remainder of the few minutes it took to get to the church, she remained as silent as the grave.

When Rich drove his patrol car into the parking lot of the church, he saw the welcoming party standing outside the office trailer.

Jim and Jasmine stood silhouetted by the late afternoon sun that made Jasmine's blonde hair glow with an ethereal halo-like effect. It was getting close to five o' clock, but most of the office staff were still present inside the office - including Pete LeTourneu.

Jim saw the patrol car approach, and stepped forward to motion to Rich, diverting him toward the church sanctuary. Rich made a left at the fork in the drive that separated the church sanctuary parking from the office parking, and the school construction site. He pulled up in front of the deserted church sanctuary building, and parked out of the view of the church office.

Jim and Jasmine strode briskly around to the front of the sanctuary, which was about a hundred and fifty feet away, and hidden from view of the office trailer. Jim fought down the impulse to glance over his shoulder to see if anyone - LeTourneu in particular, was watching them through one of the office windows. He didn't want to draw any attention to them by looking secretive, which is exactly what they were.

Rich got out of the car as they walked up, and he opened the rear door of his cruiser to let his passenger out. She was so busy hurling a string of expletives and threats at Rich that she didn't hear the DiMarios walk up.

"So, this must be Kristi," Jasmine said, with a smile on her face.

Kristi Sims halted her diatribe, and turned toward them.

"I'm Jasmine DiMario," Jasmine said, introducing herself. "And this is my husband, Jim."

Kristi regarded the two warily, looking them up and down.

"I'm Kristi," she said, avoiding eye contact with both DiMarios.

"Why don't you come inside?" Jim offered. "We can talk privately in here."

He motioned to the church sanctuary. Then he and Jasmine turned and led the way.

Kristi realized that this invitation was not voluntary, cordial as it sounded.

Most church people don't arrive in handcuffs, she thought to herself as she followed the casually-dressed middle-aged couple toward the large, imposing building. *I don't know what's worse - being thrown in jail, or being forced to go to church. I guess these two must be some kind of counselors. Doesn't matter. For all their good intentions, I'll be back in The Master's hands by this time tomorrow, just like before.*

With Rich bringing up the rear, Jim led them to a side door in the building, rather than the main entrance. He took a key ring out of his pocket, unlocked the door, and opened it for Jasmine. Jim gestured for Kristi to follow, which she did. Before her eyes could adjust to the dim interior of the room, Jasmine flicked the light switch on. The room suddenly burst into brilliance under the fluorescent panels in the ceiling, and Kristi saw that she was standing in a large kitchen. There were two large commercial refrigerators against one wall. A large expanse of tan Formica countertops ringed the rest of the room, with two large stainless steel sinks imbedded in different locations. A big food preparation island was in the center of the room, and a small folding table stood near it.

"Please, have a seat," Jasmine said, as if she were entertaining dinner guests, rather than a prisoner.

"Can we do something about these handcuffs, Deputy Harrison?" Jim asked.

Rich fished into his pocket to retrieve the key to the cuffs, which he used to free her wrists.

Kristi reached up and brushed her tousled black hair back, and gave her head a quick shake. She sat down at the table, rubbing her wrists, all the while staring smugly at the couple. Jasmine and Jim sat across from her at the rectangular folding table, Rich to her right. His seat was closest to the door, just in case she tried to make a break for freedom. Jasmine got up again and went to the first refrigerator.

"Want a drink?" she asked.

Kristi shook her head, but Jasmine opened the refrigerator door and got out a soda for herself and Jim. "Deputy?" she asked.

"Coke is fine," Rich replied.

Jasmine returned with the drinks, including a cherry coke, which she sat in front of Kristi.

Jim had learned a lot about Kristi in the phone conversation he'd had only moments before with her mother in Ohio. Because they had anticipated this moment, Rich had previously supplied Jim with the names and phone number of the girl's parents which he had lifted from the runaway's police report. As soon as Garrett had called him from the Whataburger, Jim made the phone call Kristi's parents had been praying two years to receive. One of the things he had learned from the mother was that cherry coke was Kristi's favorite drink. The other thing he'd learned - on no uncertain terms, was that her parents wanted Kristi back.

Kristi accepted the soda without comment, popped it open, and took a long drink. Then she plopped the can down on the table, hard enough to cause some of the contents to spill out.

"All right," she said, "so what am I doing here?"

"You've been away from home a long time, Kristi," Jasmine said. "We want to help you find your way back."

"Hah!" Kristi snorted. "You have no idea. That's not possible. You don't know my parents."

"True," Jim acknowledged, "but I did talk to them just a few minutes ago."

The look of sullen hardness that characterized Kristi's face abruptly gave way to stunned surprise.

"What?" she gasped. "That's impossible. You're lying."

"I'm not," Jim replied quietly. "Your mom was so happy to hear that you're alive, she broke down and cried. She had to turn the phone over to your dad."

Kristi was dumbstruck, and it appeared to Jim that he'd hit a raw nerve - one that had never healed.

"When you left home," Jim continued, "you just left behind a note saying how much you hate them and their rules, and that you hope you never see them again."

Jim paused long enough to assess her reaction to his news so far. He observed a pained look that started to form small lines around her eyes and mouth, as she fought back the tears that built up behind her eyes.

"They were devastated, of course," Jim said. "Deeply wounded. They called the state police right away, who put out an APB for you. They found out you'd gotten a ride from somebody - they never found out who, to the nearest big city, where you got on a Greyhound bus going to California. By the time they figured it out, you'd already arrived in LA and disappeared into the crowd."

"And," Rich added, "LAPD doesn't have the resources to track down the thousands of runaways and throwaways that end up here in the Southland every year."

"So, they came out to LA themselves to look for you," Jim continued. "Put up some posters with your picture on them. But no luck. Then they hired a private detective to search for you."

"They … they really did all that?" Kristi asked, her lower lip quivering.

"Yes, they did. And they took out a second mortgage on their house to keep the search going. They even approached America's Most Wanted, but they wouldn't profile the case on TV, since you weren't abducted. After a year, the private detective managed to convince them that you were probably dead, since you didn't turn up at any of the homeless shelters or usual places where runaways go."

This time when Jim looked up at Kristi, tears were running down her cheeks and her pretty face knotted up with grief and regret.

"I can't b ... believe they tried that hard to find me," Kristi stuttered between sobs. She slumped forward in her chair and hugged herself. "My parents always gave me such a hard time - I ... I figured they were glad I was gone."

"They gave you a hard time because they love you," Jim said quietly, but firmly. "They wanted the best for you, and your future. Parents aren't perfect. They're learning as they go along. But just in the short time I was on the phone to your parents, I could tell that they care very much about you, Kristi."

"Kristi, you never tried to call them in all the time you were gone?" Jasmine asked.

"Not at first. Like I said, I figured my parents were glad I was gone. After awhile, I thought about calling. Just to let them know I'm alive, you know? But someone wouldn't let me."

"Who wouldn't let you?" Jim asked.

Kristi lowered her eyes, and said nothing.

The tension in the room suddenly spiked upward, and Jim felt it. He waited as patiently as he could, in spite of the suspense. He was afraid to push her too hard; perhaps he already had. He somehow recognized that he was standing on the tip of an iceberg, and this girl was the key to a revelation of great significance.

Kristi paused a long time before answering, and looked over at Rich. "My handlers, and The Master," she replied in a low voice. "No point in denying it, I guess. The deputy has done his homework on me, for some reason."

"How did they keep you from calling," Jim asked. "Was someone watching you all the time?"

"No," Kristi admitted. "I probably could have snuck a call, but The Master would have killed me if he found out."

"Who are these people, and how did you get mixed up with them," Jasmine asked.

Kristi paused, and took a deep cleansing breath before starting her tale.

"After I got to LA, I was living on the street while I looked for a job," she started. "I figured there were plenty of jobs out here, and I wouldn't have a problem getting one. But it wasn't that easy. You need to have an address, a social security number, a work permit, all kinds of stuff. I could lie about my age, even make up a fake address and social security number. But I didn't have a telephone, and I couldn't get a work permit - turns out you can only get one at your local high school counseling office. But if you're not a student there ..." she raised her empty hands and shrugged.

"Then I went to a homeless shelter one night, and I met a guy there. He said he knew somebody who could, like, hook me up with work, and that I had the look to become a model, and this guy he knows had connections to make it happen. So I went with him to meet this guy."

Kristi looked up at the ceiling, shook her head, and let out a short, derisive laugh. "Boy, how whacked is that? Fifteen years old, straight out of the Midwest. Didn't even think about what this guy would want in return for helping me. So, I went with the guy by bus to the San Fernando Valley. It seemed so far from downtown LA, but the city like, never ended as we drove along. I had no idea until then how humongous LA is, you know?"

She collected her thoughts, and went on. As she spoke, it seemed to Jim that she was unshouldering a huge burden that she had been carrying on her young shoulders for entirely too long.

"We got to this guy's office, and I met him. He seemed pretty fly, at first. He hooked me up with some new clothes, a hot shower, makeup, and stuff. Then he took me out to dinner at bangin' restaurant, and I got my hair did at a fancy salon. Then they had this gay makeup artist do my makeup, and show me how to do it myself. Then he took me to a nail salon and I had a set of cute acrylic nails put on, and my feet pedicured. I'd never had that kind of treatment before; couldn't believe how freakin' lucky I was - so I thought."

Another short, pained laugh at the memory. "Turns out, he was just like, investing in a new asset - me. By the time we got back to his shop, I looked, you know, great and felt like a princess. But that was the last time I ever felt like that."

Kristi's eyes grew misty, and she lowered them to the table in front of her as she continued her confession. It was pouring out of her now; like a levee with a crack that has started to leak water, the long-suppressed memories and secrets that Kristi held within her had started to flow out, and there was no stopping it now.

"He ... talked me into doing things," she said haltingly. "Weird things I didn't want to do. It started that same night with some pictures. He's got a photo studio set up in the basement of his shop. It's like a one-bedroom apartment down there, but nobody lives in it. I figured out later that it's just a video and photo studio."

Jasmine passed a box of tissues over to her. Kristi took one and blew her nose.

Rich started fumbling with one of the numerous black leather cases that dotted his belt. He pulled out a tiny micro cassette recorder.

"I'd like to record this, if you don't mind," he said softly to Kristi.

She shrugged and replied, "Why not? He's going to kill me anyway when he finds out I talked to you, just like he's killed other people that crossed him. I don't care anymore, anyway. I just can't keep living like this." She shook her head despairingly, and the tears formed in her blue eyes.

"That's not going to happen," Rich promised. "We can provide you protection, and a place to stay - you never have to go back."

Kristi laughed derisively again. "Maybe you don't get just who you're dealing with," she said. "You have no clue how dangerous this guy is. He's snuffed a lot of people – I was there when he did one guy. And he's done things to other people that, you know, made them wish they were dead. He has powers that regular people don't have. It's weird."

"What's the guy's name?" asked Jim.

"Peter Durgin," Kristi replied. "That's his real name. But all of us who work for him call him *The Master* – at least to his face; he goes off on us if we don't call him that."

Jim, Rich, and Jasmine exchanged furtive glances at the mention of Pete's name, but didn't say anything.

"Go ahead, Kristi," Jasmine said softly. "Please continue."

In her own heart, Jasmine sensed that she really didn't want to hear what was coming, but, for some reason, she needed to hear it.

"Well, that first night, he was cool at first, like I said. Then he brought me down to the photo studio, and there was this photographer dude there already," Kristi said. "Pete told me to take off my clothes slowly while this guy was taking pictures. He made me pose, you know, in all kinds of different sexy positions."

"How did he make you do it?" Rich asked. "Did he force you or threaten you somehow?"

"Not exactly," Kristi admitted. "After we got back from dinner and getting all these treatments, I was feeling really buzzed and relaxed. I think he slipped something into my drink at dinner, you know? Anyway, I wasn't really scared at first, because I figured I could just go as far as I was willing to, you know? Just show as much as I wanted to, and stop at any time. But they kept asking for more … you know, graphic stuff. Anyway, after I'd been standing naked in front of these guys in ten-kinds-'a-nasty poses, I started getting afraid that they might want to … you know?"

Jim nodded silently in reply.

"Besides," she continued, "I figured out real quick that Pete isn't the kind of guy you say no to. If he tells you to do something, you do it. He has some kind of control over us … it's weird - I can't really explain it. It's like, his will is stronger than mine, and the others, too."

She studied the faces of her listeners. "That probably sounds lame," she added.

"So, did he sexually assault you?" Rich asked.

Jim shot him a look, along with a barely-noticeable shake of his head. Enough to give him the message - Jim wanted to handle this interview his own way. Rich's normal manner of questioning was akin to a bull in a china shop, and they both knew it.

Rich backed off and sat back to observe.

"No," Kristi said, "not that night. I told him that I hadn't ever done it before, and he said that we could use that to our advantage - his advantage, anyway. He said there were men who would pay a lot of money to have a teenage virgin. That's how he sold me. I had to learn how to act and dress for the meetings he would set up."

Kristi choked up for a minute as she recounted the demise of her innocence. She continued slowly, her high pitched, squeaky voice cracking with emotion.

"I was so freaked out when Pete told me what I had to do, and who I had to do it with. He gave me pills to calm me down and make me relax."

"What kind of pills?" Jim asked.

"Paxil, Quaaludes," she replied. "Later on, he got me started on Ecstasy. After awhile, I didn't care anymore. At least, that's what I told myself. The Master made a lot of money selling me as a virgin to these guys. Most of them were old enough to be my father."

At this, she broke down and cried, her tears flowing freely down her face as she wept bitterly. She pulled a tissue from the box, but it wasn't nearly adequate to stem the flow of hot tears. Jasmine moved and sat down next to her, and wrapped a comforting arm around her shoulder. After awhile, Kristi regained her composure enough to continue her story.

"Then The Master decided to use me in porn videos," she continued. "He said if I did good, I wouldn't have to keep doing tricks. So I did my best to be a good actress. After I'd been doing the porn videos for a long time, he said he had some special acting jobs for me - jobs that didn't involve any sex. I jumped at the chance. Not as if it was voluntary, anyway. Like I said, you don't say no to The Master if you want to keep breathing. You just do whatever he says."

"What kind of acting jobs were they?" Jim asked.

Kristi sighed, "Well, the deputy here knows that I was going to Westlake High School. That wasn't to, like, further my education, that's for sure. My gig was to keep an eye on two students there - a brother and sister. But I had to keep it on the down low, so they wouldn't know I was watching. After awhile, I was told to plant some weed in the guy's locker, and I did. Then my contact at the school turned him in, and he got busted."

"Who was your contact at the school?" Jim inquired.

"Mrs. McAllister, some social studies teacher," Kristi replied.

"She's working with Peter Durgin?"

"Yeah. They're both big kahunas in the temple."

The last word of Kristi's statement struck her listeners like an electric shock for a moment. Finally, Jim collected himself enough to ask.

"What temple?"

"The Temple of Anubis," Kristi replied casually. "That's what they call their group. It's some kind of weird religious cult; I don't really understand what it's all about. I never even heard the name used until after I'd been with Pete for over a year. He started to trust me more after I proved myself, I guess."

"But Pete and this teacher, McAllister, they're part of it?" Jim asked.

"Yeah, like I said, they're big players. They run a bunch of crime operations - drugs, prostitution, porno, and probably a bunch of other stuff. I don't even know what all they do. But even they have a boss that they answer to."

"Who is the boss of the group?" Jim probed.

"I don't know the dude's name," Kristi replied. "Not his real name, anyway. They call him *The Magus* - whatever that means. But I do know that he's real rich. I've been to his house."

"You've met him, then?"

"Oh, yeah," Kristi acknowledged, with a sour look. "A real scary dude. You know how I told you that The Master has some kind of power over people? The Magus has even more power. Everybody does whatever he says. Sometimes he doesn't even have to say anything, just motions or looks at somebody, and they go do what he wants. It's weird. He freaks me out. I think even The Master is a little scared of him, too."

"So, you know where he lives then?" Rich butted in.

"Well, no - not exactly," Kristi replied. "I've only been there a few times, and was blindfolded each time."

Rich looked crestfallen for a moment, but then she added, "I know it's in Westlake Village, though. His house is up on a hillside with a terrific view. It's got one of those disappearing edge swimming pools that looks like the water is flowing over the cliff. It's tight. Anyway, I picked out landmarks down below when I swam there. The Magus makes all the girls swim nude, by the way. Thinks he's some kind of Hugh Hefner type, I guess."

"What landmarks did you see from there?" Rich probed.

"Well, over to the right, I could see the lights from a bunch of car dealers. I've got good eyesight, so I could make out the names on the signs. It's the Thousand Oaks Auto Mall. Then straight ahead, there was a freeway off in the distance, and I could make out the name 'Westlake Boulevard' on the nearest exit sign."

Rich and Jim looked at each other. "That's got to be the North Ranch area," Jim said. "And who else do we know that has a house at the top of a hill in North Ranch?"

Rich nodded solemnly. "I'll see if I can find a picture of him when I get back to the station."

"Better yet," Jasmine said, "I can probably pull up a picture of him on the internet."

"Who are you talking about?" Kristi asked.

"Does the name 'Aldon Brehm' ring a bell?" Jim asked.

"Nope. Never heard of him."

After a moment, Jim said, "Okay, let's go back to your acting job at the school. You planted dope in the boy's locker. What else?"

"Well, I had to watch the brother and sister and write down their schedule, the things they did, and when they did them – that kind of thing. It was pretty easy with the boy, 'cause I think he liked me. But I could never get close to his sister. I scoped them out, and kept track of their schedules, though, like I was supposed to."

Kristi paused for a moment, then added, "And I was also supposed to find out if any girls at the school got pregnant. Then I would point them out to Mrs. McAllister."

"What for?" Jim asked.

"I don't know," Kristi replied, with a shrug. "But I do know that one girl I talked to her about isn't at school anymore."

Jasmine opened her purse and pulled her wallet out. She slipped two small photos out of their clear plastic case, and slid them across the table in front of Kristi.

"Is this the brother and sister you were supposed to watch?" she asked.

Kristi looked at the school picture of Garrett, and the formal senior portrait of Chelsea. She suddenly looked up at Jasmine with a shocked look on her face, then back down at the pictures. The realization of who she was sitting next to hit her like a ton of bricks.

"They ... they're your kids," she gasped. She looked at Jim, then at Jasmine, then back at Jim again. "Oh, my God, you're the pastor that The Master has been talking about all this time. But he made it sound like you're a bad person."

Kristi was at once overwhelmed with the realization that she had been duped and used in every possible way. Her lower lip quivered, and her throat tightened up as she came to grips with the fact that the very people she was assigned to bring down were now at her side, offering to help her. And the most shocking part was that they knew what she had done to them. Maybe not everything. If they knew everything, they would hate her, this pastor and his wife.

By all rights, they had every reason to despise her, after what she had done to them, unwitting on her part or not. But all she saw in their eyes was compassion and acceptance, not hatred. She had learned how to read the eyes of people to determine what their intentions were. It was a skill that she had groomed over the past two years. Indeed, it was part of her survival plan. It had proven to be more valuable to her success and survival than any high school diploma or college degree that she would never attain. But as she looked into the eyes of the pastor and his wife, there was no guile or secret agenda hidden carefully behind them. They were real, genuine.

"I'm ... I'm so sorry," Kristi started to say.

Any kind of apology was small and lame, she knew. But being face to face with the very people that she had hurt was now causing a strange hurt within her. She had never really concerned herself with other people's feeling before – everyone she had tripped up or set up had it coming, according to Peter Durgin. But these people provided living evidence of his lies.

"We realize that you were manipulated to do things," Jasmine said. "Please, tell us everything. It's important."

After what she had already confessed, Kristi figured there wasn't much point in holding back the rest of her misdeeds. Strangely, in only a few short minutes she had developed a deep desire to be accepted by these two. In the world of evil which she had become accustomed to, these people were different. Since the day that her Greyhound bus had disgorged her into this unforgiving land two years ago, she hadn't met anyone who genuinely cared for others, until now.

So she told them everything. About the time she'd set up the young guy to be beaten up in the dark Starbucks parking lot. And her involvement in driving the older actress to do whatever she did at the hospital, and the subsequent hasty escape. And all of the other crimes and sins she'd committed while living with Peter Durgin's harem of prostitutes. Sharing her deeds with these people was an antidote to her conscience. Like a fillet of ahi tuna, her conscience was seared on the outside, but completely raw on the inside.

The kitchen was her confessional booth, and these three her priests. Eventually, she came to the end of her long list of offenses.

"I never would have started with The Master if I knew where it would lead," Kristi said. "It would have been better if I'd just starved or died on the streets. At least I could have died keepin' it real. I can't believe that I could have become what I am."

A moment of clarity had come to Kristi, where she could actually be honest with herself and others. There was no numbing haze of alcohol or drugs. It actually felt good.

"But you say you talked to my parents, and they're coming out here?" she said.

Jim nodded.

Kristi lowered her eyes to the table in front of her. "They aren't going to accept me, you know. Not if they know even half the things I've done."

"Kristi, you might be surprised," Jim said. "The other thing your dad told me was that they started going to church for the first time, as they tried to work through their crisis of losing you. They came to put their faith in Jesus Christ, and they've been trying to live their lives for Him ever since."

"My parents, going to church?" Kristi asked, incredulous. "No way. I can't imagine it."

"Kristi, I'd like to share a bible passage with you that might be meaningful to you now. It's a story Jesus told – a parable about a young man who left his home looking for a more exciting life. He found that it wasn't what he expected, and decided to come home rather than starve to death. He might have felt the same way you do now."

Before Kristi had a chance to answer, Jim got up from his chair and went over to the Formica counter top, where he found a bible. He came back to his chair, sat down, opened up to Luke chapter fifteen, and began reading.

There was a man who had two sons. The younger one said to his father, 'Father, give me my share of the estate'. So he divided his property between them.

Not long after that, the younger son got together all he had, set off for a distant country, and there squandered his wealth in wild living. After he had spent everything, there was a severe famine in that whole country, and he began to be in need. So he went and hired himself out to a citizen of that country, who sent him out to his fields to feed pigs. He longed to fill his stomach with the pods that the pigs were eating, but no one gave him anything.

When he came to his senses, he said, 'How many of my father's hired men have food to spare, and here I am starving to death! I will set out and go back to my father and say to him: Father, I have sinned against heaven and against you. I am no longer worthy to be called your son; make me like one of your hired men.' So he got up and went to his father.

But while he was still a long way off, his father saw him and was filled with compassion for him; he ran to his son, threw his arms around him, and kissed him.

The son said to him, 'Father, I have sinned against heaven and against you. I am no longer worthy to be called your son.'

But the father said to his servants, 'Quick! Bring the best robe and put it on him. Put a ring on his finger and sandals on his feet. Bring the fattened calf and kill it. Let's have a feast and celebrate. For this son of mine was dead and is alive again; he was lost, and is found.' So they began to celebrate.

After he had finished reading the passage, Jim looked up and saw Kristi's eyes welled up with tears. She squinted, causing a teardrop to flow from each eye down her cheek.

"Do you think my parents would really be like that?" she sniffed.

"Yes, I do," Jim replied. "We'll soon find out. If you reach out to them, they'll reach out to you, and you'll find each other."

Kristi responded by weeping freely, keening and hugging her body while rocking back and forth in her chair.

Jasmine again wrapped her arm around her, and Kristi responded automatically by laying her head on Jasmine's shoulder. In that moment, Jasmine was the surrogate mother that Kristi longed for, and Kristi was the missing daughter that Jasmine's arms ached for. They sat there silently, but for the tears, dwelling in that moment of transcendence understood only by them. Jasmine's tears flowed down the girl's head and mixed with her own.

"My daughter is missing," Jasmine said softly. "She was abducted a few days ago. I can feel your hurt, and understand."

Kristi suddenly sat upright and looked her in the eye. "Oh, my God," she said, "she was abducted? The one I was supposed to watch?"

Jasmine and Jim both nodded. Jim could see the wheels turning in Kristi's mind as things started falling into place.

"It's got to be him that did it," Kristi said. "The Master – Pete. It makes perfect sense. He must have kidnapped your daughter."

"But why would he do it?" Jim wondered aloud.

"Another way to trip you up - don't you get it? He's already gone to a lot of trouble to cause you and your family harm. He had his actress set you up for a sexual harassment complaint, I know that."

"So do we," Jim interjected.

"He laughed about that with his people. I was there. Then he had me plant dope in your son's locker. And he's not working here for the money, I can tell you – he's rollin' with money – a big baller."

"Where would he be keeping her?" Rich asked.

"I don't know, but I can tell you that this is a bad time for her. Tonight is Samhain, the most unholy day of the year for them, and I know they're planning some special ceremony. I'm supposed to be the priestess in it."

"Meaning what, exactly?" Rich probed.

"Meaning that The Master, The Magus, and the others will be expecting to have sex with me during this ceremony. That's one of my expected roles. The Master says that it's an honor for me to be the priestess – some honor, huh? They've been planning this Samhain ritual for a long time, a lot more than the other ceremonies. The Magus has some kind of special book – he thinks it's got some kind of power."

"What kind of things do they do at these ceremonies?" asked Rich, forgetting his role. "Besides the sex, that is."

"Lots of chanting in languages I don't understand. Some in English. Everybody comes in wearing black satin robes, with nothing on underneath. After awhile, when they get all worked up with the chanting and stuff, they drop the robes. Then they sometimes put animal blood on each other – at least that's what Pete said it was. Then the sex. After that, they make me leave, and I guess they keep on with other stuff after that. Believe me, I'm glad to leave, so I don't ask questions."

"Kristi," Jim said, "you seem to think that Chelsea is in more danger tonight. Why is that?"

Kristi averted her eyes away from Jim and Jasmine for a moment while she answered.

"A while ago …," she started haltingly, "there was a ceremony I was in. When we came into the room, there was this girl chained up in the middle. Her mouth was taped shut, and she was naked, chained to a pipe that ran along the top of the room. I could tell that she didn't want to be there, and I didn't recognize her as being one of The Master - Pete's or The Magus' girls. She was scared to death, crying."

"What happened to her?" Rich asked.

"I don't know," Kristi replied, shaking her head.

"Did you see her afterwards?"

"No. The guards took me away, as usual. I didn't want to think about that girl – it freaked me out, but I'll never forget the look in her eyes. She was so scared. She … she could have been me."

Jim and Jasmine locked eyes and read the fear that now deepened within each other. Not knowing what had become of Chelsea was hard – the most difficult thing they had ever experienced in their lives. Now they found that knowing her situation was even worse – unbearable for any parent.

And time was quickly running out.

CHAPTER 58

The Magus' Residence: Westlake Village, California

October 31st

A ldon Brehm had been looking forward to this day for a very long time.

All the planning, all the years of searching for a genuine Necronomicon, all the money spent and people he'd killed along the way; it was all about to pay off in spades.

Relaxing at home with a fine cigar in one hand and glass of cabernet sauvignon in the other, he takes the time to reflect upon his rise to power, and mentally prepare for the coming night's activities.

Like the inevitability of death, this night had been coming slowly. But now the dark shadow of Samhain was falling upon him at last, when his powers would become full. He had the Necronomicon, and he had the virgin daughter of his enemy. Plus, what a fine looking girl she was – that was an added bonus. He was going to enjoy this night, indeed. Pity that he couldn't lay a hand on her before the ritual. But after she had been sacrificed – well, there would be no reason not to indulge then.

He imagined the sensation and scent of her warm blood being poured out over his own body even as she watched with eyes full of fear and horror, and he smiled at the thought. Indeed, tonight's Samhain ritual would not only increase his own power immeasurably and imbue his servants with power of their own, it was going to be a lot of fun – his kind of fun.

Standing on the balcony of his bedroom, Mr. Brehm takes in the view overlooking his expansive back yard and swimming pool. The usual flock of prostitutes, porn actresses, and male slaves were not bathing or milling about today; too busy for that. There were many preparations that had been made to get to this point, and everything was now in place for the special ritual night.

Brehm takes a sip of his vintage cabernet sauvignon, and raises the glass up to eye level. He swirls it around, and the alcohol content of the fine wine forms legs on the inside of his glass when he stops swirling.

Mr. Brehm never drinks white or blush wines – these are reserved for those who don't appreciate the intensity and symbolism of reds. So reminiscent of blood, the fluid of life. A person's life force is in the blood, and there was no greater thrill than to drink it, bathe in it – experience it to the fullest. Wine was the next best thing; a prelude to what would soon come.

Brehm smiles again, and takes a puff on his Havana cigar. He looks out beyond the freeway in the distance, to the hills in the north and south.

Master of all I survey, and beyond. This new personal title pleases him, and is accurate. The only things that have hindered him thus far from digging his talons deep into Ventura County, beyond the L.A. county line, have been three little things; First, the county supervisors, and their inane business zoning rules and codes, which prevented him from expanding into strip clubs, massage parlors, and other unseemly enterprises. Second, the ineptitude and lack of commitment of his indentured servants and employees. And third, the spiritual resistance emanating from one contemptible Christian church near his own home.

All three of these setbacks were now in the palm of his hand. Election day was only a couple of days henceforth, on November second, and he was favored to win a seat on the county board of supervisors. His relentless campaigning and virtually unlimited war chest had seen to that, along with some well-placed favors to the right people. He had also obtained the endorsement of some key politicians, in return for not making public the unseemly dirt that he had dug up on them. He also possessed a genuine Necronomicon, and had deciphered the incantations and understood how to use them. That, combined with the fresh blood of the girl in his basement, would gain him an untold increase in power, and empower his people with the single-minded passion to do his will.

As far as that pesky church; well, their pastor was washed up, finished. Pastor James DiMario had bigger problems to worry about now than leading his pitiful flock beside still waters. Mr. Brehm had felt the power emanating from that detestable edifice gradually waning over the past couple of weeks, he was sure of that. Soon, his right-hand man would oust Pastor DiMario once and for all, then set about his program to transform Solid Rock Community Church into an insipid social club.

Mr. Brehm smiles at the thought. *I will strike the shepherd, and the sheep will scatter.* He's always loved that bible verse.

The die was now cast, and soon The Magus Aldon Brehm would rise to a level of power, wealth, and influence that previous practitioners of the left-handed path in this generation had never known. And he deserved it, because he was more ruthless, cunning, and ambitious than all of the others put together.

The rays of the late afternoon sun were diminishing now, and the temperature had dropped to a cool, but not unpleasant briskness. Brehm takes another pull on his cigar, and finishes the last of his wine with relish, allowing the oaky flavor to linger in his cavernous mouth. A sweet sensation; a overture of things to come.

Turning, he steps inside the sliding glass door, and goes back into the house. Time for a little heart-to-heart with his girl. He might as well enjoy this day to the fullest by toying with her a bit. To a fisherman, the greatest thrill isn't in landing the fish, but playing it on the line as it desperately tries to get away. To the hunter, the excitement is not in posing for pictures with his kill, but in stalking the creature, and lining up the killing shot. Mr. Brehm is a hunter, too, and has bagged many men, women, and children over the years. Unlike the hunter of animals, he can't have the luxury of ostentatious mounted trophies on his walls. But he does keep a memento from each one he has vanquished; both for ceremonial purposes, and for the pure pleasure of reliving the moment. Mr. Brehm is sentimental to a fault.

As he descends the stairs leading to the basement, he considers what special item would make an appropriate memento of the pastor's daughter.

CHAPTER 59

Solid Rock Community Church: Westlake Village, California

Peter Durgin surreptitiously approached the church sanctuary from the backside, after making sure that he wasn't noticed by any of the office staff.

He'd waited until the old battleaxe at the reception desk went into the copy room to make up a multitude of sermon notes for next Sunday's meaningless message from the pulpit. He'd heard the distinctive *thwack, thwack* sound of the Risograph machine, which was only used for large quantities of copies. Knowing that she would be occupied for some time, he'd slipped out the door silently.

He made his way to the rear of the church, which faced the office trailer, then crept around the side, avoiding the windows as he went.

The pastor and his nettlesome wife had been over at the church sanctuary entirely too long, and there wasn't any apparent reason for them to be there. It was, after all, a weekday afternoon, and there were no "Harvest Night" activities going on at the church today – Pete had made sure of that.

Immediately after coming on board as an associate pastor, he had been given the project of organizing the annual harvest night event – the church's alternative to Halloween trick-or-treating and other traditional activities. Pete had been sure to fumble the ball at every turn, even while assuring Pastor DiMario that he had everything lined up. Just two weeks ago, he had dropped the bomb that he didn't have volunteers, the D.J. had cancelled, and the whole plan had fallen apart. He was terribly sorry, and apologized profusely for having bungled it. Of course, the unwitting church counsel was obliged to forgive him for his incompetence, and the event was cancelled.

Forgiveness, Pete mused. *The greatest weakness of these Christian fools. Revenge has much more power.*

Alistair LaVerne, the founder of the Church of Lucifer, understood and taught this concept. Incompetent people, stupid people, and fools are not to be forgiven, or have love wasted on them, like these weak Christians do. They are to be given what they deserve - not forgiveness. Pete had applied this teaching many times. But he took it further than even the milquetoast founder of the Church of Lucifer ever did. Peter Durgin had a long list of victims to his credit, people who deserved to be put out of their misery. He was a crusader of sorts, making the world a better place by removing them, one at a time. It was a testament to his own personal self control that he had kept himself from winnowing out Pastor DiMario and numerous other pitiful, soft hearted wretches in the church up until this point. He had to be patient; their time would come, just as it would tonight for the DiMario girl.

The cancellation of the harvest night event allowed Pete to boast to The Magus of another goal met. After all, young people should be out on Halloween creating mischief, rather than being supervised by a bunch of do-gooders who would deny them the right to celebrate the most unholy night; even if they didn't understand what they were celebrating.

Durgin walks around to the front of the church sanctuary and stops in his tracks at what he sees. A police cruiser is parked up front.

Not good, he thought. *This couldn't be a good omen. Especially with the DiMarios in there. I wonder what they're up to. I better check it out.*

The dark-tinted glass doors and windows all over the church building make it virtually impossible to see inside, but easy to see from the inside out. Since he doesn't know where in the building they are, he decides to enter the sanctuary from the rear, using his key ring. If he is seen, he can pretend to be checking the doors to make sure they're locked.

Rather than sneaking, Pete walks up to the rear door bold as brass, and unlocks it. Pulling it open, he steps inside the dark, cool environs. The door closer silently pulls the door shut behind him. He is alone in the hall adjacent to the nursery. Pete stands quietly, listening for any telltale sounds. Hearing none, he slowly walks to the end of the hallway, which intersects another perpendicular hallway that leads to the narthex. He creeps into the narthex and looks through the window into the large, airy main sanctuary – empty. Likewise, the crying room adjacent to the sanctuary. Durgin's keen ears pick up the faint sound of voices coming from somewhere around the corner; must be the kitchen.

Strange - why would they be in the kitchen, especially with a cop? he wondered. *On the other hand, there are a few cops in the congregation - this might just be one of them dropping by for a friendly visit.*

As he moves down the hallway to approach the kitchen, he sees that the kitchen door leading off the hallway is shut, but the window beside it spills light into the darkened hallway. The voices inside don't sound like they are engaged in casual conversation, although he can't quite make out what they are saying.

It is dim in the hallway, even where the sickly fluorescent light intrudes into the gloom. Still, Pete can't risk being observed. He steps up behind the kitchen door, just short of the window. Closing his eyes, he quietly recites a familiar incantation under his breath – the Third Enochian Key.

Behold! Saith Satan, I am a circle on whose hands stand the twelve kingdoms. Six are the seats of living breath, the rest are as sharp as sickles, or the horns of death. Therein the creatures of the earth are and are not, except in mine own hands which sleep, and shall rise!

Durgin wipes his open hands over his face, his chest, his arms.

Do not see me! he murmurs to himself, over and over.

Slowly, he steps into the hallway in front of the window, and positions himself immediately opposite the window, his back to the wall. He knows that he will not be readily visible in his current state.

Peter Durgin doesn't like what he sees – not one bit. The self-righteous pastor and his meddling wife are talking with a cop that Pete doesn't recognize, and his own little harlot, Kristi. And to make matters worse, the promiscuous waif is crying on the DiMario woman's shoulder. Not good. He can't make out the words, but he knows that nothing good can come of this tableaux.

He can't imagine how this could have happened.

What bizarre series of circumstances could have delivered her into their hands? He wonders.

Nevertheless, here she is – pouring her heart out to the pastor and the cop, by the looks of it. Best to put a stop to this session now, and deal with her later.

Durgin begins to recite another incantation, murmuring under his breath. Slowly, he raises his slender arms until they are extended in front of him, palms facing each other. His hands grasp an imaginary neck, and he utters quietly but purposefully,

Say no more!

The daemon Sekhmet lives for occasions such as this. His human subordinate has given the command for Sekhmet to show his power, and what fun it is to do so.

He had already been aroused from slumber by Durgin's incantation of invisibility, and now, he is ready for the next step. With the second incantation to give him instructions, Sekhmet passes effortlessly through the door that separates him from his target – the girl. Now he stands behind the girl seated at the table, invisible to all, including Peter Durgin.

At Durgin's command, Sekhmet wraps his scaly hands around the girl's throat, and squeezes. Immediately, she stops talking, and begins coughing violently.

Sekhmet relishes his power to reach through the time / space divide into the mortal world to produce mayhem and suffering. He has the power to torment humans, but not to kill them. Most daemons are only able to play on the minds and emotions of their human victims, but Sekhmet and others of his demonic ilk can actually cause limited physical harm. It is a power that he is always eager to flex at every opportunity.

Sekhmet's filthy, clawed hands keep their grip on the girl's throat, while his crocodilian snout sneers gleefully. Thick saliva webs between his irregularly-set fangs, and drools down from the corner of his mouth. The girl coughs, and Sekhmet feels the tremor rippling through her flesh as her body involuntarily spasms in response to his torment. He smiles widely, savoring the moment.

"Can I get you a glass of water?" Jim asks Kristi. In the middle of her detailed revelation, Kristi has begun coughing uncontrollably.

Not waiting for an answer, he gets up and quickly goes over to the sink. He finds a clean glass in the cabinet above the counter, fills it, and returns to offer it to Kristi. She accepts the glass, and struggles to swallow down a few gulps. Water drizzles off her chin as she tries to regain her composure. At last, she finally stops coughing long enough for Jim to ask,

"Kristi, what else can you tell us about the location where this ceremony was held?"

"Well, it was about forty minutes from …", she starts, before breaking into another violent coughing jag.

Peter Durgin watched intently from his vantage point in the hallway, hidden in plain sight of the four sitting in the kitchen. Each time his harlot began to speak an answer to their questions, she started to cough violently. After they got her settled down, she started coughing anew each time she tried to speak. It was greatly entertaining to watch her struggle to spit out a confession, especially since she was about to betray her master and benefactor. As soon as he got her alone, he would have more amusement with her before terminating her meaningless life. But for now, it was such fun to watch this comedic repartee. It was all he could do to keep himself from bursting out laughing as she struggled to catch her breath between bouts of deep coughs.

A bad break, no doubt. This turn of events wasn't part of Pete's plan at all. But one of the hallmarks of greatness is to take the cards we are dealt, and make a winning hand out of them. Take the lemons, and make lemonade. The girl had been a valuable player for Pete, and the temple as a whole. But in the final analysis, she was a commodity, nothing more.

Time to change the plan. Undoubtedly, she had already revealed too much. Any suspicions that might have run through the DiMario's simple and unsuspecting minds would be confirmed by now. The critical need was to eliminate the girl now, so that she couldn't be questioned further. Then, he could deny her accusations, and plead his innocence before the church council – a gullible and forgiving bunch of losers. Success now depended on speed and stealth – and ruthless execution.

Got to get her away from the others, so I can put her out of her misery. Pete thought. *Got to be ready for the opportunity, when it comes.*

***

He's up to something, and it couldn't be good, Beverly Hansen thought, watching Pete LeTourneu through the slats of the mini blinds that covered the window by her desk.

She tacitly observed his movements as he entered the large church sanctuary building through the rear door.

Bev had sensed the associate pastor's presence a few moments before when he passed by the copy room, while she had stood at the Risograph machine with her back to the door. She always felt his presence when he was near, and it never failed to send a chill down her spine. Pete LeTourneu had a powerful countenance that she could actually feel; she felt it on a spiritual level, and even on a physical level, down to the marrow of her bones. It wasn't a good power. She'd known from the first time she met him that something was wrong.

Bev decided that she should let Jim know that Pete was lurking about the church sanctuary, where she knew Jim was having a confidential meeting of some sort. She didn't know what the meeting was about – didn't need to know. But one thing she was sure of; Pete LeTourneu didn't need to know, either. Her hands found the telephone on her desk, and she punched in Jim's cell phone number.

***

Jim was still trying to help get Kristi's cough settled down when the cell phone clipped to his belt vibrated against his side.

Heck of a time for an interruption, he thought to himself, grabbing the phone off his belt.

He noticed that the caller I.D. showed the church office number. He flipped it open, pressed the green button, and put it up to his ear.

"Jim here," he said into the phone.

"Pete is inside the building," Bev's voice said through the earpiece. "I thought you might want to know."

"Where in the building?"

"He went in the back door just a minute ago."

Jim's face took on a scowl as he replied, "Okay, thanks for that tip, Bev."

He snapped the phone shut, and turned to face Rich, his back to the window.

"Durgin is in the building," Jim said quietly.

"That's interesting," Rich replied, nodding. "I think it's about time I pick him up, anyway. Looks like he's gonna save me the trouble of coming to look for him." He glanced around the room, and at the door, saying, "It's a pretty big building, and you know it like the back of your hand, even in the dark. Let's both go and find him, then I'll take him into custody. Jasmine can stay here with Kristi; Kristi can give us the positive I.D. on Durgin."

"Okay," Jim agreed, "I'll look in the sanctuary area, and you can check the nursery and childcare rooms off to the right of the hall."

Rich nodded in agreement and walked to the door, while Jim whispered their plan to Jasmine. He met Rich at the door, and Jim opened it, beckoning Rich to exit.

Once in the hallway, they went in separate directions. Pete Durgin had already moved to another darkened area down the hallway, near the narthex. His cloak of invisibility was still intact, but like the disguise of a chameleon, it wouldn't work while he moved, or under direct light. He had to concentrate to keep his mind focused on the incantation that kept the daemon Sekhmet shrouding him in the cloak of invisibility.

Jim walked right past him as Pete stood motionless in his dark corner, with his eyes closed. Durgin's closed mouth formed a tight grin as Jim unknowingly passed by.

***

After the ignorant pastor unwittingly walked by, Pete reached into his pocket for his cell phone. Time for a little fun.

After all, he figured, *if a man can't enjoy life in any circumstance, what's the point?*

The cop and the pastor thought that they were hunting him, stumbling around feebly, searching, but not seeing. It was times like this that allowed Pete to really revel in his superiority over regular men. Humanity at large could never match his skills, his power, his ability to manipulate people and circumstances to conform to his will. Pete knew his lust for blood made him superior to those who lusted merely for money, power, and sex.

He punched in a text message using the keypad, selected the phone number, and pressed the SEND button. He could barely suppress a chuckle as he put the phone back in his pocket. Now to create a plausible accident for his girl Kristi. Unfortunately, the DiMario woman was still in the kitchen with her. All the more sporting a challenge. If worst came to worst, she might have an accident, too.

Sitting next to Kristi at the kitchen table, Jasmine spoke quietly, her comforting hand draped over Kristi's shoulder. Kristi's cough had quieted, and she sat silently listening to Jasmine.

"Kristi, do you know that God wants to forgive you of your sins? You can start over, right now, today. God will wash away your sins, if you just accept His son, Jesus, as your lord and savior. He's already paid the price for your sins."

Kristi shook her head, her eyes downcast.

"You don't even know the half of what I've done," she said. "After what I told you already, how could God forgive me? There's no way."

Their talk was interrupted by a musical beep from Kristi's cell phone, which was buried somewhere in her purse. She fished it out, saying,

"Incoming text message. Let me check it."

She turned the phone in her hand so that the colored screen was facing her, then pressed a button to get the display to light up. Glancing at the screen, a look of horror quickly spread across her face. She dropped the phone on the table, where it bounced with an unpleasant clunk.

"Oh, my God!" she exclaimed, "he knows. I knew he'd find out!"

Jasmine snatched the phone up off the table top, and looked at the screen, which was still lit up. The cause of Kristi's fear was obvious – the text message on the screen read, U R GOING TO DIE.

Peter Durgin was a man of possibilities. There were so many ways he could kill the little strumpet, right here in this building; fewer if he expected to walk out alive, and fewer still if he was to remain free from prosecution and incarceration.

He decided a one-on-one meeting with Kristi in the church ladies room would work. He would get the drop on her, and break her neck quickly and quietly. Then he would slip out before anyone saw him. Unfortunately, this plan did not afford him the enjoyment of toying with her first. But it would take care of the immediate problem, and still allow him to keep up appearances. After all, a slip and fall accident on a hard tile floor is plausible. These things could, and did happen every day. People died of stranger causes than this. He could even spin it to make it appear to be DiMario's fault, for allowing an emotionally disturbed girl to walk around alone in the dim light. The DiMarios would have to explain to the police and the news media what a prostitute was doing in their church restroom. Fortunately, Pete happened to have a gram vial of cocaine on him. That would add nicely to the tableau.

Now, to get her in the restroom alone. *No problem.*

Pete stealthily slunk down the hall to the utility closet where he knew the electrical circuit breaker panel was located. Quickly stepping inside and closing the door behind him, he turned on the light in the tiny room and opened the door to the breaker panel. Pete looked intently at the labels on the circuit breakers, then deftly flipped several of them to the OFF position. He made sure not to trip any circuits that were currently on – that would draw attention, and they would know that something was wrong. Since only the kitchen lights and auxiliary lights were on, he flipped off all the other breakers in the panel.

The key to success in this plan was the element of surprise. Pete wanted to make sure the lights in the building would remain dim, but he didn't want to alarm the sheep in the process. There was a fox in the henhouse, but the hens didn't need to know about it just yet.

His work here done, he slipped out the door and glided silently down the hall, through the narthex, and to the ladies restroom.

He went inside. The church restroom featured a "modesty chamber" - a small vestibule with one door opening on the hallway, and another opening to the restroom itself. This arrangement allowed for maximum privacy and modesty.

Durgin left the light on in the vestibule, then slipped inside the restroom. He turned off the light. The room was swallowed up in pitch darkness. Pete liked the dark. He did some of his best work in the dark.

Now to summon the girl. He closes his eyes and begins to murmur quietly. In his incantation, he calls upon Sekhmet again, who still stands eagerly at the ready in the kitchen. Sekhmet receives the instruction, and moves invisibly over to the spot where Kristi Hawkins is sitting. He steps through the table, and faces Kristi. Reaching out his clawed hands, he presses gently on her lower abdomen, then releases the pressure. Again, pressing and releasing. After a few moments, his imperceptible interference has it's desired effect.

"I need to go to the bathroom," Kristi said, cutting Jasmine off in mid sentence. "Sorry, I've just got to go right now."

"Okay," Jasmine replied, "I'll show you the way."

They got up from the table and went to the door, which Jasmine held open for her. Kristi stepped into the hallway, and Jasmine gestured to the left. They walked down the hall in the dim light and rounded the corner, and continued through the narthex to the place where the restrooms were situated, next to one of the child care rooms.

"Here we go," Jasmine said, pointing at the door. "I'll just wait for you here."

"Okay," Kristi replied, reaching for the door handle.

At that moment, Rich appeared at the entrance of the child care room, which was directly across the hall from the restroom.

"What's goin' on?" he asked.

Jasmine gasped, startled. "Oh, it's you, Rich," she said. "Kristi needs to use the restroom."

Kristi already had the door to the vestibule pulled open when Rich said, "I haven't checked in there yet".

Jasmine frowned. "Well, he's not going to be in the ladies room, is he now?"

Rich had already combed this side of the large church building, and was getting the feeling that he was searching for somebody who didn't want to be found.

"Probably not, but I'll just have a quick look."

Peter Durgin stood with his back pressed against the tiled wall of the restroom interior, next to the light switch. He smirked silently in the darkness as he heard the footfalls in the hallway, and the voice of the DiMario woman. As expected, his hastily made plan was working. Fortune favors the bold.

Mr. Durgin readies himself for the moment of glory; as soon as Kristi reaches for the light switch, it will be over for her in an instant. Indeed, much too fast for his liking. Peter Durgin is not a martial artist, by any means. But he has studied techniques of how to kill both with a weapon, and empty-handed. It was a talent that had come in handy many times in the past, and it would again today.

Then, unexpectedly, he hears a man's voice joining the women in the hallway. Not Pastor DiMario. Must be the cop. Not a good development. And it sounds like he's going to come in.

Flexibility – that's the key, Pete thought to himself, *I can still come out on top, if I roll with it. And I will.*

Peter Durgin lives on the edge. Accordingly, he'll use the edge of his knife blade in this scenario, since the cop won't be as easy as the girl. But he still has the element of surprise on his side.

He'll do the cop first, take his pistol, then come out and put a round in the girl's head. Then use the knife again to stab Jasmine DiMario. He can wipe his fingerprints off the knife handle, and press it into Kristi's hand. Likewise, the pistol to the cop's hand. He'll finish up by snapping one handcuff on the girl's opposite wrist, and drop the keys on the floor right by the cop.

A quick arrangement of the bodies will suggest that the handcuffed suspect was taken to the restroom. As soon as she had one hand uncuffed, she pulled a lock-blade knife off the cop's utility belt and stabbed him and the DiMario woman with it. Before succumbing to his mortal wound, the cop gets a shot off, even as he's fading. In the event that Pastor DiMario comes along, the cop will have squeezed off a second round that accidentally hits the pastor, and they all go to meet their maker together. Pete can slip out the front, go down the steps to the parking lot below, circle around, and join the group that will be coming from the office to investigate the shot.

The tragedy will be discovered, and after grieving the loss with the parishioners, Pete will humbly rise to the occasion to fill the leadership vacuum that has so quickly and tragically occurred. Only the boy, Garrett, will remain as the sole survivor of the DiMario clan, which surely deserves to be wiped out in it's entirety. But he can be taken care of later.

The entire plan is generated by Mr. Durgin's brilliant mind in a matter of seconds, on the fly. Smiling, he reaches into his back pocket, and pulls out his three-inch lock blade tactical knife, and snaps it open with a quick motion of his thumb.

Deputy Harrison takes the door handle from Kristi, and pulls the door to the vestibule open the rest of the way.

He grins at Kristi, who is squirming with discomfort, and says, "I'll only be a minute."

He steps into the vestibule and lets the door close behind him, and pulls open the inner door to the restroom. All dark inside. Rich crosses the threshold and feels along the wall for the light switch. Before he finds it, a searing pain rips through his upper right chest, and he jerks back. Rich instantly realizes that he's under attack by an armed assailant, and he grabs for the weapon that has lunged at him in the blackness. He responds automatically without thinking by grabbing the assailant's hand with his right hand, and pulling it. In one fluid motion, Rich raises his opponents arm and steps under it, while twisting it.

Rich doesn't know if he's got his attacker's right or left arm, but it doesn't much matter. As he steps under it, he pulls the phantom hand downward, while rotating the wrist. Rich feels and hears the wrenching pop of the shoulder dislocating, a fraction of a second before a blood-curdling scream erupts in his ear. The invisible assailant falls and slams hard against the tile floor. Rich continues twisting the arm until he hears the metallic clink of the weapon hitting the tile. Then the lights come on, and Rich finds himself looking into the grimacing face of Pete Durgin.

CHAPTER 60

Solid Rock Community Church Sanctuary

When Jasmine hears the ruckus inside the restroom, she doesn't wait for an invitation. Grabbing the door pull, she snatches the door aside and dashes through the vestibule, and tears open the inner door.

The light from the vestibule casts a dim glow on two figures fighting just inside the doorway; one of them is obviously Rich, apparent by his uniform. She sees that he has thrown the other person down on the floor with bone-crushing force. She dares not step inside now, but her arm reaches around the left side of the doorway. Easily finding the light switch with her experienced fingers, she flicks it on.

The dark room suddenly becomes bathed in brilliant fluorescent light. Jasmine is at once shocked at what she sees before her, yet at the same time is strangely not surprised.

Rich is on the floor on top of another man, pinning him to the floor. The other man is Pete LeTourneu-Durgin, her husband's associate pastor. Then she sees the blood – and the knife on the floor.

"What happened, Rich?" she shouted. "Are you all right?"

"More or less," Rich replied, turning his head toward her. "He stabbed me in the chest, but I don't think he got anything critical."

"Oh, my Lord!" she exclaimed, rushing over quickly. "Let me check you."

"In a minute," he replied, waving her off.

He got up off of Durgin, who squealed like a stuck pig on the floor, his shoulder pulled out of joint. Rich roughly grabbed Durgin's other arm, and rolled him over onto his front side. As he did so, Pete let out a piercing scream that made Jasmine's skin crawl. Rich pulled out his handcuffs and deftly snapped them on his suspect. With each small movement of his arm, Pete Durgin let out a howl.

Rich gripped his other bicep, and demanded, "Get up!"

Durgin quickly complied, desperately trying to avoid any movement of his right arm. Rich turned him around and put his hand in Pete's back, shoving him up against the wall.

Jasmine saw the crimson trail that was growing progressively longer down the front of Rich's light green uniform shirt.

"That's going to need some attention," she said.

"I know."

She noticed that Pete's right arm and shoulder hung lower, and limp in comparison to the other one.

"Looks like he's going to need medical attention, too," she added.

"Heck, I can fix that myself," Rich said. To Pete, he added, "if you want me to, that is."

"Yes, yes, please help me," Durgin whimpered.

"You're my witness," Rich said to Jasmine. Turning back to Durgin, Rich grabbed his right upper arm with both hands, and shoved it abruptly and forcefully up into the shoulder socket.

Pete Durgin screamed at the top of his lungs, his face a contorted mask of pain.

"Oh, yeah," Rich said, "I forgot to tell you to take a deep breath. And considering the fact that you just stabbed me in the chest, I hope you won't mind that I didn't give you a bullet to bite on."

Jim burst into the room, with Kristi trailing right behind.

"What's going on?" he demanded. "What's all the screaming about?"

"Rich came in to check the restroom, and Pete stabbed him!" Jasmine exclaimed.

"He startled me," Pete Durgin objected. "I didn't know who he was – a robber for all I knew. I just defended myself. It was a case of mistaken identity, that's all."

"That's a filthy lie!" Jasmine countered. "You were waiting there for Kristi to come in."

"No, that's not true," Pete protested. "I was just checking the facility to make sure everything is locked up. How could I know who was going to walk in? There's not even supposed to be anyone in here."

"Just checking the facility, huh?" Rich asked sarcastically. "In the dark, with a knife in your hand? Yeah, right."

"Hey, it's a legal knife."

"Not when you use it to stab a peace officer."

At that moment, Garrett arrived from the burger joint and walked into the already crowded restroom.

"Fer shizzle!," he exclaimed, "what's goin' on?"

Immediately, a cacanophy of five voices answered excitedly all at once.

"Go get the medical kit from the office, son," Jim ordered, "and hurry up."

Garrett stared slack-jawed at the blood on Rich Harrison's uniform shirt, then quickly spun on his heel and took off.

Jasmine moved to face Durgin, while Rich applied pressure to his own knife wound. Peter Durgin was already starting to regain his attitude of smug self-assurance, now that his shoulder joint was back in place.

"Where is Chelsea?" she demanded. "Where are you keeping her?"

"I don't know what you're talking about," Pete replied casually.

"You just tried to kill Deputy Harrison, and Kristi here," Jasmine said, her voice rising in anger as she stared into his smirking face. "And you've kidnapped my daughter!"

Pete Durgin said nothing, just continued to wear his haughtiness like a gaudy cloak.

"Let me refresh your memory!" Jasmine barked.

She took a step forward and drove the instep of her foot into Durgin's crotch with enough force to rival a donkey's kick. Durgin instantly jerked forward, blowing spit forcefully out of his mouth as he doubled over in pain. He fell to the floor, and curled into the fetal position as best he could with hands cuffed behind his back.

Rich, who had witnessed this exchange with interest, said "Now, now, Mrs. DiMario. I can't allow you to abuse my prisoner. That's not legal."

In a flash, Garrett returned with the medical kit, which Jasmine took from him with trembling hands.

"Let me do it," Garrett said. "I took a first aid class, remember?"

"Good idea," Rich said. "I don't think your mom is up to it right now, anyway."

Garrett proceeded to help Rich get his uniform shirt and undershirt off, then he took a good look at the wound.

"Dang!" he said. "It looks like it went way deep into your pectoral muscle. The tip of the blade must've hit a rib bone and stopped, otherwise you'd be dead – that's lucky."

"Blessed is more like it," Jim said. "God is watching out for you, Rich."

Rich looked at him and nodded, while Garrett cleaned the wound.

"Doesn't that hurt?" Garrett asked, wiping Bactine around the gaping hole in Rich's chest.

"Yeah, it hurts like hell, actually." He looked at Jim and Jasmine, who were watching with concerned faces. "What? Hell's in the bible, isn't it?"

"Indeed it is," Jim answered. "But this knife wound is nothing compared with the torments and suffering of Hell."

Garrett finished cleaning the gash, and started rifling through the bandages in the kit with his right hand, while keeping pressure on the wound with a wad of gauze in his left.

"I'm gonna close it with some butterfly strips," he said, "But it's definitely gonna need stitches – a bunch of stitches. Maybe a tetanus shot, too, unless you're current."

"No time for that right now," Rich said. "I'm going to arrest Mac the Knife here, and take him in. I just wish we could find out exactly where his cult is keeping Chelsea."

He looked Jim in the eye. "But it looks like he's not keen on talking right now. Why don't you bring him into the kitchen for me? I have to go out to my car to call in, and get my shirt back on. You guys just keep an eye on him for me." He winked at Jim. "I'll be gone about ten minutes – comprende?"

Jim nodded.

"I get it," Garrett said.

Jim helped Peter Durgin to his feet, and grabbed his spindly upper arm to force him out of the room. One by one, the others followed him through the vestibule and down the hallway, back to the kitchen. Jim roughly shoved Pete down into a chair at the table.

Rich, with his shirt still off, said, "Ladies, would you come outside and help me put myself back together, please? I might need a gauze wrap around my chest to hold everything in place before putting my shirt back on."

"Sure," Jasmine said. "But you're going to have to take it easy on that wound until you get proper medical attention."

"I can't promise that. That's why I want you to bind it up as tight as possible."

Kristi took the medical kit from Garrett, carefully avoiding eye contact with him as she did. Jasmine found Rich's shirt, and she and Kristi followed him out of the room. Garrett and Jim turned simultaneously to look at Peter Durgin, who sat upright in his chair, a defiant smirk on his face. His hands were cuffed behind his back.

"We've got to find out where they've got Chelsea," Jim said quietly to Garrett.

"I know nothing – nnnothing!" Pete said mockingly.

Garrett turned to his dad. "I can get him to talk, Dad. Just give me a few minutes with him."

Jim looked at his son, then at Pete. "What are you going to do, son?" he asked.

"I'm just gonna 'interview' him a bit," Garrett replied, using his fingers in the quote gesture.

Jim thought about it for a moment. "Okay," he said, "do it. Do whatever you need to do."

He clapped a hand on his son's shoulder, then left the room.

Rich walked out to his patrol car with Jasmine DiMario and Kristi Hawkins in tow. He opened up the door of his car, and turned back to face Jasmine.

"Could you go ahead and wrap me up, so I can put my shirt back on? This isn't exactly appropriate attire for a sheriff's deputy, you know."

Jasmine realized that he was trying to keep the mood light, in a vain effort to combat the intense stress that squeezed them all like a vise.

"Hey, you could be a Chippendale dancer, except for that gaping knife wound in your chest," she joked.

"How would you know so much about Chippendale dancers?"

Jasmine felt her face blush. "I must have read about them somewhere."

Jasmine carefully attended to his wound, while Kristi handed her rolls of gauze, scissors, and ace bandages like a scrub nurse. Jasmine got the field dressing on his wound, and stemmed the flow of blood. Then they both helped him put the undershirt back on.

"Careful!" Kristi cautioned. "Don't raise your arms, or you might pull it open again."

He gingerly put his arms and head into the undershirt, and worked it onto his torso. Next, Kristi held his uniform shirt while he put his arms in, one by one. Jasmine insisted on buttoning his shirt up, much to Rich's chagrin.

"I'll handle the tucking in part, if you don't mind," he said, turning his back to them. He unbuttoned his trousers, tucked the shirt in, and buttoned back up. He turned back to them, and gestured with his open arms for them to look him over.

"Yeah, you look good as new," Kristi said, "'cept for the major bloodstain down the front of your shirt."

"Well, I might not have my gig line straight either, but what the heck. I'm going to call in," Rich said.

He went and sat down in the driver's seat of his car. He picked up the radio handset and held it up to his mouth.

"One x-ray nineteen, over," he said.

After a moment, the dispatcher responded. "One x-ray nineteen, see the watch commander on tack two."

"Ah man," Rich muttered under his breath. He turned the switch on the radio to the frequency reserved for more extensive one-on-one communications.

"One x-ray nineteen, over," he repeated.

"Harrison, I need you to come in, now," Mac's voice boomed through the speaker.

"What's up, Mac?" Rich asked.

The radio was silent for a moment. "Got a cell phone?" Mac asked.

"Yeah."

"Then call me at my desk."

"Ten-four," Rich replied. Then he put the mic back.

I don't like the sound of this, he thought to himself.

He plucked the cell phone off his belt, and quickly found Mac's number in his directory. He pressed the green button, and was connected.

"Mac here."

"What's going on, Mac?"

"Rich. We've got a problem. Where are you now?"

"Westlake Village. What's the problem?"

"Internal Affairs found out about your name being associated with the Angela Haskell murder, and that those LAPD detectives questioned you about it. I ran interference for you, but they suggested that I call you in on a suspension with pay, until their investigation is concluded."

Rich noticed that Mac put undue emphasis on the word 'suggested'.

"What investigation?" Rich asked.

Mac answered slowly, "The one that they're starting – on you."

"Bad timing, Mac. I'm in the process of making a key arrest in the case I was telling you about."

"Is it solid?"

"Solid enough for the suspect to stab me," Rich stated matter-of-factly.

"What!?" Mac's voice boomed so loudly through the phone that Rich had to pull it away from his ear. "What happened?"

"Long story. But I've got the suspect in custody, and I've got an eyewitness to a murder he committed, and a bunch of other crimes, too. I'm going after the head honcho of their crime organization now, but I need some help."

"Didn't you call for backup on the stabbing already?"

"No, I handled it myself."

"How much backup you need?" Mac asked.

"What I really need is a search warrant."

Mac was silent for a moment, then said, "I don't know about that, Rich – that's asking a lot. I'm supposed to pull you in from the field, not help you dig deeper into trouble. When Internal Affairs makes a suggestion, it's not really a suggestion - know what I'm sayin'? They're giving me professional courtesy right now, but that's gonna wear out quick if I don't get you back in here pronto. Then I'll end up looking bad, too. I believe in you, Rich, but I gotta answer to The Man, too."

"Mac, listen to me. These people have got a girl that they abducted a few nights ago – the DiMario girl, the pastor's daughter, remember? We passed her picture around the station a couple days ago. An Amber Alert was issued for her. They've got her, Mac, and I have good reason to believe that they're going to kill her tonight."

Rich stole a quick glance at Jasmine to see if she was watching him. She wasn't.

"What makes you think that?" Mac asked.

"Because they're a Satanic crime organization, and tonight is their most unholy night, Samhain. I've got a solid informant from inside their organization who's telling me that they intend to use her as a human sacrifice – tonight, Mac."

"Jesus!"

"Yeah, we could use His help, too." Rich was surprised at the words that just slipped out of his mouth, but he kept going. "Mac, I need a search warrant for the home of Aldon Brehm in Westlake Village. That's where they've got her, and he's in on it."

"Jesus!" Mac exclaimed again. "Are you insane? Don't you know that Brehm is a candidate for County Supervisor? He's well connected, Rich. It's gonna look political if you go fishing around through his house. That's if you could get a warrant, which you can't. No judge in his right mind is going to issue a warrant on a guy like Brehm, without hard evidence."

"One will – Linz."

The name of Superior Court Judge Howard Linz registered immediately with Mac. About a year earlier, Linz' seventeen year old daughter had been involved in a car accident. While driving home drunk after a party, she had plowed into a parked car. Nobody had been hurt, and Rich was the first officer on the scene. Instead of arresting her for felony DUI, Rich drove her home and had a serious talk with her parents around the kitchen table. It wasn't until then that Rich discovered who the father was. Although it was never mentioned, Judge Howard Linz owed Deputy Rich Harrison big time, and they both knew it. Now was the time to call in that favor.

Mac sighed audibly through the phone. "Okay, I'll talk to Linz. But this is a tall request for a judge to grant, you know?"

"I'm counting on him remembering me favorably," Rich replied.

"When does your shift end, Rich? Ten o'clock?"

"Yeah."

"Okay," Mac said, "for the record, I'm ordering you in, effective at the end of your shift. That's just a couple hours from now. Can't very well order you in when you've got your hands full. And get that knife wound treated, pronto."

"I will, as soon as I get everything wrapped up. I've got a good field dressing on it now."

"Good. You got a FAX number, just in case Linz actually comes through?"

Rich looked at Jasmine, and mouthed the word 'FAX'. She told him the number, and he repeated it to Mac.

"Okay, thanks, Mac," Rich said. "This is a big one – you're not going to regret it."

"That's what you keep saying. Be careful, Rich. I'm going to dispatch two deputies to meet you there, if and when the warrant comes through."

"Right. Talk to you soon." Rich pressed the END button, and turned to Kristi. "All right, then. So, you're one hundred percent sure that the guy in there is the one you were telling us about?"

A nod of her head.

"And that they've got Chelsea DiMario at Brehm's house?"

"Pretty sure," Kristi said. "I can't think of anywhere else they would have her, especially tonight."

Rich's mouth tightened in a grimace. "Pretty sure, huh? Okay. How much time do you figure we've got?"

Kristi looked at her watch, and pressed the backlight button. It had already started to grow dark out while they had been inside the building, and she was surprised to see that it was already eight o-clock.

"The rituals usually happen late," she said, "But definitely before midnight. My guess is, she's probably safe until ten."

Jasmine couldn't help but glance at her watch. "That's not enough time," she said nervously. "Your judge has got to come through for us. We've got enough time to pray; let's make use of it. Kristi, Rich – pray with me, will you?"

Jasmine slowly dropped to her knees right at the spot where she stood, and rested her folded hands against the bumper of the patrol car.

"Right here?" Rich asked, looking around nervously. "Shouldn't we go inside the church sanctuary?"

"Doesn't matter. You don't have to be in a special place to pray. God can hear us wherever we are. We just have to trust in Him to hear our prayer request, and act on it. If it's in alignment with His will, that is."

Rich hesitantly knelt beside Jasmine, as did Kristi.

"What if it's not in alignment with His plans?" he asked. Immediately, he silently rebuked himself. *Idiot! What a thing to say.*

"Then we just have to trust Him for the outcome, whatever the outcome is," Jasmine replied somberly.

"I don't know how you can have faith like that," Rich said, "especially at a time like this."

"How could I not?" Jasmine replied. "I've seen God's hand at work in so many circumstances over the years. Things always work out somehow, but not always the way we want. I'm scared for Chelsea, believe me. I haven't thought about anything else since she was taken. But I've got to believe that God is going to take care of this situation somehow."

Not waiting for a reply, she placed her folded hands again on the bumper of the patrol car, and bowed her head. Rich and Kristi stared at her, amazed. Then they, too, followed her lead.

CHAPTER 61

Solid Rock Community Church Sanctuary

Jim paced back and forth in the hallway outside the church kitchen, listening to the pained sounds coming from behind the closed door. It was apparent to him that Garrett was giving Pete LeTourneu – Durgin a good working over.

Jim was proud of his son. He knew that Garrett wasn't violent by nature, but he was willing to do whatever he could to save his sister, and right now that included beating information out of Durgin.

Although Garrett and Chelsea fought with each other incessantly at home; over the T.V. controller, the computer, the phone, or whatever else, Garrett was like a bulldog when it came to protecting his older sister. Any guy who wanted to date her would have to go through Garrett's scrutiny before even making it through the front door. And he wouldn't stand for any negative comments or trash talk about his sister, either. Delivering any insults or disparaging remarks about Chelsea was his job, and his alone. In public, he was her advocate, and she was his. Her 'rotten little brother' she sometimes referred to him, but the reality was, they were fiercely loyal and protective of one another.

Jim was brought back to the here and now by the sounds of shouting – Garrett's voice mostly. After awhile, the voices and the sounds of flesh being struck, along with the responsive guttural sounds, diminished.

The door opened, and Garrett stepped out into the hallway. His head hung down and his clothes were disheveled on his sweating body as he walked up to his father in the hallway. Jim saw that his son's hands were painted with smears of blood.

"It's no good," Garrett puffed, breathing heavily. "He won't talk. I tried, Dad. Believe me, he took a beat down. But he's not giving it up."

Jim rested his hand on his son's shoulder, then gently pulled him close. Jim grimaced, and nodded his head with fresh resolve.

"It's okay, son," he said resignedly, patting Garrett's back. "I'll get the information from him."

"You can't," Garrett said, with evident despair in his voice, "he was willing to take a hard beating from me. He's not going to talk now."

"Oh, he will," Jim replied with calm certainty. "I'm not leaving that room until he tells me everything I want to know. You go outside now, and make sure Rich doesn't come back too soon."

Garrett looked up at his father's face, which strangely looked to him as hard as stone. It had taken on a new appearance, one that Garrett had never seen before. It scared him a little.

Jim pulled away and strode past Garrett. He grabbed the doorknob.

No turning back, he thought to himself. *No other options.*

He took a deep breath, pulled the door open, and stepped inside.

While Jim had waited impatiently in the hallway only moments before, he was tormented by all kinds of thoughts. Thoughts about what might happen to Chelsea if they didn't find her soon; a fate worse than death, followed by death itself.

Jim didn't want to think about it – indeed, he had tried his best to push such thoughts to the far reaches of his mind before, after Chelsea had been taken. But that was before he'd met and spoken with Kristi Hawkins. Now, the grim reality of Chelsea's dire situation couldn't be denied or ignored, even for a moment.

How far will a man go to save his child? Is there anything at all a father wouldn't do?

Throughout his adult life, Jim had asked himself the rhetorical question *'what would Jesus do?'* when faced with a difficult decision or situation. As he'd paced back and forth in the hallway, he wasn't sure what Jesus would do in a situation like this. But he did decide what he would do. He was going to get his daughter's exact location from Pete, and then go there and get her. That's all there was to it – no fear, no compromise. Because in the final analysis, Jim decided that there was nothing – nothing at all, that he wouldn't do to get his daughter back in his arms. Anyone who stood in his way would be trampled under his feet.

Jim stepped inside the doorway to the kitchen, and let it shut gently behind him.

Lying on the floor near the folding table, Pete Durgin defiantly lifted his bloodied and beaten face up to Jim. He breathed deeply, and grimaced in pain as he did. Garrett had pummeled him with an assortment of hard body blows and punches to the face, and it showed. But even a hard beating had wrung out neither a confession of Chelsea's whereabouts, nor a change to his arrogant sneer. His hands remained fastened behind his back with Rich's handcuffs.

"So, DiMario," Durgin uttered, "never send a boy to do a man's job, eh?" He laughed, and spat blood out of his mouth. "Your daughter's fate is sealed, and so is yours. There's nothing you can do to change it."

"I don't believe in fate, Pete," Jim said calmly. "I believe in a God who can change circumstances, and crush evil."

"That's what makes you such an easy target, you fool," Pete said with a condescending tone. "What do you think you're going to do – pray yourself out of this situation? Do you really think your impotent God is listening? Do you think He even cares about you personally?"

"I know He hears me, and I know He cares. I have been praying. And I'll pray for forgiveness when this is all over."

A curious expression came over Peter Durgin's face, but Jim had already started to walk over to the kitchen sink.

"Yeah, pray for forgiveness for your weakness, to your weak God," Pete taunted. "What do you think you can do? You already sent your boy in to try. Maybe you should send your wife in – she can kick pretty hard."

Jim opened a drawer, with his back to Pete, who was still supine on the floor. He rooted around through the kitchen drawer, and spoke to Pete over his shoulder.

"I'd just like to know why," Jim said. "Why betray me, and do all the things you've done to my family and my church. Why did you kill my friend Bjorn? What did we ever do to you?"

"Are you still so dull?" retorted Pete. "You represent everything I hate. It's you, and others like you that hinder me from meeting my objectives. You just don't understand that we have to seize life by the short hair to get what we want out of it."

Jim's hands finally found what they were looking for – a large pair of kitchen shears and an electrical extension cord. He pulled them out of the drawer as he replied to his nemesis.

"That's a good analogy, Pete. A real good segue way."

He walked back to where Pete lay on the floor and towered over him, the shears in his right hand.

Durgin's arrogant countenance dimmed at the sight of the shears, but he tried to play it off.

"Now what? Are you gonna give me a haircut?" he said, forcing a tight laugh.

"More than that."

Jim slammed the shears and cord down on the table, then bent down and roughly grabbed his enemy by the upper arms.

"Get up," he demanded.

Jim wrestled the smaller man to his feet, and shoved him up against the kitchen island.

"Go ahead!" Durgin challenged, "do your worst."

Jim snatched up the extension cord, and quickly bent down and wrapped it firmly around Durgin's ankles. Then he grabbed Pete's belt buckle and pulled it loose. Next, he roughly unzipped and unbuttoned Pete's trousers, and pulled them down to his knees.

"Whoa!" Pete said, "I never pegged you for one of those, DiMario." But the tone of his voice lost it's haughty edge.

"Do you know what a eunuch is, Pete?" Jim asked calmly. "I realize that you're no bible scholar, but maybe you've done enough reading to know."

Pete Durgin said nothing, but his body tensed up as Jim pulled his underwear down to his knees.

"In ancient times," Jim continued, "some kings placed authority over their harems of wives and concubines to a high ranking, trusted official."

He drew his face closer to Pete's, and breathed out the words in a voice just above a whisper. "The reason a king would trust this official with such an important responsibility, is because he was made into a eunuch – that is, surgically altered so that he wouldn't be able to sin with any of the women in his charge. Basically, it's like people do these days with their dogs and cats. Spayed, neutered, fixed. Do I need to spell it out in detail for you, Pete? I actually know the steps involved in the procedure. One of my professors in seminary explained it to us. It's not pretty. Kind of makes you cringe just to think about it. I'm going to show you exactly how it works."

"You're bluffing, DiMario. I'm not afraid of you. There's no way you've got the huevos to actually do something like that -not a boy scout like you."

Jim noticed a few beads of sweat on Durgin's forehead, and the tone of his voice changed slightly, higher in pitch and intensity. He could tell that Pete's arrogant self assurance was fading.

Jim picked up the scissors with his right hand, and gripped Pete's testicles with his left. He brought the apex of the scissor blades to bear at the base of the scrotum.

"I've got news for you, Pete. Before God, I decided before I walked in this room that I would do anything – anything at all to get the information I need. I know the basic steps of how to castrate you, and make you a eunuch, and I'm prepared to do it. But I'm not a skilled surgeon, and I only have this dull, unsterilized kitchen scissor. So I can't guarantee the outcome. But I can guarantee that it'll be ugly. And slow. And more painful than you can imagine."

Jim squeezed the handles of the shears together slightly, and they bit into Pete's tender skin.

Peter Durgin turned pale and tried to twist away, but his back was up against the kitchen island, and Jim pressed him in securely from the front. There was nowhere to go.

"Help! Help me!" Pete screamed at the top of his lungs. "Get him off me!"

"Nobody's coming to help you, Pete," Jim growled, "Garrett is making sure of that. It'll all be over but the cleanup by the time you see anyone else."

"They'll put you in jail for this!" Pete sputtered.

Jim looked him coldly in the eye. "I don't care," he stated matter-of-factly. "This is your last chance. Tell me exactly where Chelsea is."

"I don't know!" Pete cried.

"Oh, we both know better than that, Pete. All right, it's time to kiss your manhood goodbye. In fact, you'll be able to literally do just that in a moment."

Peter Durgin looked fearfully into the eyes of Jim DiMario, and saw only cold, steely resolve. The compassion, love, and gentleness that characterized the pastor were gone, and replaced with a hardness he'd never seen in that face before.

"All right!" Pete shouted, "all right! She's at Aldon Brehm's house, over in North Ranch."

"Where, exactly?" Jim pressed, not backing off a bit with the shears.

"The basement," Pete whimpered fearfully. "There's a basement room. The secret entrance to it is at the back of the walk-in kitchen pantry."

Jim looked at him, and decided that he was genuinely scared and broken.

"If you're lying, Pete, as God is my witness, I will come back and finish this job – that's a promise. The police can't protect you. I know inmates in the county jail who have turned to Christ. They would consider it a service to The Lord to do anything I ask, when they find out what you've done. Do you understand my meaning, Pete?"

"Yes, yes. I understand. I swear to God I'm telling you the truth."

"You swear to God? Who's God?"

"Your God."

"All the more reason you'd better be telling the truth."

Jim relinquished his grip on the scissor, and on Pete. He set the scissor back down on the table, then proceeded to re-dress Pete – a task made more difficult by the fact that Pete was sweating profusely. He finished up, and then turned away from the young man, who slumped effete against the kitchen island.

Jim took a few steps toward the door, then stopped, turned, and walked back to Durgin.

"Just in case I don't get another chance," Jim said, stepping forward, "this is for Chelsea."

With that, he drove his right fist into Durgin's midsection. Pete doubled over in pain, and fell back against the island. Jim grabbed the hair on the back of his head, and brought his knee up into Durgin's face.

"That's for what you did to Garrett," he said, over the sickening sound of crunching nose cartilage.

Durgin let out a muffled groan, and fell to the floor, curled up. Jim untied his ankles, then turned and left him lying there, and went outside to find the others.

***

The man walking out the side door of the church building approached the small group that was gathered around Rich's patrol car. Even in the dark, Jasmine knew it was Jim, but as he drew nearer and she looked at his face in the eerie dim light cast by the mercury-vapor lamps, she barely recognized her husband.

He walked purposefully, like a soldier on a mission. His hands and clothing were marked with spatters and blotches of blood, and his face was as hard as iron. He walked directly up to Rich, ignoring the others.

"I've got the location," he said. "She's at Brehm's, like we thought. They've got her in a hidden basement room. The entrance to it is at the end of a walk-in pantry."

Rich looked at him. "You're sure?" he asked solemnly.

"I'm sure."

Rich studied the man. "Okay," he said, "I don't have a search warrant yet, and I know I'll get burned for it, but I'll deal with that later. We can't wait around at this point. Let's get Durgin in the car."

Rich and Jim hastened back to the building, followed by Garrett. Just before reaching the door, Rich's cell phone vibrated. He pulled it off his belt, pushed the green button, and held it up to his ear.

"Rich Harrison."

"Rich," said the voice of Mac, "I can't believe it myself, but I just got off the phone to Judge Linz. He remembers you, all right. He must have figured there would be a favor to repay down the line, because he actually agreed to issue the warrant. He was a bit leery at first, but I reminded him of who was asking, and told him you had a solid witness. I'm surprised he didn't give me more of a fight on it, seriously. Turns out he hates Brehm, too. Probably knows stuff about him that he can't act on. Go check that FAX machine you gave me the number for – I sent the warrant just before I called you."

"Thanks, Mac."

"Wish I could take the credit," Mac replied. "Now go make us proud. I'll dispatch two deputies over there to back you up."

"Who?"

"Vargas and Fitch are in the area, not too far away. Their ETA shouldn't be more than twenty minutes."

"Okay, good."

"Don't forget you're officially suspended as soon as you get back to the station," Mac cautioned. "Plan accordingly."

"Gotcha," Rich said. He pressed the red button, and put the phone back on his belt.

"Great news!" he said, turning to the others. "I've got the warrant – it's coming over now by FAX."

"Garrett," Jim said to his son, "run over to the office and grab it – move it!"

Garrett took off, and Jim and Rich went to retrieve Pete Durgin.

***

Rich was surprised to see the state of Peter Durgin as he and Jim walked into the kitchen. Durgin lay prostrate on the hard floor - conscious, but obviously in pain. By now, Durgin's face was swollen around his right eye and on one side of his mouth from Garrett's 'interview', and a tooth lay on the linoleum floor in front of him, his face turned toward it. Drying rivulets of blood marked the front of his face coming from his nose and mouth, and pooled below his chin.

Jeez! Rich thought to himself, *they really worked him over good. We'll have to clean him up before I take him into the station for booking. This might be a bit hard to explain.*

"Well, Durgin," Rich said, walking up to the man on the floor, "looks like you fell down and hurt yourself trying to escape."

"I want to charge him and his son with assault and battery," Durgin said weakly, pointing his chin at Jim. "Look what they did to me."

"Oh, so you want to make a charge that this pastor and his son beat you to a pulp, eh?" Rich replied. "Well, I suppose it's your word against theirs. I hope you have witnesses. No? Well, you certainly have the right to make a complaint about your treatment at the hands of the family you tried your best to destroy. I'm sure it'll fall on sympathetic ears. Of course, that can wait until after you're booked for murder, kidnapping, racketeering, pimping and pandering, drug trafficking ..."

Rich stroked his chin thoughtfully as he turned his gaze to the ceiling. He looked back at Durgin on the floor.

"Let's see," he said, his voice dripping with sarcasm, "did I miss anything? I'm sure the D.A. can come up with more once we finish our investigation of you and your little crime cult."

Jim shifted his weight back and forth impatiently. "Let's get going," he said.

"Yeah, of course," Rich replied. "Give me a hand here."

He bent down and grabbed Durgin's arm, and Jim did the same on the other side. Together, they hoisted him up. Pete let out a sharp groan as he rose to his feet.

"I'm innocent," he declared weakly, swooning slightly on his wobbly legs. "You have no evidence. You'll be in trouble for arresting me and letting them beat me up. I'll have your badge as a trophy when this is over." He stopped and stared at Rich, and a faint smile formed on his battered lips. "And what would your superiors think of your pornography addiction?" he said slyly.

Rich felt a sudden tingle like an electric shock that ran up his spine to the base of his neck.

My God, how could he know about that? he wondered to himself.

He turned his face away from Durgin, and quickly reeled his emotions in, as he had learned to do so often.

"Save the drama for your mama," Rich retorted, "let's go."

Together, they walked him outside and put him in the back of the patrol car. Jasmine stared menacingly at Peter Durgin as they shoved him in the car, but Kristi turned away to avoid eye contact with him. Garrett came trotting back around the corner, proudly waving a sheet of paper as if it were an Olympic gold medal.

"Got it," he said.

"Good, let's roll," Rich said. "You guys can go in your own car, and I'll take the girl."

Peter Durgin stared out the window at Kristi, who shifted uncomfortably under his gaze.

"I'd rather go with them," Kristi said, nodding her head toward Jasmine.

Rich frowned. "Well, you're not actually under arrest, but I'm responsible for your safety."

"Rich, she's scared to death of him," Jasmine said. "Can't you see that?"

"All right, but she stays in the car when we get there – you all do. Is that understood?"

"No, it's not," Jim said. "I want to be involved in finding Chelsea – she needs me."

"Look, Jim, I understand your position here," Rich answered. "You've already contributed a lot to this effort. I've got backup coming to meet us there. Let us professionals do our job."

"I trust you, Rich, I really do. But this is my daughter."

Rich looked at Jim and saw in the lines of his face that he was steadfast, and would not be deterred. He shook his head and sighed. "For the record," he said slowly, "I'm ordering you to stay back."

He turned away from Jim and headed to his car, not waiting for a response. Rich got into his car, and the DiMarios, along with Kristi, hastened down to the parking lot to get their car.

"I called George," Jasmine said, getting into the passenger seat of their SUV.

"Okay, good," Jim replied, "but I'm not waiting for anyone, or anything."

CHAPTER 62

KNLA Newsroom: Burbank, California

It was relatively calm inside the modestly furnished newsroom in the early evening hours. All the daytime office staff had left for the day, leaving only the broadcast news staff.

When his phone rang, George was sitting at his desk in the KNLA newsroom, getting ready to head home after a long day. His fatigue soon vanished when he heard Jasmine DiMario's voice on the line.

Their conversation was brief – just the basic facts that Jasmine rattled off. Before even hanging up with her, George was already on his feet, reaching for his sport coat.

He dashed over to the news director's office, and burst in without an invitation.

"Sy, I need a news van and cameraman, right now!" he said, dispensing with the formalities.

"No can do, George," his boss said, shaking his head. "They're all on location, except one team that just came in, and they've been out all day covering the campaigns of the county supervisor and assembly hopefuls – they're going home."

"No, they're not!" George exclaimed. "Pump 'em up with coffee, meal vouchers, anything you want. But I need to be on the road right now."

He emphasized his point by jabbing his finger at the prominent clock on Sy's wall.

"Why? Where's the fire?" Sy asked sarcastically.

"Westlake Village. This is the break I've been waiting for, Sy – and what you financed with your three hundred dollars petty cash."

Sy's eyes lit up with recognition, as he recalled the shakedown he'd endured only last week from George.

"So, this is the payday?" he asked suspiciously.

"Yeah. And I need the news van so I can uplink to the studio." He looked at the clock again, which showed that it was eight o'clock – well past the end of the standard workday. "I should have something for the ten o'clock news – eleven at the latest."

George looked expectantly at Sy, who seemed a bit hesitant. "It's an exclusive for us, remember?" George said.

Sy evidently did remember, and that got him off the fence. He picked up the phone receiver on his desk and quickly dialed a number. While it rang, he admonished George, pointing his finger.

"I'm gonna have to give them tomorrow off, you realize that?" he said.

"Yeah, I know. But it'll be worth it."

Presently, the person on the other end of the line picked up, and Sy immediately gave the orders.

"Fleming? Sy here. You and Dixon are going out again, with George." A pause. "Yeah, I know you've been out all day. It'll probably be late." He held the phone away from his ear, and George smirked and shrugged at Sy as he heard the high-pitched squabbling coming from the cameraman on the other end of the line.

"Yes, I understand," Sy answered. "You guys can have tomorrow off, okay? That more than makes up for it." Another pause. "It goes with the territory, you know that. No, he's coming down right now. You can call your wife when you get on the road. Okay, ciao."

Sy hung up and shook his head. "All right, George. Go get me some dirt."

George turned and moved out, without another word.

"And it better be good!" Sy shouted after him.

But George was already gone.

CHAPTER 63

The Magus' Estate: Westlake Village, California

Chelsea DiMario sat languidly on the king-sized bed, her back leaning against the headboard. The bedroom was elegantly appointed, with a luxurious burgundy and gold embroidered comforter spread out across the rich, oil-rubbed four-poster cherrywood bed.

She had been moved here several hours after her encounter with Roberta McAllister. Chelsea figured that since the 'softening up' technique didn't work on her, they had probably given up on trying to get her to cooperate with their repugnant pornography plans. Maybe moving her to this room was the first step toward turning her loose. Maybe not.

She still wore the same clothes she'd had on since being abducted, which had patches of ground-in dirt from the school field and the basement. Although she was disgusted with her grungy appearance and the feeling that went with it, Chelsea decided to refrain from taking a hot shower – in case there were hidden cameras in the room.

Chelsea's stomach rumbled frequently, and her mouth was dry and parched. Nobody had given her anything since she'd been in this room, and nobody had even checked in on her. The door was locked; she'd checked it immediately after she was taken here. The singular window was screwed shut, with black iron bars mounted on the outside. There were no windows in the bathroom.

With time on her hands, Chelsea alternated between singing to herself, praying, and trying to formulate an escape plan. But as she looked around the bedroom, she became disheartened to find nothing that could be used for a weapon or tool for escape. It was as if her captors had planned for any possible escape scenario. There appeared to be no way out, nothing to use to attack a guard when her door was eventually opened.

Chelsea tried to take her mind off her hunger and thirst by thinking about how good it would feel to be back at home, and to be able to sleep in her own bed. After a time, she started to grow tired again, so she got up and went into the bathroom and washed her face with cool water in the sink. Chelsea's eyes panned vacantly across the exquisite gold-plated sink fixtures – then an idea hit.

A few months ago, her dad was fixing the dripping sink in the bathroom that she shared with Garrett. She was hanging out at home that day, and was watching her dad as he reset the stopper with plumber's putty in the bottom of the sink. And she remembered something.

Chelsea reached forward and grabbed the stopper knob, between the hot and cold handles. Grasping it firmly with both hands, she twisted it hard counterclockwise. She felt the threads break loose, then continued to rotate the knob quickly, unscrewing it until she was able to pull it free from the fixture. Chelsea looked at the object she now held in her hands – a slender steel rod one-eighth of an inch in diameter, about seven inches long, with a knob at one end.

Chelsea then opened the medicine cabinet, and took out a packet of fingernail emery boards that she had seen earlier. Wasting no time, she got to work with them, first laying the rod on the edge of the sink, and filing away vigorously at the end of the rod. She continued to rotate the rod as she abrade it. It was slow and tedious work, since the sandpaper on the emery board surfaces wasn't ideal for working with metal. Eventually, after ruining all of the emery boards in the process, Chelsea realized that the rod still didn't look very sharp. She looked around the room for something else to use, and her eyes finally looked down at the floor.

Yeah, that might just work, she thought.

She quickly dropped to her knees on the tile floor, and laid the rod at an angle in one of the grout joints between the travertine tiles. Stroking it back and forth quickly, she rotated it around slowly, and stroked some more. Chelsea kept up this painstaking process for what seemed to her like a long time; rubbing the tip of the rod through the sanded grout joint. Eventually, she finished the job.

Chelsea lifted up her perfect secret weapon – a sharp-pointed, easily concealed steel rod. Long and slim like an ice pick, it was likely to do more damage because of it's larger diameter.

She held the rod in her hand, with the knob resting in her palm. Chelsea closed her fingers around the shaft of the weapon tightly, trying to get a feel of how she could use it when the time came. She laid the weapon inside the folds of the hand towel on the sink countertop, and practiced pulling it out quickly several times.

She looked for a place that she could hide it on her person, and finally decided that it could be secreted in her sock, along the inside of her leg, with the pointed tip resting against the inside of her shoe. That way, she figured, she could whip it out quickly if necessary. Placing her foot on the toilet seat, Chelsea practiced the quick extraction move, lifting her pants leg, and pulling the weapon from her sock again and again, until she was satisfied that she had it down.

Chelsea finally went back to the bedroom and assumed her position again, leaning up against the headboard of the bed. Now that she had her backup weapon, she began to wonder what she could actually do with it. She didn't know if she had it within her to hurt or even kill another person. She was well aware of the fact that '*Thou shall not kill*' was one of the big ten. The thought of stabbing somebody with her crude weapon was scary to her. Thinking about the possible scenarios that might come to pass, her body began to shake uncontrollably.

I don't know if I can do it, she thought to herself. *What if I kill one of them, then what? How many of them are there, anyway? Would I have to kill them all to get away? What if Dad doesn't come for me? I know he will come if he can find me, and I know he'll try everything he can. But what if he can't find me? Dad always said that we have the right to defend ourselves if necessary. So maybe it wouldn't be a sin in this situation if I had to do it. I don't know what these people are going to do to me.*

Her thoughts gradually drifted into prayer. *Dear Lord, please protect me. Please get me through this alive. I want to see my family again. I want to live! Deliver me from the hands of these evil people. Strengthen me, Lord, and show me what I need to do.*

She remembered the psalm that had been familiar to her since early childhood, but it had never had so much meaning to her as it did at this moment. Now it became her personal prayer.

Even though I walk through the valley of the shadow of death, I will fear no evil, for you are with me. Your rod and your staff, they comfort me. You prepare a table before me in the presence of my enemies. You anoint my head with oil; my cup overflows. Surely goodness and love will follow me all the days of my life, and I will dwell in the house of the Lord forever. Amen.

When she ended her prayer and looked up, she realized that her body wasn't shaking anymore.

She heard a sound outside the door. Sitting up straight, Chelsea heard a key slide into the lock, and turn. Her skin prickled in anticipation, waiting for the door to her freedom or doom to open.

When it did open, a middle-aged man entered the room. He had grey hair and a portly form that reminded Chelsea of an overindulged businessman. He wore a casual knit shirt with a nautical theme, and khaki trousers. The ends of his large mouth turned up in a smile.

Chelsea saw that he was flanked by a younger man who was dressed like a waiter in black pants and white shirt and tie, who carried a dinner tray laden with covered dishes and bottled beverages. Her eager nose picked up the wonderful aroma of grilled meat and onions coming from under the covered dish, the way a bloodhound locks onto the scent of her quarry.

"Hello, Chelsea," the older man said jovially. "How are you doing?"

"I don't want to be in your show," Chelsea said coldly, with a tone of bitter contempt possessed only by teenagers.

The young man came forward and placed the tray on the bed next to Chelsea, then retreated to the doorway. He didn't look at her, and his actions and mannerisms were short and jerky; she noticed his hands actually shaking as he set the tray down.

"Ah, but you are in my show, Chelsea," Aldon Brehm said. "All the world's a stage, and we are merely players. That's Shakespeare."

"Duh!" Chelsea retorted.

Brehm laughed heartily, and then turned to dismiss the young man at the door, with a wave of his hand. Brehm turned back to Chelsea, with arms crossed over his barrel-shaped chest.

"Yes, I should have guessed that you would be literate," Brehm replied to her slight. "So many young people these days are completely ignorant of classic literature – or modern literature, for that matter. It's a shame, really. A national tragedy."

Chelsea perceived that his voice was laced with a twinge of sarcasm and condescension. She watched silently as he pulled up a carved wood chair close to the edge of the bed, and sat down facing her.

"But these are exactly the kind of young people who are drawn to me, and my organization," he continued. "They have little education, usually because they spurned the opportunities that were handed to them on a silver platter. Everybody in our country has the opportunity to get a free education – even up through college, if they're from a poor upbringing. But alas, there are so many that are resistant to learning."

Chelsea didn't wait for a formal invitation – she bent forward, lifted the tray onto her lap, and lifted the lid on the plate. A fragrant puff of steam rose, revealing a filet mignon steak smothered in sliced mushrooms and béarnaise sauce, with potatoes au gratin with snow peas on the side. To a hungry girl, it was a beautiful sight.

"Yes, yes, go right ahead," Brehm said, "enjoy, by all means. As I said, so many foolish young people have fought against authority, rejected the opportunities available to them. They think that they would be better off without their family, their parents. And they're right."

Chelsea tore into the sumptuous dinner on her tray, but looked up at her captor at this last statement.

"Oh, does this surprise you?" he asked. "You, of course, being a pastor's daughter, always play by the rules, no doubt. You probably get good grades in school, follow your parents' instructions, do your chores, and are always home before curfew. And, I'm sure you expect that you'll be sent to a nice college, get a good education, and take your place among the other well-adjusted, upwardly-mobile children of privilege. Eventually, you will marry a nice clean-cut young man, have a litter of babies, and perpetuate the cycle.

"But not everyone is like you, Chelsea. Not everybody wants to wait around, play the game, be a good boy or good girl, and hope that someday all the things they have craved and desired eventually come to them. No, instead they break all the rules, fight the status quo, and go out and grab the things they want, without regard to who they step on in the process. I am one of those people, Chelsea. And I'm surrounded by other like-minded people. We know that the nice guy finishes last. The winner is the one who breaks his opponent's knees with a pipe before the race begins – like that figure skater tried to do a few years back."

Chelsea had no reply, and she continued to devour her food without pause. She wondered if she looked conspicuous with the weapon hidden in her sock. She could feel it pressing up against the inside of her leg, and she wondered if this man could somehow sense that it was there. Even though she knew in her mind that it was slender and undetectable, it felt as big as a baseball bat against her leg. Sitting cross-legged with the tray on her lap, Chelsea willed her leg not to move in any way that might betray the hidden weapon.

Aldon Brehm continued his monologue. "Many young people are drawn to my organization, Chelsea. Runaways, the disenchanted, disengaged, undisciplined, unemployed youth. They find their way to me, and I give them purpose."

"What purpose?" Chelsea asked between mouthfuls.

"To serve me," Brehm unabashedly declared. "And they serve themselves at the same time. That's what Satan is all about – power, and self service. All of us who worship the Prince of Darkness are worshipping ourselves, too; feeding our own dark nature. And our dark nature is much stronger than our light nature. I'm quite sure you've felt the pull of your dark side, Chelsea. Even a 'good girl' like you has impure thoughts, harbors hatred and grudges against somebody. Has lust for somebody else. The difference is, you have been trained all your life to suppress those kinds of thoughts and actions. You try to pray them away, but you can't – they keep coming back.

"We, and our followers have learned to embrace our dark nature, develop it. Our animal nature is our birthright. People have tried so hard over the centuries to overcome their animal nature, and for what?" Brehm asked rhetorically, raising his hands for emphasis. "Trying to fight it has only made people unhappy and miserable. Feeding the animal desires we all have is what gives us pleasure and purpose."

"Who is 'us'?" Chelsea asked.

"Myself," Brehm replied, waving his open hand across his portly torso, "and my disciples. You've already met some of them."

"Like that guy who was just in here?"

Aldon Brehm let loose a hearty laugh. "No, no. He is merely one of my servants. He, and many others like him do my bidding without any understanding of what drives me, without sharing my devotion to my god, Anubis. They fulfill various functions in my pylon, because I provide for them. I give them a home, food, work, and focus in life, Chelsea. Every one of these young people who come to me lacks discipline and purpose, and I give it to them."

"So, who are your disciples then?"

"Those who are closest to me – my inner circle," Brehm boasted. "They share my devotion to self-indulgence and power, and the accumulation of money and material goods. They also worship Satan and my god, Anubis. But they each have their own daemon as well, who directs their steps, and is their advocate and helper."

Brehm smiled mischievously, and added, "As I said, you've already met more then one."

As if on cue, a light tap was heard on the door. "Come," Brehm said loudly, without turning around.

The door opened, and a familiar-looking woman entered the room. She wore a smile on her face, with jeans with a casual top on her body, rather than a frumpy suit. Her long auburn hair was brushed straight, not pinned up tightly in a bun, and she wore uncharacteristic heavy makeup on her face. Chelsea stared at her for a moment before she realized who the woman was, because she had never seen her like this before.

"Hello, Chelsea," Roberta McAllister said, with a smile.

Chelsea's mouth fell agape as she stared at her, speechless.

"Ah, do come in, Bobbi," Brehm said. "Pull up a chair next to me."

McAllister did as she was bidden, and sat next to her master, grinning like a Cheshire cat.

Chelsea sat up straight as spear. "You!" she blurted contemptuously, "it figures."

"You've been a very stubborn girl," McAllister said. "You haven't been cooperative at all, up to now. And I had a good personal bet running, too. But," she sighed, "that doesn't really matter now. We need to get you fixed up for the big event."

"What big event?" Chelsea asked.

"Here's a hint," McAllister retorted, "it's not the prom or a debutante ball."

She and Brehm shared a private laugh.

"You're looking a bit scruffy, and that won't do," she continued. "You've got to look good for your final curtain, so we'll get you showered up, wash and style your hair, and get you in an appropriate outfit. Not that you'll be in it long, anyway." She laughed in her characteristic sharp cackle.

"But ... aren't you going to let me go? I already told you I'm not going to pose for your porno pictures, and my parents don't have money to pay you ransom. I have no value to you, so you might as well let me go."

"Oh, ho! On the contrary, Chelsea," Brehm said, "you are of great value to us. I don't need to shake down your poor church mouse parents for the few dimes and nickels they could scrape together. And I don't really need you for my websites and magazines, either. That would have been a nice bonus, definitely, but there are plenty of other young lovelies who are willing to show and use their bodies in any way I desire."

"What, then?" Chelsea demanded, "what do you want from me?"

Brehm smiled and gestured with open hands. "To die, Chelsea," he said. "I want you to die for me."

Chelsea stared at his face, waiting to see if his serious expression would break or soften, indicating that he was making a sick joke. It didn't. Her eyebrows furrowed and her mouth struggled to form words that wouldn't come. The words this man had said did not compute in Chelsea's mind – it was inconceivable. Her insides tightened up, and her throat became suddenly dry. Finally, she managed to spit out a single word.

"Why?"

Brehm's face took on a self-satisfied smirk, savoring her panicked look. He looked at Roberta McAllister in the chair next to his, and patted her gently on the hand.

"I have it on good authority that you are a virgin," he said. "And besides that, you are the daughter of my enemy. That's why you are tailor made to be my sacrificial lamb."

He paused to relish her shocked and horrified expression before continuing.

As a lamb before her shearers is silent ..., he recited silently to himself.

"You see," Brehm said, "Bobbi – that's Mrs. McAllister to you, serves an important function for our pylon. She's not working at your high school for the wages." He looked at her, and she giggled. "She's already a millionaire in her own right, thanks to our business organization."

"Chelsea," McAllister interrupted, "did you know that there were twenty-two girls from your school who got pregnant just this past year? Probably not, since I'm sure you don't hang with 'those kind' of girls. But I make it my business to find out, and I counseled most of them. Overall, I managed to convince ten of them to carry their babies to term, then turn them over to my adoption agency."

"A good yield," Brehm interjected.

"Why would you care about that?" Chelsea asked. "I always figured you to be a pro-abortion advocate."

"Oh, I am," McAllister replied, "I'm definitely in favor of eliminating unwanted children – before birth, or after. It doesn't matter to me. There are already way too many ignorant, stupid people in this world taking up space, and draining valuable resources. But we have a special use for newborn babies, Chelsea. You see, the spilling of innocent blood has great power. We use that power to advance our agenda – to increase our personal wealth, acquire more real estate holdings, to seize power over the inferior beings littering this earth, and sow corruption. We use the power to crush those who oppose us, too. Like your father, and his despicable church."

"What have we ever done to you?" Chelsea said incredulously, her voice rising with emotion. "My dad doesn't even know you."

"You and your kind do oppose us, whether you know it or not. In fact, most of you followers of Christ like to think that we don't even exist. It's more comfortable that way, I'm sure. The public doesn't want to know that there are disciples of the Prince of Darkness, Lucifer, in their schools, in elected office, in the police department – all walks of life. Just like most people refuse to believe in aliens among us because it's too scary and uncomfortable, nobody wants to acknowledge the reality of Satanists among us. But we're here, Chelsea. You 'evangelical' Christians are a stumbling stone for us, a roadblock. Our power comes from Satan and his daemons, and your presence and prayers to God's Son throw a wet blanket on our progress."

Chelsea was rendered mute by the revelation from this teacher, a respected authority figure at her school.

How could she have passed the faculty screening process? she wondered.

The remainder of Chelsea's food had gone cold, but she'd lost her appetite anyway. She sat looking back and forth alternately at McAllister and Aldon Brehm, shell shocked. Their faces smirked back at her, clearly amused by her predicament.

"And now you will be the perfect sacrifice tonight," Brehm said, "on All Hallow's eve – Samhain to us. The perfect sacrifice, at the perfect time, with the perfect incantation. You see, I've gone to great trouble to acquire an original *Necronomicon,* an ancient document that is the holy grail of the left-handed path. It contains powerful incantations that are found nowhere else. I have deciphered them, and know how to use them. Our Samhain ritual tonight will unleash a power greater than any we have ever seen. My personal power will increase greatly, and all of my followers and employees will be filled with a dark spirit of power.

"Your destiny is sealed, Chelsea. After tonight, your church will be brought down, along with your father. Our friend, Peter Durgin – that's Pete LeTourneu to you, will step in to lead your church into becoming a powerless, insipid social club. And the really funny part is, the attendance might actually increase as a result!"

Brehm turned to Roberta McAllister, and the two shared a good laugh.

"In fact," Brehm added, "Pete will be joining us soon. As it happens, you'll be able to see one of your church's pastors before you die. Perhaps you'd like to prepare a confession, or ask him to perform last rites. The one bright spot for you, Chelsea, is that, at least you'll die with your precious virginity intact. I can't guarantee anything after you're dead, though."

Again The Magus and McAllister looked at each other and laughed, more uproariously than before.

CHAPTER 64

Westlake Village, California

Rich drove his Crown Victoria police interceptor as fast as he safely could through the streets of Westlake Village, with no regard for posted speed limits. He had the spinning red and blue lights on the rack in play, but didn't have the siren on. It was now completely dark outside, and the traffic was light in this mostly-bedroom community. Rich had to be extremely alert in order to avoid the throng of trick-or-treaters that lined the sidewalks of the neighborhood streets. The evening felt festive to the children and parents who were out and about, but was just the opposite to Rich and the DiMarios.

In the back seat behind the safety cage, Pete Durgin flopped around with each aggressive turn, his bound hands unable to steady himself.

Jim stayed right behind Rich, who performed only a slight slow-down at the stop signs. The short trip across town to the posh North Ranch neighborhood took only about seven minutes at the breakneck pace that Rich set. To Jim, it seemed to take an eternity.

Rich knew the street layout like the back of his hand, and knew where the street that Aldon Brehm's home was situated on was located. Zooming up Westlake Boulevard, he saw the intersection for Deep Wood Drive, turned on it, and flew onto the residential street. Then he had to slow down for more trick-or-treaters.

"Where's the house, Durgin?" he asked his prisoner. He got no response. "Cat got your tongue, eh? No problem, I can find it myself."

Rich noticed that the house numbers were getting higher, and realized that he must have unknowingly passed the house.

"Shoot," he muttered under his breath.

He turned the car around, executing a rapid three point turn on the decidedly upscale street, while watching out for any little ghosts or goblins that might cross behind him. Jim followed suit. Rich headed back down the street, slower this time.

Kristi Hawkins said that his house is on a hill, he thought to himself, *but it doesn't look like any of these houses are on view lots. It's pretty flat at street level here.*

Then, he saw it – a narrow slice of land between two houses that had nothing more than a concrete driveway, and a mailbox which bore the address he was looking for. Neither the mailbox nor the driveway was illuminated; it was no wonder that he'd missed it the first time. He was mildly surprised that he found it at all, considering that the streetlights cast only a dim amber glow on the street.

The powerful angel who had comforted Chelsea in her darkest moments stood on the driveway, next to the mailbox. He had left Chelsea's side reluctantly, since the air in the infernal house was thick with unclean spirits. He wanted to be sure that the girl in his care would have every advantage on her side, by guiding her rescuers to her.

His heavenly body exuded a glow – not visible light, at least not visible in the physical realm. No photographer's light meter could measure any photons emanating from him. The light he provided could only be discerned on the spiritual plane. The glow reflected off the mailbox and driveway, making their presence known to those who had eyes to see. He saw the deputy stop suddenly in the street and look in his direction, and he was glad.

His task completed, he returned to Chelsea's room-cell, passing through walls and doors of the house as he went to her side.

Rich pulled into the driveway and immediately came to an abrupt halt. About thirty feet ahead on the upward-inclined driveway, his headlights illuminated an ornate iron gate. He also noticed a video camera mounted on one of the posts, pointed at his car.

He angrily hit the steering wheel with his open hand, and cursed under his breath.

"So much for the element of surprise," he muttered. "By the time I get in, they could hide everything."

A tap on his window caused him to jerk involuntarily. He turned and saw Jim standing there, wearing an eager look on his haggard face. Rich pressed a button on the inside of his police cruiser's armrest to roll the window down.

"What are we waiting for?" Jim demanded, "let's go!"

"Problem," Rich said, pointing through his windshield at the imposing gate that blocked the driveway. "I'll have to call the house to get access."

"I've got your access right here. Get out of the way."

"What?"

"Move it!"

Jim hurried back to the SUV, jumped in, and quickly backed out into the street.

Rich got the idea, and thought, *Great, another issue to explain to Mac. My report's gonna be the size of a book.*

He followed Jim's lead, and backed out of the blocked driveway, and well out of Jim's way.

Jim was behind the wheel of Jasmine's SUV – a Ford Expedition, Eddie Bauer edition. It was a behemoth machine, and Jim took a second to thank God for the fact that they had taken it, instead of Jim's smaller car.

"I'm sorry, Jasmine," he said, turning to his wife, "you're gonna have to forgive me for this."

"Oh, Lord!" Jasmine said, grabbing the door handle, and bracing her feet against the floorboard.

"This is cool!" Kristi blurted out.

"Brace for impact," Jim shouted.

He looked quickly up and down the street for any trick-or-treaters, then he stomped the accelerator to the floor.

The five-liter V-8 engine came to life, and the big SUV lurched forward with the kind of torque designed to pull large boats up a grade.

In the brief moment that it took to cross the short divide between the street and gate, the Expedition became a rolling juggernaught that had unstoppable momentum. It easily crashed through the iron gate, tearing it asunder from it's post and opening mechanism.

"Here we come!" Jim shouted.

Rich shook his head in amazement at the force with which the big SUV struck the formidable-looking iron gate, and the relative ease with which it was ripped from it's position.

He pulled in behind Jim and gunned the engine to catch up. He flew up the narrow, curving driveway, which was thankfully marked with low-voltage lights along the sides. When he was almost at the top, a flash of light appeared in his mirror, and he looked up to see another vehicle entering the driveway, about eighty feet behind him.

That's not my backup, he thought, briefly glancing at the profile of what appeared to be a large van conversion.

In another moment, he crested the top of the long driveway, which emptied into a large paved area. The Brehm residence occupied a large hilltop lot that was not readily visible from the street. The DiMario's parked haphazardly, and started to get out of the SUV. Rich met them on the driveway.

"If I had any common sense, I'd wait for backup," Rich said.

"That might be too late," Jim replied solemnly.

"I know," he replied, looking at the front door of the massive stone-faced house.

At that moment, the headlights of an approaching vehicle panned across them with brilliant light as it crested the top of the driveway – a blue Channel Four news van.

A young man glanced with disinterest at the battery of security monitors in his small, darkened room. It was the same boring view that he saw continually during his surveillance shift. He turned his eyes back to the pornographic magazine that was laid out on the desk in front of him. When he finally glanced back at the monitors, he suddenly jerked his previously relaxed body to attention in his chair. The picture in two of the monitors had changed, and he didn't like what he saw.

Looking at monitors two and three which showed views of the front of the house, he saw that someone had gained access to the property without his approval. One of the vehicles was a police car.

He immediately grabbed the walkie-talkie phone on the desk in front of him, and held it up to his face. He pressed the button, and it responded with an electronic chirp.

"Magus, we have a problem," he said into the device.

Another chirp. "What is it?" came the reply.

"Unexpected visitors. A cop car and another vehicle – an SUV, are in the front driveway. I don't know how they got in."

Chirp. "Idiot! The gate must be open. Check it."

"Sir, the gate has been closed all day. But now it looks like … I don't know – the surveillance camera down there is dead. I can't see the gate. Now I see another van pulling in, too."

Another chirp, followed by a string of obscenities. "Alert everyone in the house, quick," The Magus ordered. "Have them take their positions, like they were trained to. Stall our visitors at the door, and don't let them in unless they have a legitimate search warrant."

"Yes, sir."

The ashen-faced young man jumped to his feet and began to execute the 'Police Search' tactical plan that they had all been trained on.

Aldon Brehm turned to the woman on the chair next to him. She wasn't smiling anymore.

"Bobbi, we've got to move quick," he said. "You can fix her up later, after we get rid of the cops."

He motioned with his hand at Chelsea DiMario, who still sat at the head of the bed in her secured bedroom.

"Take her to the basement, and stay down there with her until this blows over." He stood up and pushed his chair up against the wall. "Michael is outside the door – he'll go with you," he added.

Brehm turned, and rapped hard on the door. Immediately the door opened, and the man in white and black entered.

"Help Bobbi get her into the basement, quick," Brehm commanded, pointing at Chelsea, "then get back upstairs and take your place for the police search tactical plan. Have Jason go with Bobbi to guard her down there."

With that, Aldon Brehm hastily left the room.

George hopped out of the news van as it came to a screeching halt in the Brehm mansion driveway.

"So, this is it?" he asked as he strode up to the small circle of Rich, Jim, Jasmine, Garrett, and Kristi. "It's go time?"

"Yeah," Rich replied, "I was hoping that you were my backup. No offense."

"None taken. We goin' in now?"

"Who's 'WE', Kemosabe? This is a law enforcement search, not a public event," Rich replied. To answer George's look of frustration, he added, "But if the press and family members of the abducted follow me inside, I'll probably be too busy to stop them – as long as they stay back."

"Ten-four," George replied, with a salute. "Let's go."

Rich nodded his grimacing chin, and said, "All of you wait here for now. When I enter, you guys can follow, but I want Jasmine to stay here with Kristi. I'm leaving our reverend crime lord locked up in my car."

"I don't want to go in, believe me," Kristi said.

"Tell me again exactly where this pantry is," Rich said.

"When you go in, go through the entry gallery, then turn left," Kristi replied. "At the next intersection, turn right to find the kitchen. The pantry is in the kitchen, but they always blindfolded me when they took me down there. I know the entrance is in the pantry, though, because I could smell the food and stuff. Go into the pantry walk down to the end. Down at the end, there's some kind of switch. I could hear and feel them reaching for it, so I'm pretty sure it's below waist level. The end of the pantry will open like a door. There's a staircase that goes down to the basement."

"Okay," Rich said nervously. He shook his head with trepidation. "Man, I really don't want to go in without my backup. That's bad practice."

"Have some faith, Rich," Jim said. "You take the first step, and God will provide the rest. Besides, we'll back you up."

"They could be heavily armed for all we know."

George replied, "Maybe. But Brehm wouldn't be stupid enough to shoot a cop, especially while being videotaped."

"Good point," Rich acknowledged. "Let's go for it."

He turned and rushed over to the massive oak double doors that served as the only apparent entry to the estate. George motioned to his cameraman, who quickly hoisted his video camera up onto his shoulder and turned on the attached halogen light. George followed behind Rich, keeping a distance of about fifteen feet. Jim pushed ahead, and got right behind Rich, who rapped on the ostentatious carved mahogany door with the knocker. Garrett brought up the rear.

After several long seconds, the door opened, and two burly men in white starched shirts and black trousers stood in the entryway. They said nothing – just stared at Rich.

"I'm here to serve a search warrant on these premises," Rich said, handing the paper to the nearest one.

The burly man with the shaved head took the paper and began looking it over. He didn't budge, and neither did his surly comrade.

"Watcha lookin' for?" the big man said, with a smirk.

"Read the warrant," Rich replied tersely, "It's all there. Now move."

The ogre still didn't shift from his position, but said, "I'll need to read this whole thing first, to make sure it's in order. And I'm not real good at legalese." His partner cracked a smile, and nodded.

"Read it on your own time," Rich retorted. "It's a legal search warrant. If you can't read, find somebody to read it out loud to you - I don't care. But right now, I'm coming in."

Still no movement from the human wall.

"I'll arrest you both for obstruction of justice if you don't step aside right now," Rich said, his voice rising.

"What's the problem here, Harrison?" said a voice coming from behind Rich. He turned, and saw his two backup deputies walking up to the door.

They both unsheathed their batons as they approached.

"Got a little non-compliance problem here, eh?" asked Tony Vargas, the first deputy. He tapped the end of his baton on his open palm.

"No, no problem," replied Ogre number one.

The two parted like the Red Sea before Moses, and the three deputies walked unimpeded into the large entry gallery, followed by Jim, Garrett, George, and his cameraman.

"Hey, what about all these other people?" Ogre number two shouted at their backs.

"Read the warrant," Rich answered back, without breaking stride. *Maybe they won't figure out that the others don't have any legal right to be in here,* he thought to himself hopefully.

Finding the kitchen wasn't as easy as Rich had expected, due to the sheer size of the massive estate. The entry gallery turned out to be just that; the size of a small art gallery, about fifty feet long and twenty feet wide. It was paved with an intricately-cut pattern of polished marble slabs. The walls were ornamented with artworks and paintings that looked expensive to Rich. A gracefully curving staircase with an ornate polished hardwood handrail and wrought iron balusters snaked up the wall to the right.

Rich walked through the gallery, made a left turn at the curved wall at the end, and started down the hallway. He heard the footsteps of his companions echo off the marble floor behind him. Another hallway intersected the one he was walking in, and he turned right. This short hallway opened up onto the largest kitchen Rich had ever seen in a house. The countertops and the large food preparation island in the center of the room were formed of singular, thick granite slabs. The polished black and tan speckled surface reflected the dark wood cabinetry and stainless steel appliances throughout.

Before Rich's eyes found the food pantry, a distinctive voice greeted him.

"Well, well. Look who's coming to dinner," Aldon Brehm said with a voice dripping with sarcasm, as he walked toward Rich from the gloom of the adjoining dining room. "I'm afraid you're a bit late; we've already eaten."

Before Rich could answer, Brehm added, "To what do I owe this honor?" Then, turning to the video camera, he added, "And only two days before election day. Interesting timing."

"I'm here to serve a search warrant on your premises," Rich said. "I handed it to your bodyguards at the door."

"My assistants," Brehm corrected, "and I'm sure you think you have some probable cause for this intrusion."

"Of course," Rich said. "We're looking for a missing girl who was abducted last week."

"Oh, really, now," Brehm retorted, looking amused. "I would be interested in knowing what judge is under the impression that I deal in missing children. One who has ties to my opponent, perhaps?"

"Read the warrant," Rich said. "It's all there."

Rich continued looking around the kitchen, and all the while, Brehm continued to pepper him with questions.

"Look at me," Brehm demanded. "Look me in the eye and tell me that you believe that there is a missing girl in my home. This is obviously an election-eve ploy to reverse my lead in the opinion polls."

Rich did not reply. A strange sensation came over him suddenly, making his skin tingle. It was as if a voice in his head told him, *ignore him – don't look him in the eye; there is danger there.*

"That's what we're here to find out," Rich replied, without turning to face him. "Just stand back and let me do my job."

CHAPTER 65

The Magus' Estate: Westlake Village, California

Jim stood in the entryway of the kitchen as Rich and the other two cops looked around.

In the presence of Aldon Brehm, a weird sensation came over him, too. It was like a tingle, but not on a physical level. More of a sense of heightened awareness – along with a feeling that something was very wrong with the portly man who was speaking to Rich. There was something wrong with this place in general, Jim felt. He had noticed the strange sensation the moment he stepped in the front door. A certain sense of foreboding, an uncanny feeling that he couldn't describe, and couldn't shake. The uncomfortable sensation grew the more Brehm spoke, and Jim came to realize that he was standing in the presence of evil incarnate.

Jim received a message from the Spirit of God that was twofold and clear – more clear than any other 'Spirit Thing' he had experienced before; first, the man who was obviously trying to distract Rich was a very dangerous man. Dangerous, and thoroughly evil. Jim was filled with loathing for this man, at a gut level. He couldn't explain it, but these sensations were no less real than if he'd been in the company of Adolf Hitler or Joseph Stalin.

Secondly, the message was clear that his daughter was somewhere in this house – of this he was certain. He somehow felt her presence here, in spite of the overwhelming reek of evil. Because Jim trusted his holy information source, he purposed in his heart then and there that he would take that house apart stick by stick, stone by stone if necessary, until he found Chelsea.

"All right," Aldon Brehm said to Rich in a haughty tone, "go ahead and play your little game. Search every room – and then get out. We shall let the court of public opinion decide why certain powers among their elected officials are trying to persecute me on the eve of the election. Perhaps I will write a guest editorial for the newspaper myself."

Brehm locked eyes with Deputy Tony Vargas, and fixed upon his face as he continued to speak. "You aren't going to find anything here; there's nothing to find."

"There's nothing to find," Deputy Vargas repeated. He remained transfixed by Aldon Brehm's mesmerizing gaze.

"What's that, Vargas?" Rich said, looking over his shoulder. "What did you say?"

Vargas shook his head vigorously, as if to wake himself up. He turned away from Brehm, and walked over to where Rich was looking at the cabinets.

"Nothing," Vargas said. "I mean, we probably won't find anything here."

"What makes you think that?"

Deputy Vargas was silent for a moment. "I don't know," he said, sounding surprised.

Rich looked around, and realized that the expansive kitchen was packed with people; besides himself, Vargas, and Deputy Simpson, there was Brehm, and three of his so-called 'associates' crowding the area. George, Jim, Garrett, and the cameraman weren't even in the kitchen itself, but were standing in the entry way, and the adjoining morning room.

"All right," Rich announced, turning to the assembly, "I want everybody but law enforcement out of the kitchen, right now."

"Of course," Brehm said condescendingly, "as you wish. You are the law."

He started to back out of the kitchen, and his goons followed his lead. George's cameraman continued to videotape the scene, bathing the area with the harsh halogen beam of the video light.

"Where's your pantry?" Rich demanded.

"You are searching my kitchen," Brehm retorted. "I'm sure you don't need any help from me to find anything."

Rich and the deputies continued to look around the kitchen and surrounding area for a pantry door, but saw only cabinets covering the walls, granite countertops, and high-end stainless-steel appliances. He started to sweat a bit, and felt the dew forming on his brow as he searched fruitlessly. Rich knew there had to be a pantry here, especially in a kitchen this big.

So why can't I find it? he wondered.

Jim watched the action from his spot in the morning room, about ten feet back from the kitchen. Brehm and his minions had retreated to the living room, adjacent to the kitchen opposite of where Jim and Garrett were standing, while George and his cameraman stood closer, in the doorway.

Jim started to pray silently, right where he stood. *Lord, show me the way. Show me a sign. Help me find Chelsea.*

This was no time for long-winded, eloquent prayers. Jim simply cried out silently to God. As he did, it seemed to him as if the noises and voices in the room grew quieter, and he watched with detached interest as the three deputies fumbled about the kitchen.

As he focused his gaze on the kitchen, a strange light gradually came into view. A section of kitchen cabinets right by the doorway where George stood became slightly illuminated. Jim could tell that it wasn't from the cameraman's halogen lamp; the color and tone of this light was unique.

The warm glow didn't wash over the whole area – only four cabinet doors were illuminated. Strangely, it appeared that the others didn't see this light, because they continued on doing what they were doing.

Jim walked forward, into the kitchen and right up to the bank of cabinets where the four doors were illuminated by the mysterious glow.

Brehm saw him, and shouted at Rich in protest. "Hey, what about him? What business does that guy have in my home, anyway?"

Rich looked up just as Jim reached for the side of one of the cabinet doors. Jim pulled, and a block of four doors that looked as if they were small individual cabinet doors came open as one. He opened the hidden doorway, and an inside light came on automatically, revealing shelves stocked with canned goods, cereals, and all manner of foodstuffs.

"Here's the pantry," Jim said, stating the obvious.

Rich eagerly moved in and entered what was now a standard-sized doorway. Deputy Simpson followed, and said over his shoulder to Deputy Vargas,

"Stay here and watch them."

George said to his cameraman, Dixon, "Get in there."

He did, and George followed right behind him. Jim and Garrett followed George.

Rich walked cautiously to the back of the pantry, which he found to be surprisingly deep. On both sides, food items were stacked neatly on shelves – enough to last through the next ice age. He stopped and looked around at the items lining the shelves at the end of the pantry.

The switch has got to be something solid – not loose, he figured.

Rich began to unceremoniously knock cans of vegetables, bags of rice, cartons of hamburger helper, and anything else he saw off the shelves, until most of the shelves at the end of the pantry were cleared. Then his hand hit something that wouldn't knock over – a six-pack of Coke bottles.

Rich began handling the bottles, which seemed to be glued or somehow permanently attached to their cardboard carrier and the shelf. He pushed them, squeezed them, and tried to turn them. Manipulating the bottles every which way, one of them rotated smoothly as he twisted it. When it did, the strangest thing happened.

***

Chelsea once again found herself in the cold concrete dungeon, this time in the company of the transformed Roberta – now Bobbi McAllister, and an armed guard carrying a large black handgun. The guard's weapon had a long perforated tube attached to the end. Chelsea had seen enough TV shows and movies to know it was a silencer.

The trio stood back in the far corner of the chamber, furthest from the staircase. Chelsea was pressed into the corner, with McAllister and the beefy guard blocking her from any possibility of making an end run to the stairs. Her mouth had been hastily taped shut with duct tape just before they brought her down here, but her hands were free. She figured that they would have bound her hands and feet if time had allowed. As it was, they had dragged her to this chamber through the pantry door as quickly as possible, while she resisted as much as possible.

She looked down at her forearms, where bruises were already starting to form from the rough handling she'd endured at the hands of McAllister and the guard.

The guard and McAllister kept their eyes glued on the door at the top of the stairs, just as Chelsea had done over a day ago as she laid here shivering on the hard floor.

"Well, Chelsea, maybe your moment will come a little sooner than planned," McAllister said quietly. But the haughty, self assured tone was gone from her voice.

Chelsea nervously looked at the gun hand of the guard in front of her, who kept toying with the handgun. Whenever he touched the trigger, a bright red dot appeared on the floor where the barrel was pointed. Chelsea realized that this was a laser sight, designed for low-light combat conditions - just like this one. She wondered if this guard actually had experience with a tactical combat weapon like this, or if he'd just picked it up at random when he came to help McAllister bring her down here.

She noticed that, although the guard was big, he wasn't as buff as the Marines she'd seen last summer at Oceanside Beach.

Chelsea knew that she wouldn't stand a chance against a trained military guy, even with her crude weapon. She made a quick mental assessment of the guy, and decided that if the situation called for action, she could do it. She didn't have to wait long to find out for sure.

Chelsea heard some banging and crashing noises coming from behind the door at the top of the steps. McAllister and the beefy guard moved forward slightly, as if by doing so they could somehow discern what was going on upstairs. Their movement gave Chelsea a little breathing room.

"I don't like the sound of this," Bobbi McAllister hissed to the guard next to her. "Get ready."

The guard raised the pistol in front of him. He pulled back the top and released it, chambering a .45 caliber round. He touched the trigger lightly, and the bright red dot jumped to the door, about forty feet across the room. Then the dot disappeared.

Chelsea's stomach tightened involuntarily, and she clenched her jaw behind the duct tape. More crashing, then quiet from behind the door. Then at last, the door swung open, revealing several figures standing in single file behind it. Chelsea saw a familiar-looking profile of a man at the front of the group, even though they were silhouetted by the light of the pantry behind them. Several others stood in the narrow passage behind him.

The guard raised his weapon, and the red dot fell directly on the chest of the man in front. There was no time to think, no time to weigh the moral implications of action or inaction. Chelsea quickly snatched the knob of the sharpened drain rod sticking out the top of her sock. Without hesitation, she pulled out the weapon, and thrust it forward with all her might into the guard's back.

He jerked back with a pained grunt, and his pistol discharged with a muffled high-pitched sound.

Time suddenly transformed into slow motion for Chelsea, and she was sure that she could see the glint of the bullet as it flew toward it's target. But just as the pistol fired, the dot moved up to the ceiling just above the figure at the top of the stairs. She heard the whine of the bullet ricochet off the concrete, and the man at the top of the stairs flinched.

Everything was happening at once; the guard dropped the pistol and staggered forward, clutching his back. He dropped to his knees, and fell forward into a prone position. Chelsea and Bobbi McAllister looked down at the same moment, and reacted at the same moment. Chelsea dove for the gun, which lay on the floor about six feet away. McAllister lunged for it too, coming from a slight angle on Chelsea's left. Their heads smacked together as their hands groped for the gun. McAllister got to it first, but Chelsea grabbed her wrists. They struggled to their feet, fighting for control of the gun.

Chelsea tried to twist it out of McAllister's hands, with strong arms fashioned from her years of cheerleading and tumbling. She saw the awful look of intense anger come over the face of her former teacher. It was as if McAllister had become possessed by a power not of her own; her eyes narrowed and her face contorted into tight furrows of rage. Her teeth were bared, and Chelsea couldn't have been any more surprised if she suddenly grew fangs.

McAllister managed to slowly point the end of the barrel toward Chelsea's face. She wasn't trying to pull the gun away, Chelsea realized – she was intent on using it on her. Recognizing that she was in a fight for her life, Chelsea fought with every ounce of strength she could muster, struggling to keep the weapon pointed away from her.

Chelsea was about three inches taller than McAllister, and had the advantage of youth on her side, but it wasn't enough to prevail. It seemed to her that McAllister was drawing power from some deep well. Chelsea had been certain she could overcome the older, smaller woman, but now her nemesis' burst of energy was accompanied by a grotesque change in her appearance. Her facial expression of rage and hatred intensified. Her skin took on a deep maroon color, and the furrows grew deeper. The teacher's eyes became slits, oozing with venomous contempt. She grunted with the effort of the struggle, breathing a hot, malodorous breath in Chelsea's face.

After what seemed like several minutes to Chelsea, the muzzle of the gun came within an inch of her face, relentlessly forced closer and closer by the unusually strong Bobbi McAllister. More shouting from the top of the stairs. Then McAllister hissed through clenched teeth,

"You will be sacrificed, one way or another. You won't escape us!"

A sudden, deafening boom resounded through the dim chamber as she spat out the last word. Chelsea jerked, and closed her eyes in a reflexive defense. But the gun didn't jump. Chelsea felt McAllister stiffen and stop fighting. She opened her eyes, and was face to face with her tormenter, who's eyes were open so wide they threatened to pop out. Her mouth hung open, as if to hurl one last curse. Chelsea felt McAllister's grip on the gun loosen, then she just dropped, and sprawled facedown on the floor.

Chelsea stood in shock, now holding the pistol in her trembling hands. She was numb, and her ears rang. She looked down at the body of Bobbi McAllister lying at her feet, then at the guard – not dead, but writhing on the floor in pain.

A voice - she heard a voice calling her name, but it was in the background, her ringing ears in the forefront. She stood silently, dumbfounded and still like a statue. She looked again and stared at the crumpled body of her former teacher. It seemed like only a moment that she stood there in a shocked state of paralysis, but it could have been several minutes for all she knew; time seemed to have stopped for her.

Then Chelsea heard a voice she recognized at once – her father, calling her name. She slowly turned her head toward the figures at the top of the stairs, still silhouetted from the pantry light. She pulled the duct tape off her mouth, and it tore at the tender skin of her lips as it came off.

"Daddy?"

"Chelsea!" Jim shouted, rushing down the steps, nearly trampling Rich in the process, "Chelsea, are you okay?"

Jim hit the bottom step and rushed across the concrete floor to where she stood. Rich and Deputy Simpson ran, guns drawn, to where McAllister and the guard lay. With his left hand, Rich held a bleeding shrapnel wound in his right shoulder, where he was hit by a fragment of the guard's ricocheting bullet.

Jim gently grabbed his daughter's shoulders and looked her in the face.

"Chelsea," he said more quietly, "are you all right?"

Chelsea nodded her head, and the floodgates opened. Jim pulled her to him, and she wept freely, her flow of tears dampening the front of his shirt.

Glancing at the pistol in her hand, Chelsea asked, "Daddy, did I kill her?" Her voice broke between sobs.

"No, honey. Rich – Deputy Harrison, shot her. He shot her to save you – and it looks like you saved him, too. Oh, thank God you're all right."

Rich took the handgun from Chelsea and said, "Your dad's right – you saved my life."

Jim had dozens of questions to ask her, but they would have to wait until later. Deep down, he was a bit afraid to know what had happened to his beloved daughter these last several days since she had been taken. Garrett was now behind Jim, and eager to greet his sister. She turned Jim loose and hugged her brother so hard he could hardly catch a breath.

"Hey, Sis, yer killin' me here," Garrett gasped.

Chelsea relaxed her grip, and laughed between sobs. It was a weird emotion, like nothing she had ever felt before. She cried and laughed intermittently; both stricken by grief and sadness about what had happened during her captivity and especially in the last few minutes, and yet elated at her redemption and seeing her family again. It was an emotional roller coaster for her - she was a basket case awash in contradictory feelings.

Garrett took a step back and did a quick assessment of his sister. He figured that she didn't look like she'd been physically harmed, at least, and he was thankful.

He looked at his dad and shrugged. "Hormones," he said.

Chelsea slapped him on the shoulder, and that set her off on another jag of laughing and crying. After a few moments, she pulled herself together enough to ask,

"Where's Mom?"

"Outside, with Kristi Hawkins," Garrett replied.

"Who?"

"It's a long story," Jim said. "You'll see Mom soon."

George's cameraman was taping this whole reunion scene, then he and George transitioned over to where a wounded Deputy Rich Harrison and Deputy Simpson were checking the deceased Bobbi McAllister, and cuffing the guard.

George decided that this was the moment of glory he'd been waiting for. He motioned to his cameraman to cut his taping session, then moved himself into a position where the DiMarios and the deputies were behind him. George adjusted his sport coat and tie, and wiped his brow with his handkerchief. The cameraman gave him the thumbs-up, then the red light on the front of the camera came on.

"This is George Tanaka reporting live from Westlake Village where an incredible series of events has just taken place. We are inside the home of county supervisor hopeful Aldon Brehm, where a search warrant has just been served. A teenage girl who was abducted several days ago has been found in a secret chamber below the house. In the process of finding the girl, aged seventeen, a brief gun battle ensued. One of the apparent conspirators has been shot to death, a woman identified as Roberta McAllister, a local high school teacher. Another unnamed suspect has been wounded, and the sheriff's deputy who broke this case has been wounded as well. We will continue to broadcast from the scene as the story unfolds."

The cameraman cutoff his taping, and George turned to Garrett.

"Garrett, do me a big favor and run the videocassette out to my broadcast tech in the news van, will you?"

The cameraman ejected the tape and handed it to Garrett, who took off up the stairs and went out through the pantry door, without looking at the small group gathered in the living room.

***

Deputy Tony Vargas stood in the living room of the Brehm estate, watching the master of the house and his three 'associates', who had been crowding the kitchen.

"What is your name, deputy?" Brehm asked, as he casually sauntered up to Vargas.

"Vargas, sir," he replied, looking at Brehm.

"Deputy Vargas," Brehm said slowly, staring into his eyes. "This is a most unfortunate incident we find ourselves in." His voice was relaxed and calm as he spoke. "There's really nothing to find here, nothing going on at all to be concerned about."

Vargas was immediately transfixed by Brehm's stare, and the sound of his voice. He gulped, and repeated,

"Nothing going on."

"That's right," Brehm answered. "There's no cause for concern. You might as well sit down and relax while your friends do their search. I can see that you're tired anyway."

"I am tired," Vargas said. "So tired."

"Of course you are. Just sit down in this nice chair here. Take off that uncomfortable belt – you won't be able to relax and get comfortable with that on."

Deputy Vargas, now fully entranced, moved slowly over to the leather barcolounger. He unbuckled his gun belt, and lowered it to the floor.

"I see that you don't know what to do with your hands when you're not busy," Brehm said. "My associate will help you with that, so you will be able to relax, okay?"

"Okay," Deputy Vargas replied numbly.

One of the smirking young men slowly bent down and took the handcuffs from the deputy's belt on the floor. He gently fastened Vargas' hands behind his back with the handcuffs, and guided him to sit down in the lounge chair.

"Now, isn't that better?" Brehm said.

"Better," Vargas parroted back.

Brehm and his men withdrew to the opposite side of the room, leaving the semi-catatonic deputy in the lounge chair. The four of them joined hands, and their Magus began an incantation.

CHAPTER 66

Simmons Residence: Westlake Village, California

Trey Simmons sat at his computer, digging into Aldon Brehm's personal business through the access he had gained from his data miners and keystroke-logging program.

His police scanner sat on the desk next to his computer, and he listened to the litany of calls that came across the police frequency, while at his workstation. As usual, most calls were mundane, but a few were mildly interesting.

It was still mid-evening; he'd helped his mom work the door for the trick-or-treaters, who by now had slowed to a trickle. Trey had been invited to a Halloween party in Thousand Oaks, and he was still contemplating whether or not to go.

A familiar-sounding voice came over the airwaves, immediately grabbing Trey's attention. He realized by the request for backup and the address in North Ranch that a party of another sort was about to go down, and he hadn't been invited. Trey had crashed parties plenty of times before, so he wasn't going to be shy about this one. He'd spent a lot of time on this project, and he wouldn't be denied now.

Trey carefully backed out from the bank transaction page he was viewing on the secured savings and loan web site, so as not to leave a record of his visit, then quickly logged off his computer and hopped up from his chair. He whisked through the kitchen, and gave his mom a quick peck on the cheek.

"Goin' out for a bit," he said. "Don't let the little goblins get the best of you."

"Where are you going?" his mother asked.

"I'm gonna hang out with Pastor Jim and his family for awhile," he replied. *That's a safe answer, and technically true*, he told himself.

"Oh, that's nice," Debbie Simmons replied. "Have fun."

"Yep. C-ya."

With that, Trey bounded out to his aging Honda Civic and fired it up. It didn't take him long to get over to the North Ranch neighborhood. Upon arriving, the layout of large, beautiful custom homes on spacious lots seemed a world away from his nice, but humble neighborhood.

Trey remembered exactly where the driveway to the Brehm estate was, having scouted it out a few days earlier, and found it without difficulty. He was surprised to see that the gate was not only open, but torn off the hinges. Trey decided to opt for discretion, and parked his car on the street. Then he jumped out and jogged up the driveway.

When he got to the top, he saw Jasmine DiMario standing with a girl in the midst of a bunch of haphazardly-parked cars.

He took in the girl's curvaceous figure. *Whoa, that's some hot shorty*, he thought.

"Yo, Mrs. D," he called out breathlessly, "what's up?"

Jasmine and Kristi Hawkins turned around to face him.

"Trey!" Jasmine exclaimed, "where did you come from? Never mind, I'm glad to see you." She greeted him with a hug.

"Jim, Rich, Garrett, and everybody else are inside," she continued. "We had to wait outside with him."

Jasmine pointed with her thumb over her shoulder at the police car, where Peter Durgin glared menacingly at them from the back seat.

Trey looked at him, then back at the girl who stood with Jasmine. All at once, he recognized her as the same girl who had lured him out to the dark parking lot behind the Starbucks by the college, where he'd suffered the worst beating of his life. The realization stung him like a hornet. She didn't look at him, as if she was deliberately trying to avoid eye contact with him.

"Whoa," Trey said suspiciously, "a lot must have gone down that I don't know about. What's the four-one-one, Mrs. D? Do you even know who she is?" He gestured at Kristi.

Jasmine quickly brought him up to date on the events of the past couple of hours, and made the new introductions with Kristi. Suddenly, Garrett burst forth from the front door, running with a videotape in his hand.

"What happened?" Jasmine yelled to her approaching son.

"It's all good," Garrett replied breathlessly. "We found Chelsea – she's all right!"

"Oh, thank you, Lord," Jasmine said under her breath. "Thank you so much."

He dashed past them to the news van, banged on the door, and delivered the videotape to the technician inside. His task completed, he turned back to where the others were huddled in the crisp night air.

"What's crackin', G-man?" Trey said.

Garrett caught his breath and answered, "It's just like Kristi said. There's a pantry, but it's disguised like regular cabinets. Then there's a secret switch at the end that makes the wall open – it's kind of cool. But then, oh, my God, you're not even gonna believe it. They had Chelsea down there, and a guy tried to shoot Rich, then Chelsea stabbed him, and Rich shot Mrs. McAllister, my social studies teacher."

"Hold up, Garrett," Jasmine said, grabbing his shoulders. "Slow down, you're not making sense."

Garrett took a moment to compose himself, which seemed like an hour to Jasmine and the other two, who were desperately waiting for information. After his rapid breathing slowed down a little, he quickly told them everything that had happened. After he finished his information download, he said,

"I'm goin' back in. Wait here, Mom."

"Me too, Dog," Trey quickly added.

Before Jasmine could reply, Kristi said, "I can't go in there."

Jasmine was torn by her urge to go to her daughter, and the need to comfort her new surrogate daughter. She decided to wait outside, trusting that they would soon come out.

Not content to wait, Garrett and Trey dashed back inside.

George and his cameraman taped three more short segments down in the basement; one of the formerly kidnapped girl embracing her now emotional father, another of Rich and Deputy Simpson securing their prisoner, and another brief interview of Rich, who explained in his own words what had just transpired. The taping was intrusive at a time like this, but they gave George his due, since he had contributed significantly to the effort.

After Jim and Chelsea pulled themselves together, Jim said, "Come on, honey. Let's get out of here." He turned to Rich and said, "You too, Rich. You're hurt – you seriously need to get medical attention right away. Your deputies can hold down the fort here until more backup arrives."

Deputy Simpson had already called in for an ambulance and backup. He knew that the key words "shots fired" and "officer down" would ensure that the cavalry would soon be rolling in like an overturned barrel of oranges.

Rich Harrison slowly got up to his feet, having restrained the injured guard. He recited the Miranda rights to his prisoner, to make sure some judge wouldn't throw his bust away later in the courtroom.

Rich's face looked really white to Jim, and his right sleeve was painted with blood.

"Gonna need a second ambulance for him," Rich said, nodding toward the guard. "I've got dibs on the first one, though."

"C'mon, let me help you up the stairs," Jim said.

Rich waved him off. "I can do it," he insisted.

"Why don't you just admit you could use some help from a friend who wants to help you?" Jim said. "The Proverbs say, *pity the man who has no friends, for he has no one to help him up.*"

They had made it to the foot of the stairs when they heard a voice above them, accompanied by a slow clap of hands.

"Bravo, bravo," said Aldon Brehm, his voice laced with acidic condescension. He stood at the head of the stairs with three of his men. "And isn't this a heroic scene? But I'm afraid you've really crossed me now. You're really at the top of my hate list, and that's a very bad place to be. You have upset my special plans for tonight, and now you've killed one of my key people. Quite sad about Bobbi, but we'll survive regardless. I'm afraid I can't say the same for all of you, though."

Deputy Simpson stood up from where he was kneeling next to the wounded guard, and reached for his sidearm.

"Put your hands on your heads," Rich commanded Brehm and his minions. He reached for his Sig Sauer .40 caliber pistol, and drew it out of it's holster.

Now Aldon Brehm's countenance changed from smug self-assurance to a mask of pure evil.

"Oh, please," he mocked, "the time for your impotent weapons is past."

He raised his empty hands before them, and pointed his fingers in their direction. His face furrowed with intense focus. Suddenly, Rich's pistol became too hot to hold, and he abruptly dropped it to the floor with a startled yell. The same phenomenon happened to Deputy Simpson. Rich looked in shock at his reddened palm – his third injury of the night.

"I'll have to modify my plan now, because of you," Brehm said angrily.

Jim noticed that his voice had changed – deeper and more powerful in timbre. It was like a different man was speaking.

"Make no mistake," Brehm added, "my plan will go forward. Only now I must execute it earlier than planned, but I'll have more of my enemies to sacrifice."

Rich reached down for the radio microphone that was clipped to his shirt pocket. "Vargas, come in," he said into it.

No reply.

"Vargas!"

Nothing.

He looked down at his pistol on the floor, and squatted down to touch it – still too hot to hold. It didn't make any sense, but it sent a chill down Rich's spine to think of how Brehm could have done this trick. He stood up, and turned to Deputy Simpson.

"Let's go!" he said, waving him over.

Rich unsheathed his baton and took one step toward the base of the stairs. That's as far as he got.

"Stay!" commanded Aldon Brehm, pushing his open palms toward them.

For some unknown reason, Rich, Deputy Simpson, Jim, Chelsea, George, and Dixon the cameraman suddenly found that they couldn't move from where they were standing. It was as if their feet were stuck to the floor – beyond that, they couldn't even move their leg muscles at all. It was like being paralyzed, but with their muscles in a stiff, locked position.

Rich looked up the stairs at Aldon Brehm, who's wild eyes blazed back at him, his open hands still outstretched. Rich willed his legs to move, twisting his torso in an effort to break the lock in his lower body. It was the most bizarre thing he had ever experienced. He could feel his legs. But even trying to concentrate, he couldn't make them move. He'd never had to think about walking before, but now he couldn't control his legs even by trying.

He looked around and saw that the others were in the same condition, judging by their lack of movement, and the expressions of shock and disbelief on their faces.

The Magus turned his head to his goons without moving his body or arms, and said, "Go bind their hands and feet. Take the girl, and use the manacles to secure her hands to the pipe across the ceiling. We'll sacrifice her first, while Bobbi's life force is still strong in the room. The others can watch, then they'll each have their turn – one at a time."

"With pleasure," said the largest of the three. They moved carefully past their master and clambered down the steps.

"You can't get away with this!" Rich shouted. He grabbed his microphone, but the big thug backhanded him across the face, knocking him sprawling on the floor. He snatched Rich's radio from his belt, and smashed it on the floor. One of his associates did the same to Deputy Simpson, while the third proceeded to take the video camera from Dixon.

"Wait!" The Magus shouted. "Let him continue to videotape this historic event. I do enjoy home movies."

Brehm's men proceeded to bind Jim and George using manacles they retrieved from a trunk under the stairs. They attached their bound hands to steel rings that were embedded into the walls of the chamber. Jim, George, and Rich all put up a fight as best they could, but with three against one, and an immobilized lower body, it did no good other than to earn them some lumps from their captors. They manacled Dixon's legs to one of the rings but left his hands free, so that he could still keep taping.

Then the three turned their attention to Chelsea.

CHAPTER 67

The Magus' Estate: Westlake Village, California

J asmine watched Garrett and Trey dash back into the house.

"I don't like this," she said, shaking her head. "Something's wrong."

"But they found your daughter," Kristi said. "Everything's going to be okay now."

"I'm thankful that they've found her, but why haven't they come out yet? Something's not right in there, not right about this place – I can feel it. There's a presence of evil here. I sensed it as soon as I got out of the car. I can't explain it or describe it; I just want them to come out of there so we can go home." She looked at Kristi. "Will you pray with me, Kristi?" she asked.

"I – I don't think I know how. And God probably wouldn't listen to my prayers, anyway."

"There's never been a better time to learn. And He will hear your prayers, Kristi, if you come before Him honestly and openly."

"But I don't know how to say fancy prayers like you did back at the church," Kristi protested.

"It doesn't matter. God doesn't judge our prayers and answer them based on how eloquent or knowledgeable we are. Just tell Him what's on your heart, in your own words."

"I didn't know you could pray like that," Kristi said quietly.

"You can," Jasmine said. "I'll start, and you can finish, okay?"

"Okay," Kristi agreed, with a nod.

Jasmine took Kristi's hands in hers, and bowed her head.

"Dear Lord," she began, "please have mercy on us. Please look upon my family with favor and protect us all, including Kristi, George, Trey, and Rich. Lord, I can feel the presence of evil in this place, more than any place I've ever been. Please bind the unclean spirits and keep them from harming any one of us. Rebuke them, Lord, and deliver us from this situation."

She paused and waited for Kristi to continue. Several long seconds passed before Kristi spoke quietly.

"God, I hope you can hear me, like Mrs. DiMario says. I haven't talked to you in a long time – not since I was in Sunday school, like maybe second grade. Anyway, if you still remember me, I want to pray for these people. I know this is a bad place, and I know that The Magus is a dangerous and bad man. Please let all of us get out of here safely."

She paused for a moment, then took a deep breath, and let it out slowly. "And, God, I'm sorry for all the bad stuff I've done, and been a part of," she continued haltingly, her voice breaking up. "I don't know how you can forgive me - I know that I don't deserve it. But please … forgive my sins."

At this point, Kristi broke down and sobbed openly. Jasmine put her hand on the girl's shoulder, then pulled her into a hug. Kristi cried for a long time on Jasmine's shoulder; torrents of tears, it seemed. Tears that cleansed her soul, washing out all the pent-up 'yuck' that had built up within her over the years. Kristi hadn't allowed herself to cry in a long time before today, and not at all since the day she ran away from home and landed here, way out west.

But as she wept freely on the shoulder of the woman who was the closest thing she had seen to a mother figure in two years, all the pretense of hardness in her life flowed out along with the tears. She knew for sure that, if she survived tonight, her life would never be the same as it had been these last nightmarish two years.

Garrett led Trey through the gallery and around to the kitchen at a trot. They didn't encounter any resistance - it didn't seem like anyone was around.

They rounded the wall that separated the hallway from the kitchen, and Garrett saw Deputy Vargas sitting quietly in a lounge chair with his hands behind his back, all alone in the living room. His eyes were open, but he didn't look at them.

"Hey," Garrett said to the deputy, "c'mon downstairs."

"Dude, we got issues here," Trey added.

No response from the deputy. Garrett and Trey looked at each other, then back at the entranced deputy. Garrett tapped Trey on the arm, and pointed out the entrance to the pantry.

"Check it," Garrett said.

Garrett led the way through the cluttered pantry, carefully stepping over and around various boxes, pouches, and cans of grocery items that littered the floor. When he stepped out onto the landing, he saw a scene that he didn't expect at all.

Down on the floor below, Brehm's men had Jim, Rich, George, and the other deputy held against the walls, evidently tied up. The cameraman was still taping, but he appeared to be fastened to the wall, too. And they were busy binding his sister's wrists with manacles draped over a pipe running across the ceiling. Over to Garrett's right, Brehm stood at the top of the stairs that led from the landing to the floor below, with hands outstretched in front of him. Garrett couldn't imagine how the tables could have turned so drastically in the scant few minutes that he was gone, but he didn't have time to ponder that now.

Looking at Brehm, Garrett realized that he must have done something – was even now doing something that caused this turn of events. He didn't know what that something was, but he was pretty sure how to stop it.

Without another thought, Garrett bent down into the position that had become second nature to him, even as a second-string player. He lunged forward with the zeal of a bighorn ram during rutting season, and struck Aldon Brehm hard in the lower back. Brehm's head snapped back in a violent whiplash, and his raised hands splayed apart from the impact. The force of the blow launched the portly man into the air over the steps. His body flew about halfway down the staircase, and he pitched forward, landing on his head with a loud thud. The Magus tumbled over and over, and landed in an effete heap at the bottom of the steps.

Garrett followed immediately behind, running down the steps. Trey came out of the pantry passageway, and quickly surveyed the unfolding drama below.

All three of Brehm's men looked up at the noise in time to see their master sailing through the air. When he landed at the bottom of the steps, he didn't move. It took them a moment to react – a precious moment. The three of them suddenly lost interest in Chelsea; two of Brehm's men headed toward the steps where Garrett was rapidly coming to meet them. The tall one turned his head over his shoulder, and said to the third man,

"Get the daggers out of the chest – let's waste 'em all now!"

Trey saw one thug turn and go to the chest under the stairs, directly below him. With a lump in his throat, he realized instantly what he had to do. He figured the distance to the floor to be about twelve feet from the platform he was standing on.

Trey quickly threw his right leg over the waist-high metal railing, then carefully brought his left leg over as well. He balanced himself precariously on a bit of ledge that was no more than two inches wide, clinging to the railing behind him. In a couple of seconds, the thug came out from under the stairs directly under Trey, holding long, sinister-looking daggers in both hands. He took one step toward Chelsea, then Trey made his move.

Trey released his grip on the railing and shifted his weight forward. Gauging his distance from the target, he jumped. With arms outstretched like superman, he flew down and landed hard on the back of Brehm's thug.

The momentum of Trey's lanky frame easily overwhelmed the unsuspecting man below, especially since Trey landed with his elbow in the base of the guy's neck. Brehm's thug went down hard on the unforgiving concrete floor, sending the daggers flying this way and that.

Trey scrambled up just as the guy started to raise his head, and quickly stomped him in the back of the neck,. The clear, sharp crack of his jaw breaking ensured that he was down for the count.

Garrett rounded the banister at the foot of the stairs, stepping roughly on the recumbent Aldon Brehm as he did so. He looked up and saw a human wall coming at him. Even with righteous anger on his side, he knew he was no match for these two large men. But the facts didn't matter at a time like this. He bent his body forward, and prepared for his final charge at the biggest one. Then he heard his dad shout,

"Garrett, get the gun!"

Looking down, Garrett saw Rich Harrison's service pistol right at his feet. He quickly bobbed down and grabbed it. When he did, one of his intended targets dodged over to the left, where Deputy Simpson's pistol lay. The attacker dove for it and grabbed it, but it was too late.

Garrett raised the pistol and fired. The boom was amplified by the confined room, the sound waves echoing off the hard walls. The big .40 caliber bullet struck Brehm's ogre in the right hip, instantly shattering his hipbone. The man dropped like a stone, losing his grip on Simpson's pistol. It dropped to the floor.

The second ogre stopped in his tracks. Trey quickly snatched one of the daggers from the floor, and rushed over to ogre number two. Applying the point of the dagger to his back, Trey ordered him to lie facedown on the floor.

Garrett rushed over to the man he'd just shot in the hip, and kicked the gun away from his reach. Only now did Garrett start to make sense of the cacanophy of voices that were yelling all at once.

"Pick up the other gun, Garrett!" Rich shouted.

"Trey, get the keys off that guy, and unlock us," Jim yelled.

"Dixon, tell me you're still rolling tape," George said to his cameraman. He got a nod in reply.

"Give me the keys to their cuffs, fool," Trey ordered. He applied a little pressure from the dagger tip to the man's back, eliciting a quick response. The man reached into his pocket, and produced a single key. He held it out.

"On second thought, you go ahead and unlock them," Trey added. "Start with the cops."

Ogre number two complied with Trey's demand, but not swiftly enough to avoid a red spot of blood from forming on his white shirt from the dagger's tip.

Once Rich and Deputy Simpson were set free, they immediately cuffed the three men and made them lie facedown on the floor, with their heads toward the far wall. Meanwhile, Trey continued freeing Jim, George, Chelsea, and Dixon from their restraints.

Chelsea fell into her father's arms for the second time in this dreary chamber, and cut loose tears that she didn't know she still had left. Garrett stood like a statue, looking alternately at the pistol in his hand, and the man he had shot. Rich walked over to him, and held out his hand expectantly.

"I'll take that," he said.

Garrett handed over the weapon, and Rich holstered it. "You did good, kid," he said, punching Garrett gently on the upper arm. "Real good."

Rich looked at the unmoving form of Aldon Brehm, and walked over to him. With considerable pain and effort, he bent down to check him. He felt his neck for a carotid pulse; he was alive, but the pulse was weak.

At that moment, a voice from the top of the stairs called out, "Hey, what happened here?"

They all looked up and saw Deputy Vargas on the landing, with his hands still cuffed behind his back.

"Great timing, Vargas," Rich said sarcastically, "Glad you could stop by. Where the heck have you been?"

The confused-looking deputy replied, "I don't know. It's like I just woke up and found myself sitting in a chair with my hands cuffed behind my back. I don't know how – they must've got the drop on me somehow."

"Well, get down here," Rich answered, "I need your cuffs – unless you want to keep wearing them, that is."

Vargas sheepishly walked down the steps, and turned his back to Rich, who soon made good use of his master key.

Rich transferred the cuffs from Deputy Vargas to Aldon Brehm, securing them to his chubby wrists, hands behind his back.

Rich then turned to Deputy Simpson, and said, "Looks like we've got everything pretty much under control here. Go ahead and call in the cavalry – my radio's gone. Get backup, the coroner, and another ambulance."

"Better make it a few ambulances," Jim observed, looking at Rich, who was now looking pale, and holding his bloody shoulder.

"Yeah, no kidding."

George nudged his cameraman, Dixon. "Come on," he said, "it's almost ten-forty-five. Let's work a miracle for the eleven o'clock news."

With that, the two clambered up the steps.

Outside the house, Jasmine and Kristi had just finished their prayer session, when an unmarked sedan tore up the driveway. It came to a halt near them, and it's two occupants jumped out – two clean-cut men in inexpensive-looking off-the-rack-type suits. They approached the women, and one of them pulled out a black wallet and flicked it open, exposing an I.D. card and badge.

"FBI," he said. "Who are you, and what are you doing here?"

"I'm Jasmine DiMario, and the rest of my family is inside the house. My daughter was the one who was abducted, and they've found her in a dungeon downstairs."

"Dungeon?" the other agent exclaimed, with a strange expression. "What are you talking about?"

"This man – Aldon Brehm, he's the head of a Satanic crime cult. They call themselves the Temple of Anubis. They abducted my daughter five days ago."

The two agents looked at each other, then back at Jasmine.

"It's true," Kristi chimed in.

"And who are you?" the first agent asked.

"She's with me," Jasmine replied simply. "I think we'd better get in there. It's taking too long."

"We'll go in," the agent replied, "You two stay here."

"Oh, no you don't," Jasmine replied with finality. "We're going in, too. Besides, we know where exactly in the house they are – you don't."

"We can't guarantee your safety if you go in there," Agent Number One countered.

"You can't guarantee our safety out here, either," Jasmine countered. "Come on, follow us."

She turned to Kristi and said, "Time to face your fears, honey. Let's go."

They tore off at a run toward the house with Jasmine in the lead, before the bewildered FBI agents could raise another objection. The agents drew their guns, and followed the two women inside. They all heard the sound of sirens in the distance as they crossed the threshold.

Kristi led them to the kitchen, where she saw the open pantry door. She was about to go in, but the FBI agent stopped her and entered first. They followed the path strewn with overturned and spilled food items, and came out onto the landing.

"FBI," one agent barked. "What's the situation here?"

Rich looked up. "Let's see," he said, "where to start? We've got an abduction – the victim is here, the suspects are there," he added, gesturing alternately at Brehm and his three minions.

"We've got attempted murder of a peace officer on this one here, and attempted murder on the woman there," he continued, rapid fire. "I shot her as she was trying to knife the abduction victim. This guy over here is the owner of the house, and the head of a Satanic crime organization."

The agents came down the steps, followed by Jasmine and Kristi. Jasmine rushed over to Chelsea and hugged her fiercely. They each seasoned the other's shoulder with a salty flood of tears.

The two agents walked up to Rich, surmising that he was the senior deputy by the stripes on his arm. The one in the black suit looked at Rich's name badge.

"Okay, Deputy Harrison," he said, "we'll take over from here."

"Like hell, you will!" Rich retorted. "This is my bust, and the situation's under control. I've got the search warrant and the collar on all these suspects here. They'll be coming with me."

"You're going to the ER," Simpson reminded. "I'll take them in."

"Right," Rich replied, reluctantly.

"We've been investigating Aldon Brehm for several months now," the other FBI man said. "We weren't ready to move on him yet – until we heard the call over the police frequency. Didn't even get a chance to plant the wiretapping equipment yet, because there's always somebody on the premises here. How did you know about the abduction victim?"

Rich realized that the Feds was clueless about the extent of Brehm's criminal enterprise, and the fact that he was responsible for Chelsea DiMario's abduction. He figured he'd better be circumspect about revealing too much information, lest the FBI take credit for the bust.

"I've been conducting my own investigation," Rich answered, "with the help of some civilian operatives." He looked at Trey, Jim, and George. "The investigation led here."

"What's the kidnapping victim's name?" the first agent asked, taking out a small notepad.

"Chelsea DiMario," Rich replied.

The agent jotted down the name, and nodded as if he knew that she would be found here.

"I'll need to take statements from you and the others," the FBI agent said.

"I'll make my report available to you," Rich said. "Right now, I'm about to bleed to death here, so if you'll excuse me ..."

He sat down on the floor, with the help of Deputy Simpson.

A steady column of sheriff's deputies suddenly appeared on the landing above, and began pouring down the stairs like a flood of water. They were followed by two paramedics wearing latex gloves, and carrying their first aid kits.

"Over here," Simpson called.

The paramedics came over and began attending to Rich's wounds.

The FBI agents started interviewing the DiMarios. Rich motioned for two deputies to come over to him, while the paramedics began to inspect and carefully clean his stab and shrapnel wounds.

"Get them out of here," he said, motioning toward the family. "Take them home for me."

The two deputies walked over to where the DiMarios were being questioned.

"You folks will have to come with us," one deputy said, unceremoniously cutting the FBI interview short, "right away, please."

"Hey, we're conducting an interview here," protested the agent in the black suit.

"I've got my orders," the deputy replied firmly. "LASD has jurisdiction here."

They quickly ushered the four DiMarios up the stairs, and outside to a waiting patrol car.

"Do we really need to go to the station right now?" Jim asked.

"We're under orders to take you home right now," the deputy replied. "Our command deputy apparently knows where he can find you later. What's your address, please?"

Jim and Jasmine breathed a collective sigh of relief, and gave the required directions.

"I can't wait to get home," Chelsea said, "and I've never been so glad to see all of you."

"Even me, Sis?" Garrett asked in jest.

"Yeah, even you, I suppose, little brother." Then she added, "I can't wait to feel my own bed."

"You will, honey," Jasmine said, "but first, we just want to know that you're okay. The details can wait … until you're ready to talk about it."

She put her arm around her daughter. "Are you hungry? I'll make you something to eat when we get home."

"No thanks, Mom. I'm good."

With the DiMario family gone, the FBI agents focused their attention on Trey and Kristi. They split up and interviewed them separately. Rich was helped by the paramedics as he gingerly walked up the steps, having refused their stretcher. Before his departure, he called Deputy Vargas over.

"Watch those FBI guys," he instructed. "These two are mine, too," he pointed at Trey and Kristi.

Vargas got the point, understanding that Trey and Kristi were not to be taken into custody by the Feds.

Then Rich was helped to the waiting ambulance.

Back downstairs, one of the FBI agents questioned Trey. "So, what exactly is your involvement in all of this?" he asked.

"Well, I located this house, for one thing," Trey replied. "I found the real estate holdings and corporate involvement that links Aldon Brehm, Roberta McAllister – she's the dead one, and Peter Durgin to a string of businesses. Some, or all of these businesses look to be fronts for criminal enterprises. Their organization also owns the parcel of land out in Yermo where the infant burial ground was found about three weeks ago. It was Pastor Jim, George, and Deputy Rich who found that, by the way."

The agent took out his notepad and eagerly jotted down notes. As Trey continued to explain, the agent's face held an expression of utter enthrallment as he listened intently.

"But how did you track down all this information on Brehm, and this Temple of Anubis cult?" he asked.

"I have my ways," Trey replied, with a smile. "I can't tell you everything right now, without speaking to Rich – Deputy Harrison, first. But I've got the goods on Brehm and a bunch of his henchmen, believe me."

"We're going to need your full statement, along with this evidence you claim to have," the agent said. "We'll talk to Deputy Harrison and his commander about it. Let me get all your contact info."

Trey gave him his personal information. Meanwhile, the other FBI agent continued to interview Kristi Hawkins.

"So, the reason you are here, is that you came with the victim's family?" he asked.

"Yeah, that's right. I was with them just before they came over here with the deputy."

"And why did you come along?"

"I know the layout of the house, and where their daughter would probably be hidden."

"So you've been here before, then," the agent probed. "What is your relationship with Aldon Brehm?"

"I ... I was an employee of his," Kristi replied.

After a little more Q&A time, Deputy Vargas came over.

"Okay, I'm taking these two material witnesses with me," he said.

With that, he escorted them up the stairs, while a few other deputies wrapped up and secured the basement as a crime scene. The FBI men closed their notebooks and followed, knowing that they'd been trumped on their investigation.

"I've got my car here," Trey said to Deputy Vargas, once they got outside. "I can get home myself, if that's okay. But thanks for pulling me out of there." He looked at Kristi, then back at Vargas. "I can give her a lift home, too," he added.

"Fine by me," Vargas replied, "I'll wrap up here." With that, he turned and left the pair alone.

They stood there awhile, not looking directly at each other. Finally, Trey said,

"C'mon, let's get out of here, before the Feds quiz us some more."

She followed Trey as he walked down the driveway, trailing a couple of steps behind. They got to his car and got in.

After a moment of awkward silence, he said, "So, where to?"

"Good question," she replied quietly. "I can't go back to where I was staying, obviously. I was hoping I might be able to stay with the DiMarios tonight. The pastor said that my parents are going to come out tomorrow. The deputy said he was going to put me into protective custody, but then he got hurt. I don't have anywhere else to go."

Trey thought about it for a minute, and replied, "You could probably stay at my house tonight." Then he quickly added, "My mom has an extra bedroom – it would be okay. But maybe I should take you over to the DiMario's first."

Kristi nodded in agreement, and Trey turned the key and fired up the engine. They drove away in silence. After awhile, Kristi spoke up.

"Look, Trey," she started, "I know I hurt you with what I did that night at the Starbucks by the college. I didn't want to do it. I did a lot of things I didn't want to do, 'cause they made me. I know that sounds lame. It would be impossible to explain my situation. But for what it's worth, I'm sorry. I really mean it."

She turned her head away and looked out the window at the houses passing by. "That probably doesn't count for much."

"It counts," Trey answered quietly. "You know, that was a tough time for me – the hospital and everything, I mean. Those guys almost killed me. But the bible says that we have to forgive those who sin against us – it's not an option." He turned and looked into her blue eyes. "For what it's worth, I forgive you."

They drove the rest of the way to the DiMario's house in silence, but in peace.

When Trey and Kristi left, Deputy Vargas stopped at the door of the house, and turned to watch the young pair walk down the driveway.

I guess I'd better put Harrison's other collar in my car, he thought.

But when he walked over to Rich's patrol car in the midst of the automotive jumble, he got a surprise. Peter Durgin was gone.

CHAPTER 68

Los Robles Regional Medical Center: Thousand Oaks, California

George finished up with his broadcast responsibilities at the Brehm estate, and went to the hospital to check in on Rich. News crews from other broadcast stations had got wind of the big story, and came running to the Brehm estate. But George alone had the breaking news; the action was over by the time the others arrived.

Even though most non-family members weren't permitted in the ER as a rule, George's glib patter got him through the inner door. He waited around until Doctor Henke finished putting Rich back together.

"You look like hell," George said, after seeing the state of his friend.

"You're only saying that because you haven't seen Hell," Rich replied groggily.

"I beg to differ. That house was as close as I want to come."

"Me, too," Rich said, turning serious. "If what Jim tells me is true, that's as close as I'll ever have to get."

George was quiet for a moment. He looked around at the medical equipment, the institutional plastic curtains that separated the ER beds, and finally back at Rich.

"Yeah, me too," he said at last. "I never figured myself to be a Christian, of all things. But what Jim's been talking to me about, and all the stuff I see day in and day out ... I know I need something in my life. I just didn't know it was God I needed until just recently. I need to change ..." He tightened his lips and looked away. "And there's no other way, you know? Like Jim showed me in the bible, there's no other name under heaven by which we must be saved."

They talked for awhile, then the nurse came back to say that Rich had more visitors. They couldn't all crowd into the tight ER space, so she asked George to leave. He bid Rich goodbye, and headed out the door. He met Jim on his way in.

"Hey," George said, "they just kicked me out because of you."

"Pastor's privilege," Jim replied with a smile. "I can get into any ward of any hospital, any time. Maybe it's not the most impressive perk to have, but it comes in handy."

Jim walked over to Rich's bedside.

"How are you feeling?" Jim asked him. "I didn't mean to just leave you back there, but it looked like you were in good hands."

"Yeah, they got me here pretty quick. There's nothing you could have done to help, anyway, so don't even sweat it. I owe thanks to Garrett and Jasmine, though. I probably would have lost a lot more blood if they hadn't given me a good field dressing on my stab wound."

The nurse returned, and pulled back the curtain.

"Well, you sure are the popular one," she said to Rich. Then, turning to Jim, she said, "I'm sorry, Reverend, the deputy's fiancé has just arrived, and wants to see him. I'll have to ask you to step out now, due to space constraints in here. Sorry."

Nobody looked more surprised than Rich, but he said nothing.

"Okay, no problem," Jim said.

He said his goodbyes, and left Rich's bedside. When he got to the door, he opened it and saw an attractive brunette policewoman in a dark navy uniform waiting. Her shoulder-length glossy brown hair hung down freely – uncharacteristic of an on-duty policewoman. The nurse at the triage desk said to her,

"You can go in now."

She wasted no time in doing so.

"Rhonda," Rich said, seeing her familiar form enter his narrow bay. "What are you doing here?"

His heart raced at the sight of her. Even in uniform and without makeup, she looked beautiful to him. Rhonda approached the bed and grasped Rich's hand fiercely. A flood of memories poured over him at the feel of her warm touch and familiar scent.

"Rich," she said, her voice cracking with emotion, "I heard about what happened to you. I had to come see if you're all right."

Tears began to well up in her eyes.

"How did you find out so quickly?" he asked.

"Well, I had just got off duty, and drove home," she replied. "I have a scanner there. I turned it on to your frequency before I started fixing something to eat.

"Before I finished, I heard the call come through with your call letters. I could tell you were into something heavy. Then, one of your partners made the 'officer down' call, and I didn't hear your voice anymore. I freaked out and called your station, and got hold of your watch commander. He told me that you'd been hit, and that you'd been stabbed, too."

Rhonda started to cry. She bent down and gently hugged Rich, being careful not to stress his wounds. She hovered over him, her warm tears falling upon his face. They felt good to him, more therapeutic and healing than any balm or ointment that the doctor could prescribe. A world apart from the tears of hurt she had shed when they'd broken up, over a year ago.

"Hey, don't worry," Rich said, "I'm gonna live. The gunshot wound is just shrapnel. The stab wound didn't hit any major arteries, and the tip of the blade hit a rib, so that's as deep as it went."

Rhonda pulled herself together and straightened up.

"All the way over here, I kept thinking; even though we're … not together anymore … I don't know what I'd do if something bad happened to you, Rich. I was so worried. I was afraid you might not be alive when I got here, that I wouldn't be able to tell you …"

Her hoarse voice trailed off, and she looked down at the linoleum floor.

"Tell me what?" Rich asked.

Rhonda bit her lip, then looked Rich in the eye. "That I still love you," she said softly.

Rich's mind and body absorbed the impact of this revelation, but unlike his wounds, this was a pleasant blow. Unexpected, for sure. Even though he had dreamed and longed to be together with Rhonda again, he never dared to think it possible. Especially since he heard that she had started a new relationship after they had broken up. His face softened and formed a smile, her words running through his head again and again like a stream of honey.

At last, Rich spoke. "I never stopped loving you, Rhonda," he said quietly, looking back into her welcoming face. "I've thought about you a lot since we've been apart."

He took hold of her hand and brought it to his lips. "It looks like I'm going to get a second chance to live, after all. Do you believe in second chances, Rhonda?"

She smiled, and her pretty face tightened up slightly as fresh tears began to flow. She nodded her head and said simply, "Yes, I do."

She placed her hands on Rich's cheeks, and bent down to kiss him gently on the lips.

CHAPTER 69

DiMario Residence: Westlake Village, California

Thanksgiving at the DiMario home was usually a big affair, but never as big as this year. For those in attendance, it was never so meaningful, either.

Jim's parents were there, along with Jasmine's mother and sister's family. This year the house was filled with additional guests who were making their first appearance at this holiday event.

Trey Simmons and his mother Debbie arrived in time for dinner.

Rich and his again-fiancé Rhonda became inseparable, and were on hand as well.

George and his wife Alana stopped by for awhile on their way to her parent's house in Camarillo. They had their two daughters Lydia and Jessica with them, along with an assortment of the girl's stuffed animals. George had called Alana after leaving Rich's bedside that eventful night, and asked if he could come over and talk. Watching the DiMario's reunion with Chelsea that night touched a nerve deep within him; he knew that Jim was a man that had everything he wanted. George decided that very night that he was willing to do anything to get back that which was most important. When he went over to meet Alana that night, the girls were in bed already, so the two had a serious heart-to-heart conversation about the future. Alana was happy that George at last decided to turn the focus of his priorities on his family, and one week after their talk that night, Alana and the girls moved back home.

Kristi Hawkins was not able to attend this Thanksgiving dinner, although she was welcome. As Jim had promised, her parents arrived from Ohio the day after the events at the Brehm house transpired. They came to the DiMario's home that day, and there was a tearful reunion between them and their prodigal daughter. They wanted to take Kristi home right away, but she was obligated to stay for a few days to give a deposition, and testify before the grand jury that indicted Aldon Brehm. By the time the Hawkins family returned to Ohio, they were acting like a functioning family again. All of them had learned to give a little, and forgive much. They went home to start life over, leaving Kristi's damning testimony behind for the U.S. Attorney and L.A. District Attorney to work with.

As for Aldon Brehm, he and dozens of his underlings were in the county jail in downtown L.A., awaiting trial on a multitude of felony charges. The initial attempt by his high-priced attorney to bail him out failed after the U.S. Attorney froze all of his assets. Brehm was placed in solitary confinement after it was made known that he had some kind of power to control others, which the government psychologist attributed to mind control techniques. Jim knew it was something else. The U.S. Attorney vowed to put Brehm in a federal prison, under special high-security solitary conditions as soon as he was convicted.

Peter LeTourneu-Durgin disappeared that night, and has not been found. It was if he had vanished into thin air. The FBI put out an APB on him, and notified the U.S. Customs department in case he tried to leave the country.

Chelsea was doing well, but on occasion, she woke up with nightmares. She turned down offers for counseling, preferring to work through her feelings on what had happened to her on her own. She told her family that the experience made her stronger, since she knew that she was not far from a horrible death at the hands of Brehm and his men. One of God's secrets that she was learning for the first time in her life, is that hardship and suffering lead to growth and deeper maturity. What had been meant for evil, God used for the good.

Jim had a lot of support from the church when he made the announcement before the whole assembly about what exactly had transpired, from beginning to end. He and Jasmine were inundated with phone calls and cards. Many well-wishers stopped by to share their friendship in person. Even those doubters in the congregation who stepped back and quit coming to church during the Angela Shepherd scandal started coming back once it became evident what had taken place.

Jim's sermon for the Sunday after Chelsea's rescue was titled "God is Still on the Throne". He had a lot of evidence to prove it.

Jasmine found something unexpected through it all; she came to view this entire period of trial not as a disaster, but as a growing experience. To her, it was a refining, like the bible said in Zechariah 13:9 – *I will refine them like silver, and test them like gold. They will call on my name, and I will answer them; I will say 'They are my people,' and they will say 'The Lord is our God.'*

Overall, they had all come through it stronger. Indeed, what Satan had meant for evil, God turned to good.

The FBI used information provided by Jim, Trey, Rich, and George to contact Interpol and the Brazilian authorities, who soon rounded up the members of the Temple of Anubis pylon in Rio de Janeiro. They were tried and put in prison for leaving a long trail of unspeakable crimes.

Jim sat at the head of the dining room table, which had to be supplemented by a second table alongside in order to accommodate everyone. Surrounded by family and friends who had grown dear to him, he smiled. He had everything he needed, and everything he wanted. There would be nothing to put on his Christmas list this year; everything that mattered, he already had.

Jim bowed his head and offered up a short prayer before starting dinner. "Lord, we thank you for those around this table, and for providing for our every need. In Jesus' name – amen."

He raised his head and smiled. The others echoed the *amen*, and began filling their plates, passing the food-laden dishes around.

"That was a short prayer," Jasmine commented. "You must be really hungry."

"Not really," Jim replied, "that prayer just sums it all up. If I'd gone into detail, I probably could have gone on all day."

He piled a couple slices of turkey breast onto his plate.

"It's true, you know," he added, "what I've been telling people all along."

"What's that?"

"God is still on the throne."

Jasmine smiled.

"He sure is."